Smiley's People

'The premier spy novelist of his time. Perhaps of all time'
Time

'One of those writers who will be read a century from now'
Robert Harris

'The great master of the spy story . . . the constant flow
of emotion lifts him not only above all modern suspense
novelists, but above most novelists now practising'
Financial Times

'The master'
Henning Mankell, *Daily Telegraph*

'Our greatest living master of espionage fiction . . . Le Carré
is one of our great writers of moral ambiguity, a tireless
explorer of that darkly contradictory no-man's land'
Tim Rutten, *Los Angeles Times*

'Le Carré is not just today's gold standard, but the best there
ever was'
The Huffington Post

'No other contemporary novelist has more durably enjoyed
the twin badges of being both well-read and well-regarded'
Scott Turow

'Le Carré is one of the best novelists – of any kind – we have'
Vanity Fair

'He can communicate emotion, from sweating fear to
despairing love, with terse and compassionate conviction.
Above all, he can tell a tale'
Susan Hill, *Sunday Times*

'A masterly understanding of moral complexity . . .
the signature clarity of his prose is matched only by the
distinctive murkiness of what it describes'

Guardian

'Brilliant, morally outraged works that mine rich veins of
post-Cold War venality'

Seattle Times

'The world's greatest fictional spymaster'

Newsweek

ABOUT THE AUTHOR

John le Carré was born in 1931 and attended the universities
of Bern and Oxford. He taught at Eton and served briefly in
British Intelligence during the Cold War. For the last fifty
years he has lived by his pen. He divides his time between
London and Cornwall.

JOHN LE CARRÉ

Smiley's People

PENGUIN BOOKS

PENGUIN CLASSICS

UK | USA | Canada | Ireland | Australia
India | New Zealand | South Africa

Penguin Books is part of the Penguin Random House
group of companies whose addresses can be found at
global.penguinrandomhouse.com.

Penguin
Random House
UK

First published by Hodder & Stoughton 1980
Published in Penguin Books 2018
003

Set in 11.3/14 pt Dante MT Pro
Typeset by Jouve (UK), Milton Keynes
Printed and bound in Great Britain by Clays Ltd, Elcograf S.p.A.

A CIP catalogue record for this book is available
from the British Library

ISBN: 978–0–241–32252–9

www.greenpenguin.co.uk

MIX
Paper from
responsible sources
FSC
www.fsc.org   FSC® C018179

Penguin Random House is committed to a
sustainable future for our business, our readers
and our planet. This book is made from Forest
Stewardship Council® certified paper.

For my sons,
Simon, Stephen,
Timothy and Nicholas,

with love

Two seemingly unconnected events heralded the summons of Mr George Smiley from his dubious retirement. The first had for its background Paris, and for a season the boiling month of August, when Parisians by tradition abandon their city to the scalding sunshine and the bus-loads of packaged tourists.

On one of these August days – the fourth, and at twelve o'clock exactly, for a church clock was chiming and a factory bell had just preceded it – in a *quartier* once celebrated for its large population of the poorer Russian émigrés, a stocky woman of about fifty, carrying a shopping bag, emerged from the darkness of an old warehouse and set off, full of her usual energy and purpose, along the pavement to the bus-stop. The street was grey and narrow, and shuttered, with a couple of small *hôtels de passe* and a lot of cats. It was a place, for some reason, of peculiar quiet. The warehouse, since it handled perishable goods, had remained open during the holidays. The heat, fouled by exhaust fumes and unwashed by the slightest breeze, rose at her like the heat from a lift-shaft, but her Slavic features registered no complaint. She was neither dressed nor built for exertion on a hot day, being in stature very short indeed, and fat, so that she had to roll a little in order to get along. Her black dress, of ecclesiastical severity, possessed neither a waist nor any other relief except for a dash of white

lace at the neck and a large metal cross, well fingered but of
no intrinsic value, at the bosom. Her cracked shoes, which in
walking tended outwards at the points, set a stern tattoo rattling between the shuttered houses. Her shabby bag, full since
early morning, gave her a slight starboard list and told clearly
that she was used to burdens. There was also fun in her, however. Her grey hair was gathered in a bun behind her, but there
remained one sprightly forelock that flopped over her brow to
the rhythm of her waddle. A hardy humour lit her brown eyes.
Her mouth, set above a fighter's chin, seemed ready, given half
a reason, to smile at any time.

Reaching her usual bus-stop, she put down her shopping
bag and with her right hand massaged her rump just where it
met the spine, a gesture she made often these days though it
gave her little relief. The high stool in the warehouse where
she worked every morning as a checker possessed no back,
and increasingly she was resenting the deficiency. 'Devil,' she
muttered to the offending part. Having rubbed it, she began
plying her black elbows behind her like an old town raven preparing to fly. 'Devil,' she repeated. Then, suddenly aware of
being watched, she wheeled round and peered upward at the
heavily built man towering behind her.

He was the only other person waiting, and indeed, at that
moment, the only other person in the street. She had never
spoken to him, yet his face was already familiar to her: so big,
so uncertain, so sweaty. She had seen it yesterday, she had seen
it the day before, and for all she knew, the day before that as
well – my Lord, she was not a walking diary! For the last three
or four days, this weak, itchy giant, waiting for a bus or hovering on the pavement outside the warehouse, had become
a figure of the street for her; and what was more, a figure
of a recognisable type, though she had yet to put her finger

on which. She thought he looked *traqué* – hunted – as so many Parisians did these days. She saw so much fear in their faces; in the way they walked yet dared not greet each other. Perhaps it was the same everywhere, she wouldn't know. Also, more than once, she had felt *his* interest in *her*. She had wondered whether he was a policeman. She had even considered asking him, for she had this urban cockiness. His lugubrious build suggested the police, so did the sweaty suit and the needless raincoat that hung like a bit of old uniform from his forearm. If she was right, and he *was* police, then – high time too, the idiots were finally doing something about the spate of pilfering that had made a beargarden of her stock-checking for months.

By now the stranger had been staring down at her for some time, however. And he was staring at her still.

'I have the misfortune to suffer in my back, monsieur,' she confided to him finally, in her slow and classically enunciated French. 'It is not a large back but the pain is disproportionate. You are a doctor, perhaps? An osteopath?'

Then she wondered, looking up at him, whether he was ill, and her joke out of place. An oily gloss glistened on his jaw and neck, and there was an unseeing self-obsession about his pallid eyes. He seemed to see beyond her to some private trouble of his own. She was going to ask him this – You are perhaps in love, monsieur? Your wife is deceiving you? – and she was actually considering steering him into a café for a glass of water or a *tisane* when he abruptly swung away from her and looked behind him, then over her head up the street the other way. And it occurred to her that he really was afraid, not just *traqué* but frightened stiff; so perhaps he was not a policeman at all, but a thief, though the difference, she knew well, was often slight.

'Your name is Maria Andreyevna Ostrakova?' he asked her abruptly, as if the question scared him.

He was speaking French but she knew that it was not his mother tongue any more than it was her own, and his correct pronunciation of her name, complete with patronymic, already alerted her to his origin. She recognised the slur at once and the shapes of the tongue that made it, and she identified too late, and with a considerable inward start, the type she had not been able to put her finger on.

'If it is, who on earth are *you*?' she asked him in reply, sticking out her jaw and scowling.

He had drawn a pace closer. The difference in their heights was immediately absurd. So was the degree to which the man's features betrayed his unpleasing character. From her low position Ostrakova could read his weakness as clearly as his fear. His damp chin had set in a grimace, his mouth had twisted to make him look strong, but she knew he was only banishing an incurable cowardice. He is like a man steeling himself for a heroic act, she thought. Or a criminal one. He is a man cut off from all spontaneous acts, she thought.

'You were born in Leningrad on May 8, 1927?' the stranger asked.

Probably she said yes. Afterwards she was not sure. She saw his scared gaze lift and stare at the approaching bus. She saw an indecision near to panic seize him, and it occurred to her – which in the long run was an act of near clairvoyance – that he proposed to push her under it. He didn't, but he did put his next question in Russian – and in the brutal accents of Moscow officialdom.

'In 1956, you were granted permission to leave the Soviet Union for the purpose of nursing your sick husband, the traitor Ostrakov? Also for certain other purposes?'

'Ostrakov was not a traitor,' she replied, cutting him off. 'He was a patriot.' And by instinct she took up her shopping bag and clutched the handle very tight.

The stranger spoke straight over this contradiction, and very loudly, in order to defeat the clatter of the bus: 'Ostrakova, I bring you greetings from your daughter Alexandra in Moscow, also from certain official quarters! I wish to speak to you concerning her! Do not board this car!'

The bus had pulled up. The conductor knew her and was holding his hand out for her bag. Lowering his voice, the stranger added one more terrible statement: 'Alexandra has serious problems which require the assistance of a mother.'

The conductor was calling to her to get a move on. He spoke with pretended roughness, which was the way they joked. 'Come on, mother! It's too hot for love! Pass us your bag and let's go!' cried the conductor.

Inside the bus there was laughter; then someone shouted an insult – old woman, keeps the world waiting! She felt the stranger's hand scrabbling inexpertly at her arm, like a clumsy suitor groping for the buttons. She pulled herself free. She tried to tell the conductor something but she couldn't; she opened her mouth but she had forgotten how to speak. The best she could manage was to shake her head. The conductor yelled at her again, then waved his hands and shrugged. The insults multiplied – old woman, drunk as a whore at midday! Remaining where she was, Ostrakova watched the bus out of sight, waiting for her vision to clear and her heart to stop its crazy cavorting. Now it is I who need a glass of water, she thought. From the strong I can protect myself. God preserve me from the weak.

She followed him to the café, limping heavily. In a forced-labour camp, exactly twenty-five years before, she had broken her leg in three places in a coal slip. On this August 4th – the date had not escaped her – under the extreme duress of the stranger's message to her, the old sensation of being crippled came back to her.

5

The café was the last in the street, if not in all Paris, to lack both a juke-box and neon lighting – and to remain open in August – though there were bagatelle tables that bumped and flashed from dawn till night. For the rest, there was the usual mid-morning hubbub, of grand politics, and horses, and whatever else Parisians talked; there was the usual trio of prostitutes murmuring among themselves, and a sullen young waiter in a soiled shirt who led them to a table in a corner that was reserved with a grimy Campari sign. A moment of ludicrous banality followed. The stranger ordered two coffees, but the waiter protested that at midday one does not reserve the best table in the house merely in order to drink coffee; the *patron* had to pay the rent, monsieur! Since the stranger did not follow this flow of patois, Ostrakova had to translate it for him. The stranger blushed and ordered two ham omelettes with *frites*, and two Alsatian beers, all without consulting Ostrakova. Then he took himself to the men's room to repair his courage – confident, presumably, she would not run away – and when he returned his face was dry and his ginger hair combed, but the stink of him, now they were indoors, reminded Ostrakova of Moscow subways, and Moscow trams, and Moscow interrogation rooms. More eloquently than anything he could ever have said to her, that short walk back from the men's room to their table had convinced her of what she already feared. He was one of them. The suppressed swagger, the deliberate brutalisation of the features, the ponderous style in which he now squared his forearms on the table and with feigned reluctance helped himself to a piece of bread from the basket as if he were dipping a pen in ink – they revived her worst memories of living as a disgraced woman under the weight of Moscow's malevolent bureaucracy.

'So,' he said, and started eating the bread at the same time.

He selected a crusty end. With hands like that he could have crushed it in a second, but instead he chose to prise ladylike flakes from it with his fat finger-ends, as if that were the official way of eating. While he nibbled, his eyebrows went up and he looked sorry for himself, me a stranger in this foreign land. 'Do they know here that you have lived an immoral life in Russia?' he asked finally. 'Maybe in a town full of whores they don't care.'

Her answer lay ready on the tip of her tongue: *My life in Russia was not immoral. It was your system which was immoral.*

But she did not say it, she kept rigidly silent. Ostrakova had already sworn to herself that she would restrain both her quick temper and her quick tongue, and she now physically enjoined herself to this vow by grabbing a piece of skin on the soft inside of her wrist and pinching it through her sleeve with a fierce, sustained pressure under the table, exactly as she had done a hundred times before, in the old days, when such questionings were part of her daily life – When did you last hear from your husband, Ostrakov, the traitor? Name all persons with whom you have associated in the last three months! With bitter experience she had learned the other lessons of interrogation too. A part of her was rehearsing them at this minute, and though they belonged, in terms of history, to a full generation earlier, they appeared to her now as bright as yesterday and as vital: never to match rudeness with rudeness, never to be provoked, never to score, never to be witty or superior or intellectual, never to be deflected by fury, or despair, or the surge of sudden hope that an occasional question might arouse. To match dullness with dullness and routine with routine. And only deep, deep down to preserve the two secrets that made all these humiliations bearable: her hatred of them; and her hope that one day, after endless drips of water on the stone, she would wear them down, and by a reluctant miracle of their own elephantine processes, obtain from them the freedom they were denying her.

He had produced a notebook. In Moscow it would have been her file but here in a Paris café it was a sleek black leatherbound notebook, something that in Moscow even an official would count himself lucky to possess.

File or notebook, the preamble was the same: 'You were born Maria Andreyevna Rogova in Leningrad on May 8, 1927,' he repeated. 'On September 1, 1948, aged twenty-one, you married the traitor Ostrakov Igor, a captain of infantry in the Red Army, born of an Estonian mother. In 1950, the said Ostrakov, being at the time stationed in East Berlin, traitorously defected to Fascist Germany through the assistance of reactionary Estonian émigrés, leaving you in Moscow. He took up residence, and later French citizenship, in Paris, where he continued his contact with anti-Soviet elements. At the time of his defection you had no children by this man. Also you were not pregnant. Correct?'

'Correct,' she said.

In Moscow it would have been 'Correct, Comrade Captain,' or 'Correct, Comrade Inspector,' but in this clamorous French café such formality was out of place. The fold of skin on her wrist had gone numb. Releasing it, she allowed the blood to return, then took hold of another.

'As an accomplice to Ostrakov's defection you were sentenced to five years' detention in a labour camp, but were released under an amnesty following the death of Stalin in March, 1953. Correct?'

'Correct.'

'On your return to Moscow, despite the improbability that your request would be granted, you applied for a foreign travel passport to join your husband in France. Correct?'

'He had a cancer,' she said. 'If I had not applied, I would have been failing in my duty as his wife.'

The waiter brought the plates of omelette and *frites* and the two Alsatian beers, and Ostrakova asked him to bring a *thé citron*: she was thirsty, but did not care for beer. Addressing the boy, she tried vainly to make a bridge to him, with smiles and with her eyes. But his stoniness repulsed her; she realised she was the only woman in the place apart from the three prostitutes. Holding his notebook to one side like a hymnal, the stranger helped himself to a forkful, then another, while Ostrakova tightened her grasp on her wrist, and Alexandra's name pulsed in her mind like an unstaunched wound, and she contemplated a thousand different *serious problems* that required *the immediate assistance of a mother.*

The stranger continued his crude history of her while he ate. Did he eat for pleasure or did he eat in order not to be conspicuous again? She decided he was a compulsive eater.

'Meanwhile,' he announced, eating.

'Meanwhile,' she whispered involuntarily.

'Meanwhile, despite your pretended concern for your husband, the traitor Ostrakov,' he continued through his mouthful, 'you nevertheless formed an adulterous relationship with the so-called music student Glikman Joseph, a Jew with four convictions for anti-social behaviour whom you had met during your detention. You cohabited with this Jew in his apartment. Correct or false?'

'I was lonely.'

'In consequence of this union with Glikman you bore a daughter, Alexandra, at the Lying-in Hospital of the October Revolution in Moscow. The certificate of parentage was signed by Glikman Joseph and Ostrakova Maria. The girl was registered in the name of the Jew Glikman. Correct or false?'

'Correct.'

'Meanwhile, you persisted in your application for a foreign travel passport. Why?'

'I told you. My husband was ill. It was my duty to persist.'

He ate again, so grossly that she had a sight of his many bad teeth. 'In January, 1956, as an act of clemency you were granted a passport on condition the child Alexandra was left behind in Moscow. You exceeded the permitted time limit and remained in France, abandoning your child. Correct or false?'

The doors to the street were glass, the walls too. A big lorry parked outside them and the café darkened. The young waiter slammed down her tea without looking at her.

'Correct,' she said again, and managed this time to look at her interrogator, knowing what would follow, forcing herself to show him that on this score at least she had no doubt, and no regrets. 'Correct,' she repeated defiantly.

'As a condition of your application being favourably considered by the authorities, you signed an undertaking to the organs of State Security to perform certain tasks for them during your residence in Paris. One, to persuade your husband, the traitor Ostrakov, to return to the Soviet Union—'

'To *attempt* to persuade him,' she said with a faint smile. 'He was not amenable to this suggestion.'

'Two, you undertook also to provide information concerning the activities and personalities of revanchist anti-Soviet émigré groups. You submitted two reports of no value and afterwards nothing. Why?'

'My husband despised such groups and had given up his contact with them.'

'You could have participated in the groups without him. You signed the document and neglected its undertaking. Yes or no?'

'Yes.'

'For this you abandon your child in Russia? To a Jew? In order to give your attention to an enemy of the people, a traitor of the State? For this you neglect your duty? Outstay the permitted period, remain in France?'

'My husband was dying. He needed me.'

'And the child Alexandra? She did not need you? A dying husband is more important than a living child? A traitor? A conspirator against the people?'

Releasing her wrist, Ostrakova deliberately took hold of her tea and watched the glass rise to her face, the lemon floating on the surface. Beyond it, she saw a grimy mosaic floor and beyond the floor, the loved, ferocious and kindly face of Glikman pressing down on her, exhorting her to sign, to go, to swear to anything they asked. The freedom of one is more than the slavery of three, he had whispered; a child of such parents as ourselves cannot prosper in Russia whether you stay or go; leave and we shall do our best to follow; sign anything, leave, and live for all of us; if you love me, go . . .

'They were the hard days, still,' she said to the stranger finally, almost in a tone of reminiscence. 'You are too young. They were the hard days, even after Stalin's death: still hard.'

'Does the criminal Glikman continue to write to you?' the stranger asked in a superior, knowing way.

'He never wrote,' she lied. 'How could he write, a dissident, living under restriction? The decision to stay in France was mine alone.'

Paint yourself black, she thought; do everything possible to spare those within their power.

'I have heard nothing from Glikman since I came to France twenty years ago,' she added, gathering courage. 'Indirectly, I learned that he was angered by my anti-Soviet behaviour. He did not wish to know me any more. Inwardly he was already wishing to reform by the time I left him.'

'He did not write concerning your common child?'

'He did not write, he did not send messages. I told you this already.'

'Where is your daughter now?'

'I don't know.'

'You have received communications from her?'

'Of course not. I heard only that she had entered a State orphanage and acquired another name. I assume she does not know I exist.'

The stranger ate again with one hand, while the other held the notebook. He filled his mouth, munched a little, then swilled his food down with the beer. But the superior smile remained.

'And now it is the criminal Glikman who is dead,' the stranger announced, revealing his little secret. He continued eating.

Suddenly Ostrakova wished the twenty years were two hundred. She wished that Glikman's face had never, after all, looked down on her, that she had never loved him, never cared for him, never cooked for him, or got drunk with him day after day in his one-roomed exile where they lived on the charity of their friends, deprived of the right to work, to do anything but make music and love, get drunk, walk in the woods, and be cut dead by their neighbours.

'Next time I go to prison or you do, they will take her anyway. Alexandra is forfeit in any case,' Glikman had said. 'But you can save yourself.'

'I will decide when I am there,' she had replied.

'Decide now.'

'When I am there.'

The stranger pushed aside his empty plate and once more

took the sleek French notebook in both hands. He turned a page, as if approaching a new chapter.

'Concerning now your criminal daughter Alexandra,' he announced, through his food.

'*Criminal?*' she whispered.

To her astonishment the stranger was reciting a fresh catalogue of crimes. As he did so, Ostrakova lost her final hold upon the present. Her eyes were on the mosaic floor and she noticed the husks of langoustine and crumbs of bread. But her mind was in the Moscow law court again, where her own trial was being repeated. If not hers, then Glikman's – yet not Glikman's either. Then whose? She remembered trials which the two of them had attended as unwelcome spectators. Trials of friends, if only by accident: such as people who had questioned the absolute right of the authorities; or had worshipped some unacceptable god; or had painted criminally abstract pictures; or had published politically endangering love-poems. The chattering customers in the café became the jeering claque of the State police; the slamming of the bagatelle tables, the crash of iron doors. On this date, for escaping from the State orphanage on something street, so many months' corrective detention. On that date, for insulting organs of State Security, so many more months extended for bad behaviour, followed by so many years' internal exile. Ostrakova felt her stomach turn and thought she might be sick. She put her hands to her glass of tea and saw the red pinch marks on her wrist. The stranger continued his recitation and she heard her daughter awarded another two years for refusing to accept employment at the something factory, God help her, and why shouldn't she? Where had she learnt it? Ostrakova asked herself, incredulous. What had Glikman taught the child, in the short time before they took her away from him, that had stamped her in his mould and defeated all the system's efforts? Fear, exultation, amazement jangled in Ostrakova's mind, till something that the stranger was saying to her blocked them out.

'I did not hear,' she whispered after an age. 'I am a little distressed. Kindly repeat what you just said.'

He said it again and she looked up and stared at him, trying to think of all the tricks she had been warned against, but they were too many and she was no longer clever. She no longer had Glikman's cleverness – if she had ever had it – about reading their lies and playing their games ahead of them. She knew only that to save herself and be reunited with her beloved Ostrakov, she had committed a great sin, the greatest a mother can commit. The stranger had begun threatening her, but for once the threat seemed meaningless. In the event of her non-collaboration – he was saying – a copy of her signed undertaking to the Soviet authorities would find its way to the French police. Copies of her useless two reports (done, as he well knew, solely in order to keep the brigands quiet) would be circulated among the surviving Paris émigrés – though, God knows, there were few enough of *them* about these days! Yet why should she have to submit to *pressure* in order to accept a gift of such immeasurable value – when, by some inexplicable act of clemency, this man, this system, was holding out to her the chance to redeem herself, and her child? She knew that her nightly and daily prayers for forgiveness had been answered, the thousands of candles, the thousands of tears. She made him say it a third time. She made him pull his notebook away from his gingery face, and she saw that his weak mouth had lifted into a half smile and that, idiotically, he seemed to require her absolution, even while he repeated his insane, God-given question.

'Assuming it has been decided to rid the Soviet Union of

this disruptive and unsocial element, how would you like your daughter Alexandra to follow your footsteps here to France?'

For weeks after that encounter, and through all the hushed activities which accompanied it – furtive visits to the Soviet Embassy, form-filling, signed affidavits – *certificats d'hébergement* – the laborious trail through successive French ministries – Ostrakova followed her own actions as if they were someone else's. She prayed often, but even with her prayers she adopted a conspiratorial attitude, dividing them among several Russian Orthodox churches so that in none would she be observed suffering an undue assault of piety. Some of the churches were no more than little private houses scattered round the 15th and 16th districts, with distinctive twice-struck crosses in plywood, and old, rain-sodden Russian notices on the doors, requesting cheap accommodation and offering instruction on the piano. She went to the Church of the Russian Abroad, and the Church of the Apparition of the Holy Virgin, and the Church of Saint Seraphin of Sarov. She went everywhere. She rang the bells till someone came, a verger or a frail-faced woman in black; she gave them money, and they let her crouch in the damp cold before candle-lit icons, and breathe the thick incense till it made her half drunk. She made promises to the Almighty, she thanked Him, she asked Him for advice, she practically asked Him what *He* would have done if the stranger had approached Him in similar circumstances, she reminded Him that anyway she was under pressure, and they would destroy her if she did not obey. Yet at the same time, her indomitable common sense asserted itself and she asked herself over and over again *why* she of all people, wife of the traitor Ostrakov, lover of the dissident Glikman, mother – so she was given to believe – of a turbulent and anti-social daughter, should be singled out for such untypical indulgence?

In the Soviet Embassy, when she made her first formal application, she was treated with a regard she would never have dreamed possible, which was suited neither to a defector and renegade spy nor to the mother of an untameable hell-raiser. She was not ordered brusquely to a waiting-room, but escorted to an interviewing-room, where a young and personable official showed her a positively Western courtesy, even helping her, where her pen or courage faltered, to a proper formulation of her case.

And she told nobody, not even her nearest – though her nearest was not very near. The gingery man's warning rang in her ears day and night: any indiscretion and your daughter will not be released.

And who was there, after all, apart from God, to turn to? To her half-sister Valentina who lived in Lyon and was married to a car salesman? The very thought that Ostrakova had been consorting with a secret official from Moscow would send her rushing for her smelling salts. In a *café*, Maria? In *broad daylight*, Maria? Yes, Valentina, and what he said is true. I had a bastard daughter by a Jew.

It was the nothingness that scared her most. The weeks passed; at the Embassy they told her that her application was receiving 'favoured attention'; the French authorities had assured her that Alexandra would quickly qualify for French citizenship; the gingery stranger had persuaded her to backdate Alexandra's birth so that she could be represented as an Ostrakova, not a Glikman; he said the French authorities would find this more acceptable; and it seemed that they had done so, even though she had never so much as mentioned the child's existence at her naturalisation interviews. Now, suddenly, there were no more forms to fill in, no more hurdles to be cleared, and Ostrakova waited without knowing what she was waiting for. For the gingery stranger to reappear? He no longer existed. One ham omelette and *frites*, some Alsatian beer, two pieces of crusty bread had satisfied all his needs, apparently. What he was in relation to the Embassy she could not imagine: he had told her to present herself there, and that they would be expecting her; he was right. But when she referred to 'your gentleman,' even 'your blond, large gentleman who first approached me,' she met with smiling incomprehension.

Thus gradually whatever she was waiting for ceased to exist. First it was ahead of her, then it was behind her, and she had had no knowledge of its passing, no moment of fulfilment. Had Alexandra already arrived in France? Obtained her papers, moved on or gone to ground? Ostrakova began to think she might have done. Abandoned to a new and inconsolable sense of disappointment, she peered at the faces of young girls in the street, wondering what Alexandra looked like. Returning home, her eyes would fall automatically to the doormat in the hope of seeing a handwritten note or a *pneumatique*: 'Mama, it is I. I am staying at the so-and-so hotel . . .' A cable giving a flight number, arriving Orly tomorrow, tonight; or was it not Orly airport but Charles de Gaulle? She had no familiarity with airlines, so she visited a travel agent, just to ask. It was both. She considered going to the expense of having a telephone installed so that Alexandra could ring her up. Yet what on earth was she expecting, after all these years? Tearful reunions with a grown child to whom she had never been united? The wishful remaking, more than twenty years too late, of a relationship she had deliberately turned her back on? I have no right to her, Ostrakova told herself severely; I have only my debts and my obligations. She asked at the Embassy

17

but they knew nothing more. The formalities were complete, they said. That was all they knew. And if Ostrakova wished to send her daughter money? she asked cunningly – for her fares, for instance, for her visa? – could they give her an address perhaps, an office that would find her?

We are not a postal service, they told her. Their new chilliness scared her. She did not go any more.

After that, she fell once more to worrying about the several muddy photographs, each the same, which they had given to her to pin to her application forms. The photographs were all she had ever seen. She wished now that she had made copies, but she had never thought of it; stupidly, she had assumed she would soon be meeting the original. She had not had them in her hand above an hour! She had hurried straight from the Embassy to the Ministry with them, and by the time she left the Ministry the photographs were already working their way through another bureaucracy. But she had studied them! My Lord, how she had studied those photographs, whether they were each the same or not! On the Métro, in the Ministry waiting-room, even on the pavement before she went in, she had stared at the lifeless depiction of her child, trying with all her might to see in the expressionless grey shadows some hint of the man she had adored. And failing. Always, till then, whenever she had dared to wonder, she had imagined Glikman's features as clearly written on the growing child as they had been on the new-born baby. It had seemed impossible that a man so vigorous would not plant his imprint deeply and for good. Yet Ostrakova saw nothing of Glikman in that photograph. He had worn his Jewishness like a flag. It was part of his solitary revolution. He was not orthodox, he was not even religious, he disliked Ostrakova's secret piety nearly as much as he disliked the Soviet bureaucracy – yet he had borrowed her tongs to curl his sideburns like the Hasidim, just to give focus, as he put it, to the anti-Semitism of the authorities. But in the face in the photograph she recognised not a drop of his blood, not the least spark of his fire – though his fire, according to the stranger, burned in her amazingly.

'If they had photographed a corpse to get that picture,' thought Ostrakova aloud in her apartment, 'I would not be surprised.' And with this downright observation, she gave her first outward expression of the growing doubt inside her.

Toiling in her warehouse, sitting alone in her tiny apartment in the long evenings, Ostrakova racked her brains for someone she could trust; who would not condone and not condemn; who would see round the corners of the route she had embarked on; above all, who would not talk and thus wreck – she had been assured of it – wreck her chances of being reunited with Alexandra. Then one night, either God or her own striving memory supplied her with an answer: The General! she thought, sitting up in bed and putting on the light. Ostrakov himself had told her of him! Those émigré groups are a catastrophe, he used to say, and you must avoid them like the pest. The only one you can trust is Vladimir the General; he is an old devil, and a womaniser, but he is a man, he has connections and knows how to keep his mouth shut.

But Ostrakov had said this some twenty years ago, and not even old generals are immortal. And besides – Vladimir who? She did not even know his other name. Even the name Vladimir – Ostrakov had told her – was something he had put on for his military service; since his real name was Estonian, and not suitable for Red Army usage. Nevertheless, next day, she went down to the bookshop beside the Cathedral of St Alexander Nevsky, where information about the dwindling Russian population was often to be had, and made her first enquiries. She got a name and even a phone number, but no address. The phone was disconnected. She went to the Post Office, cajoled the assistants, and finally came up with a 1956 telephone directory listing the Movement for Baltic Freedom, followed by an address in Montparnasse. She was not stupid. She looked up the address and found no less than four other organisations listed there also; the Riga Group, the Association of Victims of Soviet Imperialism, the Forty-Eight Committee for a free Latvia, the Tallinn Committee of Freedom. She remembered vividly Ostrakov's scathing opinions of such bodies, even though he had paid his dues to them. All the same, she went to the address and rang the bell, and the house was like one of her little churches: quaint, and very nearly closed for ever. Eventually an old White Russian opened the door wearing a cardigan crookedly buttoned, and leaning on a walking stick, and looking superior.

They've gone, he said, pointing his stick down the cobbled road. Moved out. Finished. Bigger outfits put them out of business, he added with a laugh. Too few of them, too many groups, and they squabbled like children. No wonder the Czar was defeated! The old White Russian had false teeth that didn't fit, and thin hair plastered all over his scalp to hide his baldness.

But the General? she asked. Where was the General? Was he still alive, or had he –

The old Russian smirked and asked whether it was business.

It was not, said Ostrakova craftily, remembering the General's reputation for philandering, and contrived a shy woman's smile. The old Russian laughed, and his teeth rattled. He laughed again and said 'Oh, the General!' Then he came back with an address in London, stamped in mauve on a bit of card, and gave it to her. The General would never change, he said; when he got to Heaven, he'd be chasing after the angels and trying to up-end them, no question. And that night while the whole neighbourhood slept, Ostrakova sat at her dead husband's desk and wrote to the General with a frankness which lonely people reserve for strangers, using French rather than Russian as an aid to greater detachment. She told him about her love for Glikman and took comfort from the knowledge that the General himself loved women just as Glikman had. She admitted immediately that she had come to France as a spy, and she explained how she had assembled the two trivial reports that were the squalid price of her freedom. It was *à contre-coeur*, she said; invention and evasion, she said; a nothing. But the reports existed, so did her signed undertaking, and they placed grave limits on her freedom. Then she told him of her soul, and of her prayers to God all round the Russian churches. Since the gingery stranger's approach to her, she said, her days had become unreal; she had a feeling of being denied a natural explanation of her life, even if it had to be a painful one. She kept nothing back from him, for whatever guilty feelings she had, they did not relate to her efforts to bring Alexandra to the West, but rather to her decision to stay in Paris and take care of Ostrakov until he died – after which event, she said, the Soviets would not let her come back anyway; she had become a defector herself.

'But General,' she wrote, 'if tonight I had to face my Maker in person, and tell Him what is deepest in my heart, I would tell Him what I now tell you. My child Alexandra was born in pain. Days and nights she fought me and I fought her back. Even in the womb she was her father's child. I had no time to love her; I only ever knew her as the little Jewish warrior her father made. But, General, this I do know: the child in the photograph is neither Glikman's, nor is she mine. They are putting the wrong egg into the nest, and though there is a part of this old woman that would like to be deluded, there is a stronger part that hates them for their tricks.'

When she had finished the letter, she sealed it immediately in its envelope so that she would not read it and change her mind. Then she stuck too many stamps on it deliberately, much as she might have lit a candle to a lover.

For the next two weeks exactly, following the posting of this document, nothing happened, and in the strange ways of women the silence was a relief to her. After the storm had come the calm, she had done the little she could do – she had confessed her weaknesses and her betrayals and her one great sin – the rest was in the hands of God, and of the General. A disruption of the French postal services did not dismay her. She saw it rather as another obstacle which those who were shaping her destiny would have to overcome if their will was strong enough. She went to work contentedly and her back ceased to trouble her, which she took as an omen. She even managed to become philosophical again. It is this way or that way, she told herself: either Alexandra was in the West and better off – if indeed it *was* Alexandra – or Alexandra was where she had been before, and no worse off. But gradually, with another part of her, she saw through this false optimism. There was a third possibility, and that was the worst and by degrees the one she considered most likely: namely, that Alexandra was being used for a sinister and perhaps wicked purpose; that they were forcing her somehow, exactly as they had forced Ostrakova, misusing the humanity and courage that her father, Glikman, had given her. So that on the fourteenth night, Ostrakova broke into a profound fit of weeping, and with the tears streaming down her face walked half-way across Paris looking for a church, any church that was open, until she came to the Cathedral of Alexander Nevsky itself. It was open. Kneeling, she prayed for long hours to St Joseph, who was after all a father and protector, and the giver of Glikman's first name, even if Glikman would have scoffed at the association. And on the day following these spiritual exertions, her prayer was answered. A letter came. It had no stamp or postmark. She had added her address at work as a precaution, and the letter was there waiting for her when she arrived, delivered by hand, presumably, some time in the night. It was a very short letter and carried neither the name of the sender nor his address. It was unsigned. Like her own, it was in a stilted French and hand-written, in the sprawl of an old and dictatorial hand, which she knew at once was the General's.

Madame! – it began, like a command – *Your letter has reached the writer safely. A friend of our cause will call upon you very soon. He is a man of honour and he will identify himself by handing to you the other half of the enclosed postcard. I urge you to speak to nobody concerning this matter until he arrives. He will come to your apartment between eight and ten o'clock in the evening. He will ring your doorbell three times. He has my absolute confidence. Trust him entirely, Madame, and we shall do everything to assist you.*

Even in her relief, she was secretly entertained by the writer's melodramatic tone. Why not deliver the letter directly to her flat? she wondered; and why should I feel safer because he gives me half an English picture? For the piece of postcard showed a part of Piccadilly Circus and was torn, not cut, with a deliberate roughness, diagonally. The side to be written on was blank.

To her astonishment the General's envoy came that night.

He rang the bell three times, as the letter promised, but he must have known she was in her apartment – must have watched her enter, and the lights go on – for all she heard was a snap of the letter-box, a snap much louder than it normally made, and when she went to the door she saw the piece of torn postcard lying on the mat, the same mat she had looked at so often when she was longing for word of her daughter Alexandra. Picking it up, she ran to the bedroom for her Bible, where her own half already lay, and yes, the pieces matched, God was on her side, St Joseph had interceded for her. (But what a needless piece of nonsense, all the same!) And when she opened the door to him, he slipped past her like a shadow: a little hobgoblin of a fellow, in a black overcoat with velvet tabs on the collar, giving him an air of operatic conspiracy. They have sent me a midget to catch a giant, was her first thought. He had arched eyebrows and a grooved face and flicked-up horns of black hair above his pointed ears, which he prinked with his little palms before the hall mirror as he took off his hat – so bright and comic that on a different occasion Ostrakova would have laughed out loud at all the life and humour and irreverence in him.

But not tonight.

Tonight he had a gravity that she sensed immediately was not his normal way. Tonight, like a busy salesman who had just stepped off an aeroplane – she had the feeling also about him that he was brand new in town: his cleanliness, his air of travelling light – tonight he wished only to do business.

'You received my letter safely, madame?' He spoke Russian swiftly, with an Estonian accent.

'I had thought it was the General's letter,' she replied, affecting – she could not save herself – a certain sternness with him.

'It is I who brought it for him,' he said gravely. He was delving in an inside pocket and she had a dreadful feeling that, like the big Russian, he was going to produce a sleek black notebook. But he drew out instead a photograph, and one look was quite enough: the pallid, glossy features, the expression that despised all womanhood, not just her own; the suggestion of longing, but not daring to take.

'Yes,' she said. 'That is the stranger.'

Seeing his happiness increase, she knew immediately that he was what Glikman and his friends called 'one of us' – not a Jew necessarily, but a man with heart and meat to him. From that moment on she called him in her mind 'the magician'. She thought of his pockets as being full of clever tricks, and of his merry eyes as containing a dash of magic.

For half the night, with an intensity she hadn't experienced since Glikman, she and the magician talked. First, she told it all again, reliving it exactly, secretly surprised to discover how much she had left out of her letter, which the magician seemed to know by heart. She explained her feelings to him, and her tears, her terrible inner turmoil; she described the crudeness of her perspiring tormentor. He was so inept – she kept repeating, in wonder – as if it were his first time, she said – he had no finesse, no assurance. So odd to think of the Devil as a fumbler! She told about the ham omelette and the *frites* and the Alsatian beer and he laughed; about her feeling that he was a man of dangerous timidity and inhibition – not a woman's man at all – to most of which the little magician agreed with her cordially, as if he and the gingery man were already well acquainted. She trusted the magician entirely, as the General had told her to; she was sick and tired of suspicion. She talked, she thought afterwards, as frankly as she once had talked to Ostrakov when they were young lovers in her own home town, on the nights they thought they might never meet again, clutching each other under siege, whispering to the sound of approaching guns; or to Glikman, while they waited for the hammering on the door that would take him back to prison yet again. She talked to his alert and understanding gaze, to the laughter in him, to the suffering which she sensed immediately was the better side of his unorthodox and perhaps anti-social nature. And gradually, as she went on talking, her woman's instinct told her that she was feeding a passion in him – not a love this time, but a sharp and particular hatred that gave thrust and sensibility to every little question he asked. What or whom it was that he hated, exactly, she could not say, but she feared for any man, whether the gingery stranger or anybody else, who had attracted this tiny magician's fire. Glikman's passion, she recalled, had been a general, sleepless passion against injustice, fixing itself almost at random upon a range of symptoms, small or large. But the magician's was a single beam, fixed upon a spot she could not see.

It is in any case a fact that by the time the magician left – my Lord, she thought, it was nearly time for her to go to work again! – Ostrakova had told him everything she had to tell, and the magician in return had woken feelings in her which for years, until this night, had belonged only to her past. Tidying away the plates and bottles in a daze, she managed, despite the complexity of her feelings regarding Alexandra, and herself, and her two dead men, to burst out laughing at her woman's folly.

'And I do not even know his name!' she said aloud, and shook her head in mockery. 'How shall I reach you?' she had asked. 'How can I warn you if he returns?'

She could not, the magician had replied. But if there was a crisis she should write to the General again, under his English name and at a different address. 'Mr Miller,' he said gravely, pronouncing it as French, and gave her a card with a London address printed by hand in capitals. 'But be discreet,' he warned. 'You must be indirect in your language.'

All that day, and for many days afterwards, Ostrakova kept her last departing image of the magician at the forefront of her memory as he slipped away from her and down the ill-lit staircase. His last fervid stare, taut with purpose and excitement: 'I promise to release you. Thank you for calling me to arms.' His little white hand, running down the broad banister of the stairwell, like a handkerchief waved from a train window, round and round in a dwindling circle of farewell, till it disappeared into the darkness of the tunnel.

2

The second of the two events that brought George Smiley from his retirement occurred a few weeks after the first, in early autumn of the same year: not in Paris at all, but in the once ancient, free, and Hanseatic city of Hamburg, now almost pounded to death by the thunder of its own prosperity; yet it remains true that nowhere does the summer fade more splendidly than along the gold and orange banks of the Alster, which nobody as yet has drained or filled with concrete. George Smiley, needless to say, had seen nothing of its languorous autumn splendour. Smiley, on the day in question, was toiling obliviously, with whatever conviction he could muster, at his habitual desk in the London Library in St James's Square, with two spindly trees to look at through the sash-window of the reading-room. The only link to Hamburg he might have pleaded – if he had afterwards attempted the connection, which he did not – was in the Parnassian field of German baroque poetry, for at the time he was composing a monograph on the bard Opitz, and trying loyally to distinguish true passion from the tiresome literary convention of the period.

The time in Hamburg was a few moments after eleven in the morning, and the footpath leading to the jetty was speckled with sunlight and dead leaves. A candescent haze hung over the flat water of the Aussenalster, and through it the spires of the Eastern bank were like green stains dabbed on the wet horizon. Along the shore, red squirrels scurried, foraging for the winter. But the slight and somewhat anarchistic-looking young man standing on the jetty wearing a tracksuit and running shoes had neither eyes nor mind for them. His red-rimmed gaze was locked tensely upon the approaching steamer, his hollow face darkened by a two-day stubble. He carried a Hamburg newspaper under his left arm, and an eye as perceptive as George Smiley's would have noticed at once that it was yesterday's edition, not today's. In his right hand he clutched a rush shopping basket better suited to the dumpy Madame Ostrakova than to this lithe, bedraggled athlete who seemed any minute about to leap into the lake. Oranges peeked out of the top of the basket, a yellow Kodak envelope with English printing lay on top of the oranges. The jetty was otherwise empty, and the haze over the water added to his solitude. His only companions were the steamer timetable and an archaic notice, which must have survived the war, telling him how to revive the half-drowned; his only thoughts concerned the General's instructions, which he was continuously reciting to himself like a prayer.

The steamer glided alongside and the boy skipped aboard like a child in a dance game – a flurry of steps, then motionless until the music starts again. For forty-eight hours, night and day, he had had nothing to think of but this moment: now. Driving, he had stared wakefully at the road, imagining, between glimpses of his wife and little girl, the many disastrous things that could go wrong. He knew he had a talent for disaster. During his rare breaks for coffee, he had packed and repacked the oranges a dozen times, laying the envelope longways, sideways – no, this angle is better, it is more appropriate, easier to get hold of. At the edge of town he had

collected small change so that he would have the fare exactly –
what if the conductor held him up, engaged him in casual conversation? There was so little time to do what he had to do!
He would speak no German, he had worked it out. He would
mumble, smile, be reticent, apologise, but stay mute. Or he
would say some of his few words of Estonian – some phrase
from the Bible he could still remember from his Lutheran
childhood, before his father insisted he learn Russian. But now,
with the moment so close upon him, the boy suddenly saw a
snag in his plan. What if his fellow passengers then came to his
aid? In polyglot Hamburg, with the East only a few miles away,
any six people could muster as many languages between them!
Better to keep silent, be blank.

He wished he had shaved. He wished he was less
conspicuous.

Inside the main cabin of the steamer, the boy looked at
nobody. He kept his eyes lowered; *avoid eye contact*, the General had ordered. The conductor was chatting to an old lady
and ignored him. He waited awkwardly, trying to look calm.
There were about thirty passengers. He had an impression of
men and women dressed alike in green overcoats and green
felt hats, all disapproving of him. It was his turn. He held out
a damp palm. One mark, a fifty-pfennig piece, a punch of little
brass tens. The conductor helped himself, not speaking. Clumsily, the boy groped his way between the seats, making for the
stern. The jetty was moving away. They suspect me of being a
terrorist, thought the boy. There was engine oil on his hands
and he wished he'd washed it off. Perhaps it's on my face as
well. *Be blank*, the General had said. *Efface yourself. Neither smile
nor frown. Be normal.* He glanced at his watch, trying to keep
the action slow. He had rolled back his left cuff in advance,
specially to leave the watch free. Ducking, though he was not

tall, the boy arrived suddenly in the stern section, which was open to the weather, protected only by a canopy. It was a case of seconds. Not of days or kilometres any more; not hours. Seconds. The timing hand of his watch flickered past the six. *The next time it reaches six, you move.* A breeze was blowing but he barely noticed it. The time was an awful worry to him. When he got excited – he knew – he lost all sense of time completely. He was afraid the seconds hand would race through a double circuit before he had realised, turning one minute into two. In the stern section all seats were vacant. He made jerkily for the last bench of all, holding the basket of oranges over his stomach in both hands, clamping the newspaper to his armpit at the same time: *it is I, read my signals.* He felt a fool. The oranges were too conspicuous by far. Why on earth should an unshaven young man in a tracksuit be carrying a basket of oranges and yesterday's newspaper? The whole boat must have noticed him! 'Captain – that young man – there – he is a bomber! He has a bomb in his basket, he intends to hijack us or sink the ship!' A couple stood arm in arm at the railing with their backs to him, staring into the mist. The man was very small, shorter than the woman. He wore a black overcoat with a velvet collar. They ignored him. *Sit as far back as you can, be sure you sit next to the aisle*, the General had said. He sat down, praying it would work first time, that none of the fallbacks would be needed. 'Beckie, I do this for *you*,' he whispered secretly, thinking of his daughter, and remembering the General's words. His Lutheran origins notwithstanding, he wore a wooden cross round his neck, a present to him from his mother, but the zip of his tunic covered it. Why had he hidden the cross? So that God would not witness his deceit? He didn't know. He wanted only to be driving again, to drive and drive till he dropped or was safely home.

Look nowhere, he remembered the General saying. He was to look nowhere but ahead of him: *you are the passive partner. You have nothing to do but supply the opportunity. No code word, nothing; just the basket and the oranges and the yellow envelope and the newspaper under your arm.* I should never have agreed to it, he thought. I have endangered my daughter Beckie. Stella will never forgive me. I shall lose my citizenship, I have put everything at risk. *Do it for our cause*, the General had said. General, I haven't got one: it was not my cause, it was your cause, it was my father's; that is why I threw the oranges overboard.

But he didn't. Laying the newspaper beside him on the slatted bench, he saw that it was drenched in sweat – that patches of print had worn off where he clutched it. He looked at his watch. The seconds hand was standing at ten. It's stopped! Fifteen seconds since I last looked – that simply is not possible! A frantic glance at the shore convinced him they were already in mid-lake. He looked at the watch again and saw the seconds hand jerking past eleven. Fool, he thought, calm yourself. Leaning to his right, he affected to read the newspaper while he kept the dial of his watch constantly in view. Terrorists. Nothing but terrorists, he thought, reading the headlines for the twentieth time. No wonder the passengers think I'm one of them. *Grossfahndung*. That was their word for massive search. It amazed him that he remembered so much German. *Do it for our cause.*

At his feet the basket of oranges was leaning precariously. *When you get up, put the basket on the bench to reserve your seat*, the General had said. What if it falls over? In his imagination he saw the oranges rolling all over the deck, the yellow envelope upside down among them, photographs everywhere, all of Beckie. The seconds hand was passing six. He stood up. Now. His midriff was cold. He tugged his tunic down to cover it and inadvertently exposed his mother's wooden cross. He closed the zip. *Saunter. Look nowhere. Pretend you are the dreamy sort*, the General had said. *Your father would not have hesitated a moment*, the General had said. *Nor will you*. Cautiously lifting the basket on to the bench he steadied it with both hands, then leaned it towards the back to give it extra stability. Then tested it. He wondered about the *Abendblatt*. To take it, to leave it where it was? Perhaps his contact had still not seen the signal? He picked it up and put it under his arm.

He returned to the main cabin. A couple moved into the stern section, presumably to take the air, older, very sedate. The first couple were a sexy pair, even from behind – the little man, the shapely girl, the trimness of them both. You knew they had a good time in bed, just to look at them. But this second couple were like a pair of policemen to him; the boy was certain they got no pleasure from their love-making at all. Where is my mind going? he thought crazily. To my wife, Stella, was the answer. To the long exquisite embraces we may never have again. Sauntering as he had been ordered to, he advanced down the aisle towards the closed-off area where the pilot sat. Looking at nobody was easy; the passengers sat with their backs to him. He had reached as far forward as passengers were allowed. The pilot sat to his left, on a raised platform. *Go to the pilot's window and admire the view. Remain there one minute exactly*. The cabin roof was lower here; he had to stoop. Through the big windscreen, trees and buildings on the move. He saw a rowing eight switch by, followed by a lone blonde goddess in a skiff. Breasts like a statue's, he thought. For greater casualness, he propped one running shoe on the pilot's platform. Give me a woman, he thought desperately, as the moment of crisis came; give me my Stella, drowsy and desiring, in the half-light of early morning. He had his left wrist forward on the railing, his watch constantly in view.

'We don't clean boots here,' the pilot growled.

Hastily the boy replaced his foot on the deck. Now he knows I speak German, he thought, and felt his face prickle in embarrassment. But they know anyway, he thought stupidly, for why else would I carry a German newspaper?

It was time. Swiftly standing to his full height again, he swung round too fast and began the return journey to his seat, and it was no use any more remembering not to stare at faces because the faces stared at him, disapproving of his two days' growth of beard, his track suit and his wild look. His eyes left one face, only to find another. He thought he had never seen such a chorus of mute ill-will. His tracksuit had parted at the midriff again and showed a line of black hair. Stella washes them too hot, he thought. He tugged the tunic down again and stepped into the air, wearing his wooden cross like a medal. As he did so, two things happened almost at the same time. On the bench, next to the basket, he saw the yellow chalk mark he was looking for, running over two slats, bright as a canary, telling him that the handover had taken place successfully. At the sight of it, a sense of glory filled him, he had known nothing like it in his life, a release more perfect than any woman could provide.

Why must we do it this way? he had asked the General; why does it have to be so elaborate?

Because the object is unique in the whole world, the General had replied. *It is a treasure without a counterpart. Its loss would be a tragedy to the free world.*

And he chose me to be his courier, thought the boy proudly: though he still, at the back of his mind, thought the old man was overdoing it. Serenely picking up the yellow envelope, he dropped it into his tunic pocket, drew the zip and ran his finger down the join to make sure it had meshed.

At the same instant exactly, he realised he was being

watched. The woman at the railing still had her back to him and he noticed again that she had very pretty hips and legs. But her sexy little companion in the black overcoat had turned all the way round to face him, and his expression put an end to all the good feelings the boy had just experienced. Only once had he seen a face like that, and that was when his father lay dying in their first English home, a room in Ruislip, a few months after they had reached England. The boy had seen nothing so desperate, so profoundly serious, so bare of all protection, in anyone else, ever. More alarming still, he knew – precisely as Ostrakova had known – that it was a desperation in contrast with the natural disposition of the features, which were those of a comedian – or, as Ostrakova had it, a magician. So that the impassioned stare of this little, sharp-faced stranger, with its message of furious entreaty – 'Boy, you have no idea what you are carrying! Guard it with your life!' – was a revelation of that same comedian's soul.

The steamer had stopped. They were on the other bank. Seizing his basket, the boy leapt ashore, and, almost running, ducked between the bustling shoppers from one side-street to another without knowing where they led.

All through the drive back, while the steering-wheel hammered his arms and the engine played its pounding scale in his ears, the boy saw that face before him in the wet road, wondering as the hours passed whether it was something he had merely imagined in the emotion of the handover. Most likely the real contact was someone completely different, he thought, trying to soothe himself. One of those fat ladies in the green felt hats – even the conductor. I was overstrung, he told himself. At a crucial moment, an unknown man turned round and looked at me and I hung an entire history on him, even imagining he was my dying father.

By the time he reached Dover he almost believed he had put the man out of his mind. He had dumped the cursed oranges in a litter bin; the yellow envelope lay snug in the pouch of his tunic, one sharp corner pricking his skin, and that was all that mattered. So he had formed theories about his secret accomplice? Forget them. And even if, by sheer coincidence, he was right, and it was that hollowed, glaring face – *then* what? All the less reason to go blabbing about it to the General, whose concern with security the boy likened to the unchallengeable passion of a seer. The thought of Stella became an aching need to him. His desire sharpened with every noisy mile. It was early morning still. He imagined waking her with his caresses; he saw her sleepy smile slowly turn to passion.

The summons came to Smiley that same night, and it is a curious fact, since he had an overall impression of not sleeping at all well during this late period of his life, that the phone had to ring a long time beside the bed before he answered it. He had come home straight from the library, then dined poorly at an Italian restaurant in the King's Road, taking the *Voyages of Olearius* with him for protection. He had returned to his house in Bywater Street and resumed work on his monograph with the devotion of a man who had nothing else to do. After a couple of hours he had opened a bottle of red Burgundy and drunk half of it, listening to a poor play on the radio. Then dozed, wrestling with troubled dreams. Yet the moment he heard Lacon's voice, he had the feeling of being hauled from a warm and treasured place, where he wished to remain undisturbed for ever. Also, though in fact he was moving swiftly, he had the sensation of taking a long time to dress; and he wondered whether that was what old men did when they heard about a death.

3

'Knew him personally at all, did you, sir?' the Detective Chief Superintendent of Police asked respectfully in a voice kept deliberately low. 'Or perhaps I shouldn't enquire.'

The two men had been together for fifteen minutes but this was the Superintendent's first question. For a while Smiley did not seem to hear it, but his silence was not offensive, he had the gift of quiet. Besides, there is a companionship about two men contemplating a corpse. It was an hour before dawn on Hampstead Heath, a dripping, misty, no-man's hour, neither warm nor cold, with a heaven tinted orange by the London glow, and the trees glistening like oilskins. They stood side by side in an avenue of beeches and the Superintendent was taller by a head: a young giant of a man, prematurely grizzled, a little pompous perhaps, but with a giant's gentleness that made him naturally befriending. Smiley was clasping his pudgy hands over his belly like a mayor at a cenotaph, and had eyes for nothing but the body lying at his feet in the beam of the Superintendent's torch. The walk this far had evidently winded him, for he puffed a little as he stared. From the darkness round them, police receivers crackled on the night air. There were no other lights at all; the Superintendent had ordered them extinguished.

'He was just somebody I worked with,' Smiley explained after a long delay.

'So I was given to understand, sir,' the Superintendent said.

He waited hopefully but nothing more came. 'Don't even speak to him,' the Deputy Assistant Commissioner (Crime and Ops) had said to him. 'You never saw him and it was two other blokes. Just show him what he wants and drop him down a hole. Fast.' Till now, the Detective Chief Superintendent had done exactly that. He had moved, in his own estimation, with the speed of light. The photographer had photographed, the doctor had certified life extinct, the pathologist had inspected the body *in situ* as a prelude to conducting his autopsy – all with an expedition quite contrary to the proper pace of things, merely in order to clear the way for the visiting *irregular*, as the Deputy Assistant Commissioner (Crime and Ops) had liked to call him. The irregular had arrived – with about as much ceremony as a meter-reader, the Superintendent noted – and the Superintendent had led him over the course at a canter. They had looked at footprints, they had tracked the old man's route till here. The Superintendent had made a reconstruction of the crime, as well as he was able in the circumstances, and the Superintendent was an able man. Now they were in the dip, at the point where the avenue turned, where the rolling mist was thickest. In the torch-beam the dead body was the centre-piece of everything. It lay face downward and spread-eagled, as if it had been crucified to the gravel, and the plastic sheet emphasised its lifelessness. It was the body of an old man, but broad-shouldered still, a body that had battled and endured. The white hair was cut to stubble. One strong, veined hand still grasped a sturdy walking-stick. He wore a black overcoat and rubber overshoes. A black beret lay on the ground beside him, and the gravel at his head was black with blood. Some loose change lay about, and a pocket handkerchief, and a small penknife that looked more like a keepsake than a tool. Most likely they had started to search him and given up, sir, the Superintendent had said. Most likely they were disturbed, Mr Smiley, sir; and Smiley had wondered what it must be like to touch a warm body you had just shot.

'If I might possibly take a look at his face, Superintendent,' Smiley said.

This time it was the Superintendent who caused the delay. 'Ah, now are you sure about that, sir?' He sounded slightly embarrassed. 'There'll be better ways of identifying him than *that*, you know.'

'Yes. Yes, I am sure,' said Smiley earnestly, as if he really had given the matter great thought.

The Superintendent called softly to the trees, where his men stood among their blacked-out cars like a next generation waiting for its turn.

'You there. Hall. Sergeant Pike. Come here at the double and turn him over.'

Fast, the Deputy Assistant Commissioner (Crime and Ops) had said.

Two men slipped forward from the shadows. The elder wore a black beard. Their surgical gloves of elbow length shone ghostly grey. They wore blue overalls and thigh-length rubber boots. Squatting, the bearded man cautiously untucked the plastic sheet while the younger constable laid a hand on the dead man's shoulder as if to wake him up.

'You'll have to try harder than that, lad,' the Superintendent warned in an altogether crisper tone.

The boy pulled, the bearded sergeant helped him, and the body reluctantly rolled over, one arm stiffly waving, the other still clutching the stick.

'Oh Christ,' said the constable. 'Oh bloody hell!' – and clapped a hand over his mouth. The sergeant grabbed his elbow and shoved him away. They heard the sound of retching.

'I don't hold with politics,' the Superintendent confided to Smiley inconsequentially, staring downward still. 'I don't hold with politics and I don't hold with politicians either. Licensed lunatics most of them, in my view. That's why I joined the Force, to be honest.' The sinewy mist curled strangely in the steady beam of his torch. 'You don't happen to know what did it, do you, sir? I haven't seen a wound like that in fifteen years.'

'I'm afraid ballistics are not my province,' Smiley replied, after another pause for thought.

'No, I don't expect they would be, would they? Seen enough, sir?'

Smiley apparently had not.

'Most people expect to be shot in the chest really, don't they, sir?' the Superintendent remarked brightly. He had learned that small talk sometimes eased the atmosphere on such occasions. 'Your neat round bullet that drills a tasteful hole. That's what most people expect. Victim falls gently to his knees to the tune of celestial choirs. It's the telly that does it, I suppose. Whereas your real bullet these days can take off an arm or a leg, so my friends in brown tell me.' His voice took on a more practical tone. 'Did he have a moustache at all, sir? My sergeant fancied a trace of white whisker on the upper jaw.'

'A military one,' said Smiley after a long gap, and with his thumb and forefinger absently described the shape upon his own lip while his gaze remained locked upon the old man's body. 'I wonder, Superintendent, whether I might just examine the contents of his pockets, possibly?'

'Sergeant Pike.'

'Sir!'

'Put that sheet back and tell Mr Murgotroyd to have his pockets ready for me in the van, will you, what they've left of them. At the double,' the Superintendent added, as a matter of routine.

'Sir!'

'And come here.' The Superintendent had taken the sergeant softly by the upper arm. 'You tell that young Constable Hall that I can't stop him sicking up but I won't have his irreverent language.' For the Superintendent on his home territory was a devoutly Christian man and did not care who knew it. 'This way, Mr Smiley, sir,' he added, recovering his gentler tone.

As they moved higher up the avenue, the chatter of the radios faded, and they heard instead the angry wheeling of rooks and the growl of the city. The Superintendent marched briskly, keeping to the left of the roped-off area. Smiley hurried after him. A windowless van was parked between the trees, its back doors open, and a dim light burning inside. Entering, they sat on hard benches. Mr Murgotroyd had grey hair and wore a grey suit. He crouched before them with a plastic sack like a transparent pillowcase. The sack had a knot at the throat, which he untied. Inside, smaller packages floated. As Mr Murgotroyd lifted them out, the Superintendent read the labels by his torch before handing them to Smiley to consider.

'One scuffed leather coin case, Continental appearance. Half inside his pocket, half out, left-side jacket. You saw the coins by his body – seventy-two pence. That's all the money on him. Carry a wallet at all, did he, sir?'

'I don't know.'

'Our guess is they helped themselves to the wallet, started on the purse, then ran. One bunch keys domestic and various, right-hand trousers . . .' He ran on but Smiley's scrutiny did not relax. Some people *act* a memory, the Superintendent thought, noticing his concentration, others *have* one. In the

Superintendent's book, memory was the better half of intelligence, he prized it highest of all mental accomplishments; and Smiley, he knew, possessed it. 'One Paddington Borough Library Card in the name of V. Miller, one box Swan Vesta matches partly used, overcoat left. One Aliens' Registration Card, number as reported, also in the name of Vladimir Miller. One bottle tablets, overcoat left. What would the tablets be for, sir, any views on that at all? Name of Sustac, whatever that is, to be taken two to three times a day?'

'Heart,' said Smiley.

'And one receipt for the sum of thirteen pounds from the Straight and Steady Minicab Service of Islington, North.'

'May I look?' said Smiley, and the Superintendent held it out so that Smiley could read the date and the driver's signature, J. Lamb, in a copy-book hand wildly underlined.

The next bag contained a stick of school chalk, yellow and miraculously unbroken. The narrow end was smeared brown as if by a single stroke, but the thick end was unused.

'There's yellow chalk powder on his left hand too,' Mr Murgotroyd said, speaking for the first time. His complexion was like grey stone. His voice too was grey, and mournful as an undertaker's. 'We did wonder whether he might be in the teaching line, actually,' Mr Murgotroyd added, but Smiley, either by design or oversight, did not answer Mr Murgotroyd's implicit question, and the Superintendent did not pursue it.

And a second cotton handkerchief, proffered this time by Mr Murgotroyd, part bloodied, part clean, and carefully ironed into a sharp triangle for the top pocket.

'On his way to a party, we wondered,' Mr Murgotroyd said, this time with no hope at all.

'Crime and Ops on the air, sir,' a voice called from the front of the van.

Without a word the Superintendent vanished into the darkness, leaving Smiley to the depressed gaze of Mr Murgotroyd.

'You a specialist of some sort, sir?' Mr Murgotroyd asked after a long sad scrutiny of his guest.

'No. No, I'm afraid not,' said Smiley.

'Home Office, sir?'

'Alas, not Home Office either,' said Smiley with a benign shake of his head, which somehow made him party to Mr Murgotroyd's bewilderment.

'My superiors are a little worried about the press, Mr Smiley,' the Superintendent said, poking his head into the van again. 'Seems they're heading this way, sir.'

Smiley clambered quickly out. The two men stood face to face in the avenue.

'You've been very kind,' Smiley said. 'Thank you.'

'Privilege,' said the Superintendent.

'You don't happen to remember which pocket the *chalk* was in, do you?' Smiley asked.

'Overcoat left,' the Superintendent replied in some surprise.

'And the searching of him – could you tell me again how you see *that* exactly?'

'They hadn't time or didn't care to turn him over. Knelt by him, fished for his wallet, pulled at his purse. Scattered a few objects as they did so. By then they'd had enough.'

'Thank you,' said Smiley again.

And a moment later, with more ease than his portly figure might have suggested him capable of, he had vanished among the trees. But not before the Superintendent had shone the torch full upon his face, a thing he hadn't done till now for reasons of discretion. And taken an intense professional look at the legendary features, if only to tell his grandchildren in his old age: how George Smiley, sometime Chief of the Secret

Service, by then retired, had one night come out of the wood-work to peer at some dead foreigner of his who had died in highly nasty circumstances.

Not *one* face at all, actually, the Superintendent reflected. Not when it was lit by the torch like that indirectly from below. More your whole range of faces. More your patchwork of different ages, people and endeavours. Even – thought the Superintendent – of different faiths.

'The best I ever met,' old Mendel, the Superintendent's one-time superior, had told him over a friendly pint not long ago. Mendel was retired now, like Smiley. But Mendel knew what he was talking about and didn't like Funnies any better than the Superintendent did – interfering la-di-da amateurs most of them, and devious with it. But not Smiley. Smiley was different, Mendel had said. Smiley was the best – simply the best case man Mendel had ever met – and old Mendel knew what he was talking about.

An abbey, the Superintendent decided. That's what he was, an abbey. He would work that into his sermon the next time his turn came around. An abbey, made up of all sorts of con-flicting ages and styles and convictions. The Superintendent liked that metaphor the more he dwelt on it. He would try it out on his wife when he got home: man as God's architecture, my dear, moulded by the hand of ages, infinite in his striving and diversity . . . But at this point the Superintendent laid a restraining hand upon his own rhetorical imagination. Maybe not, after all, he thought. Maybe we're flying a mite too high for the course, my friend.

There was another thing about that face the Superinten-dent wouldn't easily forget either. Later, he talked to old Men-del about it, as he talked to him later about lots of things. The moisture. He'd taken it for dew at first – yet if it was dew why was the Superintendent's own face bone dry? It wasn't dew and it wasn't grief either, if his hunch was right. It was a thing that happened to the Superintendent himself occasionally and happened to the lads too, even the hardest; it crept up on them and the Superintendent watched for it like a hawk. Usually in kids' cases, where the pointlessness suddenly got through to you – your child batterings, your criminal assaults, your infant rapes. You didn't break down or beat your chest or any of those histrionics. No. You just happened to put your hand to your face and find it damp and you wondered what the hell Christ bothered to die for, if He ever died at all.

And when you had that mood on you, the Superintendent told himself with a slight shiver, the best thing you could do was give yourself a couple of days off and take the wife to Margate, or before you knew where you were you found yourself getting a little too rough with people for your own good health.

'Sergeant!' the Superintendent yelled.

The bearded figure loomed before him.

'Switch the lights on and get it back to normal,' the Superintendent ordered. 'And ask Inspector Hallowes to slip up here and oblige. At the double.'

4

They had unchained the door to him, they had questioned him
even before they took his coat: tersely and intently. Were there
any compromising materials on the body, George? Any that
would link him with us? My God, you've been a time! They
had shown him where to wash, forgetting that he knew already.
They had sat him in an armchair and there Smiley remained,
humble and discarded, while Oliver Lacon, Whitehall's Head
Prefect to the intelligence services, prowled the threadbare
carpet like a man made restless by his conscience, and Lauder
Strickland said it all again in fifteen different ways to fifteen different people, over the old upright telephone in the far corner
of the room – 'Then get me back to police liaison, woman, *at
once*' – either bullying or fawning, depending on rank and clout.
The Superintendent was a life ago, but in time ten minutes. The
flat smelt of old nappies and stale cigarettes and was on the top
floor of a scrolled Edwardian apartment house not two hundred yards from Hampstead Heath. In Smiley's mind, visions of
Vladimir's burst face mingled with these pale faces of the living,
yet death was not a shock to him just now, but merely an affir-
mation that his own existence too was dwindling; that he was
living against the odds. He sat without expectation. He sat like
an old man at a country railway station, watching the express go
by. But watching all the same. And remembering old journeys.

This is how crises always were, he thought; ragtag conversations with no centre. One man on the telephone, another dead, a third prowling. The nervous idleness of slow motion.

He peered around, trying to fix his mind on the decaying things outside himself. Chipped fire extinguishers, Ministry of Works issue. Prickly brown sofas – the stains a little worse. But safe flats, unlike old generals, never die, he thought. They don't even fade away.

On the table before him lay the cumbersome apparatus of agent hospitality, there to revive the unrevivable guest. Smiley took the inventory. In a bucket of melted ice, one bottle of Stolichnaya vodka, Vladimir's recorded favourite brand. Salted herrings, still in their tin. Pickled cucumber, bought loose and already drying. One mandatory loaf of black bread. Like every Russian Smiley had known, the old boy could scarcely drink his vodka without it. Two Marks & Spencer vodka glasses, could be cleaner. One packet of Russian cigarettes, unopened: if he had come, he would have smoked the lot; he had none with him when he died.

Vladimir had none with him when he died, he repeated to himself, and made a little mental stammer of it, a knot in his handkerchief.

A clatter interrupted Smiley's reverie. In the kitchen, Mostyn the boy had dropped a plate. At the telephone Lauder Strickland wheeled round, demanding quiet. But he already had it again. What was Mostyn preparing anyway? Dinner? Breakfast? Seed-cake for the funeral? And what was Mostyn? *Who was* Mostyn? Smiley had shaken his damp and trembling hand, then promptly forgotten what he looked like except that he was so young. And yet for some reason Mostyn was known to him, if only as a type. Mostyn is our grief, Smiley decided arbitrarily.

Lacon, in the middle of his prowling, came to a sudden halt.

'George! You look worried. Don't be. We're all in the clear on this. All of us!'

'I'm not worried, Oliver.'

'You look as though you're reproaching yourself. I can tell!'

'When agents die—' said Smiley, but left the sentence incomplete, and anyway Lacon couldn't wait for him. He strode off again, a hiker with miles to go. Lacon, Strickland, Mostyn, thought Smiley as Strickland's Aberdonian brogue hammered on. One Cabinet Office factotum, one Circus fixer, one scared boy. Why not real people? Why not Vladimir's case officer, whoever he is? Why not Saul Enderby, their Chief?

A couplet of Auden's rang in his mind from the days when he was Mostyn's age: *let us honour if we can the vertical man, though we value none but the horizontal one.* Or something.

And why Smiley? he thought. Above all, why me? Of all people, when as far as they're concerned I'm deader than old Vladimir.

'Will you have tea, Mr Smiley, or something stronger?' called Mostyn through the open kitchen doorway. Smiley wondered whether he was naturally so pale.

'He'll have tea only, thank you, Mostyn!' Lacon blurted, making a sharp about-turn. 'After shock, tea is a deal safer. With sugar, right, George? Sugar replaces lost energy. Was it *gruesome*, George? How perfectly awful for you.'

No, it wasn't awful, it was the truth, thought Smiley. He was shot and I saw him dead. Perhaps you should do that too.

Apparently unable to leave Smiley alone, Lacon had come back down the room and was peering at him with clever, uncomprehending eyes. He was a mawkish creature, sudden but without spring, with youthful features cruelly aged and a raw unhealthy rash around his neck where his shirt had scuffed the skin. In the religious light between dawn and morning his black waistcoat and white collar had the glint of the soutane.

'I've hardly said hullo,' Lacon complained, as if it were Smiley's fault. 'George. Old friend. My goodness.'

'Hullo, Oliver,' said Smiley.

Still Lacon remained there, gazing down at him, his long head to one side, like a child studying an insect. In his memory Smiley replayed Lacon's fervid phone call of two hours before.

It's an emergency, George. You remember Vladimir? George, are you awake? You remember the old General, George? Used to live in Paris?

Yes, I remember the General, he had replied. Yes, Oliver, I remember Vladimir.

We need someone from his past, George. Someone who knew his little ways, can identify him, damp down potential scandal. We need you, George. Now. George, wake up.

He had been trying to. Just as he had been trying to transfer the receiver to his better ear, and sit upright in a bed too large for him. He was sprawling in the cold space deserted by his wife, because that was the side where the telephone was.

You mean he's been shot? Smiley had repeated.

George, why can't you listen? Shot dead. This evening. George, for Heaven's sake wake up, we need you!

Lacon loped off again, plucking at his signet ring as if it were too tight. *I need you*, thought Smiley, watching him gyrate. *I love you, I hate you, I need you*. Such apocalyptic statements reminded him of Ann when she had run out of money or love. The heart of the sentence is the subject, he thought. It is not the verb, least of all the object. It is the ego, demanding its feed.

Need me what for? he thought again. To console them?

Give them absolution? What have they done that they need my past to redress their future?

Down the room, Lauder Strickland was holding up an arm in Fascist salute while he addressed Authority.

'Yes, Chief, he's with us at this moment, sir . . . I shall tell him that, sir . . . Indeed, sir . . . I shall convey to him that message . . . Yes, sir . . .'

Why are Scots so attracted to the secret world? Smiley wondered, not for the first time in his career. Ships' engineers, Colonial administrators, spies . . . Their heretical Scottish history drew them to distant churches, he decided.

'George!' Strickland, suddenly much louder, calling Smiley's name like an order. 'Sir Saul sends you his warmest personal salutations, George!' He had swung round, still with his arm up. 'At a quieter moment he will express his gratitude to you more fittingly.' Back to the phone: 'Yes, Chief, Oliver Lacon is also with me and his opposite number at the Home Office is at this instant in parley with the Commissioner of Police regarding our former interest in the dead man and the preparation of the D-Notice for the press.'

Former interest, Smiley recorded. A former interest with his face shot off and no cigarettes in his pocket. Yellow chalk. Smiley studied Strickland frankly: the awful green suit, the shoes of brushed pigskin got up as suède leather. The only change he could observe in him was a russet moustache not half as military as Vladimir's when he had still had one.

'Yes, sir, "an extinct case of purely historic concern", sir,' Strickland went on, into the telephone. Extinct is right, thought Smiley. Extinct, extinguished, put out. 'That is precisely the terminology,' Strickland continued. 'And Oliver Lacon proposes to have it included word for word in the D-Notice. Am I on target there, Oliver?'

'*Historical*,' Lacon corrected him irritably. 'Not *historic* concern. That's the last thing we want! Historical.' He stalked across the room, ostensibly to peer through the window at the coming day.

'It *is* still Enderby in charge, is it, Oliver?' Smiley asked, of Lacon's back.

'Yes, yes, it is still Saul Enderby, your old adversary, and he is doing marvels,' Lacon retorted impatiently. Pulling at the curtain, he unseated it from its runners. 'Not your style, I grant you – why should he be? He's an Atlantic man.' He was trying to force the casement. 'Not an easy thing to be under a government like this one, I can tell you.' He gave the handle another savage shove. A freezing draught raced round Smiley's knees. 'Takes a lot of footwork. Mostyn, where's tea? We seem to have been waiting for ever.'

All our lives, thought Smiley.

Over the sound of a lorry grinding up the hill, he heard Strickland again, interminably talking to Saul Enderby. 'I think the point with the press is not to play him down *too far*, Chief. Dullness is all, in a case like this. Even the private-life angle is a dangerous one, here. What we want is absolute lack of contemporary relevance of any sort. Oh true, true, indeed, Chief, right—' On he droned, sycophantic but alert.

'Oliver—' Smiley began, losing patience. 'Oliver, do you mind, just—'

But Lacon was talking, not listening: 'How's Ann?' he asked vaguely, at the window, stretching his forearms on the sill. 'With you and so forth, I trust? Not roaming, is she? *God*, I hate autumn.'

'Fine, thank you. How's—' He struggled without success to remember the name of Lacon's wife.

'*Abandoned* me, dammit. Ran off with her pesky riding

instructor, blast her. Left me with the children. The girls are farmed out to boarding-schools, thank God.' Leaning over his hands, Lacon was staring up at the lightening sky. 'Is that Orion up there, stuck like a gold ball between the chimney pots?' he asked.

Which is another death, thought Smiley sadly, his mind staying briefly with Lacon's broken marriage. He remembered a pretty, unworldly woman and a string of daughters jumping ponies in the garden of their rambling house in Ascot.

'I'm sorry, Oliver,' he said.

'Why should you be? Not *your* wife. She's mine. It's every man for himself in love.'

'Could you close that window, please!' Strickland called, dialling again. 'It's bloody arctic down this end.'

Irritably slamming the window, Lacon strode back into the room.

Smiley tried a second time: 'Oliver, what's going on?' he asked. 'Why did you need me?'

'Only one who knew him for a start. Strickland, are you nearly done? He's like one of those airport announcers,' he told Smiley with a stupid grin. '*Never* done.'

You could break, Oliver, thought Smiley, noticing the estrangement of Lacon's eyes as he came under the light. You've had too much, he thought in unexpected sympathy. We both have.

From the kitchen the mysterious Mostyn appeared with tea: an earnest, contemporary-looking child with flared trousers and a mane of brown hair. Seeing him set down the tray, Smiley finally placed him in the terms of his own past. Ann had had a lover like him once, an ordinand from Wells Theological College. She gave him a lift down the M4 and later claimed to have saved him from going queer.

'What section are you in, Mostyn?' Smiley asked him quietly.

'Oddbins, sir.' He crouched, level to the table, displaying an Asian suppleness. 'Since your day, actually, sir. It's a sort of operational pool. Mainly probationers waiting for overseas postings.'

'I see.'

'I heard you lecture at the Nursery at Sarratt, sir. On the new entrants' course. "Agent handling in the field." It was the best thing of the whole two years.'

'Thank you.'

But Mostyn's calf eyes stayed on him intently.

'Thank you,' said Smiley again, more puzzled than before.

'Milk, sir, or lemon, sir? The lemon was for *him*,' Mostyn added in a low aside, as if that were recommendation for the lemon.

Strickland had rung off and was fiddling with the waistband of his trousers, making it looser or tighter.

'Yes, well, we have to temper truth, George!' Lacon bellowed suddenly, in what seemed to be a declaration of personal faith. 'Sometimes people are innocent but the circumstances can make them appear quite otherwise. There was never a golden age. There's only a golden mean. We have to remember that. Chalk it on our shaving mirrors.'

In yellow, Smiley thought.

Strickland was waddling down the room: 'You. Mostyn. Young Nigel. You, sir!'

Mostyn lifted his grave brown eyes in reply.

'Commit nothing to paper whatever,' Strickland warned him, wiping the back of his hand on his moustache as if one or the other were wet. 'Hear me? That's an order from on high. There was no encounter so you've no call to fill in the usual encounter sheet or any of that stuff. You've nothing to do but keep your mouth shut. Understand? You'll account for your expenses as general petty-cash disbursements. To me, direct. No file reference. Understand?'

'I understand,' said Mostyn.

'And no whispered confidences to those little tarts in Registry, or I'll know. Hear me? Give us some tea.'

Something happened inside George Smiley when he heard this conversation. Out of the formless indirection of these dialogues, out of the horror of the scene upon the Heath, a single shocking truth struck him. He felt a pull in his chest somewhere and he had the sensation of momentary disconnection from the room and the three haunted people he had found in it. *Encounter? Encounter* between Mostyn and Vladimir? *God in Heaven*, he thought, squaring the mad circle. *The Lord preserve, cosset and protect us. Mostyn was Vladimir's case officer! That old man, a General, once our glory, and they farmed him out to this uncut boy!* Then another lurch, more violent still, as his surprise was swept aside in an explosion of internal fury. He felt his lips tremble, he felt his throat seize up in indignation, blocking his words, and when he turned to Lacon his spectacles seemed to mist over from the heat:

'Oliver, I wonder if you'd mind finally telling me what I'm doing here,' he heard himself suggesting for the third time, hardly above a murmur.

Reaching out an arm he removed the vodka bottle from its bucket. Still unbidden, he broke the cap and poured himself a rather large tot.

Even then, Lacon dithered, pondered, hunted with his eyes, delayed. In Lacon's world, direct questions were the height of bad taste but direct answers were worse. For a moment, caught in mid-gesture at the centre of the room, he stood staring at Smiley in disbelief. A car stumbled up the hill, bringing news of the real world outside the window. Lauder Strickland slurped his tea. Mostyn was seating himself gingerly on a piano-stool to which there was no piano. But Lacon with his jerky gestures could only scratch about for words sufficiently elliptical to disguise his meaning.

'George,' he said. A shower of rain crashed against the window, but he ignored it. 'Where's Mostyn?' he asked.

Mostyn, no sooner settled, had flitted from the room to cope with a nervous need. They heard the thunder of the flush, loud as a brass band, and the gurgle of pipes all down the building.

Lacon raised a hand to his neck, tracing the raw patches. Reluctantly, he began: 'Three years ago, George – let us start there – soon after you left the Circus – your successor Saul Enderby – your *worthy* successor – under pressure from a concerned Cabinet – by *concerned* I mean newly formed – decided on certain far-reaching changes of intelligence practice. I'm giving you the *background*, George,' he explained, interrupting himself. 'I'm doing this because you're who you are, because of old times, and because—' he jabbed a finger at the window – 'because of out there.'

Strickland had unbuttoned his waistcoat and lay dozing and replete like a first-class passenger on a night plane. But his small watchful eyes followed every pass that Lacon made. The door opened and closed, admitting Mostyn, who resumed his perch on the piano-stool.

'Mostyn, I expect you to close your ears to this. I am talking high, high policy. One of these *far-reaching* changes, George, was the decision to form an inter-ministerial Steering Committee. A *mixed* committee' – he composed one in the air with his hands – 'part Westminster, part Whitehall, representing Cabinet as well as the major Whitehall customers. Known as the Wise Men. But placed – George – placed *between* the intelligence fraternity and Cabinet. As a channel, as a filter, as a brake.' One hand had remained outstretched, dealing these metaphors like cards. 'To look over the Circus's shoulder. To exercise control, George. Vigilance and accountability in the interest of a more open government. You don't like it. I can tell by your face.'

'I'm out of it,' Smiley said. 'I'm not qualified to judge.'

Suddenly Lacon's own face took on an appalled expression and his tone dropped to one of near despair.

'You should *hear* them, George, our new masters! You should *hear* the way they talk about the Circus! I'm their dogsbody, damn it: I *know*, get it every day! Gibes. Suspicion. Mistrust at every turn, even from Ministers who should know better. As if the Circus were some rogue animal outside their comprehension. As if British Intelligence were a sort of wholly owned subsidiary of the Conservative Party. Not their ally at all but some autonomous viper in their Socialist nest. The thirties all over again. Do you know, they're even reviving all that talk about a British Freedom of Information Act on the American pattern? From *within* the Cabinet? Of open hearings, revelations, all for the public sport? You'd be shocked, George. Pained. Think of the effect such a thing would have on morale alone. Would Mostyn here ever have joined the Circus after that kind of notoriety in the press and wherever? Would you, Mostyn?'

The question seemed to strike Mostyn very deep, for his grave eyes, made yet darker by his sickly colour, became graver, and he lifted a thumb and finger to his lip. But he did not speak.

'Where was I, George?' Lacon asked, suddenly lost.

'The Wise Men,' said Smiley sympathetically.

From the sofa, Lauder Strickland threw in his own pronouncement on that body: 'Wise, my Aunt Fanny. Bunch of left-wing flannel merchants. Rule our lives for us. Tell us how to run the shop. Smack our wrists when we don't do our sums right.'

Lacon shot Strickland a glance of rebuke but did not contradict him.

'One of the *less* controversial exercises of the Wise Men, George – one of their first duties – conferred upon them specifically by our masters – enshrined in a jointly drafted charter – was *stocktaking*. To review the Circus's resources world-wide and set them beside legitimate present-day targets. Don't ask me what constitutes a legitimate present-day target in their sight. That is a very moot point. However, I must not be disloyal.' He returned to his text. 'Suffice it to say that over a period of six months a review was conducted, and an axe duly laid.' He broke off, staring at Smiley. 'Are you with me, George?' he asked in a puzzled voice.

But it was hardly possible at that moment to tell whether Smiley was with anybody at all. His heavy lids had almost closed, and what remained visible of his eyes was clouded by the thick lenses of his spectacles. He was sitting upright but his head had fallen forward till his plump chins rested on his chest.

Lacon hesitated a moment longer, then continued: 'Now as a result of this axe-laying – this stocktaking, if you prefer – on the part of our Wise Men – certain categories of clandestine operation have been ruled *ipso facto* out of bounds. *Verboten*. Right?'

Prone on his sofa, Strickland incanted the unsayable: 'No coat-trailing. No honey-traps. No doubles. No stimulated defections. No émigrés. No bugger all.'

'What's that?' said Smiley, as if sharply waking from a deep sleep. But such straight talk was not to Lacon's liking and he overrode it.

'Let us not be simplistic please, Lauder. Let us reach things organically. Conceptual thinking is essential here. So the Wise Men composed a *codex*, George,' he resumed to Smiley. 'A catalogue of proscribed practices. Right?' But Smiley was waiting rather than listening. 'Ranged the whole field – on the uses and abuses of agents, on our fishing rights in Commonwealth countries – or lack of them – all sorts. Listeners, surveillance overseas, false-flag operations – a mammoth task, bravely tackled.' To the astonishment of everyone but himself, Lacon locked his fingers together, turned down the palms, and cracked the joints in a defiant staccato.

He continued: '*Also* included in their forbidden list – and it *is* a crude instrument, George, no respecter of tradition – are such matters as the classic use of double agents. *Obsession*, our new masters were pleased to call it in their findings. The old games of coat-trailing – turning and playing back our enemies' spies – in your day the very meat and drink of counter-intelligence – today, George, in the collective opinion of the Wise Men – today they are ruled obsolete. Uneconomic. Throw them out.'

Another lorry thundered giddily down the hill, or up it. They heard the bump of its wheels on the kerb.

'Christ,' Strickland muttered.

'Or – for example – I strike another blow at random – the over-emphasis on exile groups.'

This time there was no lorry at all: only the deep, accusing silence that had followed in its wake. Smiley sat as before, receiving not judging, his concentration only on Lacon, hearing him with the sharpness of the blind.

'Exile groups, you will want to know,' Lacon went on – 'or more properly the Circus's time-honoured connections with them – the Wise Men prefer to call it *dependence*, but I think that a trifle strong – I took issue with them, but was overruled – are today ruled provocative, anti-détente, inflammatory. An expensive indulgence. Those who tamper with them do so *on pain of excommunication*. I mean it, George. We have got thus far. This is the extent of their mastery. Imagine.'

With a gesture of baring his breast for Smiley's onslaught, Lacon opened his arms, and remained standing, peering down at him as he had done before, while in the background Strickland's Scottish echo once again told the same truth more brutally.

'The groups have been dustbinned, George,' Strickland said. 'The lot of them. Orders from on high. No contact, not even arm's length. The late Vladimir's death-and-glory artists included. Special two-key archive for 'em on the fifth floor. No officer access without consent in writing from the Chief. Copy to the weekly float for the Wise Men's inspection. Troubled times, George, I tell you true, troubled times.'

'George, now steady,' Lacon warned uneasily, catching something the others had not heard.

'What utter nonsense,' Smiley repeated deliberately.

His head was lifted and his eyes had turned full on Lacon, as if emphasising the bluntness of his contradiction. 'Vladimir wasn't *expensive*. He wasn't an indulgence either. Least of all was he uneconomic. You know perfectly well he loathed taking our money. We had to force it on him or he'd have starved. As to inflammatory – anti-détente, whatever those words mean – well, we had to hold him in check once in a while as one does with most good agents, but when it came down to it he took our orders like a lamb. You were a fan of his, Oliver. You know as well as I do what he was worth.'

The quietness of Smiley's voice did not conceal its tautness. Nor had Lacon failed to notice the dangerous points of colour in his cheeks.

Sharply, Lacon turned upon the weakest member present: 'Mostyn, I expect you to forget all this. Do you hear? Strickland, tell him.'

Strickland obliged with alacrity: 'Mostyn, you will present yourself to Housekeepers this morning at ten-thirty precisely and sign an indoctrination certificate which I personally shall compose and witness!'

'Yes, sir,' Mostyn said, after a slightly eerie delay.

Only now did Lacon respond to Smiley's point: 'George, I admired the *man*. Never his Group. There is an absolute distinction here. The man, yes. In many ways, a heroic figure, if you will. But not the company he kept: the fantasists, the down-at-heel princelings. Nor the Moscow Centre infiltrators they enfolded so warmly to their breasts. Never. The Wise Men have a point and you can't deny it.'

Smiley had taken off his spectacles and was polishing them on the thick end of his tie. By the pale light now breaking through the curtains, his plump face looked moist and undefended.

'Vladimir was one of the best agents we ever had,' Smiley said baldly.

'Because he was yours, you mean?' Strickland sneered, behind Smiley's back.

'Because he was good!' Smiley snapped, and there was a startled silence everywhere, while he recovered himself. 'Vladimir's father was an Estonian and a passionate Bolshevik, Oliver,' he resumed in a calmer voice. 'A professional man, a lawyer. Stalin rewarded his loyalty by murdering him in the purges. Vladimir was born Voldemar but he even changed his name to Vladimir out of allegiance to Moscow and the Revolution. He still wanted to believe, despite what they had done to his father. He joined the Red Army and by God's grace missed being purged as well. The war promoted him, he fought like a lion, and when it was over, he waited for the great Russian liberalisation that he had been dreaming of, and the freeing of his own people. It never came. Instead, he witnessed the ruthless repression of his homeland by the government he had served. Scores of thousands of his fellow Estonians went to the camps, several of his own relatives among them.' Lacon opened his mouth to interrupt, but wisely closed it. 'The lucky ones escaped to Sweden and Germany. We're talking of a population of a million sober, hard-working people, cut to bits. One night, in despair, he offered us his services. Us, the British. In Moscow. For three years after that he spied for us from the very heart of the capital. Risked everything for us, every day.'

'And needless to say, our George here ran him,' Strickland growled, still somehow trying to suggest that this very fact put Smiley out of court. But Smiley would not be stopped. At his feet, young Mostyn was listening in a kind of trance.

'We even gave him a medal, if you remember, Oliver. Not to wear or to possess, of course. But somewhere, on a bit of parchment that he was occasionally allowed to look at, there was a signature very like the Monarch's.'

'George, this is history,' Lacon protested weakly. 'This is not *today*.'

'For three long years, Vladimir was the best source we ever had on Soviet capabilities and intentions – and at the height of the cold war. He was close to their intelligence community and reported on that too. Then one day on a service visit to Paris, he took his chance and jumped, and thank God he did, because otherwise he'd have been shot a great deal sooner.'

Lacon was suddenly quite lost. 'What *do* you mean?' he asked. 'How *sooner*? What are you saying now?'

'I mean that in those days the Circus was largely run by a Moscow Centre agent,' Smiley replied with deadly patience. 'It was the sheerest luck that Bill Haydon happened to be stationed abroad while Vladimir was working for us. Another three months and Bill would have blown him sky-high.'

Lacon found nothing to say at all, so Strickland filled in for him.

'Bill Haydon this, Bill Haydon that,' he sneered. 'Just because you had that extra involvement with him—' He was going to continue but thought better of it. 'Haydon's dead, damn it,' he ended sullenly, 'so's that whole era.'

'And so is Vladimir,' said Smiley quietly, and once again there was a halt in the proceedings.

'George,' Lacon intoned gravely, as if he had belatedly found his place in the prayer book. 'We are *pragmatists*, George. We *adapt*. We are *not* keepers of some sacred flame. I ask you, I commend you, to remember this!'

Quiet but resolute, Smiley had not quite finished the old man's obituary, and he sensed already that it was the only one he was ever going to get.

'And when he did come out, all right, he was a declining asset, as all ex-agents are,' he continued.

'I'll say,' said Strickland *sotto voce*.

'He stayed on in Paris and threw himself whole-heartedly into the Baltic independence movement. All right, it was a lost cause. It so happens that to this very day, the British have refused *de jure* recognition to the Soviet annexation of the three Baltic States – but never mind that either. Estonia, you may not know, Oliver, maintains a perfectly respectable Legation and Consulate General in Queen's Gate. We don't mind supporting lost causes once they're fully lost, apparently. Not before.' He drew a sharp breath. 'And all right, in Paris he formed a Baltic Group, and the Group went downhill, as émigré groups and lost causes always will – let me go on, Oliver, I'm not often long!'

'My dear fellow,' said Lacon, and blushed. 'Be as long as you like,' he said, quelling another groan from Strickland.

'His Group split up, there were quarrels. Vladimir was in a hurry and wanted to bring all the factions under one hat. The factions had their vested interests and didn't agree. There was a pitched battle, some heads got broken and the French threw him out. We moved him to London with a couple of his lieutenants. Vladimir in his old age returned to the Lutheran religion of his forefathers, exchanging the Marxist Saviour for the Christian Messiah. We're supposed to encourage that too, I believe. Or perhaps that is not policy any more. He has now been murdered. Since we are talking background, that is Vladimir's. Now why am I here?'

The ringing of the bell could not have been more timely. Lacon was still quite pink, and Smiley, breathing heavily, was once more polishing his spectacles. Reverently, Mostyn the acolyte unchained the door and admitted a tall motor-cycle messenger dangling a bunch of keys in his gloved hand. Reverently, Mostyn bore the keys to Strickland, who signed for them and made an entry in his log. The messenger, after a long and even doting glance at Smiley, departed, leaving Smiley with the guilty feeling that he should have recognised him under all his paraphernalia. But Smiley had more pressing insights to concern him. With no reverence at all, Strickland dumped the keys into Lacon's open palm.

'All right, Mostyn, tell him!' Lacon boomed suddenly. 'Tell him in your own words.'

5

Mostyn sat with a quite particular stillness. He spoke softly. To hear him, Lacon had withdrawn to a corner, and bunched his hands judicially under his nose. But Strickland had sat himself bolt upright and seemed, like Mostyn himself, to be patrolling the boy's words for lapses.

'Vladimir telephoned the Circus at lunch-time today, sir,' Mostyn began, leaving some unclarity as to which 'sir' he was addressing. 'I happened to be Oddbins duty officer and took the call.'

Strickland corrected him with unpleasant haste: 'You mean *yesterday*. Be precise, can't you?'

'I'm sorry, sir. Yesterday,' said Mostyn.

'Well, get it right,' Strickland warned.

To be Oddbins duty officer, Mostyn explained, meant little more than covering the lunch-hour gap and checking desks and wastebins at closing time. Oddbins personnel were too junior for night duty, so there was just this roster for lunch-times and evenings.

And Vladimir, he repeated, came through in the lunch-hour, using the lifeline.

'*Lifeline?*' Smiley repeated in bewilderment. 'I don't think I quite know what you mean.'

'It's the system we have for keeping in touch with dead

64

agents, sir,' said Mostyn, then put his fingers to his temple and muttered, 'Oh, my Lord.' He started again: 'I mean agents who have run their course but are still on the welfare roll, sir,' said Mostyn unhappily.

'So he rang and you took the call,' said Smiley kindly. 'What time was that?'

'One-fifteen exactly, sir. Oddbins is like a sort of Fleet Street news-room, you see. There are these twelve desks and there's the section head's hen-coop at the end, with a glass partition between us and him. The lifeline's in a locked box and normally it's the section head who keeps the key. But in the lunch-hour he gives it to the duty dog. I unlocked the box and heard this foreign voice saying "Hullo."'

'Get on with it, Mostyn,' Strickland growled.

'I said "Hullo" back, Mr Smiley. That's all we do. We don't give the number. He said, "This is Gregory calling for Max. I have something very urgent for him. Please get me Max immediately." I asked him where he was calling from, which is routine, but he just said he had plenty of change. We have no brief to trace incoming calls and anyway it takes too long. There's an electric card selector by the lifeline, it's got all the work-names on it. I told him to hold on and typed out "Gregory". That's the next thing we do after asking where they're calling from. Up it came on the selector. "Gregory equals Vladimir, ex-agent, ex-Soviet General, ex-leader of the Riga Group." Then the file reference. I typed out "Max" and found you, sir.' Smiley gave a small nod. '"Max equals Smiley." Then I typed out "Riga Group" and realised you were their last vicar, sir.'

'Their vicar?' said Lacon, as if he had detected heresy. 'Smiley their last *vicar*, Mostyn? What on earth—'

'I thought you had heard all this, Oliver,' Smiley said, to cut him off.

'Only the essence,' Lacon retorted. 'In a crisis one deals only with essentials.'

In his pressed-down Scottish, without letting Mostyn from his sight, Strickland provided Lacon with the required explanation: 'Organisations such as the Group had by tradition two case officers. The postman, who did the nuts and bolts for them, and the vicar who stood above the fight. Their father figure,' he said, and nodded perfunctorily towards Smiley.

'And who was carded as his most recent postman, Mostyn?' Smiley asked, ignoring Strickland entirely.

'Esterhase, sir. Workname Hector.'

'And he didn't ask for him?' said Smiley to Mostyn, speaking straight past Strickland yet again.

'I'm sorry, sir?'

'Vladimir didn't ask for Hector? His postman? He asked for me. Max. Only Max. You're sure of that?'

'He wanted you and nobody else, sir,' said Mostyn earnestly.

'Did you make notes?'

'The lifeline is taped automatically, sir. It's also linked to a speaking clock, so that we get the exact timing as well.'

'Damn you, Mostyn, that's a confidential matter,' Strickland snapped. 'Mr Smiley may be a distinguished ex-member, but he's no longer family.'

'So what did you do next, Mostyn?' Smiley asked.

'Standing instructions gave me very little latitude, sir,' Mostyn replied, showing once again, like Smiley, a studied disregard for Strickland. 'Both "Smiley" and "Esterhase" were wait-listed, which meant that they could be contacted only through the fifth floor. My section head was out to lunch and not due back till two-fifteen.' He gave a light shrug. 'I stalled. I told him to try again at two-thirty.'

Smiley turned to Strickland. 'I thought you said that all the émigré files had been consigned to special keeping?'

'Correct.'

'Shouldn't there have been something on the selector card to that effect?'

'There should and there wasn't,' Strickland said.

'That is just the point, sir,' Mostyn agreed, talking only to Smiley. 'At that stage there was no suggestion that Vladimir or his Group was out of bounds. From the card, he looked just like any other pensioned-off agent raising a wind. I assumed he wanted a bit of money, or company, or something. We get quite a few of those. Leave him to the section head, I thought.'

'Who shall remain nameless, Mostyn,' Strickland said. 'Remember that.'

It crossed Smiley's mind at this point that the reticence in Mostyn – his air of distastefully stepping round some dangerous secret all the time he spoke – might have something to do with protecting a negligent superior. But Mostyn's next words put paid to this, for he went out of his way to imply that his superior was at fault.

'The trouble was, my section head didn't get back from lunch till three-fifteen, so that when Vladimir rang in at two-thirty, I had to put him off again. He was furious,' said Mostyn. 'Vladimir was, I mean. I asked whether there was anything I could do in the meantime and he said, "Find Max. Just find me Max. Tell Max I have been in touch with certain friends, also through friends with neighbours." There were a couple of notes on the card about his word code and I saw that "neighbour" meant Soviet Intelligence.'

A mandarin impassivity had descended over Smiley's face. The earlier emotion was quite gone.

'All of which you duly reported to your section head at three-fifteen?'

'Yes, sir.'

'Did you play him the tape?'

'He hadn't time to hear,' said Mostyn mercilessly. 'He had to leave straight away for a long weekend.'

The stubborn brevity in Mostyn was now so strong that Strickland apparently felt obliged to fill the gaps.

'Yes, well, there's no question but that if we're looking for scapegoats, George, that section head of Mostyn's made a monumental fool of himself, no question at all,' Strickland declared brightly. 'He omitted to send for Vladimir's papers – which would not, of course, have been forthcoming. He omitted to acquaint himself with standing orders on the handling of émigrés. He also appears to have succumbed to a severe dose of weekend fever, leaving no word of his whereabouts should he be required. God help him on Monday morning, say I. Oh, yes. Come, Mostyn, we're waiting, boy.'

Mostyn obediently took back the story. 'Vladimir rang for the third and last time at three-forty-three, sir,' he said, speaking even more slowly than before. It should have been quarter to four, but he jumped the gun by two minutes. Mostyn had by then a rudimentary brief from his section head, which he now repeated to Smiley: 'He called it a bromide job. I was to find out what, if anything, the old boy really wanted and, if all else failed, make a rendezvous with him to cool him down. I was to give him a drink, sir, pat him on the back, and promise nothing except to pass on whatever message he brought me.'

'And the "neighbours"?' Smiley asked. 'They were not an issue to your section head?'

'He rather thought that was just a bit of agent's histrionics, sir.'

'I see. Yes, I see.' Yet his eyes, in contradiction, closed completely for a moment. 'So how did the dialogue with Vladimir go this third time?'

'According to Vladimir, it was to be an immediate meeting or nothing, sir. I tried out the alternatives on him as instructed – "Write us a letter – is it money you want? Surely it can wait till Monday" – but by then he was shouting at me down the phone. "A meeting or nothing. Tonight or nothing. Moscow Rules. I insist Moscow Rules. Tell this to Max—"'

Interrupting himself, Mostyn lifted his head and with unblinking eyes returned Lauder Strickland's hostile stare.

'Tell what to Max?' said Smiley, his gaze moving swiftly from one to the other of them.

'We were speaking French, sir. The card said French was his preferred second language and I'm only Grade B in Russian.'

'Irrelevant,' Strickland snapped.

'Tell *what* to Max?' Smiley persisted.

Mostyn's eyes searched out a spot on the floor a yard or two out from his own feet: 'He meant: Tell Max I insist it's Moscow Rules.'

Lacon, who had stayed uncharacteristically quiet these last minutes, now chimed in: 'There's an important point here, George. The Circus were not the suitors here. *He* was. The ex-agent. He was doing *all* the pressing, making *all* the running. If he'd accepted our suggestion, written out his information, none of this need ever have happened. He brought it on himself entirely. George, I insist you take the point!'

Strickland was lighting himself a fresh cigarette.

'Whoever heard of Moscow Rules in the middle of bloody Hampstead anyway?' Strickland asked, waving out the match.

'Bloody Hampstead is right,' Smiley said quietly.

'Mostyn, wrap the story up,' Lacon commanded, blushing scarlet.

They had agreed a time, Mostyn resumed woodenly, now staring at his left palm as if he were reading his own fortune in it: 'Ten-twenty, sir.'

They had agreed Moscow Rules, he said, and the usual contact procedures, which Mostyn had established earlier in the afternoon by consulting the Oddbins encounter index.

'And what were the contact procedures exactly?' Smiley asked.

'A copy-book rendezvous, sir,' Mostyn replied. 'The Sarratt training course all over again, sir.'

Smiley felt suddenly crowded by the intimacy of Mostyn's respectfulness. He did not wish to be the boy's hero, or to be caressed by his voice, his gaze, his 'sirs'. He was not prepared for the claustrophobic admiration of this stranger.

'There's a tin pavilion on Hampstead Heath, ten minutes' walk from East Heath Road, overlooking a games field on the south side of the avenue, sir. The safety signal was one new drawing-pin shoved high in the first wood support on the left as you entered.'

'And the counter-signal?' Smiley asked.

But he knew the answer already.

'A yellow chalk line,' said Mostyn. 'I gather yellow was the sort of Group trade mark from the old days.' He had adopted a tone of ending. 'I put up the pin and came back here and waited. When he didn't show up, I thought, "Well, if he's secrecy-mad I'll have to go to the hut again and check out his counter-signal, then I'll know whether he's around and proposes to try the fallback."'

'Which was what?'

'A car pick-up near Swiss Cottage underground at

eleven-forty, sir. I was about to go out and take a look when Mr Strickland rang through and ordered me to sit tight until further orders.' Smiley assumed he had finished but this was not quite true. Seeming to forget everyone but himself, Mostyn slowly shook his handsome head. 'I never met him,' he said, in amazement. 'He was my first agent, I never met him, I'll never know what he was trying to tell me,' he said. 'My first agent, and he's dead. It's incredible. I feel like a complete Jonah.' His head continued shaking long after he had finished speaking.

Lacon added a brisk postscript: 'Yes, well, Scotland Yard has a computer these days, George. The Heath Patrol found the body and cordoned off the area and the moment the name was fed into the computer a light came up or a lot of digits or something, and immediately they knew he was on our special watch list. From then on it went like clockwork. The Commissioner phoned the Home Office, the Home Office phoned the Circus—'

'And you phoned me,' said Smiley. 'Why, Oliver? Who suggested you bring me in on this?'

'George, does it matter?'

'Enderby?'

'If you insist, yes, it was Saul Enderby. George, listen to me.'

It was Lacon's moment at last. The issue, whatever it might be, was before them, circumscribed if not yet actually defined. Mostyn was forgotten. Lacon was standing confidently over Smiley's seated figure and had assumed the rights of an old friend.

'George, as things now stand, I can go to the Wise Men and say: "I have investigated and the Circus's hands are clean." I can say that. "The Circus gave no encouragement to these people, nor to their leader. For a whole year they have neither paid nor welfared him!" Perfectly honestly. They don't own his flat, his car, they don't pay his rent, educate his bastards, send flowers to his mistress or have any other of the old – and lamentable – connections with him or his kind. His only link was with the past. His case officers have left the stage for good – yourself and Esterhase, both old 'uns, both off the books. I can say that with my hand on my breast. To the Wise Men, and if necessary to my Minister personally.'

'I don't follow you,' Smiley said with deliberate obtuseness. 'Vladimir was our agent. He was trying to tell us something.'

'Our *ex*-agent, George. How do we *know* he was trying to tell us something? We gave him no *brief*. He spoke of urgency – even of Soviet Intelligence – so do a lot of ex-agents when they're holding out their caps for a subsidy!'

'Not Vladimir,' Smiley said.

But sophistry was Lacon's element. He was born to it, he breathed it, he could fly and swim in it, nobody in Whitehall was better at it.

'George, we cannot be held responsible for every ex-agent who takes an injudicious nocturnal walk in one of London's increasingly dangerous open spaces!' He held out his hands in appeal. 'George. What is it to be? Choose. *You* choose. On the one hand, Vladimir asked for a chat with you. Retired buddies – a chin-wag about old times – why not? And in order to raise a bit of wind, as any of us might, he pretended he had something for you. Some nugget of information. Why not? They all do it. On that basis my Minister will back us. No heads need roll, no tantrums, Cabinet hysteria. He will help us bury the case. Not a cover-up, naturally. But he will use his judgement. If I catch him in the right mood he may even decide that there is no point in troubling the Wise Men with it at all.'

'Amen,' Strickland echoed.

'On the other hand,' Lacon insisted, mustering all his persuasiveness for the kill, 'if things were to come unstuck, George, and the Minister got it into his head that we were engaging his good offices in order to clean up the traces of some unlicensed adventure which aborted' – he was striding again, skirting an imaginary quagmire – 'and there was a scandal, George, and the Circus were proved to be currently involved – your old service, George, one you still love, I am sure – with a notoriously revanchist émigré outfit – volatile, talkative, violently anti-détente – with all manner of anachronistic fixations – a total hangover from the worst days of the cold war – the very archetype of everything our masters have told us to avoid' – he had reached his corner again, a little outside the circle of light – 'and there had been a death, George – and an attempted cover-up, as they would no doubt call it – with all the attendant publicity – well, it could be just one scandal too many. The service is a weak child still, George, a sickly one, and in the hands of these new people desperately delicate. At this stage in its rebirth, it could die of the common cold. If it does, your generation will not be least to blame. You have a duty, as we all do. A loyalty.'

Duty to *what*? Smiley wondered, with that part of himself which sometimes seemed to be a spectator to the rest. Loyalty to *whom*? 'There is no loyalty without betrayal,' Ann liked to tell him in their youth when he had ventured to protest at her infidelities.

For a time nobody spoke.

'And the weapon?' Smiley asked finally, in the tone of someone testing a theory. 'How do you account for that, Oliver?'

'What weapon? There was no weapon. He was shot. By his own buddies most likely, knowing their cabals. Not to mention his appetite for other people's wives.'

'Yes, he was shot,' Smiley agreed. 'In the face. At extremely close range. With a soft-nosed bullet. And cursorily searched. Had his wallet taken. That is the police diagnosis. But our diagnosis would be different, wouldn't it, Lauder?'

'No way,' said Strickland, glowering at him through a cloud of cigarette smoke.

'Well, mine would.'

'Then let's hear it, George,' said Lacon handsomely.

'The weapon used to kill Vladimir was a standard Moscow Centre assassination device,' Smiley said. 'Concealed in a camera, a briefcase, or whatever. A soft-nosed bullet is fired at point-blank range. To obliterate, to punish, and to discourage others. If I remember rightly they even had one on display at Sarratt in the black museum next to the bar.'

'They still have. It's horrific,' said Mostyn.

Strickland vouchsafed Mostyn a foul glance.

'But George!' Lacon cried.

Smiley waited, knowing that in this mood, Lacon could swear away Big Ben.

'These people – these émigrés – of whom this poor chap was one – don't they *come* from Russia? Haven't half of them been in *touch* with Moscow Centre – with or without our knowledge? A weapon like that – I'm not saying you're right, of course – a weapon like that, in their world, could be as common as cheese!'

Against stupidity, the gods themselves fight in vain, thought Smiley: but Schiller had forgotten the bureaucrats. Lacon was addressing Strickland.

'Lauder. There is the question of the D-Notice to the press outstanding.' It was an order. 'Perhaps you would have another shot at them, see how far it's got.'

In his stockinged feet, Strickland obediently padded down the room and dialled a number.

'Mostyn, perhaps you should take these things out to the kitchen. We don't want to leave needless traces, do we?'

With Mostyn also dismissed, Smiley and Lacon were suddenly alone.

'It's yes or no, George,' Lacon said. 'There's cleaning up to be done. Explanations to be given to tradesmen, what do I know? Mail. Milk. Friends. Whatever such people have. No one knows the course as you do. No one. The police have promised you a head start. They will not be dilatory but they will observe a certain measured order about things and let routine play its part.' With a nervous bound Lacon approached Smiley's chair and sat awkwardly on the arm. 'George. You were their vicar. Very well, I'm asking you to go and read the Offices. He wanted *you*, George. Not us. You.'

From his old place at the telephone, Strickland interrupted: 'They're asking for a signature for that D-Notice, Oliver. They'd like it to be yours, if it's all the same to you.'

'Why not the Chief's?' Lacon demanded warily.

'Seem to think yours will carry a spot more weight, I fancy.'

'Ask him to hold a moment,' Lacon said, and with a windmill gesture drove a fist into his pocket: 'I may give you the keys, George?' He dangled them in front of Smiley's face. 'On terms. Right?' The keys still dangled. Smiley stared at them and perhaps he asked 'What terms?' or perhaps he just stared; he wasn't really in a mood for conversation. His mind was on Mostyn, and missing cigarettes; on phone calls about neighbours; on agents with no faces; on sleep. Lacon was counting. He attached great merit to numbering his paragraphs. 'One, that you are a private citizen, Vladimir's Executor, not ours. Two, that you are of the past, not the present, and conduct yourself accordingly. The *sanitised* past. That you will pour oil on the waters, not muddy them. That you will suppress your old professional interest in him, naturally, for that means ours. On those terms may I give you the keys? Yes? No?'

Mostyn was standing in the kitchen doorway. He was addressing Lacon, but his earnest eyes veered constantly towards Smiley.

'What is it, Mostyn?' Lacon demanded. 'Be quick!'

'I just remembered a note on Vladimir's card, sir. He had a wife in Tallinn. I wondered whether she should be informed. I just thought I'd better mention it.'

'The card is once more not accurate,' said Smiley, returning Mostyn's gaze. 'She was with him in Moscow when he defected, she was arrested and taken to a forced labour camp. She died there.'

'Mr Smiley must do whatever he thinks fit about such things,' Lacon said swiftly, anxious to avoid a fresh outbreak, and dropped the keys into Smiley's passive palm. Suddenly everything was in movement. Smiley was on his feet, Lacon was already half-way down the room and Strickland was holding out the phone to him. Mostyn had slipped to the darkened hallway and was unhooking Smiley's raincoat from the stand.

'What else did Vladimir say to you on the telephone, Mostyn?' Smiley asked quietly, dropping one arm into the sleeve.

'He said, "Tell Max that it concerns the Sandman. Tell him I have two proofs and can bring them with me. Then perhaps he will see me." He said it twice. It was on the tape but Strickland erased it.'

'Do you know what Vladimir meant by that? Keep your voice down.'

'No, sir.'

'Nothing on the card?'

76

'No, sir.'

'Do *they* know what he meant?' Smiley asked, tilting his head swiftly towards Strickland and Lacon.

'I think Strickland may. I'm not sure.'

'Did Vladimir really not ask for Esterhase?'

'No, sir.'

Lacon was finishing on the phone. Strickland took back the receiver from him and spoke into it himself. Seeing Smiley at the door, Lacon bounded down the room to him.

'George! Good man! Fare you well! Listen, I want to talk to you about marriage some time. A seminar with no holds barred. I'm counting on you to tell me the art of it, George!'

'Yes. We must get together,' Smiley said.

Looking down, he saw that Lacon was shaking his hand.

A bizarre postscript to this meeting confounds its conspiratorial purpose. Standard Circus tradecraft requires that hidden microphones be installed in safe houses. Agents in their strange way accept this, even though they are not informed of it, even though their case officers go through motions of taking notes. For his rendezvous with Vladimir, Mostyn had quite properly switched on the system in anticipation of the old man's arrival, and nobody, in the subsequent panic, thought to turn it off. Routine procedures brought the tapes to transcriber section, who in good faith put out several texts for the general Circus reader. The luckless head of Oddbins got a copy, so did the Secretariat, so did the heads of Personnel, Operations and Finance. It was not till a copy landed in Lauder Strickland's in-tray that the explosion occurred and the innocent recipients were sworn to secrecy under all manner of dreadful threats. The tape is perfect. Lacon's restless pacing is there, so are Strickland's *sotto voce* asides, some of them obscene. Only Mostyn's flustered confessions in the hall escaped.

As to Mostyn himself, he played no further part in the affair. He resigned of his own accord a few months later, part of the wastage rate that gets everyone so worried these days.

6

The same uncertain light that greeted Smiley as he stepped gratefully out of the safe flat into the fresh air of that Hampstead morning, greeted Ostrakova also, though the Paris autumn was further on, and only a last few leaves clung like old dusters to the plane trees. Like Smiley's too, her night had not been restful. She had risen in the dark and dressed with care, and she had deliberated, since the morning looked colder, whether this was the day on which to get out her winter boots, because the draught in the warehouse would be cruel and affected her legs the most. Still undecided, she had fished them out of the cupboard and wiped them down, and even polished them, but she still had not been able to make up her mind whether to wear them or not. Which was how it always went with her when she had one big problem to grapple with: the small ones became impossible. She knew all the signs, she could feel them coming on, but there was nothing she could do. She would mislay her purse, botch her book-keeping at the warehouse, lock herself out of the flat and have to fetch the old fool of a concierge, Madame la Pierre, who pecked and snuffled like a goat in a nettle patch. She could quite easily, when the mood was on her, after fifteen years of taking the same route, catch the wrong bus and finish up, furious, in a strange neighbourhood. Pulling on the boots, finally – muttering to herself 'old fool, cretin' and the like – and, carrying the heavy shopping bag that she had prepared the previous night, she set off along her usual route, passing her three usual shops and neglecting to enter any of them, while she tried to work out whether or not she was going off her head.

I am mad. I am not mad. Somebody is trying to kill me, somebody is trying to protect me. I am safe. I am in mortal danger. Back and forth.

In the four weeks since she had received her little Estonian confessor, Ostrakova had been aware of many changes in herself and for most of them she was not at all ungrateful. Whether she had fallen in love with him was neither here nor there: his appearance was timely, and the piracy in him had revived her sense of opposition at a moment when it was in danger of going out. He had rekindled her, and there was enough of the alley cat in him to remind her of Glikman and other men as well; she had never been particularly continent. And since, on top of this, she thought, the magician is a man of looks, and knows women, and steps into my life armed with a picture of my oppressor and the determination, apparently, to eliminate him – why then, it would be positively indecent, lonely old fool that I am, if I did *not* fall in love with him on the spot!

But it was his gravity which had impressed her even more than his magic. 'You must not *decorate*,' he had told her, with uncharacteristic sharpness, when for the sake of entertainment or variety she had allowed herself to deviate just a little from the version she had written to the General. 'Merely because you yourself feel more at ease, do not make the mistake of supposing that the danger is over.'

She had promised to improve herself.

'The danger is absolute,' he had told her as he left. 'It is not yours to make greater or make less.'

People had talked to her about danger before, but when the magician talked about it, she believed him.

'Danger to my daughter?' she had asked. 'Danger to Alexandra?'

'Your daughter plays no part in this. You may be sure she knows nothing of what is going on.'

'Then danger to whom?'

'Danger to all of us who have knowledge of this matter,' he had replied, as she happily conceded, in the doorway, to their one embrace. 'Danger most of all to you.'

And now, for the last three days – or was it two? or was it ten? – Ostrakova swore she had seen the danger gather round her like an army of shadows at her own deathbed. The danger that was absolute; that was not hers to make greater or less. And she saw it again this Saturday morning as she clumped along in her polished winter boots, swinging the heavy shopping bag at her side: the same two men, pursuing her, the weekend notwithstanding. Hard men. Harder than the gingery man. Men who sit about at headquarters listening to the interrogations. And never speak a word. The one was walking five metres behind her, the other was keeping abreast of her across the street, at this moment passing the doorway of that vagabond Mercier the chandler, whose red-and-green awning hung so low it was a danger even to someone of Ostrakova's humble height.

She had decided, when she had first allowed herself to notice them, that they were the General's men. That was Monday, or was it Friday? General Vladimir has turned out his bodyguard for me, she thought with much amusement, and for a dangerous morning she plotted the friendly gestures she would make to them in order to express her gratitude: the smiles of complicity she would vouchsafe to them when there was nobody else looking; the *soupe* she would prepare and take to them, to help them while away their vigil in the doorways. Two hulking great bodyguards, she had thought, just for one old lady! Ostrakov had been right: that General was a man! On the second day she decided they were not there at all, and that her desire to appoint such men was merely an extension of her desire to be reunited with the magician: I am looking for links to him, she thought; just as I have not yet brought myself to wash up the glass from which he drank his vodka, or to puff up the cushions where he sat and lectured me on danger.

But on the third – or was it the fifth? – day she took a different and harsher view of her supposed protectors. She stopped playing the little girl. On whichever day it was, leaving her apartment early in order to check a particular consignment to the warehouse, she had stepped out of the sanctuary of her abstractions straight into the streets of Moscow, as she had too often known them in her years with Glikman. The ill-lit, cobbled street was empty but for one black car parked twenty metres from her doorway. Most likely it had arrived that minute. She had a notion, afterwards, of having seen it pull up, presumably in order to deliver the sentries to their beat. Pull up sharply, just as she came out. And douse its headlight. Resolutely she had begun walking down the pavement. 'Danger to *you*,' she kept remembering; 'danger to all of us who know.'

The car was following her.

They think I am a whore, she thought vainly, one of those old ones who work the early-morning market.

Suddenly her one aim had been to get inside a church. Any church. The nearest Russian Orthodox church was twenty minutes away, and so small that to pray in it at all was like a séance; the very proximity of the Holy Family offered a forgiveness by itself. But twenty minutes was a lifetime. Non-Orthodox churches she eschewed, as a rule, entirely – they were a betrayal of her nationhood. That morning, however, with the car crawling along behind her, she had suspended her prejudice and ducked into the very first church she came to, which turned out to be not merely Catholic, but *modern* Catholic as well, so that she heard the whole Mass twice through in bad French, read by a worker-priest who smelt of garlic and worse. But by the time she left, the men were nowhere to be seen and that was all that mattered – even though when she arrived at the warehouse she had to promise them two extra hours to make up for the inconvenience she had caused them by her lateness.

Then for three days nothing, or was it five? Ostrakova had become as incapable of hoarding time as money. Three or five, they had gone, they had never existed. It was all her 'decoration', as the magician had called it, her stupid habit of seeing too much, looking too many people in the eye, inventing too much incident. Till today again, when they were back. Except that today was about fifty thousand times worse, because today was *now*, and the street today was as empty as the Last Day or the First, and the man who was five metres behind her was drawing closer, and the man who had been under Mercier's outrageously dangerous awning was crossing the street to join him.

What happened next, in such descriptions or imaginings as had come Ostrakova's way, was supposed to happen in a flash. One minute you were upright, walking down the pavement, the next, with a flurry of lights and a wailing of horns, you were wafted to the operating table surrounded by surgeons in various-coloured masks. Or you were in Heaven, before the Almighty, mumbling excuses about certain lapses which you did not really regret; and neither – if you understood Him at all – did He. Or worst of all, you came round, and were returned, as walking wounded, to your apartment, and your boring half-sister Valentina dropped everything, with an extremely ill grace, in order to come up from Lyon and be a non-stop scold at your bedside.

Not one of these expectations was fulfilled.

What happened took place with the slowness of an underwater ballet. The man who was gaining on her drew alongside her, taking the right, or inside position. At the same moment, the man who had crossed the road from Mercier's came up on the left, walking not on the pavement, but in the gutter, incidentally splashing her with yesterday's rain-water as he strode along. With her fatal habit of looking into people's eyes Ostrakova stared at her two unwished-for companions and saw faces she had already recognised and knew by heart. They had hunted Ostrakov, they had murdered Glikman, and in her personal view they had been murdering the entire Russian people for centuries, whether in the name of the Czar, or God, or Lenin. Looking away from them, she saw the black car which had followed her on her way to church, heading slowly down the empty road towards her. Therefore she did exactly what she had planned to do all night through, what she had lain awake picturing. In her shopping bag she had put an old flat-iron, a bit of junk that Ostrakov had acquired in the days when the poor dying man had fancied he might make a few extra francs by dealing in antiques. Her shopping bag was of leather – green and brown in a patchwork – and stout. Drawing it back, she swung it round with all her strength at the man in the gutter – at his groin, the hated centre of him. He swore – she could not hear in which language – and crumpled to his knees. Here her plan went adrift. She had not expected a villain on either side of her, and she needed time to recover her own balance and get the iron swinging at the second man. He did not allow her to do this. Throwing his arms round both of hers, he gathered her together like the fat sack she was, and lifted her clean off her feet. She saw the bag fall and heard the chime as the flat-iron slipped from it onto a drain cover. Still looking down, she saw boots dangling ten centimetres from the ground, as if she had hanged herself like her brother Niki – his feet, exactly, turned into each other like a simpleton's. She noticed that one of her toe-caps, the left, was already scratched in the scuffle. Her assailant's arms now locked themselves even harder across her breast and she wondered whether her ribs would crack before she suffocated. She felt him draw her back, and she presumed that he was shaping to swing her into the car, which was now approaching at a good speed down the road: that she was being kidnapped. This notion terrified her. Nothing, least of all death, was as appalling to her at that moment as the thought that these pigs would take her back to Russia and subject her to the kind of slow, doctrinal prison death which she was certain had killed Glikman. She struggled with all her force, she managed to bite his hand. She saw a couple of bystanders who seemed as scared as she was. Then she realised that the car was not slowing down, and that the men had something quite different in mind: not to kidnap her at all, but to kill her.

He threw her.

She reeled but did not fall, and as the car swerved to knock her down, she thanked God and all His angels that she had, after all, decided on the winter boots, because the front bumper hit her at the back of the shins, and when she saw her feet again, they were straight up in front of her face, and her bare thighs were parted as for childbirth. She flew for a while, then hit the road with everything at once – with her head, her spine and her heels – then rolled like a sausage over the cobbles. The car had passed her but she heard it screech to a stop and wondered whether they were going to reverse and drive over her again. She tried to move but felt too sleepy. She heard voices and car doors slamming, she heard the engine roaring, and fading, so that either it was going away or she was losing her hearing.

'Don't touch her,' someone said.

No, *don't*, she thought.

'It's a lack of oxygen,' she heard herself say. 'Lift me to my feet and I'll be all right.'

Why on earth did she say that? Or did she only think it?

'*Aubergines*,' she said. 'Get the *aubergines*.' She didn't know whether she was talking about her shopping, or the female traffic wardens for whom aubergine was the Paris slang.

Then a pair of woman's hands put a blanket over her, and a furious Gallic argument started about what one did next. Did anyone get the number? she wanted to ask. But she was really too sleepy to bother, and besides she had no oxygen – the fall had taken it out of her body for good. She had a vision of half-shot birds she had seen in the Russian countryside, flapping helplessly on the ground, waiting for the dogs to reach them. General, she thought, did you get my second letter? Drifting off, she willed him, begged him to read it, and to respond to its entreaty. General, read my second letter.

She had written it a week before in a moment of despair. She had posted it yesterday in another.

7

There are Victorian terraces in the region of Paddington Station that are painted as white as luxury liners on the outside, and inside are dark as tombs. Westbourne Terrace that Saturday morning gleamed as brightly as any of them, but the service road that led to Vladimir's part of it was blocked at one end by a heap of rotting mattresses, and by a smashed boom, like a frontier post, at the other.

'Thank you, I'll get out here,' said Smiley politely, and paid the cab off at the mattresses.

He had come straight from Hampstead and his knees ached. The Greek driver had spent the journey lecturing him on Cyprus, and out of courtesy he had crouched on the jump seat in order to hear him over the din of the engine. Vladimir, we should have done better by you, he thought, surveying the filth on the pavements, the poor washing trailing from the balconies. The Circus should have shown more honour to its vertical man.

It concerns the Sandman, he thought. *Tell him I have two proofs and can bring them with me.*

He walked slowly, knowing that early morning is a better time of day to come out of a building than go into it. A small queue had gathered at the bus-stop. A milkman was doing his rounds, so was a newspaper boy. A squadron of grounded seagulls scavenged gracefully at the spilling dustbins. If sea-gulls are taking to the cities, he thought, will pigeons take to the sea? Crossing the service road he saw a motor-cyclist with a black official-looking side-car parking his steed a hundred yards down the kerb. Something in the man's posture remind-ed him of the tall messenger who had brought the keys to the safe flat – a similar fixity, even at that distance; a respectful at-tentiveness, of an almost military kind.

Shedding chestnut trees darkened the pillared doorway, a scarred cat eyed him warily. The doorbell was the topmost of thirty but Smiley didn't press it and when he shoved the double doors they swung open too freely, revealing the same gloomy corridors painted very shiny to defeat graffiti writers, and the same linoleum staircase which squeaked like a hospital trolley. He remembered it all. Nothing had changed, and now noth-ing ever would. There was no light switch and the stairs grew darker the higher he climbed. Why didn't Vladimir's murder-ers steal his keys? he wondered, feeling them nudging against his hip with every step. Perhaps they didn't need them. Per-haps they had their own set already. He reached a landing and squeezed past a luxurious perambulator. He heard a dog howl-ing and the morning news in German and the flushing of a communal lavatory. He heard a child screaming at its mother, then a slap and the father screaming at the child. *Tell Max it concerns the Sandman.* There was a smell of curry and cheap fat frying, and disinfectant. There was a smell of too many people with not much money jammed into too little air. He remem-bered that too. Nothing had changed.

If we'd treated him better, it would never have happened, Smiley thought. The neglected are too easily killed, he thought, in unconscious affinity with Ostrakova. He remem-bered the day they had brought him here, Smiley the vicar,

Toby Esterhase the postman. They had driven to Heathrow to fetch him: Toby the fixer, dyed in all the oceans, as he would say of himself. Toby drove like the wind but they were almost late, even then. The plane had landed. They hurried to the barrier and there he was: silvered and majestic, towering stock-still in the temporary corridor from the arrivals bay, while the common peasants swept past him. He remembered their solemn embrace – 'Max, my old friend, it is really you?' 'It's me, Vladimir, they've put us together again.' He remembered Toby spiriting them through the large back alleys of the immigration service, because the enraged French police had confiscated the old boy's papers before throwing him out. He remembered how they had lunched at Scott's, all three of them, the old boy too animated even to drink but talking grandly of the future they all knew he didn't have: 'It will be Moscow all over again, Max. Maybe we even get a chance at the Sandman.' Next day they went flat-hunting, 'just to show you a few possibilities, General,' as Toby Esterhase had explained. It was Christmas time and the resettlement budget for the year was used up. Smiley appealed to Circus Finance. He lobbied Lacon and the Treasury for a supplementary estimate, but in vain. 'A dose of reality will bring him down to earth,' Lacon had pronounced. 'Use your influence with him, George. That's what you're there for.' Their first dose of reality was a tart's parlour in Kensington, their second overlooked a shunting yard near Waterloo. Westbourne Terrace was their third, and as they squeaked up these same stairs, Toby leading, the old man had suddenly halted, and put back his great mottled head, and wrinkled his nose theatrically:

Ah! So if I get hungry I have only to stand in the corridor and sniff and my hunger is gone! he had announced in his thick French. *That way I don't have to eat for a week!*

By then even Vladimir had guessed they were putting him away for good.

Smiley returned to the present. The next landing was musical, he noticed, as he continued his solitary ascent. Through one door came rock music played at full blast, through another Sibelius and the smell of bacon. Peering out of the window he saw two men loitering between the chestnut trees who were not there when he had arrived. A team would do that, he thought. A team would post look-outs while the others went inside. Whose team was another question. Moscow's? The Superintendent's? Saul Enderby's? Farther down the road, the tall motor-cyclist had acquired a tabloid newspaper and was sitting on his bike reading it.

At Smiley's side a door opened and an old woman in a dressing gown came out holding a cat against her shoulder. He could smell last night's drink on her breath even before she spoke to him.

'Are you a burglar, dearie?' she asked.

'I'm afraid not,' Smiley replied with a laugh. 'Just a visitor.'

'Still, it's nice to be fancied, isn't it, dearie?' she said.

'It is indeed,' said Smiley politely.

The last flight was steep and very narrow and lit by real daylight from a wired skylight on the slant. There were two doors on the top landing, both closed, both very cramped. On one, a typed notice faced him: 'MR V. MILLER, TRANSLATIONS'. Smiley remembered the argument about Vladimir's alias now he was to become a Londoner and keep his head down. 'Miller' was no problem. For some reason, the old boy found Miller rather grand. 'Miller, *c'est bien*,' he had declared. 'Miller I like, Max.' But 'Mr' was anything but good. He pressed for General, then offered to settle for Colonel. But Smiley in his rôle as vicar was on this point unbudgeable: Mr was a lot less trouble than a bogus rank in the wrong army, he had ruled.

He knocked boldly, knowing that a soft knock is more conspicuous than a loud one. He heard the echo, and nothing else. He heard no footfall, no sudden freezing of a sound. He called 'Vladimir' through the letter-box as though he were an old friend visiting. He tried one Yale from the bunch and it stuck, he tried another and it turned. He stepped inside and closed the door, waiting for something to hit him on the back of the head but preferring the thought of a broken skull to having his face shot off. He felt dizzy and realised he was holding his breath. The same white paint, he noticed; the same prison emptiness exactly. The same queer hush, like a phone box; the same mix of public smells.

This is where we stood, Smiley remembered – the three of us, that afternoon. Toby and myself like tugs, nudging at the old battleship between us. The estate agent's particulars had said 'penthouse'.

'Hopeless,' Toby Esterhase had announced in his Hungarian French, always the first to speak, as he turned to open the door and leave. 'I mean completely awful. I mean, I should have come and taken a look first, I was an idiot,' said Toby when Vladimir still didn't budge. 'General, please accept my apologies. This is a complete insult.'

Smiley added his own assurances. We can do better for you than this, Vladi; much; we just have to persist.

But the old man's eyes were on the window, as Smiley's were now, on this dotty forest of chimney-pots and gables and slate roofs that flourished beyond the parapet. And suddenly he had thumped a gloved paw on Smiley's shoulder:

'Better you keep your money to shoot those swine in Moscow, Max,' he had advised.

With tears running down his cheeks, and the same determined smile, Vladimir had continued to stare at the Moscow chimneys; and at his fading dreams of ever again living under a Russian sky.

'*On reste ici,*' he had commanded finally, as if he were drawing up a last-ditch defence.

A tiny divan bed ran along one wall, a cooking ring stood on the sill. From the smell of putty Smiley guessed that the old man had kept whiteing the place himself, painting out the damp and filling the cracks. On the table he used for typing and eating lay an old Remington upright and a pair of worn dictionaries. His translating work, he thought: the few extra pennies that fleshed out his pension. Pressing back his elbows as if he were having trouble with his spine, Smiley drew himself to his full if diminutive height and launched himself upon the familiar death rites for a departed spy. An Estonian Bible lay on the pine bedside locker. He probed it delicately for cut cavities then dangled it upside down for scraps of paper or photographs. Pulling open the locker drawer he found a bottle of patent pills for rejuvenating the sexually jaded and three Red Army gallantry medals mounted on a chrome bar. So much for cover, thought Smiley, wondering how on earth Vladimir and his many paramours had managed on such a tiny bed. A print of Martin Luther hung at the bedhead. Next to it, a coloured picture called the 'Red Roofs of Old Tallinn', which Vladimir must have torn from something and backed on cardboard. A second picture showed 'The Kazari Coast', a third 'Windmills and a Ruined Castle'. He delved behind each. The bedside light caught his eye. He tried the switch and when it didn't work he unplugged it, took out the bulb and fished in the wood base, but without result. Just a dead bulb, he thought. A sudden shriek from outside sent him pulling back against the wall but when he had collected himself he realised it was more of those landborne seagulls: a whole colony had settled round the chimney-pots. He glanced over the parapet into the street again. The two loiterers had gone. They're on their way up, he thought: my head start is over. They're not police at all, he thought; they're assassins. The motor-bike with its black side-car stood unattended. He closed the window, wondering whether there was a special Valhalla for dead spies where he and Vladimir would meet and he could put things right; telling himself he had lived a long life and that this moment was as good as any other for it to end. And not believing it for one second.

The table drawer contained sheets of plain paper, a stapler, a chewed pencil, some elastic bands and a recent quarterly telephone bill, unpaid, for the sum of seventy-eight pounds, which struck him as uncharacteristically high for Vladimir's frugal lifestyle. He opened the stapler and found nothing. He put the phone bill in his pocket to study later and kept searching, knowing it was not a real search at all, that a real search would take three men several days before they could say with certainty they had found whatever was to be found. If he was looking for anything in particular, then it was probably an address book or a diary or something which did duty for one, even if it was only a scrap of paper. He knew that sometimes old spies, even the best of them, were a little like old lovers; as age crept up on them, they began to cheat, out of fear that their powers were deserting them. They pretended they had it all in the memory, but in secret they were hanging on to their virility, in secret they wrote things down, often in some home-made code which, if they only knew it, could be unbuttoned in hours or minutes by anyone who knew the game. Names and addresses of contacts, subagents. Nothing was holy. Routines, times and places of meetings, worknames, phone numbers, even safe combinations written out as social-security numbers and birthdays. In his time Smiley had seen entire networks put at risk that way because one agent no longer dared to trust his head. He didn't believe Vladimir would have done that, but there was always a first time.

Tell him I have two proofs and can bring them with me . . .

He was standing in what the old man would have called his kitchen: the window-sill with the gas ring on it, the tiny home-made food-store with holes drilled for ventilation. We men who cook for ourselves are half-creatures, he thought as he scanned the two shelves, tugged out the saucepan and the frying-pan, poked among the cayenne and paprika. Anywhere else in the house – even in bed – you can cut yourself off, read your books, deceive yourself that solitude is best. But in the kitchen the signs in incompleteness are too strident. Half of one black loaf. Half of one coarse sausage. Half an onion. Half a pint of milk. Half a lemon. Half a packet of black tea. Half a life. He opened anything that would open, he probed with his finger in the paprika. He found a loose tile and prised it free, he unscrewed the wooden handle of the frying-pan. About to pull open the clothes cupboard, he stopped as if listening again, but this time it was something he had seen that held him, not something he had heard.

On top of the food-store lay a whole parcel of Gauloises Caporal cigarettes, Vladimir's favourites when he couldn't get his Russians. Tipped, he noticed, reading the different legends. 'Duty free.' '*Filtre.*' Marked '*Exportation*' and 'Made in France.' Cellophane wrapped. He took them down. Of the ten original packets, one already missing. In the ashtray, three stubbed-out cigarettes of the same brand. In the air, now that he sniffed for it over the smell of food and putty, a faint aroma of French cigarettes.

And no cigarettes in his pocket, he remembered.

Holding the blue parcel in both hands, slowly turning it, Smiley tried to understand what it meant to him. Instinct – or better, a submerged perception yet to rise to the surface – signalled to him urgently that something about these cigarettes was wrong. Not their appearance. Not that they were stuffed with microfilm or high explosive or soft-nosed bullets or any of those weary games.

Merely the fact of their presence, here and nowhere else, was wrong.

So new, so free of dust, one packet missing, three smoked. *And no cigarettes in his pocket.*

He worked faster now, wanting very much to leave. The flat was too high up. It was too empty and too full. He had a growing sense of something being out of joint. Why didn't they take his keys? He pulled open the cupboard. It held clothes as well as papers but Vladimir possessed few of either. The papers were mostly cyclo-styled pamphlets in Russian and English and in what Smiley took to be one of the Baltic languages. There was a folder of letters from the Group's old headquarters in Paris, and posters reading 'REMEMBER LATVIA', 'REMEMBER ESTONIA', 'REMEMBER LITHUANIA', presumably for display at public demonstrations. There was a box of school chalk, yellow, a couple of pieces missing. And Vladimir's treasured Norfolk jacket, lying off its hook on the floor. Fallen there, perhaps, as Vladimir closed the cupboard door too fast.

And Vladimir so vain? thought Smiley. So military in his appearance? Yet dumps his best jacket in a heap on the cupboard floor. Or was it that a more careless hand than Vladimir's had not replaced it on the hanger?

Picking the jacket up, Smiley searched the pockets, then hung it back in the cupboard and slammed the door to see if it fell off its hook.

It did.

They didn't take the keys, and they didn't search his flat, he thought. They searched Vladimir, but in the Superintendent's opinion they had been disturbed.

Tell him I have two proofs and can bring them with me.

Returning to the kitchen area he stood before the food-store and took another studied look at the blue parcel lying on top of it. Then peered in the waste-paper basket. At the ashtray again, memorising. Then in the garbage bucket, just in case the missing packet, crumpled up, was there. It wasn't, which for some reason pleased him.

Time to go.

But he didn't, not quite. For another quarter of an hour, with his ear cocked for interruptions, Smiley delved and probed, lifting and replacing, still on the look-out for the loose floor-board, or the favoured recess behind the shelves. But this time he wanted *not* to find. This time, he wanted to confirm an absence. Only when he was as satisfied as circumstance allowed did he step quietly onto the landing and lock the door behind him. At the bottom of the first flight he met a temporary postman wearing a GPO armband emerging from another corridor. Smiley touched his elbow.

'If you've anything at all for flat 6B, I can save you the climb,' he said humbly.

The postman rummaged and produced a brown envelope. Postmark Paris, dated five days ago, the 15th district. Smiley slipped it into his pocket. At the bottom of the second flight stood a fire-door with a push-bar to open it from the inside only. He had made a mental note of it on his way up. He pushed, the door yielded, he descended a vile concrete staircase and crossed an interior courtyard to a deserted mews, still pondering the omission. Why didn't they search his flat?

he wondered. Moscow Centre, like any other large bureau-cracy, had its fixed procedures. You decide to kill a man. So you station pickets outside his house, you stake out his route with static posts, you put in your assassination team and you kill him. In the classic method. Then why not search his flat as well? – Vladimir, a bachelor, living in a building constant-ly overrun with strangers? – why not send in the pickets the moment he is on his way? *Because they knew he had it with him*, thought Smiley. And the body search, which the Super-intendent regarded as so cursory? Suppose they were not dis-turbed, but had found what they were looking for?

He hailed a taxi, telling the driver, 'Bywater Street in Chelsea, please, off the King's Road.'

Go home, he thought. Have a bath, think it through. Shave. *Tell him I have two proofs and can bring them with me.*

Suddenly, leaning forward, he tapped on the glass partition and changed his destination. As they made the U-turn, the tall motor-cyclist screeched to a stop behind them, dismounted and solemnly shunted his large black bike and side-car into the opposite lane. A footman, thought Smiley, watching him. A footman, wheeling in the trolley for tea. Like an official es-cort, arch-backed and elbows spread, the motor-cyclist fol-lowed them through the outer reaches of Camden, then, still at a regulation distance, slowly up the hill. The cab drew up, Smiley leaned forward to pay his fare. As he did so, the dark figure processed solemnly past them, one arm lifted from the elbow in a mail-fist salute.

8

He stood at the mouth of the avenue, gazing into the ranks of beech trees as they sank away from him like a retreating army into the mist. The darkness had departed reluctantly, leaving an indoor gloom. It could have been dusk already: tea-time in an old country house. The street lights either side of him were poor candles, illuminating nothing. The air felt warm and heavy. He had expected police still, and a roped-off area. He had expected journalists or curious bystanders. It never happened, he told himself, as he started slowly down the slope. No sooner had I left the scene than Vladimir clambered merrily to his feet, stick in hand, wiped off the gruesome make-up and skipped away with his fellow actors for a pot of beer at the police station.

Stick in hand, he repeated to himself, remembering something the Superintendent had said to him. Left hand or right hand? 'There's yellow chalk powder on his left hand too,' Mr Murgotroyd had said inside the van. 'Thumb and first two fingers.'

He advanced and the avenue darkened round him, the mist thickened. His footsteps echoed tinnily ahead of him. Twenty yards higher, brown sunlight burned like a slow bonfire in its own smoke. But down here in the dip the mist had collected in a cold fog, and Vladimir was very dead after all. He saw tyre marks where the police cars had parked. He noticed the absence of leaves and the unnatural cleanness of the gravel. What did they do? he wondered. Hose the gravel down? Sweep the leaves into yet more plastic pillowcases?

His tiredness had given way to a new and mysterious clarity. He continued up the avenue wishing Vladimir good morning and good night and not feeling a fool for doing so, thinking intently about drawing-pins and chalk and French cigarettes and Moscow Rules, looking for a tin pavilion by a playing field. Take it in sequence, he told himself. Take it from the beginning. Leave the Caporals on their shelf. He reached an intersection of paths and crossed it, still climbing. To his right, goal-posts appeared, and beyond them a green pavilion of corrugated iron, apparently empty. He started across the field, rain-water seeping into his shoes. Behind the hut ran a steep mud bank scoured with children's slides. He climbed the bank, entered a coppice, and kept climbing. The fog had not penetrated the trees and by the time he reached the brow it had cleared. There was still no one in sight. Returning, he approached the pavilion through the trees. It was a tin box, no more, with one side open to the field. The only furniture was a rough wood bench slashed and written on with knives, the only occupant a prone figure stretched on it, with a blanket pulled over his head and brown boots protruding. For an undisciplined moment Smiley wondered whether he too had had his face blown off. Girders held up the roof; earnest moral statements enlivened the flaking green paint. 'Punk is destructive. Society *does* not need it.' The assertion caused him a moment's indecision. 'Oh, but society *does*,' he wanted to reply; 'society is an association of minorities.' The drawing-pin was where Mostyn said it was, at head height exactly, in the best Sarratt tradition of regularity, its Circus-issue brass head as new and as unmarked as the boy who had put it there.

Proceed to the rendezvous, it said, *no danger sighted*.

Moscow Rules, thought Smiley yet again. Moscow, where it could take a fieldman three days to post a letter to a safe address. Moscow, where all minorities are punk.

Tell him I have two proofs and can bring them with me . . .

Vladimir's chalked acknowledgement ran close beside the pin, a wavering yellow worm of a message scrawled all down the post. Perhaps the old man was worried about rain, thought Smiley. Perhaps he was afraid it could wash his mark away. Or perhaps in his emotional state he leaned too heavily on the chalk, just as he had left his Norfolk jacket lying on the floor. *A meeting or nothing . . .* he had told Mostyn . . . *Tonight or nothing . . . Tell him I have two proofs and can bring them with me . . .* Nevertheless only the vigilant would ever have noticed that mark, heavy though it was, or the shiny drawing-pin either, and not even the vigilant would have found them odd, for on Hampstead Heath people post bills and messages to each other ceaselessly, and not all of them are spies. Some are children, some are tramps, some are believers in God and organisers of charitable walks, some have lost pets, and some are looking for variations of love and having to proclaim their needs from a hilltop. And not all of them, by any means, get their faces blown off at point-blank range by a Moscow Centre assassination weapon.

And the purpose of this acknowledgement? In Moscow, when Smiley from his desk in London had had the ultimate responsibility for Vladimir's case – in Moscow these signs were devised for agents who might disappear from hour to hour; they were the broken twigs along a path that could always be their last. *I see no danger and am proceeding as instructed to the agreed rendezvous*, read Vladimir's last – and fatally mistaken – message to the living world.

Leaving the hut, Smiley moved a short distance back along the route he had just come. And as he walked, he meticulously called to mind the Superintendent's reconstruction of Vladimir's last journey, drawing up his memory like an archive.

Those rubber overshoes are a Godsend, Mr Smiley, the Superintendent had declared piously: North British Century, diamond-pattern soles, sir, and barely walked on – why, you could follow him through a football crowd if you had to!

'I'll give you the authorised version,' the Superintendent had said, speaking fast because they were short of time. 'Ready, Mr Smiley?'

Ready, Smiley had said.

The Superintendent changed his tone of voice. Conversation was one thing, evidence another. As he spoke, he shone his torch in phases onto the wet gravel of the roped-off area. A lecture with magic lantern, Smiley had thought; at Sarratt I'd have taken notes: 'Here he is, coming down the hill now, sir. See him there? Normal pace, nice heel and toe movement, normal progress, everything above board. See, Mr Smiley?'

Mr Smiley had seen.

'And the stick mark there, do you see, in his right hand, sir?'

Smiley had seen that too, how the rubber-ferruled walking stick had left a deep round rip with every second footprint.

'Whereas of course he had the stick in his left when he was shot, correct? You saw that, too, sir, I noticed. Happen to know which side his bad leg was at all, sir, if he had one?'

'The right,' Smiley had said.

'Ah. Then most likely the right was the side he normally held the stick, as well. Down here, please, sir, that's the way! Walking normal still, please note,' the Superintendent had added, making a rare slip of grammar in his distraction.

For five more paces the regular diamond imprint, heel and

toe, had continued undisturbed in the beam of the Superintendent's torch. Now, by daylight, Smiley saw only the ghost of them. The rain, other feet, and the tyre tracks of illicit cyclists had caused large parts to disappear. But by night, at the Superintendent's lantern show, he had seen them vividly, as vividly as he saw the plastic-covered corpse in the dip below them, where the trail had ended.

'*Now*,' the Superintendent had declared with satisfaction, and halted, the cone of his torchbeam resting on a single scuffed area of ground.

'How old did you say he was, sir?' the Superintendent asked.

'I didn't, but he owned to sixty-nine.'

'Plus your recent heart attack, I gather. Now, sir. First he stops. In sharp order. Don't ask me why, perhaps he was spoken to. My guess is he heard something. Behind him. Notice the way the pace shortens, notice the position of the feet as he makes the half-turn, looks over his shoulder or whatever? Anyway, he *turns* and that's why I say "behind him". And whatever he saw or didn't see – or heard or didn't hear – he decides to run. Off he goes, look!' the Superintendent urged, with the sudden enthusiasm of the sportsman. 'Wider stride, heels not hardly on the ground at all. A new print entirely, and going for all he's worth. You can even see where he shoved himself off with his stick for the extra purchase.'

Peering now by daylight, Smiley no longer with any certainty *could* see, but he had seen last night – and in his memory saw again this morning – the sudden desperate gashes of the ferrule thrust downward, then thrust at an angle.

'Trouble was,' the Superintendent commented quietly, resuming his courtroom style, 'whatever killed him was out in front, wasn't it? Not behind him at all.'

It was both, thought Smiley now, with the advantage of

the intervening hours. They *drove* him, he thought, trying without success to recall the Sarratt jargon for this particular technique. They knew his route, and they *drove* him. The frightener behind the target drives him forward, the finger man loiters ahead undetected till the target blunders into him. For it was a truth known also to Moscow Centre murder teams that even the oldest hands will spend hours worrying about their backs, their flanks, the cars that pass and the cars that don't, the streets they cross and the houses that they enter. Yet still fail, when the moment is upon them, to recognise the danger that greets them face to face.

'Still running,' the Superintendent said, moving steadily nearer the body down the hill. 'Notice how the pace gets a little longer because of the steeper gradient now? Erratic too, see that? Feet flying all over the shop. Running for dear life. Literally. And the walking stick still in his right hand. See him veering now, moving towards the verge? Lost his bearings, I wouldn't wonder. Here we go. Explain *that* if you can!'

The torchbeam rested on a patch of footprints close together, five or six of them, all in a very small space at the edge of the grass between two high trees.

'Stopped again,' the Superintendent announced. 'Not so much a total *stop* perhaps, more your stutter. Don't ask me why. Maybe he just wrong-footed himself. Maybe he was worried to find himself so close to the trees. Maybe his heart got him if you tell me it was dicky. Then off he goes again same as before.'

'With the stick in his left hand,' Smiley had said quietly.

'Why? That's what I ask myself, sir, but perhaps you people know the answer. Why? Did he hear something again? Remember something? Why – when you're running for your life – why pause, do a duck-shuffle, change hands and then run on again? Straight into the arms of whoever shot him? Unless of course whatever was behind him *overtook* him there, came round through the trees perhaps, made an arc as it were? Any explanation from *your* side of the street, Mr Smiley?'

And with that question still ringing in Smiley's ears they had arrived at last at the body, floating like an embryo under its plastic film.

But Smiley, on this morning after, stopped short of the dip. Instead, by placing his sodden shoes as best he could upon each spot exactly, he set about trying to imitate the movements the old man might have made. And since Smiley did all this in slow motion, and with every appearance of concentration, under the eye of two trousered ladies walking their Alsatians, he was taken for an adherent of the new fad in Chinese martial exercises, and accounted mad accordingly.

First he put his feet side by side and pointed them down the hill. Then he put his left foot forward, and moved his right foot round until the toe pointed directly towards a spinney of young saplings. As he did so, his right shoulder followed naturally, and his instinct told him that this would be the likely moment for Vladimir to transfer the stick to his left hand. But *why*? As the Superintendent had also asked, why transfer the stick at all? Why, in the most extreme moment of his life, why solemnly move a walking stick from the right hand to the left? Certainly not to defend himself – since, as Smiley remembered, he was right-handed. To defend himself, he would only have seized the stick more firmly. Or clasped it with *both* his hands, like a club.

Was it in order to leave his right hand free? But free for what?

Aware this time of being observed, Smiley peered sharply behind him and saw two small boys in blazers who had paused to watch this round little man in spectacles performing strange antics with his feet. He glowered at them in his most schoolmasterly manner, and they moved hastily on.

To leave his right hand free for what? Smiley repeated to himself. And why start running again a moment later?

Vladimir turned to the right, thought Smiley, once again matching his action to the thought. Vladimir turned to the right. He faced the spinney, he put his stick in his left hand. For a moment, according to the Superintendent, he stood still. *Then* he ran on.

Moscow Rules, Smiley thought, staring at his own right hand. Slowly he lowered it into his raincoat pocket. Which was empty, as Vladimir's right-hand coat pocket was also empty.

Had he meant to write a message perhaps? Smiley was teasing himself with the theory he was determined to hold at bay. To write a message with the *chalk* for instance? Had he recognised his pursuer, and wished to chalk a name somewhere, or a sign? But what *on*? Not on these wet tree trunks for sure. Not on the clay, the dead leaves, the grave! Looking round him, Smiley became aware of a peculiar feature of his location. Here, almost between two trees, at the very edge of the avenue, at the point where the fog was approaching its thickest, he was as good as out of sight. The avenue descended, yes, and lifted ahead of him. But it also curved, and from where he stood the upward line of sight in both directions was masked by tree trunks and a dense thicket of saplings. Along the whole path of Vladimir's last frantic journey – a path he knew well, remember, had used for similar meetings – this was the point, Smiley realised with increasing satisfaction, where the fleeing man was out of sight from both ahead of him and behind him.

And had stopped.

Had freed his right hand.

Had put it – let us say – in his pocket.

For his heart tablets? No. Like the yellow chalk and the matches, they were in his left pocket, not his right.

For something – let us say – that was no longer in the pocket when he was found dead.

For what then?

Tell him I have two proofs and can bring them with me . . . Then perhaps he will see me . . . This is Gregory asking for Max. I have something for him, please . . .

Proofs. Proofs too precious to post. He was bringing something. Two somethings. Not just in his head – in his pocket. And was playing Moscow Rules. Rules that had been drummed into the General from the very day of his recruitment as a defector in place. By Smiley himself, no less, as well as his case officer on the spot. Rules that had been invented for his survival; and the survival of his network. Smiley felt the excitement seize his stomach like a nausea. Moscow Rules decree that, if you physically *carry* a message, you must also carry the means to discard it! That, however it is disguised or concealed – microdot, secret writing, undeveloped film, any one of the hundred risky, finicky ways – still as an *object* it must be the first and lightest thing that comes to hand, the least conspicuous when jettisoned!

Such as a medicine bottle full of tablets, he thought, calming a little. Such as a box of matches.

One box Swan Vesta matches partly used, overcoat left, he remembered. A smoker's match, note well.

And in the safe flat, he thought relentlessly – tantalising himself, staving off the final insight – there on the table waiting for him, one packet of cigarettes, Vladimir's favourite brand. And in Westbourne Terrace on the food safe, nine packets of Gauloises Caporal. Out of ten.

But no cigarettes in his pockets. None, as the good Superintendent would have said, on his person. Or not when they found him, that is to say.

So the premise, George? Smiley asked himself, mimicking Lacon – brandishing Lacon's prefectorial finger accusingly in his own intact face – the premise? The premise is thus far, Oliver, that a smoker, a habitual smoker, in a state of high nervousness, sets off on a crucial clandestine meeting equipped with matches but not even so much as an empty packet of cigarettes, though he possesses quite demonstrably a whole stock of them. So that either the assassins found it, and removed it – the proof, or proofs, which Vladimir was speaking of, or – or what? Or Vladimir changed his stick from his right hand to his left in time. And put his right hand in his pocket in time. And took it out again, also in time, at the very spot where he could not be seen. And got rid of it, or them, according to Moscow Rules.

Having satisfied his own insistence upon a logical succession, George Smiley stepped cautiously into the long grass that led to the spinney, soaking his trousers from the knees down. For half an hour or more he searched, groping in the grass and among the foliage, retreading his tracks, cursing his own blundering, giving up, beginning again, answering the fatuous enquiries of passers-by which ranged from the obscene to the excessively attentive. There were even two Buddhist monks from a local seminary, complete with saffron robes and lace-up boots and knitted woollen caps, who offered their assistance. Smiley courteously declined it. He found two broken kites, a quantity of Coca-Cola tins. He found scraps of the female body, some in colour, some in black and white, ripped from magazines. He found an old running shoe, black, and shreds of an old burnt blanket. He found four beer bottles, empty, and four empty cigarette packets so sodden and old that after one glance he discounted them. And in a branch, slipped into the fork just where it joined its parent trunk, the fifth packet, or better perhaps the tenth – that was not even empty; a relatively dry packet of Gauloises Caporal, *Filtre* and Duty Free, high up. Smiley reached for it as if it were forbidden fruit but like forbidden fruit it stayed outside his grasp. He jumped for it and felt his back rip: a distinct and unnerving parting of tissue that smarted and dug at him for days afterwards. He said 'damn' out loud and rubbed the spot, much as Ostrakova might have done. Two typists, on their way to work, consoled him with their giggles. He found a stick, poked the packet free, opened it. Four cigarettes remained.

And behind those four cigarettes, half concealed, and protected by its own skin of cellophane, something he recognised but dared not even disturb with his wet and trembling fingers. Something he dared not even contemplate until he was free of this appalling place, where giggling typists and Buddhist monks innocently trampled the spot where Vladimir had died.

They have one, I have the other, he thought. I have shared the old man's legacy with his murderers.

Braving the traffic, he followed the narrow pavement down the hill till he came to South End Green, where he hoped for a café that would give him tea. Finding none open so early, he sat on a bench across from a cinema instead, contemplating an old marble fountain and a pair of red telephone boxes, one filthier than the other. A warm drizzle was falling; a few shopkeepers had started lowering their awnings; a delicatessen store was taking delivery of bread. He sat with hunched shoulders, and the damp points of his mackintosh collar stabbed his unshaven cheeks whenever he turned his head. 'For God's

sake, mourn!' Ann had flung at Smiley once, infuriated by his
apparent composure after yet another friend had died. 'If you
won't grieve for the dead, how can you love the living?' Sitting
on his bench, pondering his next step, Smiley now transmitted to her the answer he had failed to find at the time. 'You
are wrong,' he told her distractedly. 'I mourn the dead sincere-
ly, and Vladimir, at this moment, deeply. It's loving the living
which is sometimes a bit of a problem.'

He tried the telephone boxes and the second worked. By
a miracle, even the S-Z directory was intact and, more amazing still, the Straight and Steady Minicab Service of Islington
North had paid for the privilege of heavy type. He dialled the
number and while it rang out he had a panic that he had forgotten the name of the signatory on the receipt in Vladimir's
pocket. He rang off, recovering his two pence. Lane? Lang? He
dialled again.

A female voice answered him in a bored singsong: 'Straight-
and-Stead-ee! Name-when-and-where-*to* please?'

'I'd like to speak to Mr J. Lamb, please, one of your drivers,'
Smiley said politely.

'Sorr-ee, no personal calls on this lin-*er*,' she sang and
rang off.

He dialled a third time. It wasn't personal at all, he said
huffily, now surer of his ground. He wanted Mr Lamb to
drive for him, and nobody but Mr Lamb would do. 'Tell him
it's a long journey. Stratford-on-Avon' – choosing a town at
random – 'tell him I want to go to Stratford.' *Sampson*, he replied, when she insisted on a name. Sampson with a 'p'.

He returned to his bench to wait again.

To ring Lacon? For what purpose? Rush home, open the
cigarette packet, find out its precious contents? It was the first
thing Vladimir threw away, he thought: in the spy trade we

abandon first what we love the most. I got the better end of the bargain after all. An elderly couple had settled opposite him. The man wore a stiff Homburg hat and was playing war tunes on a tin whistle. His wife grinned inanely at the passers-by. To avoid her gaze, Smiley remembered the brown envelope from Paris, and tore it open, expecting what? A bill probably, some hangover from the old boy's life there. Or one of those cyclostyled battle-cries that émigrés send each other like Christmas cards. But this was neither a bill nor a circular but a personal letter: an appeal, but of a very special sort. Unsigned, no address for the sender. In French, handwritten very fast. Smiley read it once and he was reading it a second time when an over-painted Ford Cortina, driven by a boy in a polo neck pullover, skidded to a giddy halt outside the cinema. Returning the letter to his pocket, he crossed the road to the car.

'Sampson with a "p"?' the boy yelled impertinently through the window, then shoved open the back door from inside. Smiley climbed in. A smell of aftershave mingled with the stale cigarette smoke. He held a ten-pound note in his hand and he let it show.

'Will you please switch off the engine?' Smiley asked.

The boy obeyed, watching him all the time in the mirror. He had brown Afro hair. White hands, carefully manicured.

'I'm a private detective,' Smiley explained. 'I'm sure you get a lot of us and we're a nuisance but I would be happy to pay for a little bit of information. You signed a receipt yesterday for thirteen pounds. Do you remember who your fare was?'

'Tall party. Foreign. White moustache and a limp.'

'Old?'

'Very. Walking stick and all.'

'Where did you pick him up?' Smiley asked.

'Cosmo Restaurant, Praed Street, ten-thirty, morning,' the boy said, gabbling deliberately.

Praed Street was five minutes' walk from Westbourne Terrace.

'And where did you take him, please?'

'Charlton.'

'Charlton in south-east London?'

'Saint Somebody's Church off of Battle-of-the-Nile Street. Ask for a pub called The Defeated Frog.'

'Frog?'

'Frenchman.'

'Did you leave him there?'

'One hour wait, then back to Praed Street.'

'Did you make any other stops?'

'Once at a toy-shop going, once at a phone-box coming back. Party bought a wooden duck on wheels.' He turned and, resting his chin on the back of the seat, insolently held his hands apart, indicating size. 'Yellow job,' he said. 'The phone call was local.'

'How do you know?'

'I lent him two pence, didn't I? Then he come back and borrows himself two ten p's, for in-case.'

I asked him where he was calling from but he just said he had plenty of change, Mostyn had said.

Passing the boy the ten-pound note, Smiley reached for the door handle.

'You can tell your firm I didn't turn up,' he said.

'Tell 'em what I bloody like, can't I?'

Smiley climbed quickly out, just managing to close the door before the boy drove away at the same frightful speed. Standing on the pavement, he completed his second reading of the letter, and by then he had it in his memory for good. A woman, he thought, trusting his first instinct. And she thinks she's going to die. Well, so do we all, and we're right. He was feigning light-headedness to himself, indifference. Each man has only a quantum of compassion, he argued, and mine is used up for the day. But the letter scared him all the same, and re-charged his sense of urgency.

General, I do not wish to be dramatic but some men are watching my house and I do not think they are your friends or mine. This morning I had an impression that they were trying to kill me. Will you not send me your magic friend once more?

He had things to hide. To *cache*, as they insisted on saying at Sarratt. He took buses, changing several times, watching his back, dozing. The black motor-cycle with its side-car had not reappeared; he could discern no other surveillance. At a stationer's shop in Baker Street he bought a large cardboard box, some daily newspapers, some wrapping paper and a reel of Scotch tape. He put Vladimir's packet of cigarettes into the box, together with Ostrakova's letter, and he padded out the rest of the space with newspaper. He wrapped the box and got his fingers tangled in the Scotch tape. Scotch tape had always defeated him. He wrote his own name on the lid, 'To be called for.' He paid off the cab at the Savoy Hotel, where he consigned the box to the men's-cloakroom attendant, together with a pound note.

'Not heavy enough for a bomb, is it, sir?' the attendant asked, and facetiously held the parcel to his ear.

'I wouldn't be so sure,' said Smiley and they shared a good laugh together.

Tell Max that it concerns the Sandman, he thought. Vladimir, he wondered wistfully, what was your other proof?

9

The low skyline was filled with cranes and gasometers; lazy chimneys spouted ochre smoke into the rainclouds. If it had not been Saturday, Smiley would have used public transport but on Saturdays he was prepared to drive, though he lived on terms of mutual hatred with the combustion engine. He had crossed the river at Vauxhall Bridge. Greenwich lay behind him. He had entered the flat, dismembered hinterland of the docks. While the wiper blades shuddered, large raindrops crept through the bodywork of his unhappy little English car. Glum children, sheltering in a bus-stop, said, 'Keep straight on, guv.' He had shaved and bathed, but he had not slept. He had sent Vladimir's telephone bill to Lacon, requesting a breakdown of all traceable calls as a matter of urgency. His mind, as he drove, was clear, but prey to anarchic changes of mood. He was wearing a brown tweed overcoat, the one he used for travelling. He navigated a roundabout, mounted a rise, and suddenly a fine Edwardian pub stood before him, under the sign of a red-faced warrior. Battle-of-the-Nile Street rose away from it towards an island of worn grass, and on the island stood St Saviour's Church, built of stone and flint, proclaiming God's message to the crumbling Victorian warehouses. Next Sunday's preacher, said the poster, was a female major in the Salvation Army, and in front of the poster stood the lorry: a sixty-foot giant trailer, crimson, its side windows fringed with football pennants and a motley of foreign registration stickers covering one door. It was the biggest thing in sight, bigger even than the church. Somewhere in the background he heard a motor-bike engine slow down and then start up again, but he didn't even bother to look back. The familiar escort had followed him since Chelsea; but fear, as he used to preach at Sarratt, is always a matter of selection.

Following the footpath, Smiley entered a graveyard with no graves. Lines of headstones made up the perimeter, a climbing frame and three standard-pattern new houses occupied the central ground. The first house was called Zion, the second had no name at all, the third was called Number Three. Each had wide windows but Number Three had lace curtains, and when he pushed the gate all he saw was one shadow upstairs. He saw it stationary then he saw it sink and vanish as if it had been sucked into the floor, and for a second he wondered, in a quite dreadful way, whether he had just witnessed another murder. He rang the bell and angel chimes exploded inside the house. The door was made of rippled glass. Pressing his eye to it, he made out brown stair carpet and what looked like a perambulator. He rang the bell again and heard a scream. It started low and grew louder and at first he thought it was a child, then a cat, then a whistling kettle. It reached its zenith, held it, then suddenly stopped, either because someone had taken the kettle off the boil or because it had blown its nozzle off. He walked round to the back of the house. It was the same as the front, except for the drain-pipes and a vegetable patch, and a tiny goldfish pond made of pre-cast slab. There was no water in the pond, and consequently no goldfish either, but in the concrete bowl lay a yellow wooden duck on its side. It lay with its beak open and its staring eye turned to Heaven and two of its wheels were still going round.

'Party bought a wooden duck on wheels,' the minicab driver had said, turning to illustrate with his white hands. 'Yellow job.'

The back door had a knocker. He gave a light tap with it and tried the door handle, which yielded. He stepped inside and closed the door carefully behind him. He was standing in a scullery which led to a kitchen and the first thing he noticed in the kitchen was the kettle off the gas with a thin line of steam curling from its silent whistle. And two cups and a milk jug and a teapot on a tray.

'Mrs Craven?' he called softly. 'Stella?'

He crossed the dining-room and stood in the hall, on the brown carpet beside the perambulator, and in his mind he was making pacts with God; just no more deaths, no more Vladimirs and I will worship You for the rest of our respective lives.

'Stella? It's me. Max,' he said.

He pushed open the drawing-room door and she was sitting in the corner on an easy chair between the piano and window, watching him with cold determination. She was not scared, but she looked as if she hated him. She was wearing a long Asian dress and no make-up. She was holding the child to her, boy or girl he couldn't tell and couldn't remember. She had its tousled head pressed against her shoulder and her hand over its mouth to stop it making a noise, and she was watching him over the top of its head, challenging and defying him.

'Where's Villem?' he asked.

Slowly she took her hand away and Smiley expected the child to scream but instead it stared at him in salute.

'His name's William,' she said quietly. 'Get that straight, Max. That's his choice. William Craven. British to the core. Not

Estonian, not Russian. British.' She was a beautiful woman, black-haired and still. Seated in the corner holding her child, she seemed permanently painted against the dark background.

'I want to talk to him, Stella. I'm not asking him to do anything. I may even be able to help him.'

'I've heard that before, haven't I? He's out. Gone to work where he belongs.'

Smiley digested this.

'Then what's his lorry doing outside?' he objected gently.

'He's gone to the depot. They sent a car for him.'

Smiley digested this also.

'Then who's the second cup for in the kitchen?'

'He's gone to the depot. They sent a car for him.'

He went upstairs and she let him. There was a door straight ahead of him and there were doors to his left and right, both open, one to the child's room, one to the main bedroom. The door ahead of him was closed and when he knocked there was no answer.

'Villem, it's Max,' he said. 'I have to talk to you, please. Then I'll go and leave you in peace, I promise.'

He repeated this word for word then went down the steep stairs again to the drawing-room. The child had begun crying loudly.

'Perhaps if you made that tea,' he suggested between the child's sobs.

'You're not talking to him alone, Max. I'm not having you charm him off the tree again.'

'I never did that. That was not my job.'

'He still thinks the world of you. That's enough for me.'

'It's about Vladimir,' Smiley said.

'I know what it's about. They've been ringing half the night, haven't they?'

'Who have?'

'"Where's Vladimir? Where's Vladi?" What do they think William is? Jack the Ripper? He hasn't had sound nor sight of Vladi for God knows how long. Oh Beckie, darling, *do* be quiet!' Striding across the room she found a tin of biscuits under a heap of washing and shoved one forcibly into the child's mouth. 'I'm not usually like this,' she said.

'*Who's* been asking for him?' Smiley insisted gently.

'Mikhel, who else? Remember Mikhel, our Freedom Radio ace, Prime Minister designate of Estonia, betting tout? Three o'clock this morning while Beckie's cutting a tooth, the bloody phone goes. It's Mikhel doing his heavy-breathing act. "Where's Vladi, Stella? Where's our Leader?" I said to him: "You're daft, aren't you? You think it's harder to tap the phone when people only whisper? You're barking mad," I said to him. "Stick to racehorses and get out of politics," I told him.'

'Why was he so worried?' Smiley asked.

'Vladi owed him money, that's why. Fifty quid. Probably lost it on a horse together, one of their many losers. He'd promised to bring it round to Mikhel's place and have a game of chess with him. In the middle of the night, mark you. They're insomniacs apparently, as well as patriots. Our leader hadn't shown up. Drama. "Why the hell should William know where he is?" I asked him. "Go to sleep." An hour later who's back on the line? Breathing as before? Our Major Mikhel once more, hero of the Royal Estonian Cavalry, clicking our heels and apologising. He's been round to Vladi's pad, banged on the door, rung the bell. There's nobody at home. "Look, Mikhel," I said, "he's not here, we're not hiding him in the attic, we haven't seen him since Beckie's christening, we haven't heard from him. Right? William's just in from Hamburg, he needs sleep, and I'm not waking him."'

'So he rang off again,' Smiley suggested.

'Did he hell! He's a leech. "Villem is Vladi's favourite," he says. "What for?" I say. "The three-thirty at Ascot? Look, go to bloody sleep!" "Vladimir always said to me, if ever anything went wrong, I should go to Villem," he said. "So what do you want him to do?" I said. "Drive up to town in the trailer and bang on Vladi's door as well?" Jesus!'

She sat the child on a chair. Where she stayed, contentedly cropping her biscuit.

There was the sound of a door slammed violently, followed by fast footsteps coming down the stairs.

'William's right out of it, Max,' Stella warned, staring straight at Smiley. 'He's not political and he's not slimy, and he's got over his dad being a martyr. He's a big boy now and he's going to stand on his own feet. Right? I said, "Right?"'

Smiley had moved to the far end of the room to give himself distance from the door. Villem strode in purposefully, still wearing his track suit and running shoes, about ten years Stella's junior and somehow too slight for his own safety. He perched himself on the sofa, at the edge, his intense gaze switching between his wife and Smiley as if wondering which of them would spring first. His high forehead looked strangely white under his dark, swept-back hair. He had shaved, and shaving had filled out his face, making him even younger. His eyes, red-rimmed from driving, were brown and passionate.

'Hullo, Villem,' Smiley said.

'William,' Stella corrected him.

Villem nodded tautly, acknowledging both forms.

'Hullo, Max,' said Villem. On his lap, his hands found and held each other. 'How you doing, Max? That's the way, huh?'

'I gather you've already heard the news about Vladimir,' Smiley said.

'News? What news, please?'

Smiley took his time. Watching him, sensing his stress.

'That he's disappeared,' Smiley replied quite lightly, at last. 'I gather his friends have been ringing you up at unsocial hours.'

'Friends?' Villem shot a dependent glance at Stella. 'Old émigrés, drink tea, play chess all day, politics? Talk crazy dreams? Mikhel is not my friend, Max.'

He spoke swiftly, with impatience for this foreign language which was such a poor substitute for his own. Whereas Smiley spoke as if he had all day.

'But *Vladi* is your friend,' he objected. 'Vladi was your father's friend before you. They were in Paris together. Brothers-in-arms. They came to England together.'

Countering the weight of this suggestion, Villem's small body became a storm of gestures. His hands parted and made furious arcs, his brown hair lifted and fell flat again.

'Sure! Vladimir, he was my father's friend. His good friend. Also of Beckie the godfather, okay? But not for politics. Not any more.' He glanced at Stella, seeking her approval. 'Me, I am William Craven. I got English home, English wife, English kid, English name. Okay?'

'And an English job,' Stella put in quietly, watching him.

'A good job! Know how much I earn, Max? We buy house. Maybe a car, okay?'

Something in Villem's manner – his glibness perhaps, or the energy of his protest – had caught the attention of his wife, for now Stella was studying him as intently as Smiley was, and she began to hold the baby distractedly, almost without interest.

'When did you last see him, William?' Smiley asked.

'Who, Max? See who? I don't understand you, please.'

'Tell him, Bill,' Stella ordered her husband, not moving her eyes from him for a moment.

'When did you last see Vladimir?' Smiley repeated patiently.

'Long time, Max.'

'Weeks?'

'Sure. Weeks.'

'Months?'

'Months. Six months! Seven! At christening. He was godfather, we make a party. But no politics.'

Smiley's silences had begun to produce an awkward tension.

'And not since?' he asked at last.

'No.'

'What time did William get back yesterday?'

'Early,' she said.

'As early as ten o'clock in the morning?'

'Could have been. I wasn't here. I was visiting Mother.'

'Vladimir drove down here yesterday by taxi,' he explained, still to Stella. 'I think he saw William.'

Nobody helped him, not Smiley, not his wife. Even the child kept still.

'On his way here Vladimir bought a toy. The taxi waited an hour down the lane and took him away again, back to Paddington where he lives,' Smiley said, still being very careful to keep the present tense.

Villem had found his voice at last: 'Vladi is of Beckie the godfather!' he protested with another flourish, as his English threatened to desert him entirely. 'Stella don't like him, so he must come here like a thief, okay? He bring my Beckie toy, okay? Is a crime already, Max? Is a law, an old man cannot bring to his godchild toys?'

Once again neither Smiley nor Stella spoke. They were both waiting for the same inevitable collapse.

'Vladi is old man, Max! Who knows when he sees his Beckie again? He is friend of family!'

'Not of this family,' said Stella. 'Not any more.'

'He was friend of my father! Comrade! In Paris they fight together Bolshevism. So he brings to Beckie a toy. Why not, please? Why not, Max?'

'You said you bought the bloody thing yourself,' said Stella. Putting a hand to her breast, she closed a button as if to cut him off.

Villem swung to Smiley, appealing to him: 'Stella don't like the old man, okay? Is afraid I make more politics with him, okay? So I don't tell Stella. She goes to see her mother in Staines hospital and while she is away Vladi makes a small visit to see Beckie, say hullo, why not?' In desperation he actually leapt to his feet, flinging up his arms in too much protest. 'Stella!' he cried. 'Listen to me! So Vladi don't get home last night? Please, I am so sorry! But it is not my fault, okay? Max! That Vladi is an old man! Lonely. So maybe he finds a woman once. Okay? So he can't do much with her, but he still likes her company. For this he was pretty famous, I think! Okay? Why not?'

'And before yesterday?' Smiley asked, after an age. Villem seemed not to understand, so Smiley paced out the question again: 'You saw Vladimir yesterday. He came by taxi and brought a yellow wooden duck for Beckie. On wheels.'

'Sure.'

'Very well. But before yesterday – not counting yesterday – when did you last see him?'

Some questions are hazard, some are instinct, some – like this one – are based on a premature understanding that is more than instinct, but less than knowledge.

Villem wiped his lips on the back of his hand. 'Monday,' he said miserably. 'I see him Monday. He ring me, we meet. Sure.'

Then Stella whispered, 'Oh, William,' and held the child

upright against her, a little soldier, while she peered down-ward at the haircord carpet waiting for her feelings to right themselves.

The phone began ringing. Like an infuriated infant Villem sprang at it, lifted the receiver, slammed it back on the cradle, then threw the whole telephone on to the floor and kicked the receiver clear. He sat down.

Stella turned to Smiley: 'I want you to go,' she said. 'I want you to walk out of here and never come back. Please, Max. Now.'

For a time Smiley seemed to consider this request quite seri-ously. He looked at Villem with avuncular affection; he looked at Stella. Then he delved in his inside pocket and pulled out a folded copy of the day's first edition of the *Evening Standard* and handed it to Stella rather than to Villem, partly because he guessed that Villem would break down.

'I'm afraid Vladi's disappeared for good, William,' he said in a tone of simple regret. 'It's in the papers. He's been shot dead. The police will want to ask you questions. I have to hear what happened and tell you how to answer them.'

Then Villem said something hopeless in Russian and Stella, moved by his tone if not his words, put down one child and went to comfort the other, and Smiley might not have been in the room at all. So he sat for a while quite alone, thinking of Vladimir's piece of negative film – indecipherable until he turned it to positive – nestling in its box in the Savoy Hotel with the anonymous letter from Paris that he could do noth-ing about. And of the second proof, wondering what it was, and how the old man had carried it, and supposing it was in his wallet; but believing also that he would never know.

Villem sat bravely as if he were already attending Vladimir's funeral. Stella sat at his side with her hand on his, Beckie the child lay on the floor and slept. Occasionally as Villem talked, tears rolled unashamedly down his pale cheeks.

'For the others I give nothing,' said Villem. 'For Vladi everything. I love this man.' He began again: 'After the death of my father, Vladi become father to me. Sometimes I even say him: "my father". Not uncle. Father.'

'Perhaps we could start with Monday,' Smiley suggested. 'With the first meeting.'

Vladi had telephoned, said Villem. It was the first time Villem had heard from him or from anybody in the Group for months. Vladi telephoned Villem at the depot, out of the blue, while Villem was consolidating his load and checking his trans-shipment papers with the office before leaving for Dover. That was the arrangement, Villem said, that was how it had been left with the Group. He was out of it, as they all were, more or less, but if he was ever urgently needed he could be reached at the depot on a Monday morning, not at home because of Stella. Vladi was Beckie's godfather and as godfather could ring the house any time. But not on business. Never.

'I ask him: "Vladi! What do you want? Listen, how are you?"'

Vladimir was in a call box down the road. He wanted a personal conversation immediately. Against all the employers' regulations Villem picked him up at the roundabout and Vladimir rode half the way to Dover with him: 'black,' said Villem – meaning 'illegally'. The old boy was carrying a rush basket full of oranges, but Villem had not been of a mood to ask him why he should saddle himself with pounds of oranges. At first Vladimir had talked about Paris and Villem's father, and the great struggles they had shared; then he talked about a small favour Villem could do for him. For the sake of old times a small favour. For the sake of the Group, of which Villem's father had once been such a hero.

'I tell him: "Vladi, this small favour is impossible for me. I promise Stella: is impossible!"'

Stella's hand left her husband's side and she sat alone, torn between wishing to console him for the old man's death and her hurt at his broken promise.

Just a small favour, Vladimir had insisted. Small, no trouble, no risk, but very helpful to our cause: also Villem's duty. Then Vladi produced snaps he had taken of Beckie at the christening. They were in a yellow Kodak envelope, the prints on one side and the negatives in protective cellophane on the other and the chemist's blue docket still stapled to the outside, all as innocent as the day.

For a while they admired them till Vladimir said suddenly: 'It is for Beckie, Villem. What we do, we do for Beckie's future.'

Hearing Villem repeat this, Stella clenched her fists, and when she looked up again she was resolute and somehow much older, with islands of tiny wrinkles at the corner of each eye.

Villem went on with his story: 'Then Vladimir tell to me, "Villem. Every Monday you are driving to Hanover and Hamburg, returning Friday. How long you stay in Hamburg, please?"'

To which Villem had replied as short a time as possible, depending on how long it took him to reload, depending on whether he delivered to the agent or to the addressee, depending what time of day he arrived and how many hours he already had on his sheet. Depending on his return load, if he had one. There were more questions of this sort, which Villem now related, many trivial – where Villem slept on the journey, where he ate – and Smiley knew that the old man in a rather monstrous way was doing what he would have done himself; he was talking Villem into a corner, making him answer as a prelude to making him obey. And only after this did Vladimir explain to Villem, using all his military and family authority, just what he wished Villem to do:

'He say to me: "Villem, take these oranges to Hamburg for me. Take this basket." "What for?" I ask him. "General, why do I take this basket?" Then he give me fifty pounds. "But why do I take this basket?" I ask him. "What emergency is considered here, General?"'

Then Vladimir recited to Villem his instructions, and they included fallbacks and contingencies – even, if necessary, staying an extra night on the strength of the fifty pounds – and Smiley noticed how the old man had insisted upon Moscow Rules, exactly as he had with Mostyn, and how there was *too much*, as there always had been – the older he got, the more the old boy had tied himself up in the skeins of his old conspiracies. Villem should lay the yellow Kodak envelope containing Beckie's photograph on the top of the oranges, he should take his stroll down to the front of the cabin – all as Villem, in the event had done, he said – and the envelope was the letter-box, and the sign that it had been filled would be a chalk mark 'also yellow like the envelope, which is the tradition of our Group,' said Villem.

'And the safety signal?' Smiley asked. 'The signal that says "I am not being followed?"'

'Was Hamburg newspaper from yesterday.' Villem replied swiftly – but on this subject, he confessed, he had had a small difference with Vladimir, despite all the respect he owed to him as a leader, as a General, and as his father's friend.

'He tell to me, "Villem, you carry that newspaper in your pocket." But I tell to him: "Vladi, please, look at me, I have only tracksuit, no pockets." So he say, "Villem, then carry the newspaper under your arm."'

'Bill,' Stella breathed, with a sort of awe. 'Oh Bill, you

stupid bloody fool.' She turned to Smiley. 'I mean, why didn't they just put it in the bloody post, whatever it is, and be done with it?'

Because it was a negative, and only negatives are acceptable by Moscow Rules. Because the General had a terror of betrayal, Smiley thought. The old boy saw it everywhere, in everyone around him. And if death is the ultimate judge, he was right.

'And it worked?' Smiley said finally to Villem with great gentleness. 'The handover worked?'

'Sure! It work fine,' Villem agreed heartily, and darted Stella a defiant glance.

'And did you have any idea, for instance, who might have been your contact at this meeting?'

Then with much hesitation, and after much prompting, some of it from Stella, Villem told that also: about the hollowed face that had looked so desperate and had reminded him of his father; about the warning stare which was either real or he had imagined it because he was so excited. How sometimes, when he watched football on the television, which he liked to do very much, the camera caught someone's face or expression, and it stuck in your memory for the rest of the match, even if you never saw it again – and how the face on the steamer was of this sort exactly. He described the flicked horns of hair, and with his fingertips he lightly drew deep grooves in his own unmarked cheeks. He described the man's smallness, and even his sexiness – Villem said he could tell. He described his own feelings of being *warned* by the man, warned to take care of a precious thing. Villem would look the same way himself – he told Stella with a sudden flourish of imagined tragedy – if there was another war, and fighting, and he had to give away Beckie to a stranger to look after! And this was the cue for more tears, and more reconciliation, and more lamentations about the old man's death, to which Smiley's next question inevitably contributed.

'So you brought the yellow envelope back, and yesterday when the General came down with Beckie's duck, you handed him the envelope,' he suggested, as mildly as he knew how, but it was still some while before a plain narrative emerged.

It was Villem's habit, he said, before driving home on Fridays, to sleep at the depot for a few hours in the cab, then shave and drink a cup of tea with the boys so that he arrived home feeling steady, rather than nervous and bad-tempered. It was a trick he had learned from the older hands, he said: not to rush home, you only regret it. But yesterday was different, he said, and besides – lapsing suddenly into monosyllabic nicknames – Stell had taken Beck to Staines to see her mum. So he for once came straight home, rang Vladimir and gave him the code word which they had agreed on in advance.

'Rang him where?' Smiley asked, softly interrupting.

'At flat. He told me: "Phone me only at flat. Never at library. Mikhel is good man, but he is not informed."'

And, Villem continued, within a short time – he forgot how long – Vladimir had arrived at the house by minicab, a thing he had never done before, bringing the duck for Beck. Villem handed him the yellow envelope of snapshots and Vladimir took them to the window and very slowly, 'like they were sacred from a church, Max,' with his back to Villem, Vladimir held the negatives one after the other to the light till he apparently found the one he was looking for, and after that he went on gazing at it for a long time.

'Just one?' Smiley asked swiftly – his mind upon the two proofs again – '*One* negative?'

'Sure.'

'One frame, or one strip?'

Frame: Villem was certain. One small frame. Yes, thirty-five millimetre, like his own Agfa automatic. No, Villem had not been able to see what it contained, whether writing or what. He had seen Vladimir, that was all.

'Vladi was red, Max. Wild in the face, Max, bright with his eyes. He was old man.'

'And on your journey,' Smiley said, interrupting Villem's story to ask this crucial question. 'All the way home from Hamburg, you never once thought to look?'

'Was secret, Max. Was military secret.'

Smiley glanced at Stella.

'He wouldn't,' she said in answer to his unspoken question. 'He's too straight.'

Smiley believed her.

Villem took up his story again. Having put the yellow envelope in his pocket, Vladimir took Villem into the garden and thanked him, holding Villem's hand in both of his, telling him that it was a great thing he had done, the best; that Villem was his father's son, a finer soldier even than his father – the best Estonian stock, steady, conscientious and reliable; that with this photograph they could repay many debts and do great damage to the Bolsheviks; that the photograph was a *proof*, a proof impossible to ignore. But of what, he did not say – only that Max would see it, and believe, and remember. Villem didn't quite know why they had to go into the garden but he supposed that the old man in his excitement had become scared of microphones, for he was already talking a lot about security.

'I take him to gate but not to taxi. He tell me I must not come to taxi. "Villem, I am old man," he say to me. We speak Russian. "Next week maybe I fall dead. Who cares? Today we have won great battle. Max will be greatly proud of us."'

Struck by the aptness of the General's last words to him, Villem again bounded to his feet in fury, his brown eyes smouldering. 'Was Soviets!' he shouted. 'Was Soviet spies, Max, *they* kill Vladimir! He know too much!'

'So do you,' said Stella, and there was a long and awkward silence. 'So do we all,' she added, with a glance at Smiley.

'That's all he said?' Smiley asked. 'Nothing else, about the value of what you had done, for instance? Just that Max would believe?'

Villem shook his head.

'About there being other proofs, for instance?'

Nothing, said Villem: no more.

'Nothing to explain how he had communicated with Hamburg in the first place, set up the arrangements? Whether others of the Group were involved? Please think.'

Villem thought, but without result.

'So who have you told this to, William, apart from me?' Smiley asked.

'Nobody! Max, nobody!'

'He hasn't had time,' said Stella.

'Nobody! On journey I sleep in cab, save ten pounds a night subsistence. We buy house with this money! In Hamburg I tell *nobody*! At depot, *nobody*!'

'Had Vladimir told anyone – anyone that you know of, that is?'

'From the Group nobody only Mikhel, which was necessary, but not all, even to Mikhel. I ask to him: "Vladimir, who knows I do this for you?" "Only Mikhel a very little," he say. "Mikhel lends me money, lends me photocopier, he is my friend. But even to friends we cannot trust. Enemies I do not fear, Villem. But friends I fear greatly."'

Smiley spoke to Stella: 'If the police *do* come here,' he

said. '*If* they do, they will only know that Vladimir drove down here yesterday. They'll have got on to the cabdriver, as I did.'

She was watching him with her large shrewd eyes.

'So?' she asked.

'So don't tell them the rest. They know all they need. Any more could be an embarrassment to them.'

'To them or to you?' Stella asked.

'Vladimir came here yesterday to see Beckie and bring her a present. That's the cover story, just as William first told it. He didn't know you'd taken her to see your mother. He found William here, they talked old times and strolled in the garden. He couldn't wait too long because of the taxi, so he left without seeing you or his god-daughter. That's all there was.'

'Were *you* here?' Stella was still watching him.

'If they ask about me, yes. I came here today and gave you the bad news. The police don't mind that Villem belonged to the Group. It's only the present that matters to them.'

Smiley returned his attention to Villem. 'Tell me, did you bring anything else for Vladimir?' he asked. 'Apart from what was in the envelope? A present perhaps? Something he liked and couldn't buy himself?'

Villem concentrated energetically upon the question before replying. 'Cigarettes!' he cried suddenly. 'On boat, I buy him French cigarettes as gift. Gauloises, Max. He like very much! "Gauloises Caporal, with filter, Villem." Sure!'

'And the fifty pounds he had borrowed from Mikhel?' Smiley asked.

'I give back. Sure.'

'All?' said Smiley.

'All. Cigarettes was gift. Max, I love this man.'

★

Stella saw him to the door and at the door he gently took her arm and led her a few steps into the garden out of earshot of her husband.

'You're out of date,' she told him. 'Whatever it is you're doing, sooner or later one side or the other will have to stop. You're like the Group.'

'Be quiet and listen,' said Smiley. 'Are you listening?'

'Yes.'

'William's to speak to no one about this. Whom does he like to talk to at the depot?'

'The whole world.'

'Well, do what you can. Did anybody else ring apart from Mikhel? A wrong-number call even? Ring – then ring off?'

She thought, then shook her head.

'Did anyone come to the door? Salesman, market researcher, religious evangelist. Canvasser. Anyone? You're sure?'

As she continued staring at him her eyes seemed to acquire real knowledge of him, and appreciation. Then again she shook her head, denying him the complicity he was asking for.

'Stay away, Max. All of you. Whatever happens, however bad it is. He's grown up. He doesn't need a vicar any more.'

She watched him leave, perhaps to make sure he really went. For a while as he drove, the notion of Vladimir's piece of negative film nestling in its box consumed him like hidden money – whether it was still safe, whether he should inspect it or convert it, since it had been brought through the lines at the cost of life. But by the time he approached the river he had other thoughts and purposes. Eschewing Chelsea, he joined the northbound Saturday traffic, which consisted mainly of young families with old cars. And one motor-bike with a black side-car, clinging faithfully to his tail all the way to Bloomsbury.

10

The Free Baltic Library was on the third floor over a dusty antiquarian bookshop that specialised in the Spirit. Its little windows squinted into a forecourt of the British Museum. Smiley reached the place by way of a winding wooden staircase, passing on his ponderous climb several aged hand-drawn signs pulling at their drawing-pins and a stack of brown toiletry boxes belonging to a chemist's shop next door. Gaining the top, he discovered himself thoroughly out of breath and wisely paused before pressing the bell. Waiting, he was assailed in his momentary exhaustion by a hallucination. He had the delusion that he kept visiting the same high place over and over again: the safe flat in Hampstead, Vladimir's garret in Westbourne Terrace, and now this haunted backwater from the fifties, once a rallying point of the so-called Bloomsbury Irregulars. He fancied they were all a single place, a single proving ground for virtues not yet stated. The illusion passed, and he gave three short rings, one long, wondering whether they had changed the signal, doubting it; still worrying about Villem or perhaps Stella, or perhaps just the child. He heard a close creak of floor-boards and guessed he was being examined through a spyhole by someone a foot away from him. The door swiftly opened, he stepped into a gloomy hall as two wiry arms hugged him in their grip. He smelt body-heat and sweat and cigarette smoke and an unshaven face pressed against his own – left cheek, right cheek, as if to bestow a medal – once more to the left for particular affection.

'Max,' Mikhel murmured in a voice that was itself a requiem. 'You came. I am glad. I had hoped but I did not dare expect. I was waiting for you nevertheless. I waited all day till now. He loved you, Max. You were the best. He said so always. You were his inspiration. He told me. His example.'

'I'm sorry, Mikhel,' Smiley said. 'I'm really sorry.'

'As we all are, Max. As we all are. Inconsolable. But we are soldiers.'

He was dapper, and hollow-backed, and trim as the ex-major of horse he professed to be. His brown eyes, reddened by the night watch, had a becoming droopiness. He wore a black blazer over his shoulders like a cloak and black boots much polished which could indeed have been for riding. His grey hair was groomed with military correctness, his moustache thick but carefully clipped. His face was at first glance youthful and only a close look at the crumbling of its pale surface into countless tiny deltas revealed his years. Smiley followed him to the library. It ran the width of the house and was divided by alcoves into vanished countries – Latvia, Lithuania, and not least Estonia – and in each alcove were a table and a flag and at several tables there were chess sets laid out for play, but nobody was playing, nobody was reading either; nobody was there, except for one blonde, broad woman in her forties wearing a short skirt and ankle socks. Her yellow hair, dark at the roots, was knotted in a severe bun, and she lounged beside a samovar reading a travel magazine showing birch forests in the autumn. Drawing level with her, Mikhel paused and seemed about to make an introduction, but at the sight of Smiley, her glance flared with an intense and unmistakable anger. She looked at him, her mouth curled in contempt, she looked away through the rain-smeared window. Her cheeks were shiny from weeping and there were olive bruises under her heavy-lidded eyes.

'Elvira loved him also very much,' Mikhel observed by way of explanation when they were out of her hearing. 'He was a brother to her. He instructed her.'

'Elvira?'

'My wife, Max. After many years we are married. I resisted. It is not always good for our work. But I owe her this security.'

They sat down. Around them and along the walls hung martyrs of forgotten movements. This one already in prison, photographed through wire. That one dead and – like Vladimir – they had pulled back the sheet to expose his bloodied face. A third, laughing, wore the baggy cap of a partisan and carried a long-barrelled rifle. From down the room they heard a small explosion followed by a rich Russian oath. Elvira, bride of Mikhel, was lighting the samovar.

'I'm sorry,' Smiley repeated.

Enemies I do not fear, Villem, thought Smiley. *But friends I fear greatly.*

They were in Mikhel's private alcove that he called his office. An old-fashioned telephone lay on the table beside a Remington upright typewriter like the one in Vladimir's flat. Somebody must once have bought lots of them, thought Smiley. But the focus was a high hand-carved chair with barley-twist legs and a monarchic crest embroidered on the back. Mikhel sat on it primly, knees and boots together, a proxy king too small for his throne. He had lit a cigarette, which he held vertically from below. Above him a pall of tobacco smoke hung exactly where

Smiley remembered it. In the waste-paper basket, Smiley noticed several discarded copies of *Sporting Life*.

'He was a leader, Max, he was a hero,' Mikhel declared. 'We
must try to profit from his courage and example.' He paused
as if expecting Smiley to write this down for publication. 'In
such cases it is natural to ask oneself how one can possibly
carry on. Who is worthy to follow him? Who has his stature,
his honour, his sense of destiny? Fortunately our movement is
a continuing process. It is greater than any one individual, even
than any one group.'

Listening to Mikhel's polished phrases, staring at his polished boots, Smiley found himself marvelling at the man's
age. The Russians occupied Estonia in 1940, he recalled. To
have been a cavalry officer, Mikhel would have to be sixty
if a day. He tried to assemble the rest of Mikhel's turbulent
biography – the long road through foreign wars and untrusted
ethnic brigades, all the chapters of history contained in this
one little body. He wondered how old the boots were.

'Tell me about his last days, Mikhel,' Smiley suggested.
'Was he active to the very end?'

'Completely active, Max, active in all respects. As a patriot.
As a man. As a leader.'

Her expression as contemptuous as before, Elvira put the
tea before them, two cups with lemon, and small marzipan
cakes. In motion, she was insinuating, with fluid haunches and
a sullen hint of challenge. Smiley tried to remember her background also, but it eluded him or perhaps he had never known
it. *He was a brother to her*, he thought. *He instructed her*. But
something from his own life had long ago warned him to mistrust explanations, particularly of love.

'And as a member of the Group?' Smiley asked when she
had left them. 'Also active?'

'Always,' said Mikhel gravely.

There was a small pause while each man politely waited for the other to continue.

'Who do you think did it, Mikhel? Was he betrayed?'

'Max, you know as well as I do who did it. We are all of us at risk. All of us. The call can come any time. Important is, we must be ready for it. Myself I am a soldier, I am prepared, I am ready. If I go, Elvira has her security. That is all. For the Bolshevites we exiles remain enemy number one. Anathema. Where they can, they destroy us. Still. As once they destroyed our churches and our villages and our schools and our culture. And they are right, Max. They are right to be afraid of us. Because one day we shall defeat them.'

'But why did they choose this particular moment?' Smiley objected gently after this somewhat ritualistic pronouncement. 'They could have killed Vladimir years ago.'

Mikhel had produced a flat tin box with two tiny rollers on it like a mangle, and a packet of coarse yellow cigarette papers. Having licked a paper, he laid it on the rollers and poured in black tobacco. A snap, the mangle turned, and there on the silvered surface lay one fat, loosely packed cigarette. He was about to help himself to it when Elvira came over and took it. He rolled another and returned the box to his pocket.

'Unless Vladi was *up* to something, I suppose,' Smiley continued after these staged manoeuvres. 'Unless he *provoked* them in some way – which he might have done, knowing him.'

'Who can tell?' Mikhel said and blew some more smoke carefully into the air above them.

'Well, *you* can Mikhel, if anyone can. Surely he confided in *you*. You were his right-hand man for twenty years or more. First Paris, then here. Don't tell me he didn't trust *you*,' said Smiley ingenuously.

'Our leader was a secretive man, Max. This was his strength.
He had to be. It was a military necessity.'

'But not towards *you*, surely?' Smiley insisted, in his most
flattering tone. 'His Paris adjutant. His aide-de-camp. His confidential secretary? Come, you do yourself an injustice!'

Leaning forward in his throne Mikhel placed a small hand
strictly across his heart. His brown voice took on an even deeper tone.

'Max. Even towards me. At the end, even towards Mikhel. It
was to shield me. To spare me dangerous knowledge. He said
to me, even: "Mikhel, it is better that you – even you – do not
know what the past has thrown up." I implored him. In vain.
He came to me one evening. Here. I was asleep upstairs. He
gave the special ring on the bell: "Mikhel, I need fifty pounds."'

Elvira returned, this time with an empty ashtray, and as she
put it on the table Smiley felt a surge of tension like the sudden working of a drug. He experienced it driving sometimes,
waiting for a crash that didn't happen. And he experienced it
with Ann, watching her return from some supposedly innocu-
ous engagement and knowing – simply knowing – it was not.

'When was this?' he asked when she had left again.

'Twelve days ago. One week last Monday. From his manner I am able to discern immediately that this is an official affair. He has never before asked me for money. "General," I say
to him. "You are making a conspiracy. Tell me what it is." But
he shakes his head. "Listen," I tell him, "if this is a conspiracy,
take my advice, go to Max." He refused. "Mikhel," he tells me.
"Max is a good man, but he does not have confidence any more
in our Group. He wishes, even, that we end our struggle. But
when I have landed the big fish I am hoping for, then I shall go
to Max and claim our expenses and perhaps many things besides. But this I do afterwards, not before. Meanwhile I cannot

conduct my business in a dirty shirt. Please, Mikhel. Lend me fifty pounds. In all my life this is my most important mission. It reaches far into our past." His words exactly. In my wallet I had fifty pounds – fortunately I had that day made a successful investment – I give them to him. "General," I said. "Take all I have. My possessions are yours. Please,"' said Mikhel and to punctuate this gesture – or to authenticate it – drew heavily at his yellow cigarette.

In the grimy window above them Smiley had glimpsed the reflection of Elvira standing half-way down the room, listening to their conversation. Mikhel had also seen her and had even shot her an evil frown, but he seemed unwilling, and perhaps unable, to order her away.

'That was very good of you,' Smiley said after a suitable pause.

'Max, it was my duty. From the heart. I know no other law.'

She despises me for not helping the old man, thought Smiley. She was in on it, she knew, and now she despises me for not helping him in his hour of need. *He was a brother to her*, he remembered. *He instructed her.*

'And this approach to you – this request for operational funds,' said Smiley. 'It came out of the blue? There'd been nothing before, to tell you he was up to something big?'

Again Mikhel frowned, taking his time, and it was clear that Mikhel did not care too much for questions.

'Some months ago, perhaps two, he received a letter,' he said cautiously. 'Here, to this address.'

'Did he receive so few?'

'This letter was special,' said Mikhel, with the same air of caution, and suddenly Smiley realised that Mikhel was in what the Sarratt inquisitors called the loser's corner, because he did not know – he could only guess – how much or how little

Smiley knew already. Therefore Mikhel would give up his information jealously, hoping to read the strength of Smiley's hand while he did so.

'Who was it from?'

Mikhel, as so often, answered a slightly different question.

'It was from Paris, Max, a long letter, many pages, handwritten. Addressed to the General personally, not Miller. To General Vladimir, most personal. On the envelope was written Most Personal, in French. The letter arrived, I lock it in my desk; at eleven o'clock he walks in as usual: "Mikhel, I salute you." Sometimes, believe me, we even saluted each other. I hand him the letter, he sat' – he pointed towards Elvira's end of the room – 'he sat down, opened it quite carelessly, as if he had no expectation from it, and I saw him gradually become preoccupied. Absorbed. I would say fascinated. Impassioned, even. I spoke to him. He didn't answer. I spoke again – you know his ways – he ignored me totally. He went for a walk. "I shall return," he said.'

'Taking the letter?'

'Of course. It was his fashion, when he had a great matter to consider, to go for a walk. When he returned, I noticed a deep excitement in him. A tension. "Mikhel." You know how he spoke. All must obey. "Mikhel. Get out the photocopier. Put some paper in it for me. I have a document to copy." I asked him how many copies. One. I ask him how many sheets. "Seven. Please stand at five paces' distance while I operate the machine," he tells me. "I cannot involve you in this matter."'

Once again, Mikhel indicated the spot as if it proved the absolute veracity of his story. The black copier stood on its own table, like an old steam-engine, with rollers, and holes for pouring in the different chemicals. 'The General was not mechanical, Max. I set up the machine for him – then I stood – here – so – calling out instructions to him across the room. When he had finished, he stood over the copies while they dried, then folded them into his pocket.'

'And the original?'

'This also he put in his pocket.'

'So you never read the letter?' Smiley said, in a tone of light commiseration.

'No, Max. I am sad to tell you I did not.'

'But you saw the envelope. You had it here to give to him when he arrived.'

'I told you, Max. It was from Paris.'

'Which district?'

The hesitation again: 'The fifteenth,' said Mikhel. 'I believe it was the fifteenth. Where many of our people used to be.'

'And the date? Can you be more precise about it? You said about two months.'

'Early September. I would say early September. Late August is possible. Say six weeks ago, around.'

'The address on the envelope was also handwritten?'

'It was, Max. It was.'

'What colour was the envelope?'

'Brown.'

'And the ink?'

'I suppose blue.'

'Was it sealed?'

'Please?'

'Was the envelope sealed with sealing-wax or adhesive tape? Or was it just gummed in the ordinary way?'

Mikhel shrugged, as if such details were beneath him.

'But the sender had put his name on the outside, presumably?' Smiley persisted lightly.

If he had, Mikhel was not admitting it.

For a moment Smiley allowed his mind to dwell upon the brown envelope cached in the Savoy cloakroom, and the passionate plea for help it contained. *This morning I had an impression that they were trying to kill me. Will you not send me your magic friend once more?* Postmark Paris, he thought. The 15th district. After the first letter, Vladimir gave the writer his home address, he thought. Just as he gave his home telephone number to Villem. After the first letter, Vladimir made sure he bypassed Mikhel.

A phone rang and Mikhel answered it at once, with a brief 'Yes?' then listened.

'Then put me five each way,' he muttered, and rang off with magisterial dignity.

Approaching the main purpose of his visit to Mikhel, Smiley took care to proceed with great respect. He remembered that Mikhel – who by the time he joined the Group in Paris had seen the inside of half the interrogation centres of Eastern Europe – had a way of slowing down when he was prodded, and by this means in his day had driven the Sarratt inquisitors half mad.

'May I ask you something, Mikhel?' Smiley said, selecting a line that was oblique to the main thrust of his enquiry.

'Please.'

'That evening when he called here to borrow money from you, did he stay? Did you make him tea? Play a game of chess perhaps? Could you paint it for me a little, please, that evening?'

'We played chess, but not with concentration. He was preoccupied, Max.'

'Did he say any more about the big fish?'

The drooped eyes considered Smiley soulfully.

'Please, Max?'

'The big fish. The operation he said he was planning. I wondered whether he enlarged upon it in any way.'

'Nothing. Nothing at all, Max. He was entirely secretive.'

'Did you have the impression it involved another country?'

'He spoke only of having no passport. He was wounded – Max, I tell you this frankly – he was hurt that the Circus would not trust him with a passport. After such service, such devotion – he was hurt.'

'It was for his own good, Mikhel.'

'Max, *I* understand entirely. I am a younger man, a man of the world, flexible. The General was at times impulsive, Max. Steps had to be taken – even by those who admired him – to contain his energies. Please. But for the man himself, it was incomprehensible. An insult.'

From behind him Smiley heard the thud of feet as Elvira stomped contemptuously back to her corner.

'So who did he think should do his travelling for him?' Smiley asked, again ignoring her.

'Villem,' said Mikhel with obvious disapproval. 'He does not tell me in as many words but I believe he sends Villem. That was my impression. Villem would go. General Vladimir spoke with such pride of Villem's youth and honour. Also of his father. He even made an historical reference. He spoke of bringing in the new generation to avenge the injustices of the old. He was very moved.'

'Where did he send him? Did Vladi give any hint of that?'

'He does not tell me. He tells me only, "Villem has a passport, he is a brave boy, a good Balt, steady, he can travel, but it is also necessary to protect him." I do not probe, Max. I do not pry. That is not my way. You know that.'

'Still you did form an impression, I suppose,' Smiley said.

'The way one does. There are not so many places Villem would be free to go to, after all. Least of all on fifty pounds.

There was Villem's job too, wasn't there? Not to mention his wife. He couldn't just step into the blue when he felt like it.'

Mikhel made a very military gesture. Pushing out his lips till his moustache was almost on its back, he tugged shrewdly at his nose with his thumb and forefinger. 'The General also asked me for maps,' he said firmly. 'I was in two minds whether to tell you this. You are his vicar, Max, but you are not of our cause. But as I trust you, I shall.'

'Maps of where?'

'Street maps.' He flicked a hand towards the shelves as if ordering them closer. 'City plans. Of Danzig. Hamburg, Lübeck. Helsinki. The northern seaboard. I asked him, "General, sir. Let me help you," I said to him. "Please. I am your assistant for everything. I have a right. Vladimir. Let me help you." He refused me. He wished to be entirely private.'

Moscow Rules, Smiley thought yet again. Many maps and only one of them is relevant. And once again, he noted, towards his trusted Paris adjutant Vladimir was taking measures to obscure his purpose.

'After which he left?' he suggested.

'Correct.'

'At what time?'

'It was late.'

'Can you say how late?'

'Two. Three. Even four maybe. I am not sure.'

Then Smiley felt Mikhel's gaze lift fractionally over his shoulder and beyond it and stay there and an instinct which he had lived by for as long as he could remember made him ask: 'Did Vladimir come here alone?'

'Of course, Max. Who would he bring?'

They were interrupted by a clank of crockery as Elvira at

the other end of the room went clumsily back to her chores. Daring to glance at Mikhel just then, Smiley saw him staring after her with an expression he recognised but for a split second could not place: hopeless and affectionate at once, torn between dependence and disgust. Till, with sickening empathy, Smiley found himself looking into his own face as he had glimpsed it too often, red-eyed like Mikhel's, in Ann's pretty gilt mirrors in their house in Bywater Street.

'So if he wouldn't let you help him, what did you do?' Smiley asked with the same studied casualness. 'Sit up and read – play chess with Elvira?'

Mikhel's brown eyes held him a moment, slipped away and came back to him.

'No, Max,' he replied with great courtesy. 'I gave him the maps. He desired to be left alone with them. I wished him goodnight. I was asleep by the time he left.'

But not Elvira, apparently, Smiley thought. Elvira stayed behind for instruction from her proxy brother. *Active as a patriot, as a man, as a leader*, Smiley rehearsed. *Active in all respects*.

'So what contact have you had with him since?' Smiley asked and Mikhel came suddenly to yesterday. Nothing till yesterday, Mikhel said.

'Yesterday afternoon he called me on the telephone. Max, I swear to you I had not heard him so excited for many years. Happy, I would say ecstatic. "Mikhel! Mikhel!" Max, that was a delighted man. He would come to me that night. Last night. Late maybe but he will have my fifty pounds. "General," I tell him. "What is fifty pounds? Are you well? Are you safe? Tell me." "Mikhel, I have been fishing and I am happy. Stay awake," he says to me. "I shall be with you at eleven o'clock, soon after. I shall have the money. Also it is necessary I beat you at chess to calm my nerves." I stay awake, make tea, wait for him. And wait. Max, I am a soldier, for myself I am not afraid. But for the General – for that old man, Max – I was afraid. I phone the Circus, an emergency. They hang up on me. Why? Max, why did you do that, please?'

'I was not on duty,' Smiley said, now watching Mikhel as intently as he dared. 'Tell me, Mikhel,' he began.

'Max.'

'What did you think Vladimir was going to be doing after he rang you with the good news – and before he came to repay you fifty pounds?'

Mikhel did not hesitate. 'Naturally I assumed he would be going to Max,' he said. 'He had landed his big fish. Now he would go to Max, claim his expenses, present him with his great news. Naturally,' he repeated, looking a little too straight into Smiley's eyes.

Naturally, thought Smiley; and you knew to the minute when he would leave his apartment, and to the metre the route he would take to reach the Hampstead flat.

'So he failed to appear, you rang the Circus and we were un-helpful,' Smiley resumed. 'I'm sorry. So what did you do next?'

'I phone Villem. First to make sure the boy is all right, also to ask him, where is our Leader? That English wife of his bawled me out. Finally I went to his flat. I did not like to – it was an intrusion – his private life is his own – but I went. I rang the bell. He did not answer. I came home. This morning at eleven o'clock Jüri rings. I had not read the early edition of the evening papers, I am not fond of English newspapers. Jüri had read them. Vladimir our leader was dead,' he ended.

Elvira was at his elbow. She had two glasses of vodka on a tray.

'Please,' said Mikhel. Smiley took a glass, Mikhel the other.

'To life!' said Mikhel, very loud, and drank, as the tears started to his eyes.

'To life,' Smiley repeated while Elvira watched them.

She went with him, Smiley thought. She forced Mikhel to the old man's flat, she dragged him to the door.

'Have you told anyone else of this, Mikhel?' Smiley asked when she had once more left.

'Jüri I don't trust,' said Mikhel, blowing his nose.

'Did you tell Jüri about Villem?'

'Please?'

'Did you mention Villem to him? Did you suggest to Jüri in any way that Villem might have been involved with Vladimir?'

Mikhel had committed no such sin, apparently.

'In this situation you should trust no one,' Smiley said, in a more formal tone, as he prepared to take his leave. 'Not even the police. Those are the orders. The police must not know that Vladimir was doing anything operational when he died. It is important for security. Yours as well as ours. He gave you no message otherwise? No word for Max, for instance?'

Tell Max that it concerns the Sandman, he thought.

Mikhel smiled his regrets.

'Did Vladimir mention Hector recently, Mikhel?'

'Hector was no good for him.'

'Did Vladimir say that?'

'Please, Max. I have nothing against Hector personally. Hector is Hector, he is not a gentleman, but in our work we must use many varieties of mankind. This was the General speaking. Our leader was an old man. "Hector," Vladimir says to me. "Hector is no good. Our good postman Hector is like the City banks. When it rains, they say, the banks take away your umbrella. Our postman Hector is the same." Please. This is Vladimir speaking. Not Mikhel. "Hector is no good."'

'When did he say this?'

'He said it several times.'

'Recently?'

'Yes.'

'How recently?'

'Maybe two months. Maybe less.'

'After he received the Paris letter, or before?'

'After. No question.'

Mikhel escorted him to the door, a gentleman even if Toby Esterhase was not. At her place again beside the samovar, Elvira sat smoking before the same photograph of birch trees. And as he passed her, Smiley heard a sort of hiss, made through the nose or mouth, or both at once, as a last statement of her contempt.

'What will you do now?' he asked of Mikhel in the way one asks such things of the bereaved. Out of the corner of his eye he saw her head lift at his question and her fingers spread across the page.

A last thought struck him: 'And you didn't recognise the handwriting?' Smiley started to ask.

'What handwriting is this, Max?'

'On the envelope from Paris?'

Suddenly he had no time to wait for an answer; suddenly he was sick of evasion.

'Goodbye, Mikhel.'

'Go well, Max.'

Elvira's head sank again to the birch trees. I'll never know, Smiley thought, as he made his way quickly down the wooden staircase. None of us will. Was he Mikhel the traitor who resented the old man sharing his woman, and thirsted for the crown that had been denied him for too long? Or was he Mikhel the selfless officer and gentleman, Mikhel the everloyal servant? Or was he perhaps, like many loyal servants, both?

He thought of Mikhel's cavalry pride, as terribly tender as any other hero's manhood. His pride in being the General's keeper, his pride in being his satrap. His sense of injury at being excluded. His pride again – how it split so many ways! But how far did it extend? To a pride in giving nobly to each master, for instance? *Gentlemen, I have served you both well,* says the perfect double agent in the twilight of his life. And says it with pride, too, thought Smiley, who had known a number of them.

He thought of the seven-page letter from Paris. He thought of second proofs. He wondered who the photocopy had gone to – maybe Esterhase? He wondered where the original was. So who went to Paris? he wondered. If Villem went to Hamburg, who was the little magician? He was bone tired. His tiredness hit him like a sudden virus. He felt it in the knees, the hips, his whole subsiding body. But he kept walking, for his mind refused to rest.

To walk was just possible for Ostrakova, and to walk was all she asked. To walk and wait for the magician. Nothing was broken. Though her dumpy little body, when they had given her a bath, was shaping up to become as blackened and patchy as a map of the Siberian coalfields, nothing was broken. And her poor rump, which had given her that bit of trouble at the warehouse, looked already as though the assembled secret armies of Soviet Russia had booted her from one end of Paris to the other: still, nothing was broken. They had X-rayed every part of her, they had prodded her like questionable meat for signs of internal bleeding. But in the end, they had gloomily declared her to be the victim of a miracle.

They had wanted to keep her, for all that. They had wanted to treat her for shock, sedate her – at least for one night! The police, who had found six witnesses with seven conflicting accounts of what had happened (The car was grey or was it blue? The registration number was from Marseilles or was it foreign?), the police had taken one long statement from her, and threatened to come back and take another.

Ostrakova had nevertheless discharged herself.

Then had she at least children to look after her? they had asked. Oh, but she had a mass of them! she said. Daughters who would pander to her smallest whim, sons to assist her up and down the stairs! Any number – as many as they wished! To please the sisters, she even made up lives for them, though her head was beating like a war-drum. She had sent out for clothes. Her own were in shreds and God Himself must have blushed to see the state she was in when they found her. She gave a false address to go with her false name; she wanted no follow-up, no visitors. And somehow, by sheer willpower, at the stroke of six that evening, Ostrakova became just another pale ex-patient, stepping cautiously and extremely painfully down the ramp of the great black hospital, to rejoin the very world which that same day had done its best to be rid of her for good. Wearing her boots, which like herself were battered but mysteriously unbroken; and she was quaintly proud of the way they had supported her.

She wore them still. Restored to the twilight of her own apartment, seated in Ostrakov's tattered armchair while she patiently wrestled with his old army revolver, trying to fathom how the devil it loaded, cocked, and fired itself, she wore them like a uniform. 'I am an army of one.' To stay alive: that was her one aim, and the longer she did it, the greater would be her victory. To stay alive until the General came, or sent her the magician.

To escape from them, like Ostrakov? Well, she had done that. To mock them, like Glikman, to force them into corners where they had no option but to contemplate their own obscenity? In her time, she liked to think, she had done a little of that as well. But to survive, as neither of her men had done; to cling to life, against all the efforts of that soulless, numberless universe of brutalised functionaries; to be a thorn to them every hour of the day, merely by staying alive, by breathing, eating, moving, and having her wits about her – that, Ostrakova had decided, was an occupation worthy of her mettle, and her faith, and of her two loves. She had set about it immediately, with appropriate devotion. Already she had sent the fool concierge to shop for her: disability had its uses.

'I have had a small attack, Madame la Pierre' – whether of the heart, the stomach or the Russian secret police she did not divulge to the old goat. 'I am advised to leave off work for several weeks and rest completely. I am exhausted, madame – there are times when one wishes only to be alone. And here, take this, madame – not like the others, so grasping and overvigilant.' Madame la Pierre took the note in her fist, and looked at just one corner of it before tucking it away at her waist somewhere. 'And listen, madame, if anyone asks for me, do me a favour and say I am away. I shall burn no lights on the street side. We women of sensitivity are entitled to a little peace, you agree? But, madame, please, remember who they are, these visitors, and tell me – the gasman, people from the charities – tell me everything. I like to hear that life is going on around me.'

The concierge concluded she was mad, no doubt, but there was no madness to her money, and money was what the concierge liked best, and besides, she was mad herself. In a few hours, Ostrakova had become more cunning even than in Moscow. The concierge's husband came up – a brigand himself, worse than the old goat – and, encouraged by further payments, fixed chains to her front door. Tomorrow, he would fit a peep-hole, also for money. The concierge promised to receive her mail for her, and deliver it only at certain agreed times – exactly eleven in the morning, six in the evening, two short rings – for money. By forcing open the tiny ventilator in the back lavatory, and standing on a chair, Ostrakova could look down into the courtyard whenever she wanted, at whoever came and went. She had sent a note to the warehouse saying she was indisposed. She could not move her double bed, but with pillows and her feather coverlet she made up the divan and positioned it so that it pointed like a torpedo through the open door of the drawing-room at the front door beyond it, and all she had to do was lie on it with her boots aimed at the intruder and shoot down the line of them, and if she didn't blow her own foot off, she would catch him in the first moment of surprise as he attempted to burst in on her: she had worked it out. Her head throbbed and caterwauled, her eyes had a way of darkening over when she moved her head too fast, she had a raging temperature and sometimes she half fainted. But she had worked it out, she had made her dispositions, and till the General or the magician came, it was Moscow all over again. 'You're on your own, you old fool,' she told herself aloud. 'You've nobody to rely on but yourself, so get on with it.'

With one photograph of Glikman and one of Ostrakov on the floor beside her, and an icon of the Virgin under the coverlet, Ostrakova embarked upon her first night's vigil, praying steadily to a host of saints, not least of them St Joseph, that they would send her her redeemer, the magician.

Not a single message tapped to me over the water-pipes, she thought. Not even a guard's insult to wake me up.

12

And still it was the same day; there was no end to it, no bed. For a while after leaving Mikhel, George Smiley let his legs lead him, not knowing where, too tired, too stirred to trust himself to drive, yet bright enough to watch his back, to make the vague yet sudden turnings which catch would-be followers off guard. Bedraggled, heavy-eyed, he waited for his mind to come down, trying to unwind, to step clear of the restless thrust of his twenty-hour marathon. The Embankment had him, so did a pub off Northumberland Avenue, probably The Sherlock Holmes, where he gave himself a large whisky and dithered over telephoning Stella – was she all right? Deciding there was no point – he could hardly phone her every night asking whether she and Villem were alive – he walked again until he found himself in Soho, which on Saturday nights was even nastier than usual. Beard Lacon, he thought. Demand protection for the family. But he had only to imagine the scene to know the idea was still-born. If Vladimir was not the Circus's responsibility, then still less could Villem be. And how, pray, do you attach a team of baby-sitters to a long distance Continental lorry driver? His one consolation was that Vladimir's assassins had apparently found what they were looking for: that they had no other needs. Yet what about the woman in Paris? What about the writer of the two letters?

Go home, he thought. Twice, from phone boxes, he made dummy calls, checking the pavement. Once he entered a cul-de-sac and doubled back, watching for the slurred step, the eye that ducked his glance. He considered taking a hotel room. Sometimes he did that, just for a night's peace. Sometimes his house was too much of a dangerous place for him. He thought of the piece of negative film: time to open the box. Finding himself gravitating by instinct towards Cambridge Circus, he cut hastily away eastward, finishing by his car again. Confident that he was not observed, he drove to Bayswater, well off his beaten track, but he still watched his mirror intently. From a Pakistani ironmonger who sold everything, he bought two plastic washing-up bowls and a rectangle of commercial glass three and a half inches by five; and from a cash-and-carry chemist not three doors down, ten sheets of Grade 2 resin-coated paper of the same size, and a children's pocket torch with a spaceman on the handle and a red filter that slid over the lens when you pushed a nickel button. From Bayswater, by a painstaking route, he drove to the Savoy, entering from the Embankment side. He was still alone. In the men's cloakroom, the same attendant was on duty, and he even remembered their joke.

'I'm still waiting for it to explode,' he said with a smile, handing back the box. 'I thought I heard it ticking once or twice, and all.'

At his front door the tiny wedges he had put up before his drive to Charlton were still in place. In his neighbours' windows he saw Saturday-evening candle-light and talking heads; but in his own, the curtains were still drawn as he had left them, and in the hall, Ann's pretty little grandmother clock received him in deep darkness, which he hastily corrected.

Dead weary, he nevertheless proceeded methodically.

First he tossed three fire-lighters into the drawing-room grate, lit them, shovelled smokeless coal over them and hung Ann's indoor clothes-line across the hearth. For an overall he donned an old kitchen apron, tying the cord firmly round his ample midriff for additional protection. From under the stairs he exhumed a pile of green black-out material and a pair of kitchen steps, which he took to the basement. Having blacked out the window, he went upstairs again, unwrapped the box, opened it, and no, it was not a bomb, it was a letter and a packet of battered cigarettes with Vladimir's piece of negative film fed into it. Taking it out, he returned to the basement, put on the red torch, and went to work, though Heaven knows he possessed no photographic flair whatever, and could perfectly well – in theory – have had the job done for him in a fraction of the time, through Lauder Strickland, by the Circus's own photographic section. Or for that matter he could have taken it to any one of half a dozen 'tradesmen', as they are known in the jargon: marked collaborators in certain fields who are pledged, if called upon at any time, to drop everything and, asking no questions, put their skills at the service's disposal. One such tradesman actually lived not a stone's throw from Sloane Square, a gentle soul who specialised in wedding photographs. Smiley had only to walk ten minutes and press the man's doorbell and he could have had his prints in half an hour. But he didn't. He preferred instead the inconvenience, as well as imperfection, of taking a contact print in the privacy of his home, while upstairs the telephone rang and he ignored it.

He preferred the trial and error of exposing the negative for too long, then for too little, under the main room light. Of using as a measure the cumbersome kitchen timer, which ticked and grumbled like something from *Coppélia*. He preferred grunting and cursing in irritation and sweating in the dark and wasting at least six sheets of resin-coated paper before the developer in the washing-up bowl yielded an image even half-way passable, which he laid in the rapid fixer for three minutes. And washed it. And dabbed it with a clean tea-cloth, probably ruining the cloth for good, he wouldn't know. And took it upstairs and pegged it to the clothes-line. And for those who like a heavy symbol, it is a matter of history that the fire, despite the fire-lighters, was all but out, since the coal consisted in great measure of damp slag, and that George Smiley had to puff at the flames to prevent it from dying, crouching on all fours for the task. Thus it might have occurred to him – though it didn't, for with his curiosity once more aroused he had put aside his introspective mood – that the action was exactly contrary to Lacon's jangling order to douse the flames and not to fan them.

Next, with the print safely suspended over the carpet, Smiley addressed himself to a pretty marquetry writing-desk in which Ann kept her 'things' with embarrassing openness. Such as a sheet of writing-paper on which she had written the one word 'Darling' and not continued, perhaps uncertain which darling to write to. Such as book-matches from restaurants he had never been to and letters in handwriting he did not know. From among such painful bric-à-brac he extracted a large Victorian magnifying glass with a mother-of-pearl handle, which she employed for reading clues to crosswords never completed. Thus armed – the sequence of these actions, because of his fatigue, lacked the final edge of logic – he put on a record of Mahler, which Ann had given him, and sat himself in the leather reading chair which was equipped with a mahogany book-rest designed to swivel like a bed tray across the occupant's stomach. Tired to death again, he unwisely allowed his eyes to close while he listened, part to the music, part to the occasional pat-pat of the dripping photograph, and part to the grudging crackle of the fire. Waking with a start thirty minutes later, he found the print dry, and the Mahler revolving mutely on its turntable.

He stared, one hand to his spectacles, the other slowly rotating the magnifying glass over the print.

The photograph showed a group, but it was not political, nor was it a bathing party, since nobody was wearing a swimming-suit. The group consisted of a quartet, two men and two women, and they were lounging on quilted sofas round a low table laden with bottles and cigarettes. The women were naked and young and pretty. The men, scarcely better covered, were sprawled side by side, and the girls had twined themselves dutifully around their elected mates. The lighting of the photograph was sallow and unearthly, and from the little Smiley knew of such matters he concluded that the negative was made on fast film, for the print was also grainy. Its texture, when he pondered it, reminded him of the photographs one saw too often of terrorists' hostages, except that the four in the photograph were concerned with each other, whereas hostages have a way of staring down the lens as if it were a gun barrel. Still in quest of what he would have called operational intelligence, he passed to the probable position of the camera and decided it must have been high above the subjects. The four appeared to be lying at the centre of a pit with the camera looking down on them. A shadow, very black – a balustrade, or perhaps it was a window-sill, or merely the shoulder of somebody in front – obtruded across the lower foreground. It was as if, despite the vantage point, only half the lens had dared to lift its head above the eye-line.

Here Smiley drew his first tentative conclusion. A step – not a large one; but he had enough large steps on his mind already. A technical step, call it: a modest, technical step. The photograph had every mark of being what the trade called *stolen*. And stolen moreover with a view to *burning*, meaning 'blackmail'. But the blackmail of whom? To what end?

Weighing the problem, Smiley probably fell asleep. The telephone was on Ann's little desk, and it must have rung three or four times before he was aware of it.

'Yes, Oliver?' said Smiley cautiously.

'Ah, George. I tried you earlier. You got back all right, I trust?'

'Where from?' asked Smiley.

Lacon preferred not to answer this question. 'I felt I owed you a call, George. We parted on a sour note. I was brusque. Too much on my plate. I apologise. How are things? You are done? Finished?'

In the background Smiley heard Lacon's daughters squabbling about how much rent was payable on a hotel in Park Lane. He's got them for the weekend, thought Smiley.

'I've had the Home Office on the line again, George,' Lacon went on in a lower voice, not bothering to wait for his reply. 'They've had the pathologist's report and the body may be released. An early cremation is recommended. I thought perhaps if I gave you the name of the firm that is handling things, you might care to pass it on to those concerned. Unattributably, of course. You saw the press release? What did you think of it? I thought it was apt. I thought it caught the tone exactly.'

'I'll get a pencil,' Smiley said and fumbled in the drawer once more until he found a pear-shaped plastic object with a leather thong which Ann sometimes wore around her neck. With difficulty he prised it open, and wrote to Lacon's dictation: the firm, the address, the firm again, followed yet again by the address.

'Got it? Want me to repeat it? Or should you read it back to me, make assurance double sure?'

'I think I have it, thank you,' Smiley said. Somewhat belatedly, it dawned on him that Lacon was drunk.

'Now, George, we have a date, don't forget. A seminar on marriage with no holds barred. I have cast you as my elder statesman here. There's a very decent steak-house downstairs and I shall treat you to a slap-up dinner while you give me of your wisdom. Have you a diary there? Let's pencil something in.'

With dismal foreboding Smiley agreed a date. After a lifetime of inventing cover stories for every occasion, he still found it impossible to talk his way out of a dinner invitation.

'And you found nothing?' Lacon asked, on a more curious note. 'No snags, hitches, loose ends. It was a storm in a teacup, was it, as we suspected?'

A lot of answers crossed Smiley's mind, but he saw no use to any of them.

'What about the phone bill?' Smiley asked.

'Phone bill? What phone bill? Ah, you mean *his*. Pay it and send me the receipt. No problem. Better still, slip it in the post to Strickland.'

'I already sent it to you,' said Smiley patiently. 'I asked you for a breakdown of traceable calls.'

'I'll get on to them at once,' Lacon replied blandly. 'Nothing else?'

'No. No, I don't think so. Nothing.'

'Get some sleep. You sound all in.'

'Good night,' said Smiley.

*

With Ann's magnifying glass in his plump fist once more, Smiley went back to his examination. The floor of the pit was carpeted, apparently in white; the quilted sofas were formed in a horseshoe following the line of the drapes that comprised the rear perimeter. There was an upholstered door in the background and the clothes the two men had discarded – jackets, neckties, trousers – were hanging from it with hospital neatness. There was an ashtray on the table and Smiley set to work trying to read the writing round the edge. After much manipulation of the glass he came up with what the lapsed philologist in him described as the asterisk (or putative) form of the letters 'A-C-H-T', but whether as a word in their own right – meaning 'eight' or 'attention' as well as certain other more remote concepts – or as four letters from a larger word, he could not tell. Nor did he at this stage exert himself to find out, preferring simply to store the intelligence in the back of his mind until some other part of the puzzle forced it into play.

Ann rang. Once again, perhaps, he had dozed off, for his recollection ever afterwards was that he did not hear the ring of the phone at all, but simply her voice as he slowly lifted the receiver to his ear: 'George, George,' as if she had been crying for him a long time, and he had only now summoned the energy or the caring to answer her.

They began their conversation as strangers, much as they began their love-making.

'How are you?' she asked.

'Very well, thank you. How are you? What can I do for you?'

'I meant it,' Ann insisted. 'How are you? I want to know.'

'And I told you I was well.'

'I rang you this morning. Why didn't you answer?'

'I was out.'

Long silence while she appeared to consider this feeble excuse. The telephone had never been a bother to her. It gave her no sense of urgency.

'Out working?' she asked.

'An administrative thing for Lacon.'

'He begins his administration early these days.'

'His wife's left him,' Smiley said by way of explanation.

No answer.

'You used to say she would be wise to,' he went on. 'She should get out fast, you used to say, before she became another Civil Service geisha.'

'I've changed my mind. He needs her.'

'But she, I gather, does not need him,' Smiley pointed out, taking refuge in an academic tone.

'Silly woman,' said Ann, and another longer silence followed, this time of Smiley's making while he contemplated the sudden unwished-for mountain of choice she had revealed to him.

To be together again, as she sometimes called it.

To forget the hurts, the list of lovers; to forget Bill Haydon, the Circus traitor, whose shadow still fell across her face each time he reached for her, whose memory he carried in him like a constant pain. Bill his friend, Bill the flower of their generation, the jester, the enchanter, the iconoclastic conformer; Bill the born deceiver, whose quest for the ultimate betrayal led him into the Russians' bed, and Ann's. To stage yet another honeymoon, fly away to the South of France, eat the meals, buy the clothes, all the let's-pretend that lovers play. And for how long? How long before her smile faded and her eyes grew dull and those mythical relations started needing her to cure their mythical ailments in far-off places?

'Where are you?' he asked.

161

'Hilda's.'

'I thought you were in Cornwall.'

Hilda was a divorced woman of some speed. She lived in Kensington, not twenty minutes' walk away.

'So where's Hilda?' he asked when he had come to terms with this intelligence.

'Out.'

'All night?'

'I expect so, knowing Hilda. Unless she brings him back.'

'Well, then I suppose you must entertain yourself as well as you can without her,' he said, but as he spoke he heard her whisper, 'George.'

A profound and vehement fear seized hold of Smiley's heart. He glared across the room at the reading chair and saw the contact photograph still on the book-rest beside her magnifying glass; in a single surge of memory, he reconstructed all the things that had hinted and whispered to him throughout the endless day; he heard the drum-beats of his own past, summoning him to one last effort to externalise and resolve the conflict he had lived by; and he wanted her nowhere near him. *Tell Max that it concerns the Sandman.* Gifted with the clarity that hunger, tiredness and confusion can supply, Smiley knew for certain she must have no part in what he had to do. He knew – he was barely at the threshold – yet he still knew that it was just possible, against all the odds, that he had been given, in late age, a chance to return to the rained-off contests of his life and play them after all. If that was so, then no Ann, no false peace, no tainted witness to his actions, should disturb his lonely quest. He had not known his mind till then. But now he knew it.

'You mustn't,' he said. 'Ann? Listen. You mustn't come here. It has nothing to do with choice. It's to do with practicalities. You mustn't come here.' His own words rang strangely to him.

'Then come here,' she said.

He rang off. He imagined her crying, then getting out her address book to see who from her First Eleven, as she called them, might console her in his place. He poured himself a neat whisky, the Lacon solution. He went to the kitchen, forgot why and wandered into his study. Soda, he thought. Too late. Do without. I must have been mad, he thought. I'm chasing phantoms, there is nothing there. A senile General had a dream and died for it. He remembered Wilde: the fact that a man dies for a cause does not make that cause right. A picture was crooked. He straightened it, too much, too little, stepping back each time. *Tell him it concerns the Sandman.* He returned to the reading chair and his two prostitutes, fixing on them through Ann's magnifying glass with a ferocity which would have sent them scurrying to their pimps.

Clearly they were from the upper end of their profession, being fresh-bodied and young and well-groomed. They seemed also – but perhaps it was coincidence – to be deliberately distinguished from one another by whoever had selected them. The girl at the left was blonde and fine and even classical in build, with long thighs and small high breasts, while her companion was dark-haired and stubby, with spreading hips and flared features, perhaps Eurasian. The blonde, he recorded, wore earrings in the shape of anchors, which struck him as odd because, in his limited experience of women, earrings were what they took off first. Ann had only to go out of the house without wearing them for his heart to sink. Beyond that he could think of nothing very clever to say about either girl and so, having swallowed another large gulp of raw Scotch, he transferred his attention to the men, once more – which was where it had been, if he would admit it, ever since he had started looking at the photograph in the first place. Like the girls, they were sharply differentiated from each other, though in the men – since they were a deal older – the differences had the appearance of greater depth and legibility of character. The man supporting the blonde girl was fair and at first sight dull, while the man supporting the dark girl was not merely dark-complexioned but had a Latin, even Levantine, alertness in his features, and an infectious smile that was the one engaging feature of the photograph. The fair man was large and sprawling, the dark man was small and bright enough to be his jester: a little imp of a fellow, with a kind face and flicked-up horns above his ears.

A sudden nervousness – in retrospect perhaps foreboding – made Smiley take the fair man first. It was a time to feel safer with strangers.

The man's torso was burly but not athletic, his limbs ponderous without suggesting strength. The fairness of his skin and hair emphasised his obesity. His hands, one splayed on the girl's flank, the other round her waist, were fatty and artless. Lifting the magnifying glass slowly over the naked chest, Smiley reached the head. By the age of forty, someone clever had written ominously, a man gets the face he deserves. Smiley doubted it. He had known poetic souls condemned to life imprisonment behind harsh faces, and delinquents with the appearance of angels. Nevertheless, it was not an asset as a face, nor had the camera caught it at its most appealing. In terms of character, it appeared to be divided into two parts: the lower, which was pulled into a grin of crude high spirits as, openmouthed, he addressed something to his male companion; the upper, which was ruled by two small and pallid eyes round which no mirth had gathered at all and no high spirits either, but which seemed to look out of their doughy surroundings with the cold, unblinking blandness of a child. The nose was flat, the hair-style full and mid-European.

Greedy, Ann would have said, who was given to passing absolute judgement on people merely by studying their portraits in the press. Greedy, weak, vicious. Avoid. A pity she had not reached the same conclusion about Haydon, he thought; or not in time.

Smiley returned to the kitchen and rinsed his face, then remembered that he had come to fetch water for his whisky. Settling again in the reading chair, he trained the magnifying glass on the second of the men, the jester. The whisky was keeping him awake, but it was also putting him to sleep. Why doesn't she ring again? he thought. If she rings again, I'll go to her. But in reality his mind was on this second face, because its familiarity disturbed him in much the same way that its urgent complicity had disturbed Villem and Ostrakova before him. He gazed at it and his tiredness left him, he seemed to draw energy from it. Some faces, as Villem had suggested this morning, are known to us before we see them; others we see once and remember all our lives; others we see every day, and never remember at all. But which was this?

A Toulouse-Lautrec face, Smiley thought, peering in wonder – caught as the eyes slid away to some intense and perhaps erotic distraction. Ann would have taken to him immediately; he had the dangerous edge she liked. A Toulouse-Lautrec face, caught as a stray shard of fair-ground light fired one gaunt and ravelled cheek. A hewn face, peaked and jagged, of which the brow and nose and jaw seemed all to have succumbed to the same eroding gales. A Toulouse-Lautrec face, swift and attaching. A waiter's face, never a diner's. With a waiter's anger burning brightest behind a subservient smile. Ann would like that side less well. Leaving the print where it lay, Smiley clambered slowly to his feet in order to keep himself awake, and lumbered round the room, trying to place it, failing, wondering whether it was all imagining. Some people *transmit*, he thought. Some people – you meet them, and they bring you their whole past as a natural gift. Some people are intimacy itself.

At Ann's writing-table he paused to stare at the telephone again. Hers. Hers and Haydon's. Hers and everybody's. Trimline, he thought. Or was it Slimline? Five pounds extra to the Post Office for the questionable pleasure of its outmoded futuristic lines. *My tart's phone*, she used to call it. *The little warble for my little loves, the loud woo-hoo for my big ones*. He realised it was ringing. Had been ringing a long while, the little warble for the little loves. He put down his glass, still staring at the telephone while it trilled. She used to leave it on the floor among her records when she was playing music, he remembered. She used to lie with it – there, by the fire, over there – one haunch carelessly lifted in case it needed her. When she went to bed, she unplugged it and took it with her, to comfort her in the night. When they made love, he knew he was the surrogate for all the men who hadn't rung. For the First Eleven. For Bill Haydon, even though he was dead.

It had stopped ringing.

What does she do now? Try the Second Eleven? *To be beautiful and Ann is one thing*, she had said to him not long ago; *to be beautiful and Ann's age will soon be another*. And to be ugly and mine is another again, he thought furiously. Taking up the contact print, he resumed, with fresh intensity, his contemplations.

Shadows, he thought. Smudges of light and dark, ahead of us, behind us, as we lurch along our ways. Imp's horns, devil's horns, our shadows so much larger than ourselves. Who is he? Who was he? I met him. I refused to. And if I refused to, how do I know him? He was a supplicant of some kind, a man with something to sell – Intelligence, then? Dreams? Wakefully now, he stretched out on the sofa – anything rather than go upstairs to bed – and, with the print before him, began plodding through the long galleries of his professional memory, holding the lamp to the half-forgotten portraits of charlatans, gold-makers, fabricators, pedlars, middlemen, hoods, rogues and occasionally heroes who made up the supporting cast of his multitudinous acquaintance; looking for the one hallowed face that, like a secret sharer, seemed to have swum out of the little contact photograph to board his faltering consciousness. The lamp's beam flitted, hesitated, returned. I was deceived by the darkness, he thought. I met him in the light. He saw a ghastly, neon-lit hotel bedroom – Muzak and tartan wallpaper, and the little stranger perched smiling in a corner, calling him Max. A little ambassador – but representing what cause, what country? He recalled an overcoat with velvet tabs and hard little hands, jerking out their own dance. He recalled the passionate, laughing eyes, the crisp mouth opening and closing swiftly, but he heard no words. He felt a sense of loss – of missing the target – of some other, looming shadow being present while they spoke.

Maybe, he thought. Everything is maybe. Maybe Vladimir was shot by a jealous husband after all, he thought, as the front doorbell screamed at him like a vulture, two rings.

She's forgotten her key as usual, he thought. He was in the hall before he knew it, fumbling with the lock. Her key would do no good, he realised; like Ostrakova, he had chained the door. He fished at the chain, calling 'Ann. Hang on!' and feeling nothing in his fingers. He slammed a bolt along its runner and heard the whole house tingle to the echo. 'Just coming!' he shouted. 'Wait! Don't go!'

He heaved the door wide open, swaying on the threshold,

offering his plump face as a sacrifice to the midnight air, to the shimmering black leather figure, crash helmet under his arm, standing before him like death's sentinel.

'I didn't mean to *alarm* you, sir, I'm sure,' the stranger said.

Clutching the doorway, Smiley could only stare at his intruder. He was tall and close cropped, and his eyes reflected unrequited loyalty.

'Ferguson, sir. You remember me, sir, Ferguson? I used to manage the transport pool for Mr Esterhase's lamplighters.'

His black motor-cycle with its side-car was parked on the kerb behind him, its lovingly polished surfaces glinting under the street lamp.

'I thought lamplighter section had been disbanded,' Smiley said, still staring at him.

'So they have, sir. Scattered to the four winds, I regret to say. The camaraderies, the spirit, gone for ever.'

'So who employs you?'

'Well, no one, sir. Not officially, as you might say. But still on the side of the angels, all the same.'

'I didn't know we had any angels.'

'No, well, that's true, sir. All men are fallible, I do say. Specially these days.' He was holding a brown envelope for Smiley to take. 'From certain friends of yours, sir, put it that way. I understand it relates to a telephone account you were enquiring about. We get a good response from the Post Office generally, I will say. Good night, sir. Sorry to bother you. Time you had some shut-eye, isn't it? Good men are scarce, I always say.'

'Good night,' said Smiley.

But still his visitor lingered, like someone asking for a tip. 'You did remember me really, didn't you, sir? It was just a lapse, wasn't it?'

'Of course.'

There were stars, he noticed as he closed the door. Clear stars swollen by the dew. Shivering, he took out one of Ann's many photograph albums and opened it at the centre. It was her habit, when she liked a snap, to wedge the negative behind it. Selecting a picture of the two of them in Cap Ferrat – Ann in a bathing-dress, Smiley prudently covered – he removed the negative and put Vladimir's behind it. He tidied up his chemicals and equipment and slipped the print into the tenth volume of his 1961 Oxford English Dictionary, under Y for Yesterday. He opened Ferguson's envelope, glanced wearily at the contents, registered a couple of entries and the word 'Hamburg', and tossed the whole lot into a drawer of the desk. Tomorrow, he thought; tomorrow is another riddle. He climbed into bed, never sure, as usual, which side to sleep on. He closed his eyes and at once the questions bombarded him, as he knew they would, in crazy uncoordinated salvoes.

Why didn't Vladimir ask for Hector? he wondered for the hundredth time. Why did the old man liken Esterhase, alias Hector, to the City banks who took your umbrella away when it rained?

Tell Max it concerns the Sandman.

To ring her? To throw on his clothes and hurry round there, to be received as her secret lover, creeping away with the dawn?

Too late. She was already suited.

Suddenly, he wanted her dreadfully. He could not bear the spaces round him that did not contain her, he longed for her laughing trembling body as she cried to him, calling him her only true, her best lover, she wanted none other, ever. 'Women are lawless, George,' she had told him once, when they lay in rare peace. 'So what am I?' he had asked, and she said, 'My law.' 'So what was Haydon?' he had asked. And she laughed and said, 'My anarchy.'

He saw the little photograph again, printed, like the little stranger himself, in his sinking memory. A small man, with a big shadow. He remembered Villem's description of the little figure on the Hamburg ferry, the horns of flicked-up hair, the grooved face, the warning eyes. *General*, he thought chaotically, *will you not send me your magic friend once more?*

Maybe. Everything is maybe.

Hamburg, he thought, and got quickly out of bed and put on his dressing gown. Back at Ann's desk, he set to work seriously to study the breakdown of Vladimir's telephone account, rendered in the copperplate script of a post-office clerk. Taking a sheet of paper, he began jotting down dates and notes.

Fact: in early September, Vladimir receives the Paris letter, and removes it from Mikhel's grasp.

Fact: at about the same date, Vladimir makes a rare and costly trunk-call to Hamburg, operator-dialled, presumably so that he can later claim the cost.

Fact: three days after that again, the eighth, Vladimir accepts a reverse-charge call from Hamburg, at a cost of two pounds eighty, origin, duration and time all given, and the origin is the same number that Vladimir had called three days before.

Hamburg, Smiley thought again, his mind flitting once more to the imp in the photograph. The reversed telephone traffic had continued intermittently till three days ago; nine calls, totalling twenty-one pounds, and all of them from Hamburg to Vladimir. But who was calling him? From Hamburg? Who?

Then suddenly he remembered.

The looming figure in the hotel room, the imp's vast shadow, was Vladimir himself. He saw them standing side by side, both in black coats, the giant and the midget. The vile hotel with Muzak and tartan wallpaper was near Heathrow airport, where the two men, so ill-matched, had flown in for a conference at the very moment of Smiley's life when his professional identity was crashing round his ears. *Max, we need you. Max, give us the chance.*

Picking up the telephone, Smiley dialled the number in Hamburg, and heard a man's voice the other end: the one word 'Yes', spoken softly in German, followed by a silence.

'I should like to speak to Herr Dieter Fassbender,' Smiley said, selecting a name at random. German was Smiley's second language, and sometimes his first.

'We have no Fassbender,' said the same voice coolly after a moment's pause, as if the speaker had consulted something in the meantime. Smiley could hear faint music in the background.

'This is Leber,' Smiley persisted. 'I want to speak to Herr Fassbender urgently. I'm his partner.'

There was yet another delay.

'Not possible,' said the man's voice flatly after another pause – and rang off.

Not a private house, thought Smiley, hastily jotting down his impressions – the speaker had too many choices. Not an office, for what kind of office plays soft background music and is open at midnight on a Saturday? A hotel? Possibly, but a hotel, if it was of any size, would have put him through to reception, and displayed a modicum of civility. A restaurant? Too furtive, too guarded – and surely they would have announced themselves as they picked up the phone?

Don't force the pieces, he warned himself. Store them away. Patience. But how to be patient when he had so little time?

Returning to bed, he opened a copy of Cobbett's *Rural Rides* and tried to read it while he loosely pondered, among other weighty matters, his sense of *civitas* and how much, or how little, he owed to Oliver Lacon: 'Your *duty*, George.' Yet who could seriously be Lacon's man? he asked himself. Who could regard Lacon's fragile arguments as Caesar's due?

'Émigrés in, émigrés out. Two legs good, two legs bad,' he muttered aloud.

All his professional life, it seemed to Smiley, he had listened to similar verbal antics signalling supposedly great changes in Whitehall doctrine; signalling restraint, self-denial, always another reason for doing nothing. He had watched Whitehall's skirts go up, and come down again, her belts being tightened, loosened, tightened. He had been the witness, or victim – or even reluctant prophet – of such spurious cults as lateralism, parallelism, separatism, operational devolution, and now, if he remembered Lacon's most recent meanderings correctly, of integration. Each new fashion had been hailed as a panacea: 'Now we shall vanquish, now the machine will work!' Each had gone out with a whimper, leaving behind it the familiar English muddle, of which, more and more, in retrospect, he saw himself as a lifelong moderator. He had forborne, hoping others would forbear, and they had not. He had toiled in back rooms while shallower men held the stage. They held it still. Even five years ago he would never have admitted to such sentiments. But today, peering calmly into his own heart, Smiley knew that he was unled, and perhaps unleadable; that the only restraints upon him were those of his own reason, and his own humanity. As with his marriage, so with his sense of public service. I invested my life in institutions – he thought without rancour – and all I am left with is myself.

And with Karla, he thought; with my black Grail.

He could not help himself: his restless mind would not leave

him alone. Staring ahead of him into the gloom, he imagined
he saw Karla standing before him, breaking and reforming in
the shifting specks of dark. He saw the brown, attendant eyes
appraising him, as once they had appraised him from the darkness of the interrogation cell in Delhi jail a hundred years before: eyes that at first glance were sensitive and seemed to signal
companionship; then like molten glass slowly hardened till they
were brittle and unyielding. He saw himself stepping onto the
dust-driven runway of Delhi airport, and wincing as the Indian
heat leapt up at him from the tarmac: Smiley alias Barraclough,
or Standfast, or whatever name he had fished from the bag that
week – he forgot. A Smiley of the Sixties, anyway, Smiley the
commercial traveller, they called him, charged by the Circus
to quarter the globe, offering resettlement terms to Moscow
Centre officers who were thinking of jumping ship. Centre was
holding one of its periodical purges at the time, and the woods
were thick with Russian field officers scared of going home. A
Smiley who was Ann's husband and Bill Haydon's colleague,
whose last illusions were still intact. A Smiley close to inner crisis all the same, for it was the year Ann lost her heart to a ballet
dancer: Haydon's turn was yet to come.

Still in the darkness of Ann's bedroom, he relived the rattling, honking jeep-ride to the jail, the laughing children hanging to the tailboard; he saw the ox-carts and the eternal Indian
crowds, the shanties on the brown river bank. He caught the
smells of dung and ever-smouldering fires – fires to cook and
fires to cleanse; fires to remove the dead. He saw the iron gateway of the old prison engulf him, and the perfectly pressed
British uniforms of the warders as they waded knee-deep
through the prisoners:

'This way, your honour, sir! Please be good enough to follow us, your excellency!'

One European prisoner, calling himself Gerstmann.

One grey-haired little man with brown eyes and a red calico tunic, resembling the sole survivor of an extinguished priesthood.

With his wrists manacled: 'Please undo them, officer, and bring him some cigarettes,' Smiley had said.

One prisoner, identified by London as a Moscow Centre agent, and now awaiting deportation to Russia. One little Cold War infantryman, as he appeared, who knew – knew for certain – that to be repatriated to Moscow was to face the camps or the firing squad or both; that to have been in enemy hands was in Centre's eyes to have become the enemy himself: to have talked or kept his secrets was immaterial.

Join us, Smiley had said to him across the iron table.

Join us and we will give you life.

Go home and they will give you death.

His hands were sweating – Smiley's, in the prison. The heat was dreadful. Have a cigarette, Smiley had said – here, use my lighter. It was a gold one, smeared by his own damp hands. Engraved. A gift from Ann to compensate some misdemeanour. *To George from Ann with all my love.* There are little loves and big loves, Ann liked to say, but when she had composed the inscription she awarded him both kinds. It was probably the only occasion when she did.

Join us, Smiley had said. Save yourself. You have no right to deny yourself survival. First mechanically, then with passion, Smiley had repeated the familiar arguments while his own sweat fell like raindrops onto the table. Join us. You have nothing to lose. Those in Russia who love you are already lost. Your return will make things worse for them, not better. Join us. I beg. Listen to me, listen to the arguments, the philosophy.

And waited, on and on, vainly, for the slightest response to his increasingly desperate entreaty. For the brown eyes to flicker, for the rigid lips to utter a single word through the billows of cigarette smoke – yes, I will join you. Yes, I will agree to be debriefed. Yes, I will accept your money, your promises of re-settlement, and the leftover life of a defector. He waited for the freed hands to cease their restless fondling of Ann's lighter, to George from Ann with all my love.

Yet the more Smiley implored him, the more dogmatic Gerstmann's silence became. Smiley pressed answers on him, but Gerstmann had no questions to support them. Gradually Gerstmann's completeness was awesome. He was a man who had prepared himself for the gallows; who would rather die at the hands of his friends than live at the hands of his enemies. Next morning, they parted, each to his appointed fate: Gerstmann, against all odds, flew back to Moscow to survive the purge and prosper. Smiley, with a high fever, returned to his Ann and not quite all her love; and to the later knowledge that Gerstmann was none other than Karla himself, Bill Haydon's recruiter, case officer, mentor; and the man who had spirited Bill into Ann's bed – this very bed where he now lay – in order to cloud Smiley's hardening vision of Bill's greater treason, against the service and its agents.

Karla, he thought, as his eyes bored into the darkness, what do you want with me now? *Tell Max it concerns the Sandman.*

Sandman, he thought: why do you wake me up when you are supposed to put me back to sleep?

Still incarcerated in her little Paris apartment, tormented equally in spirit and body, Ostrakova could not have slept even if she had wanted. Not all the Sandman's magic would have helped her. She turned on her side and her squeezed ribs screamed as if the assassin's arms were still flung round them while he prepared to sling her under the car. She tried her back and the pain in her rump was enough to make her vomit. And when she lay on her belly, her breasts became as sore as when she had tried to feed Alexandra in the months before she abandoned her, and she hated them.

It is God's punishment, she told herself, without too much conviction. Not till morning came, and she was back in Ostrakov's armchair, with his pistol across her knees, did the waking world, for an hour or two, release her from her thoughts.

13

The gallery was situated in what the art trade calls the naughty end of Bond Street, and Smiley arrived on its doorstep that Monday morning long before any respectable art dealer was out of bed.

His Sunday had passed in mysterious tranquillity. Bywater Street had woken late, and so had Smiley. His memory had served him while he slept, and it continued to serve him in modest spasms of enlightenment throughout the day. In terms of memory at least, his black Grail had drawn a little nearer. His telephone had not rung once, a slight but persistent hangover had kept him in the contemplative mood. There was a club he belonged to, against his better judgement, near Pall Mall, and he lunched there in imperial solitude on warmed-up steak-and-kidney pie. Afterwards, from the head porter, he had requested his box from the club safe and discreetly abstracted a few illicit possessions, including a British passport in his former workname of Standfast, which he had never quite managed to return to Circus Housekeepers; an international driving licence to match; a sizeable sum of Swiss francs, his own certainly, but equally certainly retained in defiance of the Exchange Control Act. He had them in his pocket now.

The gallery had a dazzling whiteness and the canvases in its armoured glass window were much the same: white upon white, with just the faintest outline of a mosque or St Paul's Cathedral – or was it Washington? – drawn with a finger in the thick pigment. Six months ago the sign hanging over the pavement had proclaimed The Wandering Snail Coffee Shop. Today it read 'ATELIER BENATI, GOÛT ARABE, PARIS, NEW YORK, MONACO,' and a discreet menu on the door proclaimed the new chef's specialities: '*Islam classique-moderne. Conceptual Interior Design. Contracts catered. Sonnez.*'

Smiley did as he was bidden, a buzzer screamed, the glass door yielded. A shop-worn girl, ash blonde and half-awake, eyed him warily over a white desk.

'If I could just look round,' said Smiley.

Her eyes lifted slightly towards an Islamic heaven. 'The little red spots mean sold,' she drawled, and, having handed him a typed price-list, sighed and went back to her cigarette and her horoscope.

For a few moments Smiley shuffled unhappily from one canvas to another till he stood in front of the girl again.

'If I could possibly have a word with Mr Benati,' he said.

'Oh, I'm afraid Signor Benati is *fully* involved right now. That's the trouble with being international.'

'If you could tell him it's Mr Angel,' Smiley proposed in the same diffident style. 'If you could just tell him that. Angel, Alan Angel, he does know me.'

He sat himself on the S-shaped sofa. It was priced at two thousand pounds and covered in protective cellophane which squeaked when he moved. He heard her lift the phone and sigh into it.

'Got an angel for you,' she drawled, in her pillow-talk voice. 'As in Paradise, got it, angel?'

A moment later he was descending a spiral staircase into darkness. He reached the bottom and waited. There was a click and half a dozen picture lights sprang on to empty spaces where no pictures hung. A door opened revealing a small and dapper figure, quite motionless. His full white hair was swept back with bravado. He wore a black suit with a broad stripe and shoes with pantomime buckles. The stripe was definitely too big for him. His right fist was in his jacket pocket, but when he saw Smiley he drew it slowly out, and held it at him like a dangerous blade.

'Why, Mr Angel,' he declared in a distinctly mid-European accent, with a sharp glance up the staircase as if to see who was listening. 'What pure pleasure, sir. It has been far too long. Come in, please.'

They shook hands, each keeping his distance.

'Hullo, Mr Benati,' Smiley said, and followed him to an inner room and through it to a second, where Mr Benati closed the door and gently leaned his back against it, perhaps as a bulwark against intrusion. For a while after that, neither man spoke at all, each preferring to study the other in a silence bred of mutual respect. Mr Benati's eyes were brown and swift and they looked nowhere long and nowhere without a purpose. The room had the atmosphere of a sleazy boudoir, with a chaise longue and a pink handbasin in one corner.

'So how's trade, Toby?' Smiley asked.

Toby Esterhase had a special smile for that question and a special way of tilting his little palm.

'We have been lucky, George. We had a good opening, we had a fantastic summer. Autumn, George' – the gesture again – 'autumn I would say is on the slow side. One must live off one's hump actually. Some coffee, George? My girl can make some.'

'Vladimir's dead,' said Smiley after another longish gap. 'Shot dead on Hampstead Heath.'

'Too bad. That old man, huh? Too bad.'

'Oliver Lacon has asked me to sweep up the bits. As you were the Group's postman, I thought I'd have a word with you.'

'Sure,' said Toby agreeably.

'You knew, then? About his death?'

'Read it in the papers.'

Smiley let his eye wander round the room. There were no newspapers anywhere.

'Any theories about who did it?' Smiley asked.

'At *his* age, George? After a lifetime of disappointments, you might say? No family, no prospects, the Group all washed up – I assumed he had done it himself. Naturally.'

Cautiously Smiley sat himself on the chaise longue and, watched by Toby, picked up a bronze maquette of a dancer that stood on the table.

'Shouldn't this be *numbered* if it's a Degas, Toby?' Smiley asked.

'Degas, that's a very grey area, George. You've got to know exactly what you are dealing with.'

'But this one is genuine?' Smiley asked, with an air of really wishing to know.

'Totally.'

'Would you sell it to me?'

'What's that?'

'Just out of academic interest. Is it for sale? If I offered to buy it, would I be out of court?'

Toby shrugged, slightly embarrassed.

'George, listen, we're talking thousands, know what I mean? Like a year's pension or something.'

'When was the last time you had anything to do with Vladi's network, actually, Toby?' Smiley asked, returning the dancer to its table.

Toby digested this question at his leisure.

'Network?' he echoed incredulously at last. 'Did I hear network, George?' Laughter in the normal run played little part in Toby's repertoire but now he did manage a small if tense outburst. 'You call that crazy Group a network? Twenty cuckoo Balts, leaky like a barn, and they make a *network* already?'

'Well we have to call them something,' Smiley objected equably.

'Something, sure. Just not network, okay?'

'So what's the answer?'

'What answer?'

'When did you last have dealings with the Group?'

'Years ago. Before they sacked me. Years ago.'

'How many years?'

'I don't know.'

'Three?'

'Maybe.'

'Two?'

'You trying to pin me down, George?'

'I suppose I am. Yes.'

Toby nodded gravely as if he had suspected as much all along: 'And have you forgotten, George, how it was with us in lamplighters? How overworked we were? How my boys and I played postman to half the networks in the Circus? Remember? In one week how many meetings, pick-ups? Twenty, thirty? In the high season once – forty? Go to Registry, George. If you've got Lacon behind you, go to Registry, draw the file, check the encounter sheets. That way you see exactly. Don't come here trying to trip me up, know what I mean? Degas, Vladimir – I don't like these questions. A friend, an old boss, my own house – it upsets me, okay?'

His speech having run for a deal longer than either of them

apparently expected, Toby paused, as if waiting for Smiley to provide the explanation for his loquacity. Then he took a step forward, and turned up his palms in appeal.

'George,' he said reproachfully. 'George, my name is Benati, okay?'

Smiley seemed to have lapsed into dejection. He was peering gloomily at the stacks of grimy art catalogues strewn over the carpet.

'I'm not called Hector, definitely not Esterhase,' Toby insisted. 'I got an alibi for every day of the year – hiding from my bank manager. You think I want trouble round my neck? Émigrés, police even. This an interrogation, George?'

'You know me, Toby.'

'Sure. I know you, George. You want matches so you can burn my feet?'

Smiley's gaze remained fixed upon the catalogues. 'Before Vladimir died – hours before – he rang the Circus,' he said. 'He said he wanted to give us information.'

'But this Vladimir was an old man, George!' Toby insisted – protesting, at least to Smiley's ear, altogether too much. 'Listen, there's a lot of guys like him. Big background, been on the payroll too long; they get old, soft in the head, start writing crazy memoirs, seeing world plots everywhere, know what I mean?'

On and on, Smiley contemplated the catalogues, his round head supported on his clenched fists.

'Now why do you say that exactly, Toby?' he asked critically. 'I don't follow your reasoning.'

'What do you mean, why I say it? Old defectors, old spies, they get a bit cuckoo. They hear voices, talk to the dicky-birds. It's normal.'

'Did Vladimir hear voices?'

'How should I know?'

'That's what I was asking you, Toby,' Smiley explained reasonably, to the catalogues. 'I told you Vladimir claimed to have news for us, and *you* replied to me that he was going soft in the head. I wondered how you knew. About the softness of Vladimir's head. I wondered how recent was your information about his state of mind. And why you pooh-poohed whatever he might have had to say. That's all.'

'George, these are very old games you are playing. Don't twist my words. Okay? You want to ask me, ask me. Please. But don't twist my words.'

'It wasn't suicide, Toby,' Smiley said, still without a glance at him. 'It *definitely* wasn't suicide. I saw the body, believe me. It wasn't a jealous husband either – not unless he was equipped with a Moscow Centre murder weapon. What used we to call them, those gun things? "Inhumane killers", wasn't it? Well, that's what Moscow used. An inhumane killer.'

Smiley once more pondered, but this time – even if it was too late – Toby had the wit to wait in silence.

'You see, Toby, when Vladimir made that phone call to the Circus he demanded *Max*. Myself, in other words. Not his postman, which would have been you. Not Hector. He demanded his vicar, which for better or worse was me. Against all protocol, against all training, and against all precedent. Never done it before. I wasn't there of course, so they offered him a substitute, a silly little boy called Mostyn. It didn't matter because in the event they never met anyway. But can *you* tell me why he didn't ask for Hector?'

'George, I mean *really*! These are shadows you are chasing! Should I know why he *doesn't* ask for me? We are responsible for the omissions of others, suddenly? What is this?'

'Did you quarrel with him? Would that be a reason?'

'Why should I quarrel with Vladimir? He was being dramatic, George. That's how they are, these old guys, when they retire.' Toby paused as if to imply that Smiley himself was not above these foibles. 'They get bored, they miss the action, they want stroking, so they make up some piece of mickey-mouse.'

'But not all of them get shot, do they, Toby? That's the worry, you see: the cause and effect. Toby quarrels with Vladimir one day, Vladimir gets shot with a Russian gun the next. In police terms that's what one calls an embarrassing chain of events. In our terms too, actually.'

'George, are you crazy? What the hell is quarrel? I told you: I never quarrel with the old man in my life!'

'Mikhel said you did.'

'Mikhel? You go talking to *Mikhel*?'

'According to Mikhel, the old man was very bitter about you. "Hector is no good," Vladimir kept telling him. He quoted Vladimir's words exactly. "Hector is no good." Mikhel was very surprised. Vladimir used to think highly of you. Mikhel couldn't think what had been going on between the two of you that could produce such a severe change of heart. "Hector is no good." *Why* weren't you any good, Toby? What happened that made Vladimir so passionate about you? I'd like to keep it away from the police if I could, you see. For all our sakes.'

But the fieldman in Toby Esterhase was by now fully awake, and he knew that interrogations, like battles, are never won but only lost.

'George, this is absurd,' he declared with pity rather than hurt. 'I mean it's so obvious you are fooling me. Know that? Some old man builds castles in the air, so you want to go to the police already? Is that what Lacon is hiring you for? Are these the bits you are sweeping up? George?'

This time, the long silence seemed to create some resolution in Smiley, and when he spoke again it was as if he had not much time left. His tone was brisk, even impatient.

'Vladimir came to see you. I don't know when but within the last few weeks. You met him or you talked to him over the phone – call box to call box, whatever the technique was. He asked you to do something for him. You refused. That's why he demanded Max when he rang the Circus on Friday night. He'd had Hector's answer already and it was no. That's also why Hector was "no good". You turned him down.'

This time Toby made no attempt to interrupt.

'And if I may say so, you're scared,' Smiley resumed, studiously not looking at the lump in Toby's jacket pocket. 'You know enough about who killed Vladimir to think they might kill you too. You even thought it possible I wasn't the right Angel.' He waited, but Toby didn't rise. His tone softened. 'You remember what we used to say at Sarratt, Toby – about fear being information without the cure? How we should respect it? Well, I respect yours, Toby. I want to know more about it. Where it came from. Whether I should share it. That's all.'

Still at the door, his little palms pressed flat against the panels, Toby Esterhase studied Smiley most attentively and without the smallest decline in his composure. He even contrived to suggest, by the depth and question of his glance, that his concern was now for Smiley rather than himself. Next, in line with this solicitous approach, he took a pace, then another, into the room – but tentatively, and somewhat as if he were visiting an ailing friend in hospital. Only then, with a passable imitation of a bedside manner, did he respond to Smiley's accusations with a most perceptive question, one which Smiley himself, as it happened, had deliberated in some depth over the last two days.

'George. Kindly answer me something. Who is speaking here actually? Is it George Smiley? Is it Oliver Lacon? Mikhel? Who is speaking, please?' Receiving no immediate answer, he continued his advance as far as a grimy satin-covered stool where he perched himself with a catlike trimness, one hand over each knee. 'Because for an official fellow, George, you are asking some pretty damn unofficial questions, it strikes me. You are taking rather an unofficial attitude, I think.'

'You saw Vladimir and you spoke to him. What happened?' Smiley asked, quite undeflected by this challenge. 'You tell me that, and I'll tell you who is speaking here.'

In the farthest corner of the ceiling there was a yellowed patch of glass about a metre square and the shadows that played over it were the feet of passers-by in the street. For some reason Toby's eyes had fixed on this strange spot and he seemed to read his decision there, like an instruction flashed on a screen.

'Vladimir put up a distress rocket,' Toby said in exactly the same tone as before, of neither conceding nor confiding. Indeed, by some trick of tone or inflection, he even managed to bring a note of warning to his voice.

'Through the Circus?'

'Through friends of mine,' said Toby.

'When?'

Toby gave a date. Two weeks ago. A crash meeting. Smiley asked where it took place.

'In the Science Museum,' Toby replied with new-found confidence. 'The café on the top floor, George. We drank coffee, admired the old aeroplanes hanging from the roof. You going to report all this to Lacon, George? Feel free, okay? Be my guest. I got nothing to hide.'

'And he put the proposition?'

'Sure. He put me a proposition. He wanted me to do a

lamplighter job. To be his camel. That was our joke, back in the old Moscow days, remember? To collect, carry across the desert, to deliver. "Toby, I got no passport. *Aidez-moi. Mon ami, aidez-moi.*" You know how he talked. Like de Gaulle. We used to call him that – "The other General." Remember?'

'Carry what?'

'He was not precise. It was documentary, it was small, no concealment was needed. This much he tells me.'

'For somebody putting out feelers, he seems to have told you a lot.'

'He was asking a hell of a lot too,' said Toby calmly, and waited for Smiley's next question.

'And the where?' Smiley asked. 'Did Vladimir tell you that too?'

'Germany.'

'Which one?'

'Ours. The north of it.'

'Casual encounter? Dead-letter-boxes? Live? What sort of meeting?'

'On the fly. I should take a train ride. From Hamburg north. The handover to be made on the train, details on acceptance.'

'And it was to be a private arrangement. No Circus, no Max?'

'For the time being very private, George.'

Smiley picked his words with tact. 'And the compensation for your labours?'

A distinct scepticism marked Toby's answer: 'If we get the document – that's what he called it, okay? Document. If we get the document, and the document is genuine, which he swore it was, we win immediately a place in Heaven. We take first the document to Max, tell Max the story. Max would know its meaning, Max would know the crucial importance – of the document. Max would reward us. Gifts, promotion, medals, Max will put us in the House of Lords. Sure. Only problem was, Vladimir didn't know Max was on the shelf and the Circus has joined the Boy Scouts.'

'Did he know that Hector was on the shelf?'

'Fifty-fifty, George.'

'What does that mean?' Then with a 'never mind', Smiley cancelled his own question and again lapsed into prolonged thought.

'George, you want to drop this line of enquiry,' Toby said earnestly. 'That is my strong advice to you, abandon it,' he said, and waited.

Smiley might not have heard. Momentarily shocked, he seemed to be pondering the scale of Toby's error.

'The point is, you sent him packing,' he muttered and remained staring into space. 'He appealed to you and you slammed the door in his face. How could you do that, Toby? You of all people?'

The reproach brought Toby furiously to his feet, which was perhaps what it was meant to do. His eyes lit up, his cheeks coloured, the sleeping Hungarian in him was wide awake.

'And you want to hear why, maybe? You want to know why I told him, "Go to hell, Vladimir. Leave my sight, please, you make me sick"? You want to know who his connect is out there – this magic guy in North Germany with the crock of gold that's going to make millionaires of us overnight, George – you want to know his full identity? Remember the name Otto Leipzig, by any chance? Holder many times of our Creep of the Year award? Fabricator, intelligence pedlar, confidence man, sex maniac, pimp, also various sorts of criminal? Remember *that* great hero?'

Smiley saw the tartan walls of the hotel again, and the

dreadful hunting prints of Jorrocks in full cry; he saw the two black-coated figures, the giant and the midget, and the General's huge mottled hand resting on the tiny shoulder of his protégé. *Max, here is my good friend Otto. I have brought him to tell his own story.* He heard the steady thunder of the planes landing and taking off at Heathrow Airport.

'Vaguely,' Smiley replied equably. 'Yes, vaguely I do remember an Otto Leipzig. Tell me about him. I seem to remember he had rather a lot of names. But then so do we all, don't we?'

'About two hundred, but Leipzig he ended up with. Know why? Leipzig in East Germany: he liked the jail there. He was that kind of crazy joker. Remember the stuff he peddled, by any chance?' Believing he had the initiative, Toby stepped boldly forward and stood over the passive Smiley while he talked down at him: 'George, do you not even remember the incredible and total bilge which year after year that creep would push out under fifteen different source names to our West European stations, mainly German? Our expert on the new Estonian order? Our top source on Soviet arms shipments out of Leningrad? Our inside ear at Moscow Centre, our principal Karla-watcher, even?' Smiley did not stir. 'How he took our Berlin resident alone for two thousand Deutschmarks for a rewrite from *Stern* magazine? How he foxed that old General, worked on him like a sucking-leech, time and again – "us fellow Balts" – that line? "General, I just got the Crown jewels for you – only trouble, I don't have the air fare"? Jesus!'

'It wasn't *all* fabrication, though, was it, Toby?' Smiley objected mildly. 'Some of it, I seem to remember – in certain areas, at least – turned out to be rather good stuff.'

'Count it on one finger.'

'His Moscow Centre material, for instance. I don't remember that we faulted him on that, ever?'

'Okay! So Centre gave him some decent chicken-feed occasionally, so he could pass us the other crap! How else does anyone play a double, for God's sake?'

Smiley seemed about to argue this point, then changed his mind.

'I see,' he said finally, as if overruled. 'Yes, I see what you mean. A plant.'

'Not a plant, a creep. A little of this, a little of that. A dealer. No principles. No standards. Work for anyone who sweetens his pie.'

'I take the point,' said Smiley gravely, in the same diminished tone. 'And of course he settled in North Germany, too, didn't he? Up towards Travemünde somewhere.'

'Otto Leipzig never settled anywhere in his life,' said Toby with contempt. 'George, that guy's a drifter, a total bum. Dresses like he was a Rothschild, owns a cat and bicycle. Know what his last job was, this great spy? Night-watchman in some lousy Hamburg cargo house somewhere! Forget him.'

'And he had a partner,' Smiley said, in the same tone of innocent reminiscence. 'Yes, that comes back to me too. An immigrant, an East German.'

'Worse than East German: Saxon. Name of Kretzschmar, first name was Claus. Claus with a "C", don't ask me why. I mean these guys have got no logic at all. Claus was also a creep. They stole together, pimped together, faked reports together.'

'But that was long ago, Toby,' Smiley put in gently.

'Who cares? It was a perfect marriage.'

'Then I expect it didn't last,' said Smiley, in an aside to himself.

But perhaps Smiley had for once overdone his meekness; or perhaps Toby simply knew him too well. For a warning light had come up in his swift, Hungarian eye, and a tuck of suspicion formed on his bland brow. He stood back and, contemplating Smiley, passed one hand thoughtfully over his immaculate white hair.

'George,' he said. 'Listen, who are you fooling, okay?'

Smiley did not speak, but lifted the Degas, and turned it round, then put it down.

'George, listen to me once. Please! Okay, George? Maybe I give you once a lecture.'

Smiley glanced at him, then looked away.

'George, I owe you. You got to hear me. So you pulled me from the gutter once in Vienna when I was a stinking kid. I was a Leipzig. A bum. So you got me my job with the Circus. So we had a lot of times together, stole some horses. You remember the first rule of retirement, George? "No moonlighting. No fooling with loose ends? No private enterprise ever?" You remember who preached this rule? At Sarratt? In the corridors? George Smiley did. "When it's over, it's over. Pull down the shutters, go home!" So now what do you want to do, suddenly? Play kiss-kiss with an old crazy General who's dead but won't lie down and a five-sided comedian like Otto Leipzig! What is this? The last cavalry charge on the Kremlin suddenly? We're over, George. We got no licence. They don't want us any more. Forget it.' He hesitated, suddenly embarrassed. 'So okay, Ann gave you a bad time with Bill Haydon. So there's Karla, and Karla was Bill's big daddy in Moscow. George, I mean, this gets very crude, know what I mean?'

His hands fell to his sides. He stared at the still figure before him. Smiley's eyelids were nearly closed. His head had dropped forward. With the shifting of his cheeks deep crevices had appeared round his mouth and eyes.

'We never faulted Leipzig's reports on Moscow Centre,' Smiley said, as if he hadn't heard the last part. 'I remember distinctly that we never faulted them. Nor on Karla. Vladimir trusted him implicitly. On the Moscow stuff, so did we.'

'George, who ever faulted a report on Moscow Centre? Please? So okay, once in a while we got a defector, he tells you: "This thing is crap and that thing is maybe true." So where's the collateral? Where's the hard base, you used to say? Some guy feeds you a story: "Karla just built a new spy nursery in Siberia." So who's to say they didn't? Keep it vague, you can't lose.'

'That was why we put up with him,' Smiley went on, as if he hadn't heard. 'Where the Soviet Service was involved, he played a straight game.'

'George,' said Toby softly, shaking his head. 'You got to wake up. The crowds have all gone home.'

'Will you tell me the rest of it now, Toby? Will you tell me exactly what Vladimir said to you? Please?'

So in the end, as a reluctant gift of friendship, Toby told it as Smiley asked, straight out, with a frankness that was like defeat.

The maquette which might have been by Degas portrayed a ballerina with her arms above her head. Her body was curved backward and her lips were parted in what might have been ecstasy and there was no question but that, fake or genuine, she bore an uncomfortable if superficial resemblance to Ann. Smiley had taken her in his hands again and was slowly turning her, gazing at her this way and that with no clear appreciation. Toby was back on his satin stool. In the ceiling window, the shadowed feet walked jauntily.

Toby and Vladimir had met in the café of the Science Museum on the aeronautical floor, Toby repeated. Vladimir was in a state of high excitement and kept clutching Toby's arm, which Toby didn't like, it made him conspicuous. Otto Leipzig had managed the impossible, Vladimir kept saying. It was the big one, the chance in a million, Toby; Otto Leipzig had landed the one Max had always dreamed of, 'the full settlement of all our claims,' as Vladimir had put it. When Toby asked him somewhat acidly what claims he had in mind, Vladimir either wouldn't or couldn't say: 'Ask Max,' he insisted. 'If you do not believe me, ask Max, tell Max it is the big one.'

'So what's the deal?' Toby had asked – knowing, he said, that where Otto Leipzig was concerned the bill came first and the goods a long, long way behind. 'How much does he want, the great hero?'

Toby confessed to Smiley that he had found it hard to conceal his scepticism – 'which put a bad mood on the meeting from the start.' Vladimir outlined the terms. Leipzig had the story, said Vladimir, but he also had certain material proofs that the story was true. There was first a document and the document was what Leipzig called a *Vorspeise*, or appetiser. There was also a second proof, a letter, held by Vladimir. There was then the story itself, which would be given by other materials which Leipzig had entrusted to safe keeping. The document showed how the story was obtained, the materials themselves were incontrovertible.

'And the subject?' Smiley asked.

'Not revealed,' Toby replied shortly. 'To Hector, not revealed. Get Max and okay – then Vladimir reveals the subject. But Hector for the time being got to shut up and run the errands.'

For a moment Toby appeared about to launch upon a second speech of discouragement. 'George, I mean look here, the old boy was just totally cuckoo,' he began. 'Otto Leipzig was taking him a complete ride.' Then he saw Smiley's expression, so inward and inaccessible, and contented himself instead with a repetition of Otto Leipzig's totally outrageous demands.

'The document to be taken personally to Max by Vladimir, Moscow Rules at all points, no middle men, no correspondence. The preparations they made already on the telephone—'

'Telephone between London and Hamburg?' Smiley interrupted, suggesting by his tone that this was new and unwelcome information.

'They used word code, he tells me. Old pals, they know how to fox around. But not with the proof, says Vladi; with the proof there's no foxing at all. No phones, no mails, no trucks, they got to have a camel, period. Vladi's security-crazy, okay, this we know already. From now on, only Moscow Rules apply.'

Smiley remembered his own phone call to Hamburg of Saturday night, and wondered again what kind of establishment Otto Leipzig had been using as his telephone exchange.

'Once the Circus has declared its interest,' Toby continued, 'they pay a down payment to Otto Leipzig of five thousand Swiss for an audition fee. George! Five thousand Swiss! For openers! Just to be in the game! Next – George, you got to hear this – next, Otto Leipzig to be flown to a safe house in England for the audition. George, I mean I never heard such craziness. You want the rest? If, following the audition, the Circus wants to buy the material itself – you want to hear how much?'

Smiley did.

'Fifty grand Swiss. Maybe you want to sign me a cheque?'

Toby waited for a cry of outrage but none came.

'All for Leipzig?'

'Sure. They were Leipzig's terms. Who else would be so cuckoo?'

'What did Vladimir ask for himself?'

A small hesitation. 'Nothing,' said Toby reluctantly. Then,

as if to leave that point behind, set off on a fresh wave of indignation.

'*Basta*. So now all Hector got to do is fly to Hamburg at his own expense, take a train north and play rabbit for some crazy entrapment game that Otto Leipzig has lined up for himself with the East Germans, the Russians, the Poles, the Bulgarians, the Cubans, and also no doubt, being modern, the Chinese. I said to him – George, listen to me – I said to him: "Vladimir, old friend, excuse me, pay attention to me once. Tell me what in life is so important that the Circus pays five thousand Swiss from its precious reptile fund for one lousy audition with Otto Leipzig? Maria Callas never got so much and believe me she sings a damn lot better than Otto does." He's holding my arm. Here.' Demonstrating, Toby grasped his own bicep. 'Squeezing me like I am an orange. That old boy had some strength still, believe me. "Fetch the document for me, Hector." He is speaking Russian. That's a very quiet place, that museum. Everyone has stopped to listen to him. I had a bad feeling. He is weeping. "For the sake of God, Hector, I am an old man. I got no legs, no passport, no one I can trust but Otto Leipzig. Go to Hamburg and fetch the document. When he sees the proof, Max will believe me, Max has faith." I try to console him, make some hints. I tell him émigrés are bad news these days, change of policy, new government. I advise him, "Vladimir, go home, play some chess. Listen, I come round to the library one day, have a game maybe." Then he says to me: "Hector, I began this. It was me sent the order to Otto Leipzig telling him to explore the position. Me who sent the money to him for the groundwork, all I had." Listen, that was an old, sad man. Past it.'

Toby made a pause but Smiley did not stir. Toby stood up, went to a cupboard, poured two glasses of an extremely indifferent sherry, and put one on the table beside the Degas maquette. He said 'Cheers' and drank back his glass, but still Smiley did not budge. His inertia rekindled Toby's anger.

'So I killed him, George, okay? It's Hector's fault, okay. Hector is personally and totally responsible for the old man's death. That's all I need.' He flung out both hands, palms upward. 'George! Advise me! George, for this story I should go to Hamburg, unofficial, no cover, no baby-sitter? Know where the East German border is up there? From Lübeck two kilometres? Less? Remember? In Travemünde you got to stay on the left of the street or you've defected by mistake.' Smiley did not laugh. 'And in the unlikely event I come back, I should call up George Smiley, go round to Saul Enderby with him, knock on the back door like a bum – "Let us in, Saul, please, we got hot information totally reliable from Otto Leipzig, only five grand Swiss for an audition concerning matters totally forbidden under the Boy Scout laws?" I should do this, George?'

From an inside pocket, Smiley drew a battered packet of English cigarettes. From the packet he drew the home-made contact print which he passed silently across the table for Toby to look at.

'Who's the second man?' Smiley asked.

'I don't know.'

'Not his partner, the Saxon, the man he stole with in the old days? Kretzschmar?'

Shaking his head, Toby Esterhase went on looking at the picture.

'So who's the second man?' Smiley asked again.

Toby handed back the photograph. 'George, pay attention to me, please,' he said quietly. 'You listening?'

Smiley might have been and might not. He was threading the print back into the cigarette packet.

'People forge things like that these days, you know that? That's very easy done, George. I want to put a head on another guy's shoulders, I got the equipment, it takes me maybe two minutes. You're not a technical guy, George, you don't understand these matters. You don't buy photographs from Otto Leipzig, you don't buy Degas from Signor Benati, follow me?'

'Do they forge negatives?'

'Sure. You forge the print, then you photograph it, make a new negative – why not?'

'Is this a forgery?' Smiley asked.

Toby hesitated a long time. 'I don't think so.'

'Leipzig travelled a lot. How did we raise him if we needed him?' Smiley asked.

'He was strictly arm's length. Totally.'

'So how did we raise him?'

'For a routine rendezvous the *Hamburger Abendblatt* marriage ads. Petra, aged twenty-two, blonde, petite, former singer – that crap. George, listen to me. Leipzig is a dangerous bum with very many lousy connections, mostly still in Moscow.'

'What about emergencies? Did he have a house, a girl?'

'He never had a house in his life. For crash meetings, Claus Kretzschmar played key-holder. George, for God's sake, hear me once—'

'So how did we reach Kretzschmar?'

'He's got a couple of night-clubs. Cat houses. We left a message there.'

A warning buzzer rang and from upstairs they heard the sound of voices raised in argument.

'I'm afraid Signor Benati has a conference in Florence today,' the blonde girl was saying. 'That's the trouble with being international.'

But the caller refused to believe her; Smiley could hear the rising tide of his protest. For a fraction of a second Toby's brown eyes lifted sharply to the sound; then with a sigh he pulled open a wardrobe and drew out a grimy raincoat and a brown hat, despite the sunlight in the ceiling window.

'What's it called?' Smiley asked. 'Kretzschmar's nightclub – what's it called?'

'The Blue Diamond. George, don't do it, okay? Whatever it is, drop it. So the photo is genuine, then what? The Circus has a picture of some guy rolling in the snow, courtesy of Otto Leipzig. You think that's a gold-mine suddenly? You think that makes Saul Enderby horny?'

Smiley looked at Toby, and remembered him, and remembered also that in all the years they had known each other and worked together, Toby had never once volunteered the truth, that information was money to him; even when he counted it valueless, he never threw it away.

'What else did Vladimir tell you about Leipzig's information?' Smiley asked.

'He said it was some old case come alive. Years of investment. Some crap about the Sandman. He was a child again, remembering fairy tales, for God's sake. See what I mean?'

'What about the Sandman?'

'To tell you it concerned the Sandman. That's all. The Sandman is making a legend for a girl. Max will understand. George, he was weeping, for Christ's sake. He'd have said anything that came into his head. He wanted the action. He was an old spy in a hurry. You used to say they were the worst.'

Toby was at the far door, already half-way gone. But he turned and came back despite the approaching clamour from upstairs, because something in Smiley's manner seemed to trouble him – 'a definitely harder stare', he called it afterwards, 'like I'd completely insulted him somehow.'

'George? George, this is Toby, remember? If you don't get the hell out of here, that guy upstairs will sequester you in part-payment, hear me?'

Smiley hardly did. 'Years of investment and the Sandman was making a legend for a girl?' he repeated. 'What else? Toby, what else!'

'He was behaving like a crazy man again.'

'The General was? Vladi was?'

'No, the Sandman. George, listen. "The Sandman is behaving like a crazy man again, the Sandman is making a legend for a girl, Max will understand." *Finito*. The total garbage. I've told you every word. Go easy now, hear me?'

From upstairs, the sounds of argument grew still louder. A door slammed, they heard footsteps stamping towards the staircase. Toby gave Smiley's arm a last, swift pat.

'Goodbye, George. Hear me. You want a Hungarian baby-sitter some day, call me. Hear that? You're messing around with a creep like Otto Leipzig, then you better have a creep like Toby look after you. Don't go out alone nights, you're too young.'

Climbing the steel ladder back to the gallery, Smiley all but knocked over an irate creditor on his way down. But this was not important to Smiley; neither was the insolent sigh of the ash-blonde girl as he stepped into the street. What mattered was that he had put a name to the second face in the photograph; and to the name, the story, which like an undiagnosed pain had been nagging at his memory for the last thirty-six hours – as Toby might have said, the story of a legend.

And that, indeed, is the dilemma of those would-be historians who are concerned, only months after the close of the affair, to chart the interplay of Smiley's knowledge and his actions.

Toby told him this much, they say, so he did that much. Or: if so-and-so had not occurred, then there would have been no resolution. Yet the truth is more complex than this, and far less handy. As a patient tests himself on coming out of the anaesthetic – this leg, that leg, do the hands still close and open? – so Smiley by a succession of cautious movements grew into his own strength of body and mind, probing the motives of his adversary as he probed his own.

14

He was driving on a high plateau and the plateau was above the tree-line because the pines had been planted low in the valley's cleft. It was early evening of the same day and in the plain the first lights were pricking the wet gloom. On the horizon lay the city of Oxford, lifted by ground mist, an academic Jerusalem. The view from that side was new to him and increased his sense of unreality, of being conveyed rather than determining his own journey; of being in the grasp of thoughts which were not his to command. His visit to Toby Esterhase had fallen, arguably, within the crude guide-lines of Lacon's brief; but this journey, he knew, led for better or worse to the forbidden province of his secret interest. Yet he was aware of no alternative, and wanted none. Like an archaeologist who has delved all his life in vain, Smiley had begged for one last day, and this was it.

At first he had watched his rear-view mirror constantly, how the familiar motor cycle had hung behind him like a gull at sea. But when he left the last roundabout the man called Ferguson had not followed him, and when he pulled up to read the map nothing passed him either; so either they had guessed his destination or, for some arcane reason of procedure, they had forbidden their man to cross the county border. Sometimes, as he drove, a trepidation gripped him. Let her be, he thought. He had heard things; not much, but enough to guess the rest. Let her be, let her find her own peace where she can. But he knew that peace was not his to give, that the battle he was involved in must be continuous to have any meaning at all.

The kennel sign was like a painted grin: 'MERRILLEE BOARD-ING ALL PETS WELCOME EGGS'. A daubed yellow dog wearing a top hat pointed one paw down a cart-track; the track, when he took it, led so steeply downward that it felt like a free fall. He passed a pylon and heard the wind howling in it; he entered the plantation. First came the young trees; then the old ones darkened over him and he was in the Black Forest of his German childhood heading for some unrevealed interior. He switched on his headlights, rounded a steep bend, and another, and a third, and there was the cabin much as he had imagined it – her *dacha*, as she used to call it. Once she had had the house in Oxford and the *dacha* as a place away from it. Now there was only the *dacha*; she had quitted towns for ever. It stood in its own clearing of tree trunks and trodden mud, with a ramshackle veranda and a wood-shingle roof and a tin chimney with smoke coming out of it. The clapboard walls were blackened with creosote, a galvanised iron feed-tub almost blocked the front porch. On a bit of lawn stood a home-made bird-table with enough bread to feed an ark, and dotted round the clearing, like allotment huts, stood the asbestos sheds and wire runs which held the chickens and all the pets welcome without discrimination.

Karla, he thought. What a place to look for you.

He parked, and his arrival set loose a bedlam as dogs sobbed in torment and thin walls thundered to desperate bodies. He walked to the house, carrier-bag in hand, the bottles bumping against his legs. Above the din he heard his own feet rattling up the six steps of the veranda. A notice on the door read: 'If out do not leave pets on spec.' and underneath, seemingly added in a fury, 'No bloody monkeys.'

The bell-pull was a donkey's tail in plastic. He reached for it but the door had already opened and a frail pretty woman peered at him from the interior darkness of the cabin. Her eyes were timid and grey, she had that period English beauty which had once been Ann's: accepting, and grave. She saw him and stopped dead. 'Oh, Lord,' she whispered. 'Gosh.' Then looked downward at her brogues, brushing back her forelock with one finger, while the dogs barked themselves hoarse at him from behind their wire.

'I'm sorry, Hilary,' said Smiley, with great gentleness. 'It's only for an hour, I promise. That's all it is. An hour.'

A deep, masculine voice, very slow, issued out of the darkness behind her. 'What is it, Hils?' growled the voice. 'Bog-weevil, budgie or giraffe?'

The question was followed by a slow thud like the movement of cloth over something hollow.

'It's human, Con,' Hilary called over her shoulder, and went back to looking at her brogues.

'*She* human or the other thing?' the voice demanded.

'It's George, Con. Don't be cross, Con.'

'*George*? Which George? George the Lorry, who waters my coal, or George the Meat, who poisons my dogs?'

'It's just some questions,' Smiley assured Hilary in the same deeply compassionate tone. 'An old case. Nothing momentous, I promise you.'

'It doesn't matter, George,' Hilary said, still looking downward. 'Honestly. It's fine.'

'Stop all that flirting!' the voice from inside the house commanded. 'Unhand her, whoever you are!'

As the thudding grew gradually nearer Smiley leaned past

Hilary and spoke into the doorway. 'Connie, it's me,' he said. And once again, his voice did everything possible to signal his goodwill.

First came the puppies – four of them, probably whippets – in a fast pack. Next came a mangy old mongrel with barely life enough to reach the veranda and collapse. Then the door shuddered open to its fullest extent and revealed a mountainous woman propped crookedly between two thick wooden crutches, which she did not seem to hold. She had white hair clipped short as a man's, and watery, very shrewd eyes that held him fiercely in their stare. So long was her examination of him, in fact, so leisured and minute – his earnest face, his baggy suit, the plastic carrier-bag dangling from his left hand, his whole posture of waiting meekly to be admitted – that it gave her an almost regal authority over him, to which her stillness, and her troubled breathing, and her crippled state only contributed greater strength.

'Oh my giddy aunts,' she announced, still studying him, and blew out a stream of air. 'Jumping whatevers. Damn you, George Smiley. Damn you and all who sail in you. Welcome to Siberia.'

Then she smiled, and her smile was so sudden, and fresh, and little-girl, that it almost washed away the long questioning that had gone before it.

'Hullo, Con,' said Smiley.

Her eyes, notwithstanding her smile, stayed on him still. They had the pallor of a new-born baby's.

'Hils,' she said, at last. 'I said *Hils*!'

'Yes, Con?'

'Go feed the doggy-wogs, darling. When you've done that, feed the filthy chickadees. Glut the brutes. When you've done that, mix tomorrow's meal, and when you've done *that*, bring me the humane killer so that I can despatch this interfering whatsit to an early Paradise. George, follow me.'

Hilary smiled but seemed unable to move till Connie softly pushed an elbow into her to get her going.

'Hoof it, darling. There's nothing he can do to you now. He's shot his bolt, and so have you, and, God knows, so have I.'

It was a house of day and night at once. At the centre, on a pine table littered with the remains of toast and Marmite, an old oil lamp shed a globe of yellow light, intensifying the darkness round it. The gleam of blue rain clouds, streaked by sunset, filled the far French windows. Gradually, as Smiley followed Connie's agonisingly slow procession, he realised that this one wooden room was all there was. For an office, they had the roll-top desk laden with bills and flea powder; for a bedroom the brass double bedstead with its heap of stuffed toy animals lying like dead soldiers between the pillows; for a drawing-room Connie's rocking-chair and a crumbling wicker sofa; for a kitchen a gas ring fired from a cylinder; and for decoration the unclearable litter of old age.

'Connie's not coming back, George,' she called as she hobbled ahead of him. 'Wild horses can puff and blow their snivelling hearts out, the old fool has hung up her boots for good.' Reaching her rocking-chair, she began the ponderous business of turning herself round until she had her back to it. 'So if that's what you're after, you can tell Saul Enderby to shove it up his smoke and pipe it.' She held out her arms to him and he thought she wanted him to kiss her. 'Not *that*, you sex maniac. Batten on to my hands!'

He did so, and lowered her into the rocking-chair.

'That's not what I came for, Con,' said Smiley. 'I'm not trying to woo you away, I promise.'

'For one good reason, she's dying,' she announced firmly, not seeming to notice his interjection. 'The old fool's for the shredder, and high time too. The leech tries to fool me, of course. That's because he's a funk. Bronchitis. Rheumatism. Touch of the weathers. Balls, the lot of it. It's death, that's what I'm suffering from. The systematic encroachment of the big D. Is that booze you're toting in that bag?'

'Yes. Yes, it is,' said Smiley.

'Goody. Let's have lots. How's the demon Ann?'

On the draining-board, amid a permanent pile of washing-up, he found two glasses, and half filled them.

'Flourishing, I gather,' he replied.

Reciprocating, by his own kindly smile, her evident pleasure at his visit, he held out a glass to her and she grappled it between her mittened hands.

'You gather,' she echoed. 'Wish you *would* gather. Gather her up for good is what you should do. Or else put powdered glass in her coffee. All right, what are you after?' she demanded, all in the same breath. 'I never knew you yet do anything without a reason. Mud in your eye.'

'And in yours, Con,' said Smiley.

To drink, she had to lean her whole trunk towards the glass. And as her huge head lurched into the glare of the lamplight, he saw – he knew from too much experience – that she was telling no less than the truth, and her flesh had the leprous whiteness of death.

'Come on. Out with it,' she ordered, in her sternest tone. 'I'm not sure I'll help you, mind. I've discovered love since we parted. Addles the hormones. Softens the teeth.'

He had wanted time to know her again. He was unsure of her.

'It's one of our old cases, Con, that's all,' he began apologetically. 'It's come alive again, the way they do.' He tried to raise the pitch of his voice to make it sound casual. 'We need more details. You know how you used to be about keeping records,' he added, teasingly.

Her eyes did not stir from his face.

'*Kirov*,' he went on, pronouncing the name very slowly. 'Kirov, first name Oleg. Ring a bell? Soviet Embassy, Paris, three or four hundred years ago, Second Secretary? We thought he was some sort of Moscow Centre man.'

'He was,' she said, and sat back a little, still watching him.

She motioned for a cigarette. A packet of ten lay on the table. He wedged one between her lips and lit it, but still her eyes would not leave his face.

'Saul Enderby threw that case out of the window,' she said and, forming her lips as if to play a flute, blew a lot of smoke straight downward in order to avoid his face.

'He ruled it should be dropped,' Smiley corrected her.

'What's the difference?'

Smiley had not expected to find himself defending Saul Enderby.

'It ran awhile, then in the transition time between my tenure and his, he ruled, quite understandably, that it was unproductive,' Smiley said, picking his words with measured care.

'And now he's changed his mind,' she said.

'I've got bits, Con. I want it all.'

'You always did,' she said. 'George,' she muttered. 'George Smiley. Lord alive. Lord bless us and preserve us. *George*.' Her gaze was half possessive, half disapproving, as if he were an erring son she loved. It held him a while longer, then switched to the French windows and the darkening sky outside.

'Kirov,' he said again, reminding her, and waited, wondering seriously whether it was all up with her; whether her mind was dying with her body, and this was all there was.

'Kirov, Oleg,' she repeated, in a musing tone. 'Born Lenin-grad October, 1929, according to his passport, which doesn't mean a damn thing except that he probably never went near Leningrad in his life.' She smiled, as if that were the way of the wicked world. 'Arrived Paris June 1, 1974, in the rank and qual-ity of Second Secretary, Commercial. Three to four years ago, you say? Dear Lord, it could be twenty. That's right, darling, he was a hood. 'Course he was. Identified by the Paris lodge of the poor old Riga Group, which didn't help us any, special-ly not on the fifth floor. What was his real name? *Kursky*. Of course it was. Yes, I think I remember Oleg Kirov, né Kursky all right.' Her smile returned, and was once more very pretty. 'Must have been Vladimir's last case, near enough. How is the old stoat?' she asked, and her moist clever eyes waited for his answer.

'Oh, fighting fit,' said Smiley.

'Still terrifying the virgins of Paddington?'

'I'm sure he is.'

'Bless you, darling,' said Connie, and turned her head till it was in profile to him, very dark except for the one fine line from the oil lamp, while she again stared out of the French windows.

'Go and see how the mad bitch is, will you, heart?' she asked fondly. 'Make sure the idiot hasn't thrown herself into the mill-race or drunk the universal weed-killer.'

Stepping outside, Smiley stood on the veranda, and in the thickening gloom made out the figure of Hilary loping awk-wardly among the coops. He heard the clanking of her spoon on the bucket, and shreds of her well-bred voice on the night air as she called out childish names: Come on Whitey, Flopsy, Bo.

'She's fine,' said Smiley, coming back. 'Feeding the chickens.'

'I should tell her to bugger off, shouldn't I, George?' she

remarked, ignoring his information entirely. '"Go forth into the world, Hils my dear." That's what I should say. "Don't tie yourself to a rotting old hulk like Con. Marry a chinless fool, spawn brats, fulfil your foul womanhood."' She had voices for everybody, he remembered: even for herself. She had them still. 'I'll be damned if I will, George. I want her. Every gorgeous bit of her. I'd take her with me if I'd half a chance. You want to try it some time.' A break. 'How *are* all the boys and girls?'

For a second, he didn't understand her question; his thoughts were with Hilary still, and Ann.

'His Grace Saul Enderby is still top of the heap, I take it? Eating well, I trust? Not moulting?'

'Oh, Saul goes from strength to strength, thanks.'

'That toad Sam Collins still Head of Operations?'

There was an edge to her questions, but he had no choice except to answer.

'Sam's fine too,' he said.

'Toby Esterhase still oiling round the corridors?'

'It's all pretty much as usual.'

Her face was now so dark to him that he could not tell whether she was proposing to speak again. He heard her breathing and the rasp of her chest. But he knew he was still the object of her scrutiny.

'*You'd* never work for that bunch, George,' she remarked at last, as if it were the most self-evident of platitudes. 'Not you. Give me another drink.'

Glad of the movement, Smiley went down the room again.

'*Kirov*, you said?' Connie called to him.

'That's right,' said Smiley cheerfully, and returned with her glass replenished.

'That little ferret Otto Leipzig was the first hurdle,' she

remarked with relish, when she had taken a deep draught. 'The fifth floor wouldn't believe *him*, would they? Not our little Otto – *oh* no! Otto was a fabricator, and that was that!'

'But I don't think Leipzig ever lied to us about the *Moscow* target,' Smiley said, taking up her tone of reminiscence.

'No, darling, he did *not*,' she said with approval. 'He had his weaknesses, I'll grant you. But when it came to the big stuff he always played a straight bat. And *you* understood that, alone of all your tribe, I'll say that for you. But you didn't get much support from the *other* barons, did you?'

'He never lied to Vladimir, either,' Smiley said. 'It was Vladimir's escape lines that got him out of Russia in the first place.'

'Well, well,' said Connie, after another long silence. 'Kirov né Kursky, the Ginger Pig.'

She said it again – 'Kirov, né Kursky' – a rallying call spoken to her own mountainous memory. As she did so, Smiley saw in his mind's eye the airport hotel room again, and the two strange conspirators seated before him in their black overcoats: the one so huge, the other tiny; the old General using all his bulk to enforce his passionate imploring; little Leipzig with his burning eyes, watching like an angry leash-dog at his side.

She was seduced.

The glow of the oil lamp had grown into a smoky lightball, and Connie in her rocking-chair sat at the edge of it, Mother Russia herself, as they had called her in the Circus, her wasting face hallowed with reminiscence as she unfolded the story of just one of her unnumbered family of erring children. Whatever suspicions she was harbouring about Smiley's motive in coming here, she had suspended them: this was what she had lived for; this was her song, even if it was her last; these monumental acts of recollection were her genius. In the old days, Smiley remembered, she would have teased him, flirted with her voice, taken huge arcs through seemingly extraneous chunks of Moscow Centre, all to lure him nearer. But tonight her narrative had acquired an awesome sobriety, as if she knew she had very little time.

Oleg Kirov arrived in Paris direct from Moscow, she repeated – that June, darling, same as I told you – the one when it poured and poured and the annual Sarratt cricket match had to be scrapped three Sundays in a row. Fat Oleg was listed as single, and he didn't replace anyone. His desk was on the second floor overlooking the Rue Saint-Simon – trafficky but *nice*, darling – whereas the Moscow Centre Residency hogged the third and fourth, to the rage of the Ambassador, who felt he was being squeezed into a cupboard by his unloved neighbours. To outward appearances, therefore, Kirov looked at first sight like that rare creature of the Soviet diplomatic community – namely, a straight diplomat. But it was the practice in Paris in those days – and for all Connie knew in *these* days too, heart – whenever a new face showed up at the Soviet Embassy, to distribute his photograph among the émigré tribal chiefs. Brother Kirov's photograph duly found its way to the groups, and in no time that old devil Vladimir was banging on his case officer's door in a state of fine excitement – Steve Mackelvore had Paris in those days, bless him, and dropped dead of a heart attack soon after, but that's another story – insisting that 'his people' had identified Kirov as a former *agent provocateur* named Kursky, who, while a student at Tallinn Polytechnical Institute, had formed a circle of dissident Estonian dock workers, something called 'the unaligned discussion club', then shopped its members to the secret police. Vladimir's source, presently visiting Paris, had been one of those unfortunate workers, and for his sins he had personally befriended Kursky right up to the moment of his betrayal.

So far so good, except that Vladi's source – said Connie – was none other than wicked little Otto, which meant that the fat was in the fire from the start.

As Connie went on speaking, Smiley's memory once again began to supplement her own. He saw himself in his last months as caretaker Chief of the Circus, wearily descending the rickety wooden staircase from the fifth floor for the Monday meeting, a bunch of dog-eared files jammed under his arm. The Circus in those days was like a bombed-out building, he remembered; its officers scattered, its budget hamstrung, its agents blown or dead or laid off. Bill Haydon's unmasking was an open wound in everyone's mind: they called it the Fall and shared the same sense of primeval shame. In their secret hearts, perhaps, they even blamed Smiley for having caused it, because it was Smiley who had nailed Bill's treachery. He saw himself at the head of the conference, and the ring of hostile faces already set against him as one by one the week's cases were introduced, and subjected to the customary questions: Do we or do we not develop this? Shall we give it another week? Another month? Another year? Is it a trap, is it deniable, is it within our Charter? What resources will be needed and are they better applied elsewhere? Who will authorise? Who will be informed? How much will it cost? He remembered the intemperate outburst which the mere name, or workname, of Otto Leipzig immediately called forth among such uncertain judges as Lauder Strickland, Sam Collins and their kind. He tried to recall who else would have been there apart from Connie and her cohorts from Soviet Research. Director of Finance, director Western Europe, director Soviet Attack, most of them already Saul Enderby's men. And Enderby himself, still nominally a Foreign Servant, put in by his own palace guard in the guise of Whitehall linkman, but whose smile was already their laughter, whose frown, their disapproval. Smiley saw himself listening to the submission – Connie's own – much as she now repeated it, together with the results of her preliminary researches.

Otto's story figured, she had insisted. This far, it couldn't be faulted. She had shown her workings:

Her own Soviet Research Section had confirmed from printed sources that one Oleg Kursky, a law student, was at Tallinn Polytechnic during the relevant period, she said.

Foreign Office contemporary archives spoke of unrest in the docks.

A defector report from the American Cousins gave a Kursky query Karsky, lawyer, first name Oleg, as graduating from a Moscow Centre training course at Kiev in 1971.

The same source, though suspect, suggested Kursky had later changed his name on the advice of his superiors, 'owing to his previous field experience'.

Routine French liaison reports, though notoriously unreliable, indicated that for a Second Secretary, Commercial, in Paris, Kirov did indeed enjoy unusual freedoms, such as shopping alone and attending Third World receptions without the customary fifteen companions.

All of which, in short – Connie had ended, far too vigorously for the fifth-floor taste – all of which confirmed the Leipzig story, and the suspicion that Kirov had an intelligence rôle. Then she had slapped the file on the table and passed round her photographs – the very stills, picked up as a matter of routine by French surveillance teams, that had caused the original uproar in the Riga Group headquarters in Paris. Kirov enters an Embassy car. Kirov emerges from the Moscow Narodny carrying a brief-case. Kirov pauses at the window of a saucy bookshop in order to scowl at the magazine covers.

But none, Smiley reflected – returning to the present – none showing Oleg Kirov and his erstwhile victim Otto Leipzig disporting themselves with a pair of ladies.

'So that was the *case*, darling,' Connie announced, when she had taken a long pull at her drink. 'We had the evidence of little Otto with plenty on his file to prove him right. We had a spot of collateral from other sources, not oodles, I grant you, but a start. Kirov was a hood, he was newly appointed, but what *sort* of hood was anybody's guess. And that made him *interesting*, didn't it, darling?'

'Yes,' Smiley said distractedly. 'Yes, Connie, I remember that it did.'

'He wasn't residency mainstream, we knew that from day one. He didn't ride about in residency cars, do night-shifts or twin up with identified fellow hoods, or use their cipher room or attend their weekly prayer-meetings or feed the residency cat or whatever. On the other hand, Kirov wasn't Karla's man, was he, heart? That was the rum thing.'

'Why not?' Smiley asked, without looking at her.

But Connie looked at Smiley all right. Connie made one of her long pauses in order to consider him at her leisure, while outside in the dying elms, the roofs wisely chose the sudden lull to sound a Shakespearean omen of screams. 'Because Karla already *had* his man in Paris, darling,' she explained patiently. 'As you are very well aware. That old stickler Pudin, the assistant military attaché. *You* remember how Karla always loved a soldier. Still does, for all I know.' She broke off, in order once more to study his impassive face. He had put his chin in his hands. His eyes, half closed, were turned towards the floor. 'Besides, Kirov was an idiot, and the one thing Karla *never* did like was idiots, did he? You weren't too kindly towards them either, come to think of it. Oleg Kirov was foul-mannered, stank, sweated, and stuck out like a fish in a tree wherever he went. Karla would have run a *mile* before hiring an oaf like that.' Again she paused. 'So would you,' she added.

Lifting a palm, Smiley placed it against his brow, fingers upwards, like a child at an exam. 'Unless,' he said.

'Unless *what*? Unless he'd gone off his turnip, I suppose! That'll be the day, I must say.'

'It was the time of the rumours,' Smiley said from far inside his thoughts.

'What rumours? There were always rumours, you dunder-head.'

'Oh, just defector reports,' he said disparagingly. 'Stories of strange happenings in Karla's court. Secondary sources, of course. But didn't they—'

'Didn't they what?'

'Well, didn't they suggest that he was taking rather strange people onto his pay-roll? Holding interviews with them at dead of night? It was all low-grade stuff, I know. I only mention it in passing.'

'And we were ordered to discount them,' Connie said very firmly. 'Kirov was the target. Not Karla. That was the fifth-floor ruling, George, and you were party to it. "Stop moon-gazing and get on with earthly matters," says you.' Twisting her mouth and putting back her head, she produced an uncomfortably realistic likeness of Saul Enderby: '"This Service is in the business of collectin' intelligence,"' she drawled. '"Not conductin' feuds agin the opposition." Don't tell me he's changed his tune, darling. Has he? *George?*' she whispered. 'Oh *George*, you are bad!'

He fetched her another drink and when he came back he saw her eyes glistening with mischievous excitement. She was plucking at the tufts of her white hair the way she used to when she wore it long.

'The point is, we licensed the operation, Con,' said Smiley, in a factual tone intended to rein her in. 'We overruled the doubters, and we gave you permission to take Kirov to first base. How did it run after that?'

The drink, the memories, the revived excitement of the chase were driving her at a speed he could not control. Her breathing had quickened. She was rasping like an old engine with the restraints dangerously removed. He realised she was telling Leipzig's story the way Leipzig had told it to Vladimir. He had thought he was in the Circus with her still, with the operation against Kirov just about to be launched. But in her imagination she had leapt instead to the ancient city of Tallinn a quarter of a century earlier. In her extraordinary mind, she had been there; she had known both Leipzig and Kirov in the time of their friendship. A love story, she insisted. Little Otto and fat Oleg. This was the pivot, she said; let the old fool tell it the way it was, she said, and you pursue your wicked purposes as I go along, George.

'The tortoise and the hare, darling, that's who they were. Kirov the big sad baby, reading away at his law books at the Poly, and using the beastly secret police as Daddy; and little Otto Leipzig the proper devil, a finger in all the rackets, bit of prison behind him, working in the docks all day, at night preaching sedition to the unaligned. They met in a bar and it was love at first sight. Otto pulled the girls, Oleg Kirov slipstreamed along behind him, picking up his leavings. What are you trying to do, George? Joan-of-Arc me?'

He had lighted a fresh cigarette for her and put it into her mouth in the hope of calming her, but her feverish talking had already burned it low enough to scorch her. Taking it quickly from her, he stubbed it on the tin lid she used for an ashtray.

'They even shared a girl-friend for a time,' she said, so loud she was nearly yelling. 'And *one* day, if you can believe it, the poor ninny came to little Otto and warned him outright. "Your fat friend is jealous of you and he's a toady of the secret police," says she. "The unaligned discussion club is for the high jump. Beware the Ides of March!"'

'Go easy, Con,' Smiley warned her anxiously. 'Con, come down!'

Her voice grew still louder: 'Otto threw the girl out and a week later the whole bunch were arrested. Including fat Oleg, of course, who'd set them up – but *they* knew. Oh, they knew!' She faltered as if she had lost her way. 'And the fool girl who'd tried to warn him died,' she said. 'Missing believed interrogated. Otto combed the forests for her till he found someone who'd been with her in the cells. Dead as a dodo. Two dodos. Dead as I'll be, damn soon.'

'Let's go on later,' Smiley said.

He would have stopped her, too – made tea, talked weather, anything to halt the mounting speed of her. But she had taken a second leap and was already back in Paris, describing how Otto Leipzig, with the fifth floor's grudging approval and the old General's passionate help, set about arranging the reunion, after all those lost years, with Second Secretary Kirov, whom she dubbed the Ginger Pig. Smiley supposed it was her name for him at the time. Her face was scarlet and her breath was not enough for her story, so that it kept running out in a wheeze, but she forced herself to continue.

'Connie,' he begged her again, but it was not enough either, and perhaps nothing would have been.

First, she said, in search of the Ginger Pig, little Otto trotted along to the various Franco-Soviet friendship societies that Kirov was known to frequent.

'That poor little Otto must have seen *The Battleship Potemkin* fifteen times, but the Ginger Pig never showed up once.'

Word came that Kirov was showing a serious interest in émigrés, and even representing himself as their secret sympathiser, enquiring whether, as a junior official, there was anything he could do to help their families in the Soviet Union. With Vladimir's help Leipzig tried to put himself in Kirov's path, but once more luck was against him. Then Kirov started travelling – travelling everywhere, my dear, a positive Flying Dutchman – so that Connie and her boys began to wonder whether he was some sort of clerical administrator for Moscow Centre, not on the operational side at all: the accountant-auditor for a group of Western residencies, for instance, with Paris as their centre – Bonn, Madrid, Stockholm, Vienna.

'For Karla or for the mainstream?' Smiley asked quietly.

Whisper who dares, said Connie, but for her money, it was for Karla. Even though Pudin was already there. Even though Kirov was an idiot, and not a soldier; it still *had* to be for Karla, Connie said, perversely doubling back upon her own assertions to the contrary. If Kirov had been visiting the mainstream residencies, he would have been entertained and put up by identified intelligence officers. But instead, he lived his cover, and stayed only with his national counterparts in the Commercial sections, she said.

Anyway, the flying did it, said Connie. Little Otto waited till Kirov had booked himself on a flight to Vienna, made sure he was travelling alone, then boarded the same flight, and they were in business.

'A straight copybook honey-trap, that's what we were aiming for,' Connie sang, very loud indeed. 'Your real old-fashioned burn. A big operator might laugh it off, but not Brother Kirov, least of all if he was on Karla's books. Naughty photographs and information with menaces, that was what we were after. And when we'd done with him, and found out what he was up to, and who his nasty friends were, and who was giving him all that heady freedom, we'd either buy him in as a defector or bung him back in the pond, depending on how much was left of him!'

She stopped dead. She opened her mouth, closed it, drew some breath, held out her glass to him.

'Darling, get the old soak another drinkie, double-quick, will you? Connie's getting her lurgies. No, don't. Stay where you are.'

For a fatal second, Smiley was lost.

'George?'

'Connie, I'm here! What is it?'

He was fast but not fast enough. He saw the stiffening of her face, he saw her distorted hands fly out in front of her, and her eyes screw up in disgust, as if she had seen a horrible accident.

'Hils, quick!' she cried. 'Oh, my hat!'

He embraced her and felt her forearms lock over the back of his neck to hold him tighter. Her skin was cold, she was shaking, but from terror not from chill. He stayed against her, smelling Scotch and medicated powder and old lady, trying to comfort her. Her tears were all over his cheeks, he could feel them and taste their salty sting as she pushed him away from her. He found her handbag and opened it for her, then went quickly back to the veranda and called to Hilary. She ran out of the darkness with her fists half clenched, elbows and hips rotating, in a way that makes men laugh. She hurried past him, grinning with shyness, and he stayed on the veranda, feeling the night cold pricking his cheeks while he stared at the gathering rain-clouds and the pine trees silvered by the rising moon. The dogs' screaming had subsided. Only the wheeling rooks sounded their harsh warnings. Go, he told himself. Get out of here. Bolt. His car waited not a hundred feet from him, frost already forming on the roof. He imagined himself leaping into it and driving up the hill, through the plantation, and away, never to return. But he knew he couldn't.

'She wants you back now, George,' Hilary said sternly from the doorway, with the special authority of those who nurse the dying.

But when he went back, everything was fine.

15

Everything was fine. Connie sat powdered and austere in her rocking-chair, and her eyes, as he entered, were as straight upon him as when he had first come here. Hilary had calmed her, Hilary had sobered her, and now Hilary stood behind her with her hands on Connie's neck, thumbs inward, while she gently massaged the nape.

'Spot of *timor mortis*, darling,' Connie explained. 'The leech prescribes Valium but the old fool prefers the juice. You won't mention that bit to Saul Enderby when you report back, will you, heart?'

'No, of course not.'

'When *will* you be reporting back, by the by, darling?'

'Soon,' said Smiley.

'Tonight, when you get home?'

'It depends what there is to tell.'

'Con did write it all *up*, you know, George. The old fool's accounts of the case were very *full*, I thought. Very *detailed*. Very *circumstantial*, for once. But you haven't consulted them.' Smiley said nothing. 'They're lost. Destroyed. Eaten by mealy-bugs. You haven't had time. Well, well. And you such a devil for the paperwork. *Higher*, Hils,' she ordered, without taking her gleaming eyes away from Smiley. 'Higher, darling. The bit where the vertebrae get stuck in the tonsils.'

Smiley sat down on the old wicker sofa.

'I used to love those double-double games,' Connie confessed dreamily, rolling her head in order to caress Hilary's hands with it. 'Didn't I, Hils? All human life was there. You wouldn't know that any more, would you? Not since you blew your gasket.'

She returned to Smiley. 'Want me to go on, dearie?' she asked in her East End tart's voice.

'If you could just take me through it briefly,' Smiley said. 'But not if it's—'

'Where were we? I know. Up in that aeroplane with the Ginger Pig. He's on his way to Vienna, he's got his trotters in a trough of beer. Looks up, and who does he see standing in front of him like his own bad conscience but his dear old buddy of twenty-five years ago, little Otto, grinning like Old Nick. What does Brother Kirov né Kursky *feel*? we ask ourselves, assuming he's got any feelings. Does Otto *know* – he wonders – that it was naughty me who sold him into the Gulag? So what does he do?'

'What does he do?' said Smiley, not responding to her banter.

'He decides to play it hearty, dearie. Doesn't he, Hils? Whistles up the caviar, and says "Thank God."' She whispered something and Hilary bent her head to catch it, then giggled. '"Champagne!" he says. And my God, they have it, and the Ginger Pig pays for it, and they drink it, and they share a taxi into town, and they even have a quick snifter in a café before the Ginger Pig goes about his furtive duties. Kirov *likes* Otto,' Connie insisted. '*Loves* him, doesn't he, Hils? They're a proper pair of raving whatsits, same as us. Otto's sexy, Otto's fun, Otto's dishy, and anti-authoritarian, and light on his feet – and – oh, everything the Ginger Pig could never be, not in a thousand years! Why did the fifth floor always think people had to have one motive only?'

'I'm sure I didn't,' said Smiley fervently.

But Connie was back talking to Hilary, not to Smiley at all. 'Kirov was *bored*, heart. Otto was life for him. Same as you are for me. You put the spring into my stride, don't you, lovey? Hadn't prevented him from shopping Otto, of course, but that's only Nature, isn't it?'

Still gently swaying at Connie's back, Hilary nodded in vague assent.

'And what did Kirov mean to Otto Leipzig?' Smiley asked.

'Hate, my darling,' Connie replied, without hesitation. 'Pure, undiluted hatred. Plain, honest-to-God, black loathing. Hate and money. Those were Otto's best two things. Otto always felt he was *owed* for all those years he'd spent in the slammer. He wanted to collect for the girl, too. His great dream was that one day he would sell Kirov né Kursky for lots of money. Lots and lots and *lots* of money. Then spend it.'

A waiter's anger, Smiley thought, remembering the contact print. Remembering the tartan room again, at the airport, and Otto's quiet German voice with its caressing edge; remembering his brown, unblinking eyes, that were like windows on his smouldering soul.

After the Vienna meeting, said Connie, the two men had agreed to meet again in Paris, and Otto wisely played a long hand. In Vienna, Otto had not asked a single question to which the Ginger Pig could take exception; Otto was a pro, said Connie. Was Kirov married? he had asked. Kirov had flung up his hands and roared with laughter at the question, indicating that he was prepared not to be at any time. *Married but wife in Moscow*, Otto had reported – which would make a honey-trap that

223

much more effective. Kirov had asked Leipzig what his job was these days, and Leipzig had replied magnanimously 'import-export', proposing himself as a bit of a wheeler-dealer, Vienna one day, Hamburg the next. In the event, Otto waited a whole month – after twenty-five years, said Connie, he could afford to take his time – and during that one month, Kirov was observed by the French to make three separate passes at elderly Paris-based Russian émigrés: one a taxi-driver, one a shopkeeper, one a restaurateur, all three with dependants in the Soviet Union. He offered to take letters, messages, addresses; he even offered to take money and, if they were not too bulky, gifts. And to operate a two-way service next time he returned. Nobody took him up. In the fifth week Otto rang Kirov at his flat, said he had just flown in from Hamburg, and suggested they had some fun. Over dinner, picking his moment, Otto said the night was on him; he had just made a big killing on a certain shipment to a certain country, and had money to burn.

'This was the bait we had worked out for him, darling,' Connie explained, addressing Smiley directly at last. 'And the Ginger Pig rose to it, didn't he, as they all do, don't they, bless them, salmon to the fly every time?'

What sort of shipment? Kirov had asked Otto. What sort of country? For reply, Leipzig had drawn in the air a hooked nose on the end of his own, and broken out laughing. Kirov laughed too, but he was clearly very interested. To *Israel*? he said; then what sort of shipment? Leipzig pointed his same forefinger at Kirov and pretended to pull a trigger. *Arms* to Israel? Kirov asked in amazement, but Leipzig was a pro and would say no more. They drank, went to a strip club, and talked old times. Kirov even referred to their shared girl-friend, asking whether Leipzig knew what had become of her. Leipzig said he didn't. In the early morning, Leipzig had proposed they pick up some company and take it to his flat, but Kirov, to his disappointment, refused: not in Paris, too dangerous. In Vienna or Hamburg, sure. But not in Paris. They parted, drunk, at breakfast time, and the Circus was a hundred pounds poorer.

'Then the bloody infighting started,' said Connie, suddenly changing track completely. 'The Great Head Office Debate, my arse. You were away, Saul Enderby put one manicured hoof in, and the rest of them promptly got the vapours – that's what happened.' Her baron's voice again: '"Otto Leipzig's taking us for a ride . . . We haven't cleared the operation with the Frogs . . . Foreign Office worried about implications . . . Kirov is a plant . . . the Riga Group a totally unsound base from which to make a ploy of this scale." Where were you, anyway? Beastly Berlin, wasn't it?'

'Hong Kong.'

'Oh, there,' she said vaguely, and slumped in her chair while her eyelids drooped.

Smiley had sent Hilary to make tea, and she was clanking dishes at the other end of the room. He glanced at her, wondering whether he should call her, and saw her standing exactly as he had last seen her in the Circus the night they sent for him – her knuckles backed against her mouth, suppressing a silent scream. He had been working late – it was about that time; yes, he was preparing his departure to Hong Kong – when suddenly his internal phone rang and he heard a man's voice, very strained, asking him to come immediately to the cipher room, Mr Smiley, sir, it's urgent. Moments later he was hurrying down a bare corridor, flanked by two worried janitors. They pushed open the door for him, he stepped inside, they hung back. He saw the smashed machinery, the files and card indices and telegrams flung around the room like rubbish at a football ground, he saw the filthy graffiti daubed in lipstick on the wall. And at the centre of it all, he saw Hilary herself, the culprit – exactly as she was now – staring through the thick net curtains at the free white sky outside: Hilary our Vestal, so well-bred; Hilary our Circus bride.

'Hell are you up to, Hils?' Connie demanded roughly from her rocking-chair.

'Making tea, Con. George wants a cup of tea.'

'To hell with what *George* wants,' she retorted, flaring. 'George is *fifth floor*. George put the kibosh on the Kirov case and now he's trying to get it right, flying solo in his old age. Right, George? Right? Even lied to me about that old devil Vladimir, who walked into a bullet on Hampstead Heath, according to the newspapers, which he apparently doesn't read, any more than my reports!'

They drank the tea. A rainstorm was getting up. The first hard drops were hammering on the wood roof.

Smiley had charmed her, Smiley had flattered her, Smiley had willed her to go on. She had drawn the thread half-way out for him. He was determined that she should draw it all the way.

'I've got to have it all, Con,' he repeated. 'I've got to hear everything, just as you remember it, even if the end is painful.'

'The end bloody well is painful,' she retorted.

But already her voice, her face, the very lustre of her memory were flagging, and he knew it was a race against time.

Now it was Kirov's turn to play the classic card, she said wearily. At their next meeting, which was in Brussels a month later, Kirov referred to the Israeli arms shipment thing and said he had happened to mention their conversation to a friend of his in the Commercial Section of the Embassy who was contributing to a special study of the Israeli military economy, and even had funds available for researching it. Would Leipzig consider – no, but seriously, Otto – talking to the fellow or, better still, giving the story to his old buddy Oleg here and now, who might even get a little credit for it on his own account? Otto said, 'Provided it pays and didn't hurt anyone.' Then he solemnly fed Kirov a bag of chickenfeed prepared by Connie and the Middle Eastern people – all of it true, of course, and eminently checkable, even if it wasn't a lot of use to anyone – and Kirov solemnly wrote it all down, though both of them, as Connie put it, knew perfectly well that neither Kirov nor his master, whoever that was, had the smallest interest in Israel, or shipments, or her military economy – not in *this* case, anyway. What Kirov was aiming to do was create a conspiratorial relationship, as their next meeting back in Paris showed. Kirov evinced huge enthusiasm for the report, insisted that Otto accept five hundred dollars for it, against the minor formality of signing a receipt. And when Otto had done this, and was squarely hooked, Kirov sailed straight in with all the crudity he could command – which was a lot, said Connie – and asked Otto how well placed he was with the local Russian émigrés.

'Please, Con,' he whispered. 'We're almost there!' She was so near but he could feel her drifting farther and farther away.

Hilary was lying on the floor with her head against Connie's knees. Absently, Connie's mittened hands had taken hold of her hair for comfort, and her eyes had fallen almost shut.

'Connie!' he repeated.

Opening her eyes, Connie gave a tired smile.

'It was only the fan dance, darling,' she said. 'The he-knows-I-know-you-know. The usual fan dance,' she repeated indulgently, and her eyes closed again.

'So how did Leipzig answer him? *Connie!*'

'He did what we'd do, darling,' she murmured. 'Stalled.

Admitted he was well in with the émigré groups, and hugger-mugger with the General. Then stalled. Said he didn't visit Paris that much. "Why not hire someone local?" he said. He was teasing, Hils, darling, you see. Asked again: Would it hurt anyone? Asked what the job was, anyway? What did it pay? Get me some booze, Hils.'

'No,' said Hilary.

'Get it.'

Smiley poured two fingers of whisky and watched her sip.

'What did Kirov want Otto to do with the émigrés?' he said.

'Kirov wanted a legend,' she replied. 'He wanted a legend for a girl.'

Nothing in Smiley's manner suggested he had heard the phrase from Toby Esterhase only a few hours ago. Four years ago, Oleg Kirov wanted a legend, Connie repeated. Just as the Sandman, according to Toby and the General – thought Smiley – wanted one today. Kirov wanted a cover story for a female agent who could be infiltrated into France. That was the nub of it, Connie said. Kirov didn't say this, of course; he put it quite differently, in fact. He told Otto that Moscow had issued a secret instruction to all Embassies announcing their split Russian families might in certain circumstances be reunited abroad. If enough families could be found who wished it, said the instruction, then Moscow would go public with the idea and thus enhance the Soviet Union's image in the field of human rights. Ideally, they wanted cases with a compassionate ring: daughters in Russia, say, cut off from their families in the West, single girls, perhaps of marriageable age. Secrecy was essential, said Kirov, until a list of suitable cases had been assembled – think of the outcry there would be, Kirov said, if the story leaked ahead of time!

The Ginger Pig made his pitch so badly, said Connie, that Otto had at first to deride the proposal simply for the sake of verisimilitude: it was too crazy, too hole-in-corner, he said – secret lists, what nonsense! Why didn't Kirov approach the émigré organisations themselves and swear them to secrecy? Why employ a total outsider to do his dirty work? As Leipzig teased, Kirov grew more heated. It was not Leipzig's job to make fun of Moscow's secret edicts, said Kirov. He began shouting at him, and somehow Connie discovered the energy to shout too, or at least to lift her voice above its weary level, and to give it the guttural Russian ring she thought Kirov ought to have: '"Where is your compassion?" he says. "Don't you want to help people? Why do you sneer at a human gesture merely because it comes from Russia!"' Kirov said he had approached some families himself, but found no trust, and made no headway. He began to put pressure on Leipzig, first of a personal kind – 'Don't you want to help me in my career?' – and when this failed, he suggested to Leipzig that since he had already supplied secret information to the Embassy for money, he might consider it prudent to continue, lest the West German authorities somehow got to hear of this connection and threw him out of Hamburg – maybe out of Germany altogether. How would Otto like that? And finally, said Connie, Kirov offered money, and that was where the wonder lay. 'For each successful reunion effected, ten thousand US dollars,' she announced. 'For each suitable candidate, whether a reunion takes place or not, one thousand US on the nail. Cash-cash.'

At which point, of course, said Connie, the fifth floor decided Kirov was off his head, and ordered the case abandoned immediately.

'And I returned from the Far East,' said Smiley.

'Like poor King Richard from the Crusades, you did,

darling!' Connie agreed. '*And* found the peasants in uproar and your nasty brother on the throne. Serves you right.' She gave a gigantic yawn. 'Case dustbinned,' she declared. 'The Kraut police wanted Leipzig extradited from France; we could perfectly well have begged them off but we didn't. No honey-trap, no dividend, no bugger-all. Fixture cancelled.'

'And how did Vladimir take all that?' Smiley asked, as if he really didn't know.

Connie opened her eyes with difficulty. 'Take what?'

'Cancelling the fixture.'

'Oh, *roared*, what do you expect? Roar, roar. Said we'd spoilt the kill of the century. Swore to continue the war by other means.'

'What *kind* of kill?'

She missed his question. 'It's not a *shooting* war any more, George,' she said, as her eyes closed again. 'That's the trouble. It's grey. Half-angels fighting half-devils. No one knows where the lines are. No bang-bangs.'

Once again, Smiley in his memory saw the tartan hotel bedroom and the two black overcoats side by side, as Vladimir appealed desperately to have the case reopened: 'Max, hear us one more time, hear what has happened since you ordered us to stop!' They had flown from Paris at their own expense to tell him, because Finance Section on Enderby's orders had closed the case account. 'Max, hear us, please,' Vladimir had begged. 'Kirov summoned Otto to his apartment late last night. They had another meeting, Otto and Kirov. Kirov got drunk and said amazing things!'

He saw himself back in his old room at the Circus, Enderby already installed in his desk. It was the same day, just a few hours later.

'Sounds like little Otto's last-ditch effort at keeping out of the hands of the Huns,' Enderby said when he had heard Smiley out. 'What do they want him for over there, theft or rape?'

'Fraud,' Smiley had replied hopelessly, which was the wretched truth.

Connie was humming something. She tried to make a song of it, then a limerick. She wanted more drink but Hilary had taken away her glass.

'I want you to go,' Hilary said, straight into Smiley's face.

Leaning forward on the wicker sofa, Smiley asked his last question. He asked it, one might have thought, reluctantly; almost with distaste. His soft face had hardened with determination, but not enough to conceal the marks of disapproval. 'Do you remember a story old Vladimir used to tell, Con? One we never shared with anyone? Stored away, as a piece of private treasure? That Karla had a mistress, someone he loved?'

'His Ann,' she said dully.

'That in all the world, she was his one thing, that she made him act like a crazy man?'

Slowly her head came up, and he saw her face clear, and his voice quickened and gathered strength.

'How that was the rumour they passed around in Moscow Centre – those in the know? Karla's invention – his creation, Con? How he found her when she was a child, wandering in a burnt-out village in the war? Adopted her, brought her up, fell in love with her?'

He watched her and despite the whisky, despite her deathly weariness, he saw the last excitement, like the last drop in the bottle, slowly rekindle her features.

'He was behind the German lines,' she said. 'It was the forties. There was a team of them, raising the Balts. Building networks, stay-behind groups. It was a big operation. Karla was boss. She became their mascot. They carted her from pillar to post. A kid. Oh, George!'

He was holding his breath to catch her words. The din on the roof grew louder. His face was near to hers, very; its animation matched her own.

'And then what?' he said.

'Then he bumped her off, darling. That's what.'

'Why?' He drew still closer, as if he feared her words might fail her at the crucial moment. '*Why*, Connie? Why kill her when he loved her?'

'He'd done everything for her. Found foster-parents for her. Educated her. Had her all got up to be his ideal hag. Played Daddy, played lover, played God. She was his toy. Then one day she ups and gets ideas above her station.'

'What sort of ideas?'

'Soft on revolution. Mixing with bloody intellectuals. Wanting the State to wither away. Asking the big "Why?" and the big "Why not?" He told her to shut up. She wouldn't. She had a devil in her. He had her shoved in the slammer. Made her worse.'

'And there was a child,' Smiley prompted, taking her mittened hand in both of his. 'He gave her a child, remember?' Her hand was between them, between their faces. 'You researched it, didn't you, Con? One silly season, I gave you your head. "Track it down, Con," I said to you. "Take it wherever it leads." Remember?'

Under Smiley's intense encouragement, her story had acquired the fervour of a last love. She was speaking fast, eyes streaming. She was backtracking, zigzagging everywhere in her memory. Karla had this hag . . . yes, darling, that was the story, do you hear me? – Yes, Connie, go on, I hear you. Then listen. He brought her up, made her his mistress, there was a brat, and the quarrels were about the brat. George, darling, do you love me like the old days? – Come on, Con, give me the rest, yes of course I do. – He accused her of warping its precious mind with dangerous ideas, like freedom for instance. Or love. A girl, her mother's image, said to be a beauty. In the end the old despot's love turned to hatred and he had his ideal carted off and spavined: end of story. We had it from Vladimir first, then a few scraps, never the hard base. Name unknown, darling, because he destroyed all records of her, killed whoever might have heard, which is Karla's way, bless him, isn't it, darling, always was? Others said she wasn't dead at all, the story of her murder was disinformation to end the trail. There, she did it, didn't she? The old fool remembered!

'And the child?' Smiley asked. 'The child in her mother's image? There was a defector's report – what was *that* about?' She didn't pause. She had remembered that as well, her mind was galloping ahead of her, just as her voice was outrunning her breath.

A don of some sort from Leningrad University, said Connie. Claimed he'd been ordered to take on a weird girl for special political instruction in the evenings, a sort of private patient who was showing anti-social tendencies, the daughter of a high official. Tatiana, he was only allowed to know her as Tatiana. She'd been raising hell all over town, but her father was a big beef in Moscow and she couldn't be touched. The girl tried to seduce him, probably did, then told him some story about how Daddy had had Mummy killed for showing insufficient faith in the historical process. Next day his professor called him in and said if he ever repeated a word of what had happened at that interview, he would find himself tripping on a very big banana skin . . .

Connie ran on wildly, describing clues that led nowhere, the sources that vanished at the moment of discovery. It seemed impossible that her racked and drink-sodden body could have once more summoned so much strength.

'Oh, George, darling, take me with you! That's what you're after, I've got it! Who killed Vladimir, and why! I saw it in your ugly face the moment you walked in. I couldn't place it, now I can. You've got your Karla look! Vladi had opened up the vein again, so Karla had him killed! That's your banner, George. I can see you marching. Take me with you, George, for God's sake! I'll leave Hils, I'll leave anything, no more of the juice, I swear. Get me up to London and I'll find his hag for you, even if she doesn't exist, if it's the last thing I do!'

'Why did Vladimir call him the Sandman?' Smiley asked, knowing the answer already.

'It was his joke. A German fairy tale Vladi picked up in Estonia from one of his Kraut forebears. "Karla is our Sandman. Anyone who comes too close to him has a way of falling asleep." We never knew, darling, how could we? In the Lubianka, someone had met a man who'd met a woman who'd met her. Someone else knew someone who'd helped to bury her. That hag was Karla's shrine, George. And she betrayed him. Twin cities, we used to say you were, you and Karla, two halves of the same apple. George, darling, don't! Please!'

She had stopped, and he realised that she was staring up at him in fear, that her face was somehow beneath his own; he was standing, glaring down at her. Hilary was against the wall, calling 'Stop, stop!' He was standing over her, incensed by her cheap and unjust comparison, knowing that neither Karla's methods nor Karla's absolutism were his own. He heard himself say '*No, Connie!*' and discovered that he had lifted his hands to the level of his chest, palms downward and rigid, as if he were pressing something into the ground. And he realised his passion had scared her; that he had never betrayed so much conviction to her – or so much feeling – before.

'I'm getting old,' he muttered, and gave a sheepish smile.

He relaxed, and as he did so, slowly Connie's own body became limp also, and the dream died in her. The hands which had clutched him seconds earlier lay on her lap like bodies in a trench.

'It was all bilge,' she said sullenly. A deep and terminal listlessness descended over her. 'Bored émigrés, crying into their vodka. Drop it, George. Karla's beaten you all ends up. He foxed you, he made a fool of your time. *Our* time.' She drank, no longer caring what she said. Her head flopped forward again and for a moment he thought she really was asleep. 'He foxed *you*, he foxed *me*, and when you smelt a rat he got Bloody Bill Haydon to fox Ann and put you off the scent.' With difficulty she lifted her head to stare at him one more time. 'Go home, George. Karla won't give you back your past. Be like the old fool here. Get yourself a bit of love and wait for Armageddon.'

She began coughing again, hopelessly, one hacking retch after another.

The rain had stopped. Gazing out of the French windows, Smiley saw again the moonlight on the cages, touching the frost on the wire; he saw the frosted crowns of the fir trees climbing the hill into a black sky; he saw a world reversed, with the light things darkened into shadow, and the dark things picked out like beacons on the white ground. He saw a sudden moon, stepping clear before the clouds, beckoning him into seething crevices. He saw one black figure in Wellington boots and a headscarf running up the lane, and realised it was Hilary; she must have slipped out without his noticing. He remembered he had heard a door slam. He went back to Connie and sat on the sofa beside her. Connie wept and drifted, talking about love. Love was a positive power, she said vaguely – ask Hils. But Hilary was not there to ask. Love was a stone thrown into the water, and if there were enough stones and we all loved together, the ripples would eventually be strong enough to reach across the sea and overwhelm the haters and the cynics – 'even beastly Karla, darling,' she assured him. 'That's what Hils says. Bilge, isn't it? It's bilge, Hils!' she yelled.

Then Connie closed her eyes again, and after a while, by the breathing, appeared to doze off. Or perhaps she was only pretending in order to avoid the pain of saying goodbye to him. He tiptoed into the cold evening. The car's engine, by a miracle, started; he began climbing the lane, keeping a look-out for Hilary. He rounded a bend and saw her in the headlights. She was cowering among the trees, waiting for him to leave before she went back to Connie. She had had her hands to her face again and he thought he saw blood; perhaps she had scratched herself with her fingernails. He passed her and saw her in the mirror, staring after him in the glow of his rear lights, and for a moment she resembled for him all those muddy ghosts who are the real victims of conflict: who lurch out of the smoke of war, battered and starved and deprived of all they ever had or loved. He waited until he saw her start down the hill again, towards the lights of the *dacha*.

At Heathrow airport he bought his air ticket for the next morning, then lay on his bed in the hotel, for all he knew the same one, though the walls were not tartan. All night long the hotel stayed awake, and Smiley with it. He heard the clank of plumbing and the ringing of phones and the thud of lovers who would not or could not sleep.

Max, hear us one more time, he rehearsed; *it was the Sandman himself who sent Kirov to the émigrés to find the legend.*

16

Smiley arrived in Hamburg in mid-morning and took the airport bus to the city centre. Fog lingered and the day was very cold. In the Station Square, after repeated rejections, he found an old, thin terminus hotel with a lift licensed for three persons at a time. He signed in as Standfast, then walked as far as a car-rental agency, where he hired a small Opel, which he parked in an underground garage that played softened Beethoven out of loudspeakers. The car was his back door. He didn't know whether he would need it, but he knew it needed to be there. He walked again, heading for the Alster, sensing everything with a particular sharpness: the manic traffic, the toy-shops for millionaire children. The din of the city hit him like a fire-storm, causing him to forget the cold. Germany was his second nature, even his second soul. In his youth, her literature had been his passion and his discipline. He could put on her language like a uniform and speak with its boldness. Yet he sensed danger in every step he took, for Smiley as a young man had spent half the war here in the lonely terror of the spy, and the awareness of being on enemy territory was lodged in him for good. In boyhood he had known Hamburg as a rich and graceful shipping town, which hid its volatile soul behind a cloak of Englishness; in manhood as a city smashed into medieval darkness by thousand-bomber air raids. He had seen it in the first years of peace, one endless smouldering bomb-site and the survivors tilling the rubble like fields. And he saw it today, hurtling into the anonymity of canned music, high-rise concrete and smoked glass.

Reaching the sanctuary of the Alster he walked the pleasant footpath to the jetty where Villem had boarded the steamer. On weekdays, he recorded, the first ferry was at 7.10, the last at 20.15, and Villem had been here on a weekday. There was a steamer due in fifteen minutes. Waiting for it, he watched the sculls and the red squirrels much as Villem had done, and when the steamer arrived he sat in the stern where Villem had sat, in the open air under the canopy. His companions consisted of a crowd of schoolchildren and three nuns. He sat with his eyes almost closed by the dazzle, listening to their chatter. Half-way across, he stood, walked through the cabins to the forward window, looked out, apparently to confirm something, glanced at his watch, then returned to his seat until the Jungfernstieg, where he landed.

Villem's story tallied. Smiley had not expected otherwise, but in a world of perpetual doubt, reassurance never came amiss.

He lunched then went to the main Post Office and studied old telephone directories for an hour, much as Ostrakova had done in Paris, though for different reasons. His researches complete, he settled himself gratefully in the lounge of the Four Seasons Hotel and read newspapers till dusk.

In a Hamburg guide to houses of pleasure, the Blue Diamond was not listed under night-clubs but under 'amour' and earned three stars for exclusivity and cost. It was situated in St Pauli, but discreetly apart from the main beat, in a cobbled alley that was tilted and dark and smelt of fish. Smiley rang the doorbell and it opened on an electric switch. He stepped inside and stood at once in a trim ante-room filled with grey machinery manned by a smart young man in a grey suit. On the walls, grey reels of tape turned slowly, though the music they played was mostly somewhere else. On the desk an elaborate telephone system, also grey, flickered and ticked.

'I should like to pass some time here,' Smiley said.

This is where they answered my phone call, he thought, when I telephoned Vladimir's Hamburg correspondent.

The smart young man drew a printed form from his desk and in a confiding murmur explained the procedure, much as a lawyer would, which possibly was his daytime profession anyway. Membership cost one hundred and seventy-five marks, he said softly. This was a one-time annual subscription entitling Smiley to enter free for a full year, as many times as he wished. The first drink would cost him a further twenty-five marks and thereafter prices were high but not unreasonable. A first drink was obligatory and, like the membership fee, payable before entry. All other forms of entertainment came without charge, though the girls received gifts appreciatively. Smiley should complete the form in whatever name he wished. It would be filed here by the young man personally. All he had to do on his next visit was remember the name under which he had joined and he would be admitted without formalities.

Smiley put down his money and added one more false name to the dozens he had used in his lifetime. He descended a staircase to a second door which once more opened electronically, revealing a narrow passage giving on to a row of cubicles, still empty because in that world the night was only now beginning. At the end of the passage stood a third door and, once through it, he entered total darkness filled with the full blast of the music from the smart young man's tape-recorders.

A male voice spoke to him, a pin-light led him to a table. He was handed a list of drinks. 'Proprietor C. Kretzschmar', he read at the foot of the page in small print. He ordered whisky.

'I wish to remain alone. No company.'

'I shall advise the house, sir,' the waiter said with confiding dignity, and accepted his tip.

'Concerning Herr Kretzschmar. He is from Saxony, by any chance?'

'Yes, sir.'

Worse than East German, Toby Esterhase had said. *Saxon. They stole together, pimped together, faked reports together. It was a perfect marriage.*

He sipped his whisky, waiting for his eyes to grow accustomed to the light. From somewhere a blue glow shone, picking out cuffs and collars eerily. He saw white faces and white bodies. There were two levels. The lower, where he sat, was furnished with tables and armchairs. The upper consisted of six *chambres séparées*, like boxes at the theatre, each with its own blue glow. It was in one of these, he decided, that, knowingly or not, the quartet had posed for its photograph. He recalled the angle from which the picture had been taken. It was from above – from well above. But 'well above' meant somewhere in the blackness of the upper walls where no eye could penetrate, not even Smiley's.

The music died and over the same speakers a cabaret was announced. The title, said the *compère*, was Old Berlin, and the *compère*'s voice was also Old Berlin: hectoring, nasal and suggestive. The smart young man has changed the tape, thought Smiley. A curtain lifted revealing a small stage. By the light it released, he peered quickly upward again and this time saw what he was looking for: a small observation window of smoked glass set very high in the wall. The photographer used special cameras, he thought vaguely; these days, he had been told, darkness was no longer a hindrance. I should have asked Toby, he thought; Toby knows those gadgets by heart. On the stage, a demonstration of lovemaking had begun, mechanical, pointless, dispiriting. Smiley turned his attention to his fellow members scattered round the room. The girls were beautiful and naked and young, in the way the girls in the photograph were young. Those who had partners sat entwined with them, seemingly delighted by their senility and ugliness. Those who had none sat in a silent group like American footballers waiting to be called. The noise from the speakers grew very loud, a mixture of music and hysterical narrative. And in Berlin they are playing Old Hamburg, Smiley thought. On the stage the couple increased their efforts, but to little account. Smiley wondered whether he would recognise the girls in the photographs if they should appear. He decided he would not. The curtain closed. He ordered another whisky in relief.

'Is Herr Kretzschmar in the house tonight?' he asked the waiter.

Herr Kretzschmar was a man of commitments, the waiter explained. Herr Kretzschmar was obliged to divide his time between several establishments.

'If he comes, have the goodness to let me know.'

'He will be here at eleven exactly, sir.'

At the bar, naked couples had begun dancing. He endured another half-hour of this before returning to the front office by way of the cubicles, some of which were now occupied. The smart young man asked whom he might announce.

'Tell him it's a special request,' Smiley said.

The smart young man pressed a button and spoke extremely quietly, much as he had spoken to Smiley.

The upstairs office was clean as a doctor's surgery with a polished plastic desk and a lot more machinery. A closed-circuit television supplied a daylight version of the scene downstairs. The same observation window that Smiley had already noticed looked down into the *séparées*. Herr Kretzschmar was what the Germans call a serious person. He was fiftyish, groomed and thickset, with a dark suit and pale tie. His hair was straw blond like a good Saxon's, his bland face neither welcomed nor rejected. He shook Smiley's hand briskly and motioned him to a chair. He seemed well accustomed to dealing with special requests.

'Please,' Herr Kretzschmar said, and the preliminaries were over.

There was nowhere to go but forward.

'I understand you were once business partner to an acquaintance of mine named Otto Leipzig,' Smiley said, sounding a little too loud to himself. 'I happen to be visiting Hamburg and I wondered whether you could tell me where he is. His address does not appear to be listed anywhere.'

Herr Kretzschmar's coffee was in a silver pot with a paper napkin round the handle to protect his fingers when he poured. He drank and put his cup down carefully, to avoid collision.

'Who are you, please?' Herr Kretzschmar asked. The Saxon twang made his voice flat. A small frown enhanced his air of respectability.

'Otto called me Max,' Smiley said.

Herr Kretzschmar did not respond to this information but he took his time before putting his next question. His gaze, Smiley noticed again, was strangely innocent. *Otto never had a house in his life*, Toby had said. *For crash meetings, Kretzschmar played key-holder*.

'And your business with Herr Leipzig, if I may ask?'

'I represent a large company,' Smiley said. 'Among other

interests, we own a literary and photographic agency for free-lance reporters.'

'So?'

'In the distant past, my parent company has been pleased to accept occasional offerings from Herr Leipzig – through intermediaries – and pass them out to our customers for processing and syndication.'

'So?' Herr Kretzschmar repeated. His head lifted slightly, but his expression had not altered.

'Recently the business relationship between my parent company and Herr Leipzig was revived.' He paused lightly. 'Initially by means of the telephone,' he said, but Herr Kretzschmar might never have heard of the telephone. 'Through intermediaries again, he sent us a sample of his work which we were pleased to place for him. I came here to discuss terms and to commission further work. Assuming of course that Herr Leipzig is in a position to provide it.'

'Of what nature was this work, please – that Herr Leipzig sent you – please, Herr Max?'

'It was a negative photograph of erotic content. My firm always insists on negatives. Herr Leipzig knew this, naturally.' Smiley pointed carefully across the room. 'I rather think it must have been taken from that window. A peculiarity of the photograph is that Herr Leipzig himself was modelling in it. One therefore assumes that a friend or business partner may have operated the camera.'

Herr Kretzschmar's blue gaze remained as direct and innocent as before. His face, though strangely unmarked, struck Smiley as courageous, but he didn't know why.

You're messing around with a creep like Leipzig, then you better have a creep like me to look after you, Toby had said.

'There is another aspect,' Smiley said.

'Yes?'

'Unhappily the gentleman who was acting as intermediary on this occasion met with a serious accident shortly after the negative was put into our care. The usual line of communication with Herr Leipzig was therefore severed.'

Herr Kretzschmar did not conceal his anxiety. A frown of what seemed to be genuine concern clouded his smooth face and he spoke quite sharply.

'How so an accident? What sort of accident?'

'A fatal one. I came to warn Otto and talk to him.'

Herr Kretzschmar owned a fine gold pencil. Taking it deliberately from an inside pocket he popped out the point and, still frowning, drew a pure circle on the pad before him. Then he set a cross on top, then he drew a line through his creation, then he tutted and said 'Pity,' and when he had done all this he straightened up, and spoke tersely into a machine. 'No disturbances,' he said. In a murmur, the voice of the grey receptionist acknowledged the instruction.

'You said Herr Leipzig was an old acquaintance of your parent company?' Herr Kretzschmar resumed.

'As I believe you yourself were, long ago, Herr Kretzschmar.'

'Please explain this more closely,' Herr Kretzschmar said, turning the pencil slowly in both hands as if studying the quality of the gold.

'We are talking old history, of course,' said Smiley deprecatingly.

'This I understand.'

'When Herr Leipzig first escaped from Russia he came to Schleswig-Holstein,' Smiley said. 'The organisation which had arranged his escape was based in Paris, but as a Balt, he preferred to live in northern Germany. Germany was still occupied and it was difficult for him to make a living.'

'For anyone,' Herr Kretzschmar corrected him. 'For anyone at all to make a living. Those were fantastically hard times. The young of today have no idea.'

'None,' Smiley agreed. 'And they were particularly hard for refugees. Whether they came from Estonia or from Saxony, life was hard for them.'

'This is absolutely correct. The refugees had it worst. Please continue.'

'In those days there was a considerable industry in information. Of all kinds. Military, industrial, political, economic. The victorious powers were prepared to pay large sums of money for enlightening material about each other. My parent company was involved in this commerce, and kept a representative here whose task was to collect such material and pass it back to London. Herr Leipzig and his partner became occasional clients. On a freelance basis.'

News of the General's fatal accident notwithstanding, a swift and most unexpected smile passed like a breeze across the surface of Herr Kretzschmar's features.

'Free lance,' he said, as if he liked the words, and was new to them. 'Free lance,' he repeated. 'That's what we were.'

'Such relationships are naturally of a temporary nature,' Smiley continued. 'But Herr Leipzig, being a Balt, had other interests and continued over a long period to correspond with my firm through intermediaries in Paris.' He paused. 'Notably a certain General. A few years ago, following a dispute, the General was obliged to move to London, but Otto kept in touch with him. And the General on his side remained the intermediary.'

'Until his accident,' Herr Kretzschmar put in.

'Precisely,' Smiley said.

'It was a traffic accident? An old man – a bit careless?'

'He was shot,' said Smiley and saw Herr Kretzschmar's face once more wince with displeasure. 'But murdered,' Smiley added, as if to reassure him. 'It wasn't suicide or an accident or anything like that.'

'Naturally,' said Herr Kretzschmar, and offered Smiley a cigarette. Smiley declined, so he lit one for himself, took a few puffs, and stubbed it out. His pale complexion was a shade paler.

'You have met Otto? You know him?' Herr Kretzschmar asked in the tone of one making light conversation.

'I have met him once.'

'Where?'

'I am not at liberty to say.'

Herr Kretzschmar frowned, but in perplexity rather than disapproval.

'Tell me, please. If your parent company – okay, London – wanted to reach Herr Leipzig directly, what steps did it take?' Herr Kretzschmar asked.

'There was an arrangement involving the *Hamburger Abendblatt*.'

'And if they wished to contact him very urgently?'

'There was you.'

'You are police?' Herr Kretzschmar asked quietly. 'Scotland Yard?'

'No.' Smiley stared at Herr Kretzschmar and Herr Kretzschmar returned his gaze.

'Have you brought me something?' Herr Kretzschmar asked. At a loss, Smiley did not immediately reply. 'Such as a letter of introduction? A card, for instance?'

'No.'

'Nothing to show? That's a pity.'

'Perhaps when I have seen him, I shall understand your question better.'

'But you have seen it evidently, this photograph? You have it with you, maybe?'

Smiley took out his wallet, and passed the contact print across the desk. Holding it by the edges, Herr Kretzschmar studied it for a moment, but only by way of confirmation, then laid it on the plastic surface before him. As he did so, Smiley's sixth sense told him that Herr Kretzschmar was about to make a statement, in the way that Germans sometimes do make statements – whether of philosophy, or personal exculpation, or in order to be liked, or pitied. He began to suspect that Herr Kretzschmar, in his own estimation at least, was a companionable if misunderstood man; a man of heart; even a good man; and that his initial taciturnity was something he wore like a professional suit, reluctantly, in a world which he frequently found unsympathetic to his affectionate character:

'I wish to explain to you that I run a decent house here,' Herr Kretzschmar remarked, when he had once more, by the clinical modern lamp, glanced at the print on his desk. 'I am not in the habit of photographing clients. Other people sell ties, I sell sex. The important thing to me is to conduct my business in an orderly and correct manner. But this was not business. This was friendship.'

Smiley had the wisdom to keep silent.

Herr Kretzschmar frowned. His voice dropped and became confiding: 'You knew him, Herr Max? That old General? You were personally connected with him?'

'Yes.'

'He was something, I understand?'

'He was indeed.'

'A lion, huh?'

'A lion.'

'Otto is still crazy about him. My name is Claus. "Claus,"

he would say to me. "That Vladimir, I love that man." You follow me? Otto is a very loyal fellow. The General too?'

'He was,' said Smiley.

'A lot of people do not believe in Otto. Your parent company also, they do not always believe in him. This is understandable. I make no reproach. But the General, he believed in Otto. Not in every detail. But in the big things.' Holding up his forearm, Herr Kretzschmar clenched his fist and it was suddenly a very big fist indeed. 'When things got hard, the old General believed in Otto absolutely. I too believe in Otto, Herr Max. In the big things. But I am German, I am not political, I am a businessman. These refugee stories are finished for me. You follow me?'

'Of course.'

'But not for Otto. Never. Otto is a fanatic. I can use that word. Fanatic. This is one reason why our lives have diverged. Nevertheless he is my friend. Anyone harms him, they get a bad time from Kretzschmar.' His face clouded in momentary mystification. 'You are sure you have nothing for me, Herr Max?'

'Beyond the photograph, I have nothing for you.'

Reluctantly Herr Kretzschmar once more dismissed the matter, but it took him time; he was uneasy.

'The old General was shot in England?' he asked finally.

'Yes.'

'But you consider nevertheless that Otto too is in danger?'

'Yes, but I think he has chosen to be.'

Herr Kretzschmar was pleased with this answer and nodded energetically twice.

'So do I. I also. This is my clear impression of him. I told him many times: "Otto, you should have been a high-wire acrobat." To Otto, in my opinion, no day is worth living unless it threatens on at least six separate occasions to be his last. You permit me to make certain observations on my relationship with Otto?'

'Please,' said Smiley politely.

Putting his forearms on the plastic surface, Herr Kretzschmar settled himself into a more comfortable posture for confession.

'There was a time when Otto and Claus Kretzschmar did everything together – stole a lot of horses, as we say. I was from Saxony, Otto came from the East. A Balt. Not Russia – he would insist – Estonia. He had had a tough time, studied the interior of a good few prisons, some bad fellow had betrayed him back in Estonia. A girl had died, and he was pretty mad about that. There was an uncle near Kiel but he was a swine. I may say that. We had no money, we were comrades and fellow thieves. This was normal, Herr Max.'

Smiley acknowledged the instructive point.

'One of our lines of business was to sell information. You have said correctly that information was a valuable commodity in those days. For example, we would hear of a refugee who had just come over and had not yet been interviewed by the Allies. Or maybe a Russian deserted. Or the master of a cargo ship. We hear about him, we question him. If we are ingenious, we contrive to sell the same report in different versions to two or even three different buyers. The Americans, the French, the British. The Germans themselves, already back in the saddle, yes. Sometimes, as long as it was inaccurate, even *five* buyers.' He gave a rich laugh. 'But only if it was inaccurate, okay? On other occasions, when we were out of sources, we invented – no question. We had maps, good imagination, good contacts. Don't misunderstand me: Kretzschmar is an enemy of Communism. We are talking old history, like you said, Herr Max. It was necessary to survive. Otto had the idea,

Kretzschmar did the work. Otto was not the inventor of work, I would say.' Herr Kretzschmar frowned. 'But in one respect Otto was a very serious man. He had a debt to settle. Of this he spoke repeatedly. Maybe against the fellow who betrayed him and killed his girl, maybe against the whole human race. What do I know? He had to be active. Politically active. So for this purpose he went to Paris, on many occasions. Many.'

Herr Kretzschmar allowed himself a short period of reflection.

'I shall be frank,' he announced.

'And I shall respect your confidence,' said Smiley.

'I believe you. You are Max. The General was your friend, Otto told me this. Otto met you once, he admired you. Very well. I shall be frank with you. Many years ago Otto Leipzig went to prison for me. In those days I was not respectable. Now that I have money I can afford to be. We stole something, he was caught, he lied and took the whole rap. I wanted to pay him. He said, "What the hell? If you are Otto Leipzig, a year in prison is a holiday." I visited him every week, I bribed the guards to take him special food – even once a woman. When he came out, I again tried to pay him. He declined my offers. "One day I'll ask you something," he said. "Maybe your wife." "You shall have her," I told him. "No problem." Herr Max, I assume you are an Englishman. You will appreciate my position.'

Smiley said he did.

'Two months ago – what do I know, maybe more, maybe less – the old General comes through on the telephone. He needs Otto urgently. "Not tomorrow, but tonight." Sometimes he used to call that way from Paris, using code-names, all this nonsense. The old General is a secretive fellow. So is Otto. Like children, know what I mean? Never mind.'

Herr Kretzschmar made an indulgent sweep of his big hand

across his face, as if he were wiping away a cobweb. '"Listen," I tell him. "I don't know where Otto is. Last time I heard of him, he was in bad trouble with some business he started. I've got to find him, it will take time. Maybe tomorrow, maybe ten days." Then the old man tells me, "I sent you a letter for him. Guard it with your life." Next day a letter comes, express for Kretzschmar, postmark London. Inside, a second envelope. "Urgent and top secret for Otto." *Top Secret*, okay? So the old guy's crazy. Never mind. You know that big handwriting of his, strong like an army order?'

Smiley did.

'I find Otto. He's hiding from trouble again, no money. One suit he's got, but dresses like a film star. I give him the old man's letter.'

'Which is a fat one,' Smiley suggested, thinking of the seven pages of photocopy paper. Thinking of Mikhel's black machine parked like an old tank in the library.

'Sure. A long letter. He opened it while I was there—'

Herr Kretzschmar broke off and stared at Smiley and from his expression seemed, reluctantly, to recognise a restraint.

'A long letter,' he repeated. 'Many pages. He read it, he got pretty excited. "Claus," he said. "Lend me some money. I got to go to Paris." I lend him some money, five hundred marks, no problem. After this I don't see him much for a time. A couple of occasions he comes here, makes a phone call. I don't listen. Then a month ago he came to see me.' Again he broke off, and again Smiley felt his restraint. 'I am being frank,' he said, as if once again enjoining Smiley to secrecy. 'He was – well, I would say excited.'

'He wanted to use the night-club,' Smiley suggested helpfully.

'"Claus," he said. "Do what I ask and you have paid your

debt to me." He called it a honey-trap. He would bring a man to the club, an Ivan, someone he knew well, had been cultivating for many years, he said, a very particular swine. This man was the target. He called him "the target". He said it was the chance of his life, everything he had waited for. The best girls, the best champagne, the best show. For one night, courtesy of Kretzschmar. The climax of his efforts, he said. The chance to pay old debts and make some money as well. He was owed, he said. Now he would collect. He promised there would be no repercussions. I said "No problem." "Also, Claus, I wish you to photograph us," he tells me. I said "No problem" again. So he came. And brought his target.'

Herr Kretzschmar's narrative had suddenly become uncharacteristically sparse. In the hiatus, Smiley slipped in a question, of which the purpose went far beyond the context: 'What language did they speak?'

Herr Kretzschmar hesitated, frowned, but finally answered: 'At first his target pretended to be French, but the girls did not speak much French so he spoke German to them. But with Otto he spoke Russian. He was disagreeable, this target. Smelt a lot, sweated a lot, and was in certain other ways not a gentleman. The girls did not like to stay with him. They came to me and complained. I sent them back but they still grumbled.'

He seemed embarrassed.

'Another small question,' said Smiley, as the awkwardness returned.

'Please.'

'How could Otto Leipzig promise there would be no repercussions since he was presumably setting out to blackmail this man?'

'The target was not the *end*,' Herr Kretzschmar said, pursing his lips to assist the intellectual point. 'He was the means.'

'The means to someone else?'

'Otto was not precise. "A step on the General's ladder," was his expression. "For me, Claus, the target is enough. The target and afterwards the money. But for the General, he is only a step on the ladder. For Max also." For reasons I did not understand, the money was also dependent upon the General's satisfaction. Or perhaps yours.' He paused, as if hoping Smiley might enlighten him. Smiley did not. 'It was not my wish to ask questions or make conditions,' Herr Kretzschmar continued, picking his words with much greater severity. 'Otto and his target were admitted by the back entrance, and shown straight to a *séparée*. We arranged to display nothing that would indicate the name of the establishment. Not long ago, a night-club down the road went bankrupt,' Herr Kretzschmar said, in a tone which suggested he might not be wholly desolated by the event. 'Place called the Freudenjacht. I had bought certain equipment at the sale. Matches. Plates, we spread them around the *séparée*.' Smiley remembered the letters ACHT on the ashtray in the photograph.

'Can you tell me what the two men discussed?'

'No.' He changed his answer: 'I have no Russian,' he said. He made the same disowning wave of his hand. 'In German they talked about God and the world. Everything.'

'I see.'

'That's all I know.'

'How was Otto in his manner?' Smiley asked. 'Was he still excited?'

'I never saw Otto like that before in my life. He was laughing like an executioner, speaking three languages at once, not drunk but extremely animated, singing, telling jokes, I don't know what. That's all I know,' Herr Kretzschmar repeated, with embarrassment.

Smiley glanced discreetly at the observation window and at the grey boxes of machinery. He glimpsed once more in Herr Kretzschmar's little television screen the soundless twining and parting of the white bodies on the other side of the wall. He saw his last question, he recognised its logic, he sensed the wealth it promised. Yet the same lifetime's instinct that had brought him this far now held him back. Nothing at this moment, no short-term dividend, was worth the risk of alienating Kretzschmar, and closing the road to Otto Leipzig.

'And Otto gave you no other description of his target?' Smiley asked, for the sake of asking something; to help him run their conversation down.

'During the evening he came to me once. Up here. He excused himself from the company and came up here to make sure the arrangements were in order. He looked at the screen there and laughed. "Now I have taken him over the edge and he can't get back," he said. I did not ask any more. That is all that happened.'

Herr Kretzschmar was writing his instructions for Smiley on a leather-backed jotting pad with gold corners.

'Otto lives in bad circumstances,' he said. 'One cannot alter that. Giving him money does not improve his social standards. He remains—' Herr Kretzschmar hesitated – 'he remains at heart, Herr Max, a *gypsy*. Do not misunderstand me.'

'Will you warn him that I am coming?'

'We have agreed not to use the telephone. The official link between us is completely closed.' He handed him the sheet of paper. 'I strongly advise you to take care,' Herr Kretzschmar said. 'Otto will be very angry when he hears the old General has been shot.' He saw Smiley to the door. 'What did they charge you down there?'

'I'm sorry?'

'Downstairs. How much did they take from you?'

'A hundred and seventy-five marks for membership.'

'With the drinks inside, at least two hundred. I'll tell them to give it back to you at the door. You English are poor these days. Too many trade unions. How'd you like the show?'

'It was very artistic,' said Smiley.

Herr Kretzschmar was once again very pleased with Smiley's answer. He patted Smiley on the shoulder: 'Maybe you should have more fun in life.'

'Maybe I should have done,' Smiley agreed.

'Greet Otto for me,' said Herr Kretzschmar.

'I will,' Smiley promised.

Herr Kretzschmar hesitated, and the same momentary bewilderment came over him.

'And you have nothing for me?' he repeated. 'No papers, for example?'

'No.'

'Pity.'

As Smiley left, Herr Kretzschmar was already at the telephone, attending to other special requests.

He returned to the hotel. A drunken night porter opened the door to him, full of suggestions about the wonderful girls he could send to Smiley's room. He woke, if he had ever slept, to the chime of church bells and the honk of shipping in the harbour, carried to him on the wind. But there are nightmares that do not go away with daylight, and as he drove northward over the fens in his hired Opel, the terrors which hovered in the mist were the same as those that had plagued him in the night.

17

The roads were as empty as the landscape. Through breaks in the mist, he glimpsed now a patch of cornfield, now a red farmhouse crouched low against the wind. A blue notice said 'KAI'. He swung sharply into a slip-road, dropping two flights, and saw ahead of him the wharf, a complex of low grey barracks dwarfed by the decks of cargo ships. A red-and-white pole guarded the entrance, there was a customs notice in several languages, but not a human soul in sight. Stopping the car, Smiley got out and walked lightly to the barrier. The red push-button was as big as a saucer. He pressed it and the shriek of its bell set a pair of herons flapping into the white mist. A control tower stood to his left on tubular legs. He heard a door slam and a ring of metal and watched a bearded figure in blue uniform stomp down the iron staircase to the bottom step. The man called to him, 'What do you want then?' Not waiting for an answer, he released the boom and waved Smiley through. The tarmac was like a vast bombed area cemented in, bordered by cranes and pressed down by the fogged white sky. Beyond it, the low sea looked too frail for the weight of so much shipping. He glanced in the mirror and saw the spires of a sea town etched like an old print half-way up the page. He glanced out to sea and saw through the mist the lines of buoys and winking lamps that marked the water border to

East Germany and the start of seven and a half thousand miles of Soviet Empire. That's where the herons went, he thought. He was driving at a crawl between red-and-white traffic cones towards a container-park heaped with car tyres and logs. 'Left at the container-park,' Herr Kretzschmar had said. Obediently, Smiley swung slowly left, looking for an old house, though an old house in this Hanseatic dumping ground seemed a physical impossibility. But Herr Kretzschmar had said, 'Look for an old house marked "Office",' and Herr Kretzschmar did not make errors.

He bumped over a railway track and headed for the cargo ships. Beams of morning sun had broken through the mist, making their white paintwork dazzle. He entered an alley comprised of control rooms for the cranes, each like a modern signal-box, each with green levers and big windows. And there at the end of the alley, exactly as Herr Kretzschmar had promised, stood the old tin house with a high tin gable cut like fretwork and crowned with a peeling flag-post. The electric wires that led into it seemed to hold it up; there was an old water pump beside it, dripping, with a tin mug chained to its pedestal. On the wooden door, in faded Gothic lettering, stood the one word 'BUREAU', in the French spelling, not the German, above a newer notice saying, 'P. K. BERGEN, IMPORT-EXPORT'. *He works there as the night clerk*, Herr Kretzschmar had said. *What he does by day only God and the Devil know.*

He rang the bell, then stood well back from the door, very visible. He was keeping his hands clear of his pockets and they were very visible too. He had buttoned his overcoat to the neck. He wore no hat. He had parked the car sideways to the house so that anyone indoors could see the car was empty. *I am alone and unarmed*, he was trying to say. *I am not their man, but yours.* He rang the bell again and called 'Herr Leipzig!' An upper window opened, and a pretty woman looked out blearily, holding a blanket round her shoulders.

'I'm sorry,' Smiley called up to her politely. 'I was looking for Herr Leipzig. It's rather important.'

'Not here,' she replied, and smiled.

A man joined her. He was young and unshaven with tattoo marks on his arms and chest. They spoke together a moment, Smiley guessed in Polish.

'*Nix hier*,' the man confirmed guardedly. '*Otto nix hier*.'

'We're just the temporary tenants,' the girl called down. 'When Otto's broke he moves to his country villa and rents us the apartment.'

She repeated this to her man, who this time laughed.

'*Nix hier*,' he repeated. 'No money. Nobody has money.'

They were enjoying the crisp morning, and the company.

'How long since you saw him?' Smiley asked.

More conference. Was it this day or that day? Smiley had the impression they had lost track of time.

'Thursday,' the girl announced, smiling again.

'Thursday,' her man repeated.

'I've got news for him,' Smiley explained cheerfully, catching her mood. He patted his side pocket. 'Money, *Pinkapinka*. All for Otto. He's earned it in commission. I promised to bring it to him yesterday.'

The girl interpreted all this and the man argued with her, and the girl laughed again.

'My friend says don't give it to him or Otto will come back and move us out and we'll have nowhere to make love!'

Try the water camp, she suggested, pointing with her bare arm. Two kilometres along the main road, over the railway and past the windmill, then right – she looked at her hands, then curved one prettily towards her lover – yes, right; right towards the lake, though you don't see the lake till you get to it.

'What is the place called?' Smiley asked.

'It has no name,' she said. 'It's just a place. Ask for holiday houses to let, then drive on towards the boats. Ask for Walther. If Otto is around, Walther will know where to find him.'

'Thank you.'

'Walther knows everything!' she called. 'He is like a professor!'

She translated this also, but this time her man looked angry.

'*Bad* professor!' he called down. 'Walther bad man!'

'Are you a professor too?' the girl asked Smiley.

'No. No, unfortunately not.' He laughed and thanked them, and they watched him get into his car as if they were children at a celebration. The day, the spreading sunshine, his visit – everything was fun for them. He lowered the window to say goodbye and heard her say something he couldn't catch.

'What was that?' he called up to her, still smiling.

'I said, "Then Otto is twice lucky for a change!"' the girl repeated.

'Why?' asked Smiley, and stopped the engine. 'Why is he twice lucky?'

The girl shrugged. The blanket was slipping from her shoulders and the blanket was all she wore. Her man put an arm round her and pulled it up again for decency.

'Last week the unexpected visit from the East,' she said. 'And today the money.' She opened her hands. 'Otto is Sunday's child for once. That's all.'

Then she saw Smiley's face, and the laughter went clean out of her voice.

'Visitor?' Smiley repeated. 'Who was the visitor?'

'From the East,' she said.

Seeing her dismay, terrified she might disappear altogether, Smiley with difficulty resurrected his appearance of good humour.

'Not his brother, was it?' he asked gaily, all enthusiasm. He held out one hand, cupping it over the mythical brother's head. 'A small chap? Spectacles like mine?'

'No, *no*! A big fellow. With a chauffeur. Rich.'

Smiley shook his head, affecting light-hearted disappointment. 'Then I don't know him,' he said. 'Otto's brother was certainly never rich.' He succeeded in laughing outright. 'Unless he was the chauffeur, of course,' he added.

He followed her directions exactly, with the secret calmness of emergency. To be conveyed. To have no will of his own. To be conveyed, to pray, to make deals with your Maker. Oh God, don't make it happen, not another Vladimir. In the sunlight the brown fields had turned to gold, but the sweat on Smiley's back was like a cold hand stinging his skin. He followed her directions seeing everything as if it were his last day, knowing the big fellow with the chauffeur had gone ahead of him. He saw the farmhouse with the old horse-plough in the barn, the faulty beer sign with its neon blinking, the window-boxes of geraniums like blood. He saw the windmill like a giant pepper-mill and the field full of white geese all running with the gusty wind. He saw the herons skimming like sails over the fens. He was driving too fast. I should drive more often, he thought; I'm out of practice, out of control. The road changed from tarmac to gravel, gravel to dust and the dust blew up round the car like a sandstorm. He entered some pine trees and on the other side of them saw a sign saying 'HOLIDAY HOUSES TO LET', and a row of shuttered asbestos bungalows waiting for their summer paint. He kept going and in the distance saw a coppice of masts, and brown water low in its basin. He headed for the masts, bumped over a pot-hole and heard a frightful crack from under the car. He supposed it was the exhaust, because the noise of his engine was suddenly much louder, and half the water birds in Schleswig-Holstein had taken fright at his arrival.

He passed a farm and entered the protective darkness of trees, then emerged in a stark and brilliant frame of whiteness of which a broken jetty and a few faint olive-coloured reeds made up the foreground, and an enormous sky the rest. The boats lay to his right, beside an inlet. Shabby caravans were parked along the track that led to them, grubby washing hung between the television aerials. He passed a tent in its own vegetable patch and a couple of broken huts that had once been military. On one, a psychedelic sunrise had been painted, and it was peeling. Three old cars and some heaped rubbish stood beside it. He parked and followed a mud path through the reeds to the shore. In the grass harbour lay a cluster of improvised houseboats, some of them converted landing-craft from the war. It was colder here, and for some reason darker. The boats he had seen were day boats, moored in a huddle apart, mostly under tarpaulins. A couple of radios played, but at first he saw nobody. Then he noticed a backwater and a blue dinghy made fast in it. And, in the dinghy, one gnarled old man in a sailcloth jacket and a black peaked cap, massaging his neck as if he had just woken up.

'Are you Walther?' Smiley asked.

Still rubbing his neck, the old man seemed to nod.

'I'm looking for Otto Leipzig. They told me at the wharf I might find him here.'

Walther's eyes were cut almond-shaped into the crumpled brown paper of his skin.

'*Isadora,*' he said.

He pointed at a rickety jetty farther down the shore. The *Isadora* lay at the end of it, a forty-foot motor launch down on her luck, a Grand Hotel awaiting demolition. The portholes were curtained, one of them was smashed, another was repaired with Scotch tape. Once he nearly fell, and twice, to bridge the gaps, he had to stride much wider than seemed safe to his short legs. At the end of the jetty, he realised that the *Isadora* was adrift. She had slipped her moorings at the stern and shifted twelve feet out to sea, which was probably the longest journey she would ever make. The cabin doors were closed, their windows curtained. There was no small boat.

The old man sat sixty yards off, resting on his oars. He had rowed out of the backwater to watch. Smiley cupped his hands and yelled: 'How do I get to him?'

'If you want him, call him,' the old man replied, not seeming to lift his voice at all.

Turning to the old launch, Smiley called, 'Otto.' He called softly, then more loudly, but inside the *Isadora* nothing stirred. He watched the curtains. He watched the oily water tossing against the rotting hull. He listened and thought he heard music like the music in Herr Kretzschmar's club, but it might have been an echo from another boat. From the dinghy, Walther's brown face still watched him.

'Call again,' he growled. 'Keep calling, if you want him.'

But Smiley had an instinct against being commanded by the old man. He could feel his authority and his contempt and he resented both.

'Is he in here or not?' Smiley called. 'I said, "Is he in here?"'

The old man did not budge.

'Did you see him come aboard?' Smiley insisted.

He saw the brown head turn and knew the old man was spitting into the water.

'The wild pig comes and goes,' Smiley heard him say. 'What the hell do I care?'

'So when did he come last?'

At the sound of their voices a couple of heads had lifted out of other boats. They stared at Smiley without expression: the little fat stranger standing at the end of the broken jetty. On the shore a ragtag group had formed: a girl in shorts, an old woman; two blond teen-aged boys dressed alike. There was something that linked them in their disparity: a prison look; submission to the same bad laws.

'I'm looking for Otto Leipzig,' Smiley called to all of them. 'Can anyone tell me, please, whether he's around?' On a houseboat not too far away, a bearded man was lowering a bucket into the water. Smiley's eye selected him. 'Is there anyone aboard the *Isadora*?' he asked.

The bucket gurgled and filled. The bearded man pulled it out, but didn't speak.

'You should see his car,' a woman shouted shrilly from the shore, or perhaps it was a child. 'They took it to the wood.'

The wood lay a hundred yards back from the water, mostly saplings and birch trees.

'Who did?' Smiley asked. 'Who took it there?'

Whoever had spoken chose not to speak again. The old man was rowing himself towards the jetty. Smiley watched him approach, watched him back the stern towards the jetty steps. Without hesitating, Smiley clambered aboard. The old man pulled him the few strokes to the *Isadora*'s side. A cigarette was jammed between his cracked old lips and, like his eyes, it shone unnaturally against the evil gloom of his weathered face.

'Come far?' the old man asked.

'I'm a friend of his,' Smiley said.

There was rust and weed on the *Isadora*'s ladder, and as Smiley reached the deck it was slippery with dew. He looked for signs of life and saw none. He looked for footprints in the dew, in vain. A couple of fixed fishing-lines hung into the water, made fast to the rusted balustrade, but they could have been there for weeks. He listened, and heard again, very faintly, the strains of slow band music. From the shore? Or from farther out? From neither. The sound came from under his feet, and it was as if someone were playing a seventy-eight record on thirty-three.

He looked down and saw the old man in his dinghy, leaning back, and the peak of his cap pulled over his eyes, while he slowly conducted to the beat. He tried the cabin door and it was locked, but the door did not seem strong – nothing did – so he walked around the deck till he found a rusted screwdriver to use as a jemmy. He shoved it into the gap, worked it backwards and forwards, and suddenly to his surprise the whole door went, frame, hinges, lock, and everything else, with a bang like an explosion, followed by a shower of red dust from the rotten timber. A big slow moth thudded against his cheek and left it stinging strangely for a good while afterwards, till he began to wonder whether it was a bee. Inside, the cabin was pitch dark, but the music was a little louder. He was on the top rung of the ladder and even with the daylight behind him the darkness below remained absolute. He pressed a light switch. It didn't work, so he stepped back and spoke to the old man in his dinghy: 'Matches.'

For a moment Smiley nearly lost his temper. The peaked cap didn't stir, nor did the conducting cease. He shouted, and this time a box of matches landed at his feet. He took them into the cabin and lit one, and saw the exhausted transistor radio that was still putting out music with the last of its energy, and it was about the one thing intact, the only thing still functioning, in all the devastation round it.

The match had gone out. He pulled the curtains, but not on the landward side, before he lit another. He didn't want the old man looking in. In the grey sideways light, Leipzig was ridiculously like his tiny portrait in the photograph taken by Herr Kretzschmar. He was naked, he was lying where they had trussed him, even if there was no girl and no Kirov either. The hewn Toulouse-Lautrec face, blackened with bruising and gagged with several strands of rope, was as jagged and articulate in death as Smiley had remembered it in life. They must have used the music to drown the noise while they tortured him, Smiley thought. But he doubted whether the music would have been enough. He went on staring at the radio as a point of reference, a thing to go back to with his ears and eyes when the body became too much to look at before the match went out. Japanese, he noticed. Odd, he thought. Fix on the oddness of it. How odd of the technical Germans to buy Japanese radios. He wondered whether the Japanese returned the compliment. Keep wondering, he urged himself ferociously; keep your whole mind on this interesting economic phenomenon of the exchange of goods between highly industrialised nations.

Still staring at the radio, Smiley righted a folding stool and sat on it. Slowly, he returned his gaze to Leipzig's face. Some dead faces, he reflected, have the dull, even stupid look of a patient under anaesthetic. Others preserve a single mood of the once varied nature – the dead man as lover, as father, as car driver, bridge player, tyrant. And some, like Vladimir's, have ceased to preserve anything. But Leipzig's face, even without the ropes across it, had a mood, and it was anger: anger intensified by pain, turned to fury by it; anger that had increased and become the whole man as the body lost its strength.

Hate, Connie had said.

Methodically, Smiley peered about him, thinking as slowly as he could manage, trying, by his examination of the debris, to reconstruct their progress. First the fight before they overpowered him, which he deduced from the smashed table-legs and chairs and lamps and shelves, and anything else that could be ripped from its housing and either wielded or thrown. Then the search, which took place after they had trussed him and in the intervals while they questioned him. Their frustration was written everywhere. They had ripped out wall-boards and floor-boards and cupboard drawers and clothes and mattresses and by the end anything that came apart, anything that was not a minimal component, as Otto Leipzig still refused to talk. He noticed also that there was blood in surprising places – in the washbasin, over the stove. He liked to think it was not all Otto Leipzig's. And finally, in desperation, they had killed him, because those were Karla's orders, that was Karla's way. 'The killing comes first, the questioning second,' Vladimir used to say.

I too believe in Otto, Smiley thought stupidly, recalling Herr Kretzschmar's words. *Not in every detail but in the big things*. So do I, he thought. He believed in him, at that moment, as surely as he believed in death, and in the Sandman. As for Vladimir, so for Otto Leipzig: death had ruled that he was telling the truth.

From the direction of the shore, he heard a woman yelling: 'What's he found? Has he found something? Who is he?'

He returned aloft. The old man had shipped his oars and let the dinghy drift. He sat with his back to the ladder, head hunched into his big shoulders. He had finished his cigarette and lit a cigar as if it were Sunday. And at the same moment as Smiley saw the old man, he saw also the chalk mark. It was in the same line of vision, but very close to him, swimming in the misted lenses of his spectacles. He had to lower his head and look over the top of them to fix on it. A chalk mark, sharp and yellow. One line, carefully drawn over the rust of the balustrade, and a foot away from it the reel of fishing-line, made fast with a sailors' knot. The old man was watching him; so, for all he knew, was the growing group of watchers on the shore, but he had no option. He pulled at the line and it was heavy. He pulled steadily, hand over hand, till the line changed to gut, and he found himself pulling that instead. The gut grew suddenly tight. Cautiously he kept pulling. The people on the shore had grown expectant; he could feel their interest even across the water. The old man had put back his head and was watching through the black shadow of his cap. Suddenly, with a plop, the catch jumped clear of the water and a peal of ribald laughter rose from the spectators: one old gym-shoe, green, with the lace still in it, and the hook which held it to the line was big enough to beach a shark. The laughter slowly died. Smiley unhooked the shoe. Then, as if he had other business there, he lumbered back into the cabin till he was out of sight, leaving the door ajar for light.

But happening to take the gym-shoe with him.

An oilskin packet was hand-stitched into the toe of the shoe. He pulled it out. It was a tobacco pouch, stitched along the top and folded several times. *Moscow Rules*, he thought woodenly. *Moscow Rules all the way*. How many more dead men's legacies must I inherit? he wondered. *Though we value none but the horizontal one*. He had unpicked the stitching. Inside the pouch was another wrapping, this time a latex rubber sheath knotted at the throat. And secreted inside the sheath, one hard wad of cardboard smaller than a book of matches. Smiley opened it. It was half a picture postcard. Black and white, not even coloured. Half a dull picture of Schleswig-Holstein landscape with half a herd of Friesian cattle grazing in grey sunlight. Ripped with a deliberate jaggedness. No writing on the back, no address, no stamp. Just half a boring, unposted postcard; but they had tortured him, then killed him for it, and still not found it, or any of the treasures it unlocked. Putting it, together with its wrapping, into the inside pocket of his jacket, he returned to the deck. The old man in his dinghy had drawn alongside. Without a word Smiley climbed slowly down the ladder. The crowd of camp people on the shore had grown still larger.

'Drunk?' the old man asked. 'Sleeping it off?'

Smiley stepped into the dinghy and, as the old man pulled away, looked back at the *Isadora* once more. He saw the broken porthole, he thought of the wreckage in the cabin, the paper-thin sides that allowed him to hear the very shuffle of feet on the shore. He imagined the fight and Leipzig's screams filling the whole camp with their din. He imagined the silent group standing where they were standing now, without a voice or a helping hand between them.

'It was a party,' the old man said carelessly while he made the dinghy fast against the jetty. 'Lots of music, singing. They warned us it would be loud.' He tugged at a knot. 'Maybe they quarrelled. So what? Many people quarrel. They made some noise, played some jazz. So what? We are musical people here.'

'They were police,' a woman called from the group on the shore. 'When police go about their business it is the duty of the citizen to keep his trap shut.'

'Show me his car,' Smiley asked.

They moved in a rabble, no one leading. The old man strode at Smiley's side, half custodian, half bodyguard, making a way for him with facetious ceremony. The children ran everywhere but they kept well clear of the old man. The Volkswagen stood in a coppice and it was ripped apart like the cabin of the *Isadora*. The roof lining hung in shreds, the seats had been pulled out and split open. The wheels were missing but Smiley guessed that had happened since. The camp people stood round it reverently as if it were their show-piece. Someone had tried to burn it but the fire had not caught.

'He was scum,' the old man explained. 'They all are. Look at them. Polacks, criminals, subhumans.'

Smiley's Opel stood where he had parked it, at the edge of the track, close to the dustbins, and the two blond boys who were dressed alike were standing over the boot beating the lid with hammers. As he walked towards them he could see their forelocks bouncing with each blow. They wore jeans and black boots studded with love-daisies.

'Tell them to stop hitting my car,' Smiley said to the old man.

The camp people were following at a distance. He could hear again the furtive shuffle of their feet, like a refugee army. He reached his car and had the keys in his hand, and the two boys were still bent over the back hitting with all their might. But when he walked round to take a look, all they had done was beat the lid of the boot right off its hinges, then fold it and beat it flat again till it lay like a crude parcel on the floor. He looked at the wheels but nothing seemed amiss. He didn't know what else to look for. Then he saw that they had tied a dustbin to the rear bumper with string. Keeping clear, he tugged at the string to break it, but it refused to yield. He tried it with his teeth, without success. The old man lent him a penknife and he cut it, keeping clear of the boys with their hammers. The camp people had made a half ring and they were holding up their children for the farewell. Smiley got into the car and the old man slammed the door after him with a tremendous heave. Smiley had the key in the ignition but by the time he turned it, one of the boys had draped himself over the bonnet as languidly as a model at a motorshow and the other was tapping politely at the window.

Smiley lowered the window.

'What do you want?' Smiley asked.

The boy held out his palm. 'Repairs,' he explained. 'Your boot didn't shut properly. Time and materials. Overheads. Parking.' He indicated his thumb-nail. 'My colleague here hurt his hand. It could have been serious.'

Smiley looked at the boy's face and saw no human instinct that he understood.

'You have repaired nothing. You have done damage. Ask your friend to get off the car.'

The boys conferred, seeming to disagree. They did this under the full gaze of the crowd, in a reasoned manner, slowly pushing each other's shoulders and making rhetorical gestures which did not coincide with their words. They talked about nature and about politics, and their platonic dialogue might have gone on indefinitely if the boy who was on the car had not stood up in order to make the best of a debating point. As he did so, he broke off a windscreen wiper as if it were a flower and handed it to the old man. Driving away, Smiley looked in his mirror and saw a ring of faces staring after him with the old man at their centre. Nobody waved goodbye.

He drove without haste, weighing the chances, while the car clanged like an old fire-engine. He supposed they had done something else to it as well; something he had failed to notice. He had left Germany before, he had come and gone illicitly, he had hunted while on the run, and though he was old and in a different Germany, he felt as if he had been returned to the wild. He had no way of knowing whether anybody from the water camp had telephoned the police, but he took it for an accomplished fact. The boat was open and its secret out. Those who had looked away would now be the first to come forward as good citizens. He had seen that before as well.

He entered a sea town, the boot – if it *was* the boot – still clanking behind him. Or perhaps it's the exhaust, he thought; the pot-hole I crashed into on the way to the camp. A hot, unseasonable sun had replaced the morning mists. There were no trees. An amazing brilliance was opening around him. It was still early, and empty horse carriages stood waiting for the first tourists. The sand was a pattern of craters dug in the summer by sun-worshippers to escape the wind. He could hear the tinny echo of his own progress bouncing between the painted shop-fronts and the sunlight seemed to make it even louder. Where he passed people, he saw their heads lift to stare after him because of the row the car made.

'They'll know the car,' he thought. Even if nobody at the water camp remembered the number, the smashed boot would give him away. He turned off the main street. The sun was really very bright indeed. 'A man came, Herr Wachtmeister,' they would be saying to the police patrol. 'This morning, Herr Wachtmeister. He said he was a friend. He looked in the boat and then drove away. He asked us nothing, Captain. He was unmoved. He fished a shoe, Herr Wachtmeister. Imagine – a shoe!'

He was heading for the railway station, following the signs, looking for a place where you could park a car all day. The station was red brick and massive, he supposed from before the war. He passed it and found a big car-park to his left. A line of shedding trees ran through it, and there were leaves on some of the cars. A machine took his money and issued him with a ticket to stick on his windscreen. He backed into the middle of a line, the boot as far out of sight as possible against a mud bank. He stepped out and the extraordinary sun hit him like a slap. There was not a breath of wind. He locked the car and put the keys in the exhaust-pipe, he didn't quite know why, except that he felt apologetic towards the hire company. He kicked up the leaves and sand till the front number-plate was almost hidden. In an hour, in this St Luke's summer, there would be a hundred and more cars in the park.

He had noticed a men's clothes shop in the main street. He bought a linen jacket there but nothing more, because people who buy whole outfits are remembered. He did not wear it, but carried it in a plastic bag. In a side-street full of boutiques he bought a gaudy straw hat and, from a stationer's, a holiday map of the area, and a railway timetable of the region Hamburg, Schleswig-Holstein and Lower Saxony. He didn't wear the hat either, but kept it in its bag like the jacket. He was sweating from the unexpected heat. The heat was upsetting him; it was as absurd as snow in summer. He went to a telephone box and again consulted local directories. Hamburg had no Claus Kretzschmar, but one of the Schleswig-Holstein directories had a Kretzschmar who lived in a place Smiley had never heard of. He studied the map and found a small town by that name on the main railway line to Hamburg. This pleased him very much.

Calmly, all other thoughts bound down with iron bands, Smiley once more did his sums. Within moments of finding the car, the police would be talking to the hire firm in Hamburg. As soon as they had spoken to the hire firm and obtained his name and description, they would put a watch on the airport and other crossing places. Kretzschmar was a night-bird and would sleep late. The town where he lived was an hour away by stopping train.

He returned to the railway station. The main concourse was a Wagnerian fantasy of a Gothic court, with an arched roof, and a huge stained-glass window that poured out coloured sunbeams onto the ceramic floor. From a telephone box, he rang Hamburg Airport, giving his name as 'Standfast, initial J', which was the name on the passport he had collected from his London club. The first available flight to London was this evening at six but only first-class was open. He booked a first-class seat and said he would upgrade his economy ticket on arrival at the airport. The girl said, 'Then please come half an hour before check-in.' Smiley promised he would – he wanted to make an impression – but no, alas, Mr Standfast had no phone number where he could be reached meanwhile. There was nothing in her tone to suggest she had a security officer standing behind her with a telex in his hand, whispering instructions in her ear, but he guessed that within a couple of hours Mr Standfast's seat reservation was going to ring a lot of bells, because it was Mr Standfast who had hired the Opel car. He stepped back into the concourse, and the shafts of coloured light. There were two ticket counters and two short queues. At the first, an intelligent girl attended him and he bought a second-class single ticket to Hamburg. But it was a deliberately laboured purchase, full of indecision and nervousness, and when he had made it he insisted on writing down times of departure and arrival: also on borrowing her ball-point and a pad of paper.

In the men's room, having first transferred the contents of his pockets, beginning with the treasured piece of postcard from Leipzig's boat, he changed into the linen jacket and straw hat, then went to the second ticket counter where, with a minimum of fuss, he bought a ticket on the stopping train to Kretzschmar's town. To do this, he avoided looking at the attendant at all, concentrated instead on the ticket and his change, from under the brim of his loud straw hat. Before leaving he took one last precaution. He made a wrong-number phone call to Herr Kretzschmar and established from an indignant wife that it was a scandal to telephone anybody so early. As a last measure, he folded the plastic carrier-bags into his pocket.

The town was leafy and secluded, the lawns large, the houses carefully zoned. Whatever there had been of country life had long fallen before the armies of suburbia, but the brilliant sunlight made everything beautiful. Number 8 was on the right-hand side, a substantial two-storey residence with steep Scandinavian roofs, a double garage and a wide selection of young trees planted much too close together. There was a swing chair in the garden with a flowered plastic seat and a new fish-pond in the romantic idiom. But the main attraction, and Herr Kretzschmar's pride, was an outdoor swimming-pool in its own patio of shrieking red tile, and it was there that Smiley found him, in the bosom of his family, on this unlikely autumn day, entertaining a few neighbours at an impromptu party. Herr Kretzschmar himself, in shorts, was preparing the barbecue and as Smiley dropped the latch on the gate he paused from his labours and looked round to see who had come. But the new straw hat and the linen jacket confused him and he called instead to his wife.

Frau Kretzschmar strode down the path bearing a champagne glass. She was clad in a pink bathing-dress and a diaphanous pink cape, which she allowed to flow behind her daringly.

'Who *is* that then? Who is the nice surprise?' she kept asking in a playful voice. She could have been talking to her puppy.

She stopped in front of him. She was tanned and tall and,

like her husband, built to last. He could see little of her face, for she wore dark glasses with a white plastic beak to protect her nose from burning.

'Here is family Kretzschmar, going about its pleasures,' she said not very confidently, when he had still not introduced himself. 'What can we do for you, sir? In what way can we *serve*?'

'I have to speak to your husband,' Smiley said. It was the first time he had spoken since he bought his ticket, and his voice was thick and unnatural.

'But Cläuschen does no business in the daytime,' she said firmly, still smiling. 'In the daytime by family decree the profit motive has its sleep. Shall I put handcuffs on him to prove to you he is our prisoner till sunset?'

Her bathing-dress was in two parts and her smooth, full belly was oily with lotion. She wore a gold chain round her waist, presumably as a further sign of naturalness. And gold sandals with very high heels.

'Kindly tell your husband that this is not business,' Smiley said. 'This is friendship.'

Frau Kretzschmar took a sip of her champagne, then removed her dark glasses and beak, as if she were declaring herself at the *bal masqué*. She had a snub nose. Her face, though kindly, was a good deal older than her body.

'But how can it be friendship when I don't know your name?' she demanded, no longer sure whether to be winsome or discouraging.

But by then Herr Kretzschmar himself had walked down the path after her, and stopped before them, staring from his wife to Smiley, then at Smiley again. And perhaps the sight of Smiley's set face and manner, and the fixity of his gaze, warned Herr Kretzschmar of the reason for his coming.

'Go and take care of the cooking,' he said curtly.

Guiding Smiley by the arm, Herr Kretzschmar led him to a drawing-room with brass chandeliers and a picture window full of jungle cacti.

'Otto Leipzig is dead,' Smiley said without preliminary as soon as the door was closed. 'Two men killed him at the water camp.'

Herr Kretzschmar's eyes opened very wide; then unashamedly he swung his back to Smiley and covered his face with his hands.

'You made a tape-recording,' Smiley said, ignoring this display entirely. 'There was the photograph which I showed you, and somewhere there is also a tape-recording which you are keeping for him.' Herr Kretzschmar's back showed no sign that he had heard. 'You talked about it to me yourself last night,' Smiley went on, in the same sentinel tone. 'You said they discussed God and the world. You said Otto was laughing like an executioner, speaking three languages at once, singing, telling jokes. You took the photographs for Otto, but you also recorded their conversation for him. I suspect you also have the letter which you received on his behalf from London.'

Herr Kretzschmar had swung round and he was staring at Smiley in outrage.

'Who killed him?' he asked. 'Herr Max, I ask you as a soldier!'

Smiley had taken the torn piece of picture postcard from his pocket.

'Who killed him?' Herr Kretzschmar repeated. 'I insist!'

'This is what you expected me to bring last night,' said Smiley ignoring the question. 'Whoever brings it to you may have the tapes and whatever else you were keeping for him. That was the way he worked it out with you.'

Kretzschmar took the card.

'He called it his Moscow Rules,' Kretzschmar said. 'Both Otto and the General insisted on it, though it struck me personally as ridiculous.'

'You have the other half of the card?' Smiley asked.

'Yes,' said Kretzschmar.

'Then make the match and give me the material. I shall use it exactly as Otto would have wished.'

He had to say this twice in different ways before Kretzschmar answered. 'You promise this?' Kretzschmar demanded.

'Yes.'

'And the killers? What will you do with them?'

'Most likely they are already safe across the water,' Smiley said. 'They have only a few kilometres to drive.'

'Then what good is the material?'

'The material is an embarrassment to the man who sent the killers,' Smiley said, and perhaps at this moment the iron quietness of Smiley's demeanour advised Herr Kretzschmar that his visitor was as distressed as he was – perhaps, in his own very private fashion, more so.

'Will it kill him also?' Herr Kretzschmar asked.

Smiley took quite a time to answer this question. 'It will do worse than kill him,' he said.

For a moment Herr Kretzschmar seemed disposed to ask what was worse than being killed; but he didn't. Holding the half postcard lifelessly in his hand, he left the room. Smiley waited patiently. A perpetual brass clock laboured on its captive course, red fish gazed at him from an aquarium. Kretzschmar returned. He held a white cardboard box. Inside it, padded in hygienic tissue, lay a folded wad of photocopy paper covered with a now familiar handwriting, and six miniature cassettes, blue plastic, of a type favoured by men of modern habits.

'He entrusted them to me,' Herr Kretzschmar said.

'He was wise,' said Smiley.

Herr Kretzschmar laid a hand on Smiley's shoulder. 'If you need anything let me know,' he said. 'I have my people. These are violent times.'

From a call box Smiley once more rang Hamburg Airport, this time to re-confirm Standfast's flight to London Heathrow. This done, he bought stamps and a strong envelope and wrote on it a fictional address in Adelaide, Australia. He put Mr Standfast's passport inside it and dropped it in a letterbox. Then, travelling as plain Mr George Smiley, profession clerk, he returned to the railway station, passing without incident across the border into Denmark. During the journey, he took himself to the lavatory and there read Ostrakova's letter, all seven pages of it, the copy made by the General himself on Mikhel's antiquated liquid copier in the little library next door to the British Museum. What he read, added to what he had that day already seen, filled him with a growing and almost uncontainable alarm. By train, ferry and finally taxi, he hastened to Copenhagen's Castrup Airport. From Castrup he caught a mid-afternoon plane to Paris and though the flight lasted only an hour, in Smiley's world it took a lifetime, conveying him across an entire range of his memories, emotions, and anticipation. His anger and revulsion at Leipzig's murder, till now suppressed, welled over, only to be set aside by his fears for Ostrakova: if they had done so much to Leipzig and the General, what would they not do to her? The dash through Schleswig-Holstein had given him the swiftness of revived youth, but now, in the anti-climax of escape, he was assailed by the incurable indifference of age. With death so close, he thought, so ever-present, what is the point of struggling any longer? He thought of Karla again, and of his absolutism, which at least gave point to the perpetual chaos that was life's condition; point to violence, and to death; of Karla for whom killing had never been more than the necessary adjunct of a grand design.

How can I win? he asked himself; alone, restrained by doubt and a sense of decency – how can any of us – against this remorseless fusillade?

The plane's descent – and the promise of the renewed chase – restored him. There are two Karlas, he reasoned, remembering again the stoic face, the patient eyes, the wiry body waiting philosophically upon its own destruction. There is Karla the professional, so self-possessed that he could allow, if need be, ten years for an operation to bear fruit: in Bill Haydon's case, twenty; Karla the old spy, the pragmatist, ready to trade a dozen losses for one great win.

And there is this other Karla, Karla of the human heart after all, of the one great love, the Karla flawed by humanity. I should not be deterred if, in order to defend his weakness, he resorts to the methods of his trade.

Reaching in the compartment above him for his straw hat, Smiley happened to remember a cavalier promise he had once made concerning Karla's eventual downfall. 'No,' he had replied, in answer to a question much like the one he had just put to himself. 'No, Karla is not fireproof. Because he's a fanatic. And one day, if I have anything to do with it, that lack of moderation will be his downfall.'

Hastening to the cab rank, he recalled that his remark had been made to one Peter Guillam, who at this present moment happened to be much upon his mind.

18

Lying on the divan, Ostrakova glanced at the twilight and seriously wondered whether it signalled the world's end.

All day long the same grey gloom had hung over the courtyard, consigning her tiny universe to a perpetual evening. At dawn a sepia glow had thickened it; at midday, soon after the men came, it was a celestial power-cut, deepening to a cavernous black in anticipation of her own end. And now, at evening, fog had further strengthened the grip of darkness upon the retreating forces of light. And so it goes with Ostrakova also, she decided without bitterness: with my bruised, black-and-blue body, and my siege, and my hopes for the second coming of the redeemer; so it goes exactly, an ebbing of my own day.

She had woken this morning to find herself seemingly bound hand and foot. She had tried to move one leg and, immediately, burning cords had tightened round her thighs and chest and stomach. She had raised an arm, but only against the tugging of iron ligatures. She had taken a lifetime to crawl to the bathroom and another to get herself undressed and into the warm water. And when she entered it, she was frightened that she had fainted from the pain, her flailed flesh hurt so terribly where the road had grazed it. She heard a hammering and had thought it was inside her head, till she realised it was the work of a furious neighbour. When she counted the church clock's chimes, they stopped at four, so no wonder the neighbour was protesting at the thunder of running water in the old pipes. The labour of making coffee had exhausted her but sitting down was suddenly unbearable, lying down just as bad. The only way for her to rest was to lean herself forward, elbows on the draining-board. From there she could watch the courtyard, as a pastime and as a precaution, and from there she had seen the men, the two creatures of darkness, as she now thought of them, mouthing to the concierge, and the old goat of a concierge, Madame la Pierre, mouthing back, shaking her fool head – 'No, Ostrakova is not here, not here' – not here in ten different ways, that echoed like an aria round the courtyard – *is not here* – drowning the clipping of carpet-beaters and the clatter of children and the gossip of the two turbaned old wives on the third floor, leaning out of their windows two metres apart – *is not here!* Till a child would not have believed her.

If she wanted to read, she had to put the book on the draining-board, which, after the men came, was where she kept the gun as well, till she noticed the swivel on the buttend, and with a woman's practicality improvised a lanyard out of kitchen string. In that way, with the pistol round her neck, she had both her arms free when she needed to hand herself across the room. But when it prodded her breasts she thought she would retch from the agony. After the men left again, she had started reciting aloud while she went about the chores she had promised herself she would observe during her imprisonment. 'One *tall* man, one leather *coat*, one Homburg *hat*,' she had murmured, helping herself to a generous ration of vodka to restore her. 'One *broad* man, one balding *pate*, grey *shoes* with perforations!' Make songs of my memory, she had thought; sing them to the magician, to the General – oh, why don't they answer my second letter?

She was a child again, falling off her pony, and the pony came back and trampled her. She was a woman again, trying to be a mother. She remembered the three days of impossible pain in which Alexandra fiercely resisted being born into the grey and dangerous light of an unwashed Moscow nursing home – the same light that was outside her window now, and lay like unnatural dust over the polished floors of her apartment. She heard herself calling for Glikman – 'Bring him to me, bring him to me.' She remembered how it had seemed to her that sometimes it was he, Glikman her lover, whom she was bearing, and not their child at all – as if his whole sturdy, hairy body were trying to fight its way out of her – or was it into her? – as if to give birth at all would be to deliver Glikman into the very captivity she dreaded for him.

Why was he not there, why would he not come? she wondered, confusing Glikman with the General and the magician equally. Why don't they answer my letter?

She knew very well why Glikman had not come to her as she wrestled with Alexandra. She had begged him to keep away. 'You have the courage to suffer, and that is enough,' she had told him. 'But you have not the courage to witness the suffering of others, and for that I love you also. Christ had it too easy,' she told him. 'Christ could cure the lepers, Christ could make the blind see and the dead come alive. He could even die in a sensible cause. But you are not Christ, you are Glikman, and there's nothing you can do about my pain except watch and suffer too, which does nobody any good whatever.'

But the General and his magician were different, she argued, with some resentment; they have set themselves up as physicians of my disease, and I have a right to them!

At her appointed time, the cretinous, braying concierge had come up, complete with her troglodyte husband with his screwdriver. They were full of excitement for Ostrakova, and joy at being able to bring such heartening news. Ostrakova had composed herself carefully for the visit, putting on music, making up her face, and heaping books beside the divan, all to create an atmosphere of leisured introspection.

'Visitors, madame, *men* . . . No, they would not leave their names . . . here for a short visit from abroad . . . knew your *husband*, madame. Émigrés, they were, like yourself . . . No, they wished to keep it a *surprise*, madame . . . They said they had *gifts* for you from relations, madame . . . a secret, madame, and one of them so big and strong and good-looking . . . No, they will come back another time, they are here on business, many appointments, they said . . . No, by taxi, and they kept it waiting – the expense, imagine!'

Ostrakova had laughed, and put her hand on the concierge's arm, physically drawing her into a great secret, while the troglodyte stood and puffed cigarette and garlic over both of them.

'Listen,' she said. 'Both of you. Attend to me, Monsieur and Madame la Pierre. I know very well who they are, these rich and handsome visitors. They are my husband's no-good nephews from Marseilles, lazy devils and great vagabonds. If they are bringing a present for me, you may be sure they will also want beds and most likely dinner too. Be so kind and tell them I am away in the country for a few more days. I love them dearly, but I must have my peace.'

Whatever doubts or disappointments remained in their goatish heads, Ostrakova bought them away with money, and now she was alone again – the lanyard round her neck. She was stretched out on the divan, her hips hoisted into a position that was half-way tolerable. The gun was in her hand and pointed at the door, and she could hear the footsteps coming up the stairs, two pairs, the one heavy, the other light.

She rehearsed: 'One *tall* man, one leather *coat* . . . One *broad* man, *grey* shoes with perforations . . .'

Then the knocking, timid as a childhood proposition of love. And the unfamiliar voice, speaking French with an unfamiliar accent, slow and classical like her husband Ostrakov's and with the same alluring tenderness.

'Madame Ostrakova. Please admit me. I am here to help you.'

With a sense of everything ending, Ostrakova deliberately cocked her dead husband's pistol, and advanced with firm if painful steps, upon the door. She advanced crabwise and she wore no shoes and she mistrusted the fisheye peep-hole. Nothing would convince her it couldn't peep in both directions. Therefore she made this detour round the room in the hope of escaping its eyeline, and on the way she passed Ostrakov's blurry portrait and resented very much that he had had the selfishness to die so early instead of staying alive so that he could protect her. Then she thought: No. I have turned the corner. I possess my own courage.

And she did possess it. She was going to war, every minute could be her last, but the pains had vanished, her body felt as ready as it had been for Glikman, always, any time; she could feel his energy running into her limbs like reinforcements. She had Glikman beside her and she remembered his strength without wishing for it. She had a Biblical notion that all his tireless love-making had invigorated her for this moment. She had the calm of Ostrakov and the honour of Ostrakov; she had his gun. But her desperate, solitary courage was finally her own, and it was the courage of a mother roused, and deprived, and furious: Alexandra! The men who had come to kill her were the same men who had taunted her with her secret motherhood, who had killed Ostrakov and Glikman, and would kill the whole poor world if she did not stop them.

She wanted only to aim before she fired, and she had realised that as long as the door was closed and chained and the peep-hole was in place, she could aim from very close – and the closer she aimed, the better, for she was sensibly modest about her marksmanship. She put her finger over the peep-hole to stop them looking in, then she put her eye to it to see who they were, and the first thing she saw was her own foolish concierge, very close, round as an onion in the distorted lens, with green hair from the glow of the ceramic tiles in the landing, and a huge rubber smile and a nose that came out like a duck's bill. And it occurred to Ostrakova that the light footsteps had been hers – lightness, like pain and happiness, being always relative to whatever has come before, or after. And the second thing she saw was a small gentleman in spectacles, who in the fisheye was as fat as the Michelin tyre man. And while she watched him, he earnestly removed a straw hat that came straight out of a novel by Turgenev, and held it at his side as if he had just heard his national anthem being played. And she inferred from this gesture that the small gentleman was telling her that he knew she was afraid, and knew that a shadowed face was what she was afraid of most, and that by baring his head he was in some way revealing his goodwill to her.

His stillness and his gravity had a sense of dutiful submission about them, which, like his voice, again reminded her of Ostrakov; the lens might make him into a frog, but it could not take away his bearing. His spectacles also reminded her of Ostrakov, being as necessary to vision as a walking-stick to a cripple. All this, with a thumping heart but a very steady eye, Ostrakova took in at her first long inspection, while she kept the gun barrel clamped to the door and her finger on the trigger, and considered whether or not to shoot him then and there, straight through the door – 'Take *that* for Glikman, *that* for Ostrakov, *that* for Alexandra!'

For, in her state of suspicion, she was ready to believe that they had selected the man for his very air of humanity; because they knew that Ostrakov himself had had this same capacity to be at once fat and dignified.

'*I do not need help*,' Ostrakova called back at last, and watched in terror to see what effect her words would have on him. But while she watched, the fool concierge decided to start yelling on her own account.

'Madame, he is a gentleman! He is English! He is concerned for you! You are ill, madame, the whole street is frightened for you! Madame, you cannot lock yourself away like this any more.' A pause. 'He is a doctor, madame – aren't you, monsieur? A distinguished doctor for maladies of the spirit!' Then Ostrakova heard the idiot whisper to him: 'Tell her, monsieur. Tell her you're a doctor.'

But the stranger shook his head in disapproval, and replied: 'No. It is not true.'

'Madame, open up or I shall fetch the police!' the concierge cried. 'A Russian, making such a scandal!'

'I *do not need help*,' Ostrakova repeated, much louder.

But she knew already that help, more than anything else, was what she did need; that without it she would never kill, any more than Glikman would have killed. Not even if she had the Devil himself in her sights could she kill another woman's child.

As she continued her vigil, the little man took a slow step forward till his face, distorted like a face under water, was all she could see in the lens; and she saw for the first time the fatigue in it, the redness of the eyes behind the spectacles, the heavy shadows under them; and she sensed in him a passionate caring for herself that had nothing to do with death, but with survival; she sensed that she was looking at a face that was concerned, rather than one that had banished sympathy for ever. The face came closer still and the snap of the letter-box alone almost made her pull the trigger by mistake and this appalled her. She felt the convulsion in her hand and stayed it only at the very instant of completion; then stopped to pick the envelope from the mat. It was her own letter, addressed to the General – her second, saying 'Someone is trying to kill me,' written in French. As a last-ditch gesture of resistance, she pretended to wonder whether the letter was a trick, and they had intercepted it, or bought it, or stolen it, or done whatever deceivers do. But seeing her letter, recognising its opening words and its despairing tone, she became utterly weary of deceit, and weary of mistrust, and weary of trying to read evil where she wished more than anything to read good. She heard the fat man's voice again, and a French well-taught but a little rusty, and it reminded her of rhymes from school she half remembered. And if it was a lie he was telling, then it was the most cunning lie she had ever heard in her life.

'The magician is dead, madame,' he said, fogging the fish-eye with his breath. 'I have come from London to help you in his place.'

For years afterwards, and probably for all his life, Peter Guillam would relate, with varying degrees of frankness, the story of his home-coming that same evening. He would emphasise that the circumstances were particular. He was in a bad temper – one – he had been so all day. Two – his Ambassador had publicly rebuked him at the weekly meeting for a remark of unseemly levity about the British balance of payments.

He was newly married – three – and his very young wife was pregnant. Her phone call – four – came moments after he had decoded a long and extremely boring signal from the Circus reminding him for the fifteenth time that *no*, repeat, no operations could be undertaken on French soil without advance permission in writing from Head Office. And – five – *le tout Paris* was having one of its periodical scares about kidnapping. Last, the post of Circus head resident in Paris was widely known to be a laying-out place for officers shortly to be buried, offering little more than the opportunity to lunch interminably with a variety of very corrupt, very boring chiefs of rival French Intelligence services who spent more time spying on each other than on their supposed enemies. All of these factors, Guillam would afterwards insist, should be taken into account before anyone accused him of impetuosity. Guillam, it may be added, was an athlete, half French, but more English on account of it; he was slender, and near enough handsome – but though he fought it every inch of the way, he was also close on fifty, which is the watershed that few careers of ageing fieldman survive. He also owned a brand-new German Porsche car, which he had acquired, somewhat shamefacedly, at diplomatic rates, and parked, to the Ambassador's strident disapproval, in the Embassy car-park.

Marie-Claire Guillam, then, rang her husband at six exactly, just as Guillam was locking away his code-books. Guillam had two telephone lines to his desk, one of them in theory operational and direct. The second went through the Embassy switchboard. Marie-Claire rang on the direct line, a thing they had always agreed she would only ever do in emergency. She spoke French, which, true, was her native language, but they had recently been communicating in English in order to improve her fluency.

'Peter,' she began.

He heard at once the tension in her voice.

'Marie-Claire? What is it?'

'Peter, there's someone here. He wants you to come at once.'

'Who?'

'I can't say. It's important. Please come home at once,' she repeated and rang off.

Guillam's chief clerk, a Mr Anstruther, had been standing at the strong-room door when the call came, waiting for him to spin the combination lock before they each put in their keys. Through the open doorway to Guillam's office he saw him slam down the phone, and the next thing he knew, Guillam had tossed to Anstruther – a long throw, probably fifteen feet – the Head Resident's sacred *personal key*, near enough the symbol of his office, and Anstruther by a miracle had caught it: put up his left hand and caught it in his palm, like an American baseball player; he couldn't have done it again if he'd tried it a hundred times, he told Guillam later.

'Don't budge from here till I ring you!' Guillam shouted. 'You sit at my desk and you man those phones. Hear me?'

Anstruther did, but by then Guillam was half-way down the absurdly elegant spiral staircase of the Embassy, barging between typists and Chancery guards and bright young men setting out on the evening cocktail round. Seconds later, he was at the wheel of his Porsche, revving the engine like a racing driver, which in another life he might well have been. Guillam's home was in Neuilly, and in the ordinary way these sporting dashes through the rush hour rather amused him, reminding him twice a day – as he put it – that however mind-bendingly boring the Embassy routine, life around him was hairy, quarrelsome, and fun. He was even given to timing himself over the distance. If he took the Avenue Charles de Gaulle and got a fair wind at the traffic lights, twenty-five minutes through the evening traffic was not unreasonable. Late at night or early in the morning, with empty roads and CD plates, he could cut it to fifteen, but in the rush hour thirty-five minutes was fast going and forty the norm. That evening, hounded by visions of Marie-Claire held at pistol point by a bunch of crazed nihilists, he made the distance in eighteen minutes cold. Police reports later submitted to the Ambassador had him jumping three sets of lights and touching around a hundred and forty kilometres as he entered the home stretch; but these were of necessity something of a reconstruction, since no one felt inclined to try to keep up with him. Guillam himself remembers little of the drive, beyond a near squeak with a furniture van, and a lunatic cyclist who took it into his head to turn left when Guillam was a mere hundred and fifty metres behind him.

His apartment was in a villa, on the third floor. Braking hard before he reached the entrance, he cut the engine and coasted to a halt in the street outside, then pelted to the front door as quietly as haste allowed. He had expected a car parked somewhere close, probably with a get-away driver waiting at the wheel, but to his momentary relief there was none in sight. A light was burning in their bedroom, however, so that he now imagined Marie-Claire gagged and tied to the bed, and her captors sitting over her, waiting for Guillam to arrive. If it was Guillam they wanted, he did not propose to disappoint them. He had come unarmed; he had no choice. The Circus Housekeepers had a holy terror of weapons, and his illicit revolver was in the bedside locker, where no doubt they had by now found it. He climbed the three flights silently and at the front door threw off his jacket and dropped it on the floor beside him. He had his door-key in his hand, and now, as softly as he knew how, he fed it into the lock, then pressed the bell and called '*Facteur*' – postman – through the letter-box and then '*Exprès.*' His hand on the key, he waited till he heard approaching footsteps, which he knew at once were not those of Marie-Claire. They were slow, even ponderous, and, to Guillam's ear, too self-assured by half. And they came from the direction of the bedroom. What he did next, he did all at once. To open the door from inside, he knew, required two distinct movements: first the chain must be shot, then the spring catch must be freed. In a half-crouch, Guillam waited till he heard the chain slip, then used his weapon of surprise: he turned his own key and threw all his weight against the door and, as he did so, had the intense satisfaction of seeing a plump figure spin wildly back against the hall mirror, knocking it clean off its moorings, while Guillam seized his arm and swung it into a vicious breaking lock – only to see the startled face of his lifelong friend and mentor, George Smiley, staring helplessly at him.

The aftermath of that encounter is described by Guillam somewhat hazily; he had, of course, no forewarning of Smiley's coming, and Smiley – perhaps out of fear of microphones – said little inside the flat to enlighten him. Marie-Claire was in the bedroom, but neither bound nor gagged; it was Ostrakova who, at Marie-Claire's insistence, was lying on the bed, still in her old black dress, and Marie-Claire was ministering to her in any way she could think of – jellied breast of chicken, mint tea, all the invalid foods she had diligently laid in for the wonderful day, alas not yet at hand, when Guillam would also fall ill on her. Ostrakova, Guillam noticed (though he had yet to learn her name) seemed to have been beaten up. She had broad grey bruises round the eyes and lips, and her fingers were cut to bits where she had apparently tried to defend herself. Having briefly admitted Guillam to this scene – the battered lady tended by the anxious child bride – Smiley conducted Guillam to his own drawing-room and, with all the authority of Guillam's old chief, which he indeed had been, rapidly set out his requirements. Only now, it developed, was Guillam's earlier haste warranted. Ostrakova – Smiley referred to her only as 'our guest' – should leave Paris tonight, he said. The station's safe house outside Orléans – he called it 'our country mansion' – was not safe enough; she needed somewhere that provided care and protection. Guillam remembered a French couple in Arras, a retired agent and his wife, who in the past had provided shelter for the Circus's occasional birds of passage. It was agreed he would telephone them, but not from the apartment: Smiley sent him off to find a public call box. By the time Guillam had made the necessary arrangements and returned, Smiley had written out a brief signal on a sheet of Marie-Claire's awful notepaper with its grazing bunnies, which he wished Guillam to have transmitted immediately to the Circus, 'Personal for Saul Enderby, decipher yourself.' The text, which Smiley insisted that Guillam should read (but not aloud), politely asked Enderby – 'in view of a second death no doubt by now reported to you' – for a meeting at Ben's Place forty-eight hours hence. Guillam had no idea where Ben's Place was.

'And, Peter.'

'Yes, George,' said Guillam, still dazed.

'I imagine there exists an official directory of locally accredited diplomats. Do you happen to have such a thing in the house by any chance?'

Guillam did. Indeed, Marie-Claire lived by it. She had no memory for names at all, so it lay beside the bedroom telephone for every time a member of a foreign embassy telephoned her with yet another invitation to drinks, to dinner, or, most ghastly of all, to a National Day festivity. Guillam fetched it, and a moment later was peering over Smiley's shoulder. 'Kirov,' he read – but not, once more, aloud – as he followed the line of Smiley's thumb-nail – 'Kirov, Oleg, Second Secretary (Commercial), Unmarried.' Followed by an address in the Soviet Embassy ghetto in the 7th district.

'Ever bumped into him?' Smiley asked.

Guillam shook his head. 'We took a look at him a few years back. He's marked "hands off",' he replied.

'When was this list compiled?' Smiley asked. The answer was printed on the cover: December of the previous year.

Smiley said, 'Well, when you get to the office—'

'I'll take a look at the file,' Guillam promised.

'There is also *this*,' said Smiley sharply, and handed Guillam a plain carrier-bag containing, when he looked later, several micro-cassettes and a fat brown envelope.

'By first bag tomorrow, please,' Smiley said. 'The same grading and the same addressee as the telegram.'

Leaving Smiley still poring over the list, and the two women cloistered in the bedroom, Guillam hastened back to the Embassy and, having released the bemused Anstruther from his vigil at the telephones, consigned the carrier-bag to him, together with Smiley's instructions. The tension in Smiley had affected Guillam considerably, and he was sweating. In all the years he had known George, he said later, he had never known him so inward, so intent, so elliptical, so desperate. Re-opening the strong-room, he personally encoded and despatched the telegram, waiting only as long as it took him to receive the Head Office acknowledgement before drawing the file on Soviet Embassy movements and browsing through back numbers of old watch lists. He had not far to look. The third serial, copied to London, told him all that he needed to know. Kirov, Oleg, Second Secretary (Commercial), described this time as 'married but wife not en poste', had returned to Moscow two weeks ago. In the panel reserved for miscellaneous comments, the French liaison service added that, according to informed Soviet sources, Kirov had been 'recalled to the Soviet Ministry of Foreign Affairs at short notice in order to take up a senior appointment which had become vacant unexpectedly.' The customary farewell parties had therefore not been feasible.

Back in Neuilly, Smiley received Guillam's intelligence in utter silence. He did not seem surprised, but he seemed in some way appalled, and when he finally spoke – which did not occur until they were all three in the car and speeding towards Arras – his voice had an almost hopeless ring. 'Yes,' he said – as if Guillam knew the whole history inside out. 'Yes, that is of course exactly what he *would* do, isn't it? He would call Kirov back under the pretext of a promotion, in order to make sure he really came.'

George had not sounded that way, said Guillam – no doubt with the wisdom of hindsight – since the night he unmasked Bill Haydon as Karla's mole as well as Ann's lover.

Ostrakova also, in retrospect, had little coherent recollection of that night, neither of the car journey, on which she contrived to sleep, nor of the patient but persistent questioning to which the little plump man subjected her when she woke late the next morning. Perhaps she had temporarily lost her capacity to be impressed – and, accordingly, to remember. She answered his questions, she was grateful to him, she gave him – without the zest or 'decoration' – the same information that she had given to the magician, though he seemed to possess most of it already.

'The magician,' she said once. 'Dead. My God.'

She asked after the General, but scarcely heeded Smiley's non-committal reply. She was thinking of Ostrakov, then Glikman, now the magician – and she never knew his name. Her host and hostess were kind to her also, but as yet made no impression on her. It was raining and she could not see the distant fields.

Little by little, all the same, as the weeks passed, Ostrakova permitted herself an idyllic hibernation. The deep winter came early and she let its snows embrace her; she walked a little, and then a great deal, retired early, spoke seldom, and as her body repaired itself so did her spirit. At first a pardonable confusion reigned in her mind, and she found herself thinking of her daughter in the terms by which the gingery stranger had described her: as the tearaway dissenter and untameable rebel. Then slowly the logic of the matter presented itself to her. Somewhere, she argued, there was the real Alexandra who lived and had her being, as before. Or who, as before, did not. In either case, the gingery man's lies concerned a different creature altogether, one whom they had invented for their own needs. She even managed to find consolation in the likelihood that her daughter, if she lived at all, lived in complete ignorance of their machinations. Perhaps the hurts which had been visited on her – of the mind as well as of the body – did what years of prayer and anxiety had failed to do, and purged her of her self-recriminations regarding Alexandra. She mourned Glikman at her leisure, she was conscious of being quite alone in the world, but in the winter landscape her solitude was not disagreeable to her. A retired brigadier proposed marriage to her but she declined. It turned out later that he proposed to everybody. Peter Guillam visited her at least every week and sometimes they walked together for an hour or two. In faultless French he talked to her mainly of landscape gardening, a subject on which he possessed an inexhaustible knowledge. That was Ostrakova's life, where it touched upon this story. And it was lived out in total ignorance of the events that her own first letter to the General had set in train.

19

'Do you know his name really *is* Ferguson?' Saul Enderby drawled in that lounging Belgravia cockney which is the final vulgarity of the English upper-class.

'I never doubted it,' Smiley said.

'He's about all we've got left of that whole lamplighter stable. Wise Men don't hold with domestic surveillance these days. Anti-Party or some damn thing.' Enderby continued his study of the bulky document in his hand. 'So what's *your* name, George? Sherlock Holmes dogging his poor old Moriarty? Captain Ahab chasing his big white whale? Who are you?'

Smiley did not reply.

'Wish I had an enemy, I must say,' Enderby remarked, turning a few pages. 'Been looking for one for donkey's years. Haven't I, Sam?'

'Night and day, Chief,' Sam Collins agreed heartily, and sent his master a confiding grin.

Ben's Place was the back room of a dark hotel in Knightsbridge and the three men had met there an hour ago. A notice on the door said 'MANAGEMENT STRICTLY PRIVATE' and inside was an ante-room for coats and hats and privacy, and beyond it lay this oak-panelled sanctum full of books and musk, which in turn gave on to its own rectangle of walled garden stolen from the park, with a fish-pond and a marble angel and a path for contemplative walks. Ben's identity, if he ever had one, was lost in the unwritten archives of Circus mythology. But this place of his remained, as an unrecorded perquisite of Enderby's appointment, and of George Smiley's before him – and as a trysting ground for meetings that afterwards have not occurred.

'I'll read it again, if you don't mind,' Enderby said. 'I'm a bit slow on the uptake this time of day.'

'I think that would be jolly helpful, actually, Chief,' said Collins.

Enderby shifted his half-lens spectacles, but only by way of peering over the top of them, and it was Smiley's secret theory that they were plain glass anyway.

'Kirov is doing the talking. This is after Leipzig has put the bite on him, right, George?' Smiley gave a distant nod. 'They're still sitting in the cat house with their pants down, but it's five in the morning and the girls have been sent home. First we get Kirov's tearful how-could-you-do-this-to-me? "I thought you were my friend, Otto!" he says. Christ, he picked a wrong 'un there! Then comes his statement, put into bad English by the translators. They've made a concordance – that the word, George? Um's and ah's omitted.'

Whether it was the word or not, Smiley offered no answer. Perhaps he was not expected to. He sat very still in a leather armchair leaning forward over his clasped hands, and he had not taken off his brown tweed overcoat. A set of the Kirov typescripts lay at his elbow. He looked drawn, and Enderby remarked later that he seemed to have been on a diet. Sam Collins, Head of Operations, sat literally in Enderby's shadow, a dapper man with a dark moustache and a flashy, ever-ready smile. There had been a time when Collins was the Circus hard-man, whose years in the field had taught him to despise the cant of the fifth floor. Now he was the poacher turned gamekeeper, nurturing his own pension and security in the way he had once nurtured his networks. A wilful blankness had overcome him; he was smoking brown cigarettes down to the half-way mark, then stubbing them into a cracked sea shell, while his doglike gaze rested faithfully on Enderby, his master. Enderby himself stood propped against the pillar of French windows, silhouetted by the light outside, and he was using a bit of matchstick to pick his teeth. A silk handkerchief peeked from his left sleeve and he stood with one knee forward and slightly bent as if he were in the members' enclosure at Ascot. In the garden, shreds of mist lay stretched like fine gauze across the lawn. Enderby put back his head and held the document away from him like a menu.

'Here we go. I'm Kirov. "As a finance officer working in Moscow Centre from 1970 to 1974 it was my duty to unearth irregularities in the accounts of overseas residencies and bring the culprits to book."' He broke off and peered over his glasses again. 'This is all before Kirov was posted to Paris, right?'

'Dead right,' said Collins keenly and glanced at Smiley for support, but got none.

'Just working it out, you see, George,' Enderby explained. 'Just getting my ducks in a row. Haven't got your little grey cells.'

Sam Collins smiled brightly at his chief's show of modesty.

Enderby continued: '"As a result of conducting these extremely delicate and confidential enquiries, which in some cases led to the punishment of senior officers of Moscow Centre, I made the acquaintance of the head of the independent Thirteenth Intelligence Directorate, subordinated to the Party's Central Committee, who is known throughout Centre only by his workname Karla. This is a woman's name and is said to belong to the first network he controlled." That right, George?'

'It was during the Spanish Civil War,' said Smiley.

'The great playground. Well, well. To continue. "The Thirteenth Directorate is a separate service within Moscow Centre, since its principal duty is the recruitment, training and placing of illegal agents under deep cover in Fascist countries, known also as moles . . . blah . . . blah . . . blah. Often a mole will take many years to find his place inside the target country before he becomes active in secret work." Shades of Bloody Bill Haydon. "The task of servicing such moles is not entrusted to normal overseas residencies but to a Karla representative, as he is known, usually a military officer, whose daywork is to be an attaché of an Embassy. Such representatives are handpicked by Karla personally and constitute an élite . . . blah . . . blah . . . enjoying privileges of trust and freedom not given to other Centre officers, also travel and money. They are accordingly objects of jealousy to the rest of the service."'

Enderby affected to draw breath: '*Christ*, these translators!' he exclaimed. 'Or maybe it's just Kirov being a perishing little bore. You'd think a man making his deathbed confession would have the grace to keep it brief, wouldn't you? But not our Kirov, oh no. How you doing, Sam?'

'Fine, Chief, fine.'

'Here we go again,' said Enderby, and resumed his ritual tone: '"In the course of my general investigations into financial irregularities, the integrity of a Karla resident came into question, the resident in Lisbon, Colonel Orlov. Karla convened a secret tribunal of his own people to hear the case, and as a result of my evidence Colonel Orlov was liquidated in Moscow on June 10, 1973." That checks, you say, Sam?'

'We have an unconfirmed defector report that he was shot by firing-squad,' said Collins breezily.

'Congratulations, Comrade Kirov, the embezzler's friend.

Jesus. What a snake pit. Worse than us.' Enderby continued: '"For my part in bringing the criminal Orlov to justice I was personally congratulated by Karla, and also sworn to secrecy, since he considered the irregularity of Colonel Orlov a shame on his Directorate, and damaging to his standing within Moscow Centre. Karla is known as a comrade of high standards of integrity, and for this reason has many enemies among the ranks of the self-indulgent."'

Enderby deliberately paused, and yet again glanced at Smiley over the top of his half-lenses.

'We all spin the ropes that hang us, right, George?'

'We're a bunch of suicidal spiders, Chief,' said Collins heartily, and flashed an even broader smile at a place somewhere between the two of them.

But Smiley was lost in his reading of Kirov's statement and not accessible to pleasantries.

'Skip the next year of Brother Kirov's life and loves, and let's come to his next meeting with Karla,' Enderby proposed, undeterred by Smiley's taciturnity. 'The nocturnal summons . . . that's standard, I gather.' He turned a couple of pages. Smiley, following Enderby, did the same. 'Car pulls up outside Kirov's Moscow apartment – why can't they say *flat* for God's sake, like anyone else? – he's hauled out of bed and driven to an unknown destination. They lead a rum life, don't they, those gorillas in Moscow Centre, never knowing whether they're getting a medal or a bullet?' He referred to the report again. 'All that tallies, does it, George? The journey and stuff? Half an hour by car, small plane, and so forth?'

'The Thirteenth Directorate has three or four establishments, including a large training camp near Minsk,' Smiley said.

Enderby turned some more pages.

'So here's Kirov back in Karla's presence again: middle

of nowhere, the same night. Karla and Kirov totally alone. Small wooden hut, monastic atmosphere, no trimmings, no witnesses – or none visible. Karla goes straight to the nub. How would Kirov like a posting to Paris? Kirov would like one very much, sir –' He turned another page. 'Kirov always admired the Thirteenth Directorate, sir, blah, blah – always been a great fan of Karla's – creep, crawl, creep. Sounds like you, Sam. Interesting that Kirov thought Karla looked tired – notice that point? – twitchy. Karla under stress, smoking like a chimney.'

'He always did that,' said Smiley.

'Did what?'

'He was always an excessive smoker,' Smiley said.

'Was he, by God? Was he?'

Enderby turned another page. 'Now Kirov's brief,' he said. 'Karla spells it out for him. "For my daywork I should have the post of a Commercial officer of the Embassy, and for my special work I would be responsible for the control and conduct of financial accounts in all outstations of the Thirteenth Directorate in the following countries . . ." Kirov goes on to list them. They include Bonn, but not Hamburg. With me, Sam?'

'All the way, Chief.'

'Not losing you in the labyrinth?'

'Not a bit, Chief.'

'Clever blokes, these Russkies.'

'Devilish.'

'Kirov again: "He impressed upon me the extreme importance of my task – blah, blah – reminded me of my excellent performance in the Orlov case, and advised me that in view of the great delicacy of the matters I was handling, I would be reporting directly to Karla's private office and would have a separate set of ciphers . . ." Turn to page fifteen.'

'Page fifteen it is, Chief,' Collins said.

Smiley had already found it.

'"In addition to my work as West European auditor to the Thirteenth Directorate outstations, however, Karla also warned me that I would be required to perform certain clandestine activities with a view to finding cover backgrounds, or legends for future agents. All members of his Directorate took a hand in this, he said, but legend work was extremely secret nevertheless, and I should not under any circumstances discuss it with anybody at all. Not my Ambassador, not with Major Pudin who was Karla's permanent operational representative inside our Embassy in Paris. I naturally accepted the appointment and, having attended a special course in security and communications, took up my post. I had not been in Paris long when a personal signal from Karla advised me that a legend was required urgently for a female agent, age about twenty-one years. Now we're at the bone,' Enderby commented with satisfaction. '"Karla's signal referred me to several émigré families who might be persuaded by pressure to adopt such an agent as their own child, since blackmail is considered by Karla a preferable technique to bribery." Damn right it is,' Enderby assented heartily. 'At the present rate of inflation, blackmail's about the only bloody thing that keeps its value.'

Sam Collins obliged with a rich laugh of appreciation.

'Thank you, Sam,' said Enderby pleasantly. 'Thanks very much.'

A lesser man than Enderby – or a less thick-skinned one – might have skated over the next few pages, for they consisted mainly of a vindication of Connie Sachs's and Smiley's pleas of three years ago that the Leipzig-Kirov relationship should be exploited.

'Kirov dutifully trawls the émigrés, but without result,' Enderby announced, as if he were reading out subtitles at the cinema. 'Karla exhorts Kirov to greater efforts, Kirov strives still harder, and goofs again.'

Enderby broke off, and looked at Smiley, this time very straight. 'Kirov was no bloody good, was he, George?' he said.

'No,' said Smiley.

'Karla couldn't trust his own chaps, that's your point. He had to go out into the sticks and recruit an irregular like Kirov.'

'Yes.'

'A clod. Sort of bloke who'd never make Sarratt.'

'That's right.'

'Having set up his apparatus, in other words, trained it to accept his iron rules, you might say, he didn't dare use it for this particular deal. That your point?'

'Yes,' said Smiley. 'That is my point.'

Thus, when Kirov bumped into Leipzig on the plane to Vienna – Enderby resumed, paraphrasing Kirov's own account now – Leipzig appeared to him as the answer to all his prayers. Never mind that he was based in Hamburg, never mind that there'd been a bit of nastiness back in Tallinn: Otto was an émigré, in with the groups. Otto the Golden Boy. Kirov signalled urgently to Karla proposing that Leipzig be recruited as an émigré and source talent-spotter. Karla agreed.

'Which is another rum thing, when you work it out,' Enderby remarked. 'Jesus, I mean who'd back a horse with Leipzig's record when he was sober and of sound mind? Specially for a job like that?'

'Karla was under stress,' Smiley said. 'Kirov said so and we have it from elsewhere also. He was in a hurry. He had to take risks.'

'Like bumping chaps off?'

'That was more recent,' Smiley said, in a tone of such casual exoneration that Enderby glanced at him quite sharply.

'You're bloody forgiving these days, aren't you, George?' said Enderby suspiciously.

'Am I?' Smiley sounded puzzled by the question. 'If you say so, Saul.'

'And bloody meek, too.' He returned to the transcript. 'Page twenty-one and we're home free.' He read slowly to give the passage extra point. 'Page twenty-one, he repeated. '"Following the successful recruitment of Ostrakova, and the formal issuing of a French permit to her daughter Alexandra, I was instructed to set aside immediately ten thousand American dollars a month from the Paris imprest for the purpose of servicing this new mole, who was henceforth awarded the workname KOMET. The agent KOMET also received the highest classification of secrecy within the Directorate, requiring all communications regarding her to be sent to the Director personally, using person-to-person ciphers, and without intermediaries. Preferably, however, such communications should go by courier, since Karla is an opponent of the excessive use of radio." Any truth in that one, George?' Enderby asked casually.

'It was how we caught him in India,' said Smiley without lifting his head from the script. 'We broke his codes and he later swore that he would never use radio again. Like most promises, it was subject to review.'

Enderby bit off a bit of matchstick, and smeared it onto the back of his hand. 'Don't you want to take your coat off, George?' he asked. 'Sam, ask him what he wants to drink.'

Sam asked, but Smiley was too absorbed in the script to answer.

Enderby resumed his reading aloud. '"I was also instructed to make sure that no reference to KOMET appeared on the annual accounts for Western Europe which, as auditor, I was obliged to sign and present to Karla for submission to the

Collegium of Moscow Centre at the close of each financial year . . . No, I never met the agent KOMET, nor do I know what became of her, or in which country she is operating. I know only that she is living under the name of Alexandra Ostrakova, the daughter of naturalised French parents . . ."' More turning of pages. '"The monthly payment of ten thousand dollars was not expended by myself, but transferred to a bank in Thun in the Swiss canton of Berne. The transfer is made by standing orders to the credit of a Dr Adolf Glaser. Glaser is the nominal account holder, but I believe that Dr Glaser is only the work-name for a Karla operative at the Soviet Embassy in Berne, whose real name is Grigoriev. I believe this because once when I sent money to Thun, the sending bank made an error, and it did not arrive; when this became known to Karla, he ordered me to send a second sum immediately to Grigoriev personally while bank enquiries were continuing. I did as I was ordered and later recovered the duplicated amount. This is all I know. Otto, my friend, I beg you to preserve these confidences, they could kill me." He's bloody right. They did.' Enderby chucked the transcript on to a table, and it made a loud slap. 'Kirov's last will and testament, as you might say. That's it. George?'

'Yes, Saul.'

'Really no drink?'

'Thank you, I'm fine.'

'I'm still going to spell it out because I'm thick. Watch my arithmetic. It's nowhere near as good as yours. Watch my *every move*.' Recalling Lacon, he held up a white hand and spread the fingers as a prelude to counting on them.

'One, Ostrakova writes to Vladimir. Her message rings old bells. Probably Mikhel intercepted and read it, but we'll never know. We could sweat him, but I doubt if it would help, and it would most certainly put the cat among Karla's pigeons in a big way if we did.' He grabbed a second finger. 'Two, Vladimir sends a copy of Ostrakova's letter to Otto Leipzig, urging him to re-warm the Kirov relationship double-quick. Three, Leipzig roars off to Paris, sees Ostrakova, gets himself alongside his dear old buddy Kirov, tempts him to Hamburg – where Kirov is free to go, after all, since Leipzig is still down in Karla's books as Kirov's agent. Now there's a thing, George.'

Smiley waited.

'In Hamburg, Leipzig burns Kirov rotten. Right? Proof right here in our sweaty hands. But I mean – how?'

Did Smiley really not follow, or was he merely intent upon making Enderby work a little harder? In either case, he preferred to take Enderby's question as rhetorical.

'*How* does Leipzig burn him precisely?' Enderby insisted. 'What's the pressure? Dirty pix – well, okay. Karla's a puritan, so's Kirov. But I mean, Christ, this isn't the fifties, is it? Everyone's allowed a bit of leg-sliding these days, what?'

Smiley offered no comment on Russian mores; but on the subject of pressure he was as precise as Karla might have been: 'It's a different ethic to ours. It suffers no fools. We think of ourselves as more susceptible to pressure than the Russians. It's not true. It's simply not true.' He seemed very sure of this. He seemed to have given the matter a lot of recent thought:

'Kirov had been incompetent and indiscreet. For his indiscretion alone, Karla would have destroyed him. Leipzig had the proof of that. You may remember that when we were running the original operation against Kirov, Kirov got drunk and talked out of turn about Karla. He told Leipzig that it was Karla personally who had ordered him to compose the legend for a female agent. You discounted the story at the time, but it was true.'

Enderby was not a man to blush, but he did have the grace

to pull a wry grin before fishing in his pocket for another matchstick.

'*And he that rolleth a stone, it will return upon him,*' he remarked contentedly, though whether he was referring to his own dereliction or to Kirov's was unclear. '"Tell us the rest, buddy, or I'll tell Karla what you've told me already," says little Otto to the fly. Jesus, you're right, he really *did* have Kirov by the balls!'

Sam Collins ventured a soothing interjection. 'I think George's point meshes pretty neatly with the reference on page two, Chief,' he said. 'There's a passage where Leipzig actually refers to "our discussions in Paris". Otto's twisting the Karla knife there, no question. Right, George?'

But Sam Collins might have been speaking in another room for all the attention either of them paid him.

'Leipzig also had Ostrakova's letter,' Smiley added. 'Its contents did not speak well for Kirov.'

'Another thing,' said Enderby.

'Yes, Saul?'

'Four years, right? It's fully four years since Kirov made his original pass at Leipzig. Suddenly he's all over Ostrakova, wanting the same thing. Four years later. You suggesting he's been swanning around with the same brief all this time, and got no forrader?'

Smiley's answer was curiously bureaucratic. 'One can only suppose that Karla's requirement ceased and was then revived,' he replied primly, and Enderby had the sense not to press him.

'Point is, Leipzig burns Kirov rotten and gets word to Vladimir that he's done so,' Enderby resumed as the spread fingers came up again for counting. 'Vladimir despatches Villem to play courier. Meanwhile back at the Moscow ranch, Karla is either smelling a rat or Mikhel has peached, probably the latter. In either case, Karla calls Kirov home under the pretext of promotion and swings him by his ears. Kirov sings, as I would, fast. Karla tries to put the toothpaste back in the tube. Kills Vladimir while he's on the way to our rendezvous armed with Ostrakova's letter. Kills Leipzig. Takes a pot at the old lady, and fluffs it. What's his mood now?'

'He's sitting in Moscow waiting for Holmes or Captain Ahab to catch up with him,' Sam Collins suggested, in his velvet voice, and lit yet another of his brown cigarettes.

Enderby was unamused. 'So why doesn't Karla dig up his treasure, George? Put it somewhere else? If Kirov has confessed to Karla what he's confessed to Leipzig, Karla's first move should be to brush over the traces!'

'Perhaps the treasure is not movable,' Smiley replied. 'Perhaps Karla's options have run out.'

'But it would be daylight madness to leave that bank account intact!'

'It was daylight madness to use a fool like Kirov,' Smiley said, with unusual harshness. 'It was madness to let him recruit Leipzig and madness to approach Ostrakova, and madness to believe that by killing three people he could stop the leak. Presumptions of sanity are therefore not given. Why should they be?' He paused. 'And Karla does believe it, apparently, or Grigoriev would not still be in Berne. Which you say he is, I gather?' The smallest glance at Collins.

'As of today he's sitting pretty,' Collins said, through his all-weather grin.

'Then moving the bank account would hardly be a logical step,' Smiley remarked. And he added: 'Even for a madman.'

And it was strange – as Collins and Enderby afterwards privily agreed – how everything that Smiley said seemed to pass through the room like a chill; how in some way that they failed to understand, they had removed themselves to a higher order of human conduct for which they were unfit.

'So who's his dark lady?' Enderby demanded. 'Who's worth ten grand a month and his whole damn career? Forcing him to use boobies instead of his own regular cut-throats? Must be quite a gal.'

Again there is mystery about Smiley's decision not to reply to this question. Perhaps only his wilful inaccessibility can explain it; or perhaps we are staring at the stubborn refusal of the born caseman to reveal anything to his controller that is not essential to their collaboration. Certainly there was philosophy in his decision. In his mind already, Smiley was accountable to nobody but himself: why should he act as if things were otherwise? 'The threads lead all of them into my own life,' he may have reasoned. 'Why pass the ends to my adversary merely so that he can manipulate me?' Again, he may well have assumed – and probably with justice – that Enderby was as familiar as Smiley was with the complexities of Karla's background; and that even if he was not, he had had his Soviet Research Section burrowing all night until they found the answers he required.

In any case, the fact is that Smiley kept his counsel.

'George?' said Enderby, finally.

An aeroplane flew over quite low.

'It's simply a question of whether you want the product,' Smiley said at last. 'I can't see that anything else is ultimately of very much importance.'

'Can't you, by God!' said Enderby, and pulled his hand from his mouth and the matchstick with it. 'Oh I *want* him all right,' he went on, as if that were only half the point. 'I *want* the Mona Lisa, and the Chairman of the Chinese People's Republic, and next year's winner of the Irish Sweep. I *want* Karla sitting in the hot seat at Sarratt, coughing out his life story to the inquisitors. I *want* the American Cousins to eat out of my hand for years to come. I *want* the whole ball game, of course I do. Still doesn't get me off the hook.'

But Smiley seemed curiously unconcerned by Enderby's dilemma.

'Brother Lacon told you the facts of life, I suppose? The stalemate and all?' Enderby asked. 'Young, idealistic Cabinet, mustard for détente, preaching open government, all that balls? Ending the conditioned reflexes of the cold war? Sniffing Tory conspiracies under every Whitehall bed, ours specially? Did he? Did he tell you they're proposing to launch a damn great Anglo-Bolshie peace initiative, yet another, which will duly fall on its arse around Christmas next?'

'No. No, he didn't tell me that part.'

'Well, they are. And we're not to jeopardise it, tra-la. Mind you, the very chaps who go hammering the peace-drums are the ones who scream like hell when we don't deliver the goods. I suppose that stands to reason. They're already asking what the Soviet posture will be, even now. Was it always like that?'

Smiley took so long to answer that he might have been passing the Judgement of Ages. 'Yes. I suppose it was. I suppose that in one form or another it always *was* like that,' he said at last, as if the answer mattered to him deeply.

'Wish you'd warned me.'

Enderby sauntered back towards the centre of the room and poured himself some plain soda from the sideboard; he stared at Smiley with what seemed to be honest indecision. He stared at him, he shifted his head and stared again, showing all the signs of being faced with an absolute problem.

'It's a tough one, Chief, it really is,' said Sam Collins, unremarked by either man.

'And it's not all a wicked Bolshie plot, George, to lure us to our ultimate destruction – you're sure of *that*?'

'I'm afraid we're no longer worth the candle, Saul,' Smiley said, with an apologetic smile.

Enderby did not care to be reminded of the limitations of British grandeur, and for a moment his mouth set into a sour grimace.

'All right, Maud,' he said finally. 'Let's go into the garden.'

They walked side by side. Collins, on Enderby's nod, had stayed indoors. Slow rain puckered the surface of the pool and made the marble angel glisten in the dusk. Sometimes a breeze passed and a chain of water slopped from the hanging branches onto the lawn, soaking one or the other of them. But Enderby was an English gentleman, and while God's rain might be falling on the rest of mankind, he was damned if it was going to fall on him. The light came at them in bits. From Ben's French windows, yellow rectangles fell across the pond. From over the brick wall, they had the sickly green glow of a modern street lamp. They completed a round in silence before Enderby spoke.

'Led us a proper dance, you did, George, I'll tell you that for nothing. Villem, Mikhel, Toby, Connie. Poor old Ferguson hardly had time to fill in his expense claims before you were off again. "Doesn't he ever sleep?" he asked me. "Doesn't he ever drink?"'

'I'm sorry,' said Smiley, for something to say.

'Oh, no, you're not,' said Enderby, and came to a sudden halt. '*Bloody* laces,' he muttered, stooping over his boot, 'they always do this with suède. Too few eyeholes, that's the problem. You wouldn't think even the bloody Brits would manage to be mean with *holes*, would you?'

Enderby replaced one foot and lifted the other.

'I want his body, George, hear me? Hand me a live, talking Karla and I'll accept him and make my excuses later. Karla asks for asylum? Well, um, yes, most reluctantly he can have it. By the time the Wise Men are loading their shot-guns for me I'll have enough out of him to shut them up for good. His body or nothing, you got me?'

They were strolling again, Smiley trailing behind, but Enderby, though he was speaking, did not turn his head.

'Don't you ever go thinking they'll go away, either,' he warned. 'When you and Karla are stuck on your ledge on the Reichenbach Falls and you've got your hands round Karla's throat, Brother Lacon will be right there behind you holding your coat-tails and telling you not to be beastly to the Russians. Did you get that?'

Smiley said yes, he had got it.

'What have you got on him so far? Misuse of the facilities of his office, I suppose. Fraud. Peculation of public funds, the very thing he topped that Lisbon fellow for. Unlawful operations abroad, including a couple of assassination jobs. I suppose there's a whole bloody bookful when you work it out. *Plus* all those jealous beavers at Centre longing for an excuse to knife him. He's right: blackmail's a *bloody* sight better than bribery.'

Smiley said, yes, it seemed so.

'You'll need people. Baby-sitters, lamplighters, all the forbidden toys. Don't talk to me about it, find your own. Money's another matter. I can lose you in the accounts for years the way these clowns in Treasury work. Just tell me when and how much and where, and I'll do a Karla for you and fiddle the accounts. How about passports and stuff? Need some addresses?'

'I think I can manage, thank you.'

'I'll watch you day and night. If the ploy aborts and there's a scandal, I'm not going to have people telling me I should have staked you out. I'll say I suspected you might be slipping the leash on the Vladimir thing and I decided to have you checked in case. I'll say the whole catastrophe was a ludicrous piece of private enterprise by a senile spy who's lost his marbles.'

Smiley said he thought that was a good idea.

'I may not have much to put on the street, but I can still tap your phone, steam open your mail, and if I want to, I'll bug your bedroom too. We've been listening in since Saturday as it is. Nothing of course, but what do you expect?'

Smiley gave a small nod of sympathy.

'If your departure abroad strikes me as hasty or mysterious, I shall report it. I also need a cover story for your visits to the Circus Registry. You'll go at night but you may be recognised and I'm not having *that* catch up with me, either.'

'There was a project once to commission an in-house history of the service,' Smiley said helpfully. 'Nothing for publication, obviously, but some sort of continuing record which could be available to new entrants and certain liaison services.'

'I'll send you a formal letter,' Enderby said. 'I'll bloody well backdate it too. If you happen to misuse your licence while you're inside the building, it's no fault of mine. That chap in Berne whom Kirov mentioned. Grigoriev, Commercial Counsellor. The chap who's been getting the cash?'

Smiley seemed lost in thought. 'Yes, yes, of course,' he said. 'Grigoriev?'

'I suppose he's your next stop, is he?'

A shooting star ran across the sky and for a second they both watched it.

Enderby pulled a plain piece of folded paper from his inside pocket. 'Well, that's Grigoriev's pedigree, far as we know it. He's clean as a whistle. One of the very rare ones. Used to be an economics don at some Bolshie university. Wife's a harridan.'

'Thank you,' said Smiley politely. 'Thank you very much.'

'Meanwhile, you have my totally deniable blessing,' said Enderby as they started back towards the house.

'Thank you,' said Smiley again.

'Sorry you've become an instrument of the imperial hypocrisy, but there's rather a lot of it about.'

'Not at all,' said Smiley.

Enderby stopped to let Smiley draw up beside him.

'How's Ann?'

'Well, thank you.'

'How much—' He was sufficiently off his stroke. 'Put it this way, George,' he suggested, when he had savoured the night air for a moment. 'You travelling on business, or for pleasure in this thing? Which is it?'

Smiley's reply was also slow in coming, and as indirect: 'I was never conscious of pleasure,' he said. 'Or perhaps I mean: of the distinction.'

'Karla still got that cigarette-lighter she gave you? It's true, isn't it? That time you interviewed him in Delhi – tried to get him to defect – they say he pinched your cigarette-lighter. Still got it, has he? Still using it? Pretty grating, I'd find that, if it was mine.'

'It was just an ordinary Ronson,' Smiley said. 'Still they're made to last, aren't they?'

They parted without saying goodbye.

20

In the weeks that followed this encounter with Enderby, George Smiley found himself in a complex and variable mood to accompany his many tasks of preparation. He was not at peace; he was not, in a single phrase, definable as a single person, beyond the one constant thrust of his determination. Hunter, recluse, lover, solitary man in search of completion, shrewd player of the Great Game, avenger, doubter in search of reassurance – Smiley was by turns each one of them, and sometimes more than one. Among those who remembered him later – old Mendel, the retired policeman, one of his few confidants; a Mrs Gray, the landlady of the humble bed-and-breakfast house for gentlemen only, in Pimlico, which for security reasons he made his temporary headquarters; or Toby Esterhase, alias Benati, the distinguished dealer in Arab art – most, in their various ways, spoke of an ominous *going in, a quietness*, an economy of word and glance, and they described it according to their knowledge of him, and their station in life.

Mendel, a loping, dourly observant man with a taste for keeping bees, said outright that George was pacing himself before his big fight. Mendel had been in the amateur ring in his time, he had boxed middleweight for the Division, and he claimed to recognise the eve-of-match signs: a sobriety, a clarifying loneliness, and what he called a staring sort of look, which showed that Smiley was 'thinking about his hands'. Mendel seems to have taken him in occasionally, and fed him meals. But Mendel was too perceptive not to observe the other sides of him also: the perplexity, often cloaked as social inhibition; his habit of slipping away, on a frail excuse, as if the sitting-still had suddenly become too long for him; as if he needed movement in order to escape himself.

To his landlady, Mrs Gray, Smiley was, quite simply, bereaved. She knew nothing of him as a man, except that his name was Lorimer and he was a retired librarian by trade. But she told her other gentlemen she could feel he had had a *loss*, which was why he left his bacon, why he went out a lot but always alone, and why he slept with his light on. He reminded her of her father, she said, 'after Mother went'. And this was perceptive of Mrs Gray, for the aftermath of the two violent deaths hung heavily on Smiley in the lull, though it did the very reverse of slow his hand. She was also right when she called him *divided*, constantly changing his mind about small things; like Ostrakova, Smiley found life's lesser decisions increasingly difficult to take.

Toby Esterhase, on the other hand, who dealt with him a great deal, took a more informed view, and one that was naturally brightened by Toby's own excitement at being back in the field. The prospect of playing Karla 'at the big table', as he insisted on describing it, had made a new man of Toby. Mr Benati had become international indeed. For two weeks, he toured the byways of Europe's seedier cities, mustering his bizarre army of discarded specialists – the pavement artists, the sound-thieves, the drivers, the photographers – and every day, from wherever he happened to be, using an agreed word code, he telephoned Smiley at a succession of numbers within walking distance of the boarding house in order to report his progress. If Toby was passing through London, Smiley would drive to an airport hotel, and debrief him in one of its now familiar bedrooms. George – Toby declared – was making a *Flucht nach vorn*, which nobody has ever quite succeeded in translating. Literally it means 'an escape forward', and it implies a desperation certainly, but also a weakness at one's back, if not an actual burning of boats. Quite what this weakness was, Toby could not describe. 'Listen,' he would say, 'George always bruised easy, know what I mean? You see a lot – your eyes get very painful. George saw too much, maybe.' And he added, in a phrase which found a modest place in Circus folklore – 'George has got too many heads under his hat.' Of his generalship, on the other hand, Toby had no doubt whatever. 'Meticulous to a fault,' he declared respectfully – even if the fault included checking Toby's imprest down to the last Swiss *Rappen*, a discipline he accepted with a rueful grace. George was nervous, he said, as they all were; and his nervousness came to a natural head as Toby began concentrating his teams, in twos and threes, on the target city of Berne, and very, very cautiously taking the first steps towards the quarry. 'He got too detailed,' Toby complained. 'Like he wanted to be on the pavement with us. A caseman, he finds it hard to delegate, know what I mean?'

Even when the teams were all assembled, all accounted for and briefed, Smiley from his London base still insisted on three days of virtual inactivity while everybody 'took the temperature of the city', as he called it, acquiring local clothes and transport, and rehearsed the systems of communication. 'It's lace curtain all the way, Toby,' he repeated anxiously. 'For every week that nothing happens, Karla will feel that much more secure. But frighten the game just once, and Karla will panic and we're done for.' After the first operational swing Smiley summoned Toby home to report yet again: 'Are you sure there was no eye contact? Did you ring the changes enough? Do you need more cars, more people?' Then, said Toby, he had to take him through the whole manoeuvre yet again, using street maps and still photographs of the target house, explaining exactly where the static posts were laid, where the one team had peeled off to make room for the next. 'Wait till you've got his pattern,' said Smiley as they parted. 'When you've got his behaviour pattern, I'll come. Not before.'

Toby says he made damn sure to take his time.

Of Smiley's visits to the Circus during this trying period there is, naturally, no official memory at all. He entered the place like his own ghost, floating as if invisible down the familiar corridors. At Enderby's suggestion, he arrived at a quarter past six in the evening, just after the day-shift had ended, and before the night staff had got into its stride. He had expected barriers; he had queasy notions of janitors he had known for twenty years telephoning the fifth floor for clearance. But Enderby had arranged things differently, and when Smiley presented himself, passless, at the hardboard chicane, a boy he had never seen before nodded him carelessly to the open lift. From there, he made his way unchallenged to the basement. He got out, and the first thing he saw was the welfare club noticeboard and they were the same notices from his own days exactly, word for word: free kittens available to good home; the junior staff drama group would read *The Admirable Crichton*, misspelt, on Friday in the canteen. The same squash competition, with players enrolled under worknames in the interest of security. The same ventilators emitting their troubled hum. So that, by the time he pushed the wired-glass door of Registry and scented the printing-ink and library dust, he half expected to see his own rotund shape bowed over the corner desk in the glow of the chipped green reading-lamp, as it had been often enough in the days when he was charting Bill Haydon's rampages of betrayal, and trying, by a reverse process of logic, to point to the weaknesses in Moscow Centre's armour.

'Ah, now, you're writing up our glorious past, I hear,' the night registrar sang indulgently. She was a tall girl and county, with Hilary's walk: she seemed to topple even when she sat. She plonked an old tin deed-box on the table. 'Fifth floor sent you this lot with their love,' she said. 'Squeal if you need ferrying around, won't you?'

The label on the handle read 'Memorabilia'. Lifting the lid, Smiley saw a heap of old buff files bound together with green string. Gently, he untied and lifted the cover of the first volume to reveal Karla's misted photograph staring up at him like a corpse from the darkness of its coffin. He read all night, he hardly stirred. He read as far into his own past as into Karla's, and sometimes it seemed to him that the one life was merely the complement to the other; that they were causes of the same incurable malady. He wondered, as so often before, how he would have turned out if he had had Karla's childhood, had been fired in the same kilns of revolutionary upheaval. He tried but, as so often before, failed to resist his own fascination at the sheer scale of the Russian suffering, its careless savagery, its flights of heroism. He felt small in the face of it, and soft by comparison, even though he did not consider his own life wanting in its pains. When the night-shift ended, he was still there, staring into the yellow pages 'the way a horse sleeps standing up,' said the same night registrar, who rode in gymkhanas. Even when she took the files from him to return them to the fifth floor, he went on staring till she gently touched his elbow.

He came the next night and the next; he disappeared, and

returned a week later without explanation. When he had done with Karla, he drew the files on Kirov, on Mikhel, on Villem, and on the Group at large, if only to give, in retrospect, a solid documentary heart to all he had heard and remembered of the Leipzig-Kirov story. For there was yet another part of Smiley, call it pedant, call it scholar, for which the file was the only truth, and all the rest a mere extravagance until it was matched and fitted to the record. He drew the files on Otto Leipzig and the General, too, and, as a service to their memory, if nothing else, added to each a memorandum which calmly set out the true circumstances of his death. The last file he drew was Bill Haydon's. There was hesitation at first about releasing it, and the fifth-floor duty officer, whoever he was that night, called Enderby out of a private ministerial dinner party in order to clear it with him. Enderby, to his credit, was furious: 'God Almighty, man, he *wrote* the damn thing in the first place, didn't he? If George can't read his own reports, who the hell can?' Smiley didn't really *read* it, even then, the registrar reported, who had a secret watching brief on everything he drew. It was more browsing, she said – and described a slow and speculative turning of the pages, 'like someone looking for a picture they'd seen and couldn't find again.' He only kept the file for an hour or so, then gave it back with a polite 'Thank you very much.' He did not come again after that, but there is a story the janitors tell that some time after eleven on the same night, when he had tidied away his papers and cleared his desk and consigned his few scribbled notes to the bin for secret waste, he was observed to stand for a long time in the rear courtyard – a dismal place, all white tiles and black drain-pipes and a stink of cat – staring at the building he was about to take his leave of, and of the light that was burning weakly in his former room, much as old men will look at the houses where they were born, the schools where they were educated, and the churches where they were married. And from Cambridge Circus – it was by then eleven-thirty – he startled everybody, took a cab to Paddington and caught the night sleeper to Penzance, which leaves just after midnight. He had not bought a ticket in advance, nor ordered one by telephone; nor did he have any night things with him, not even a razor, though in the morning he did manage to borrow one from the attendant. Sam Collins had put together a ragtag team of watchers by then, an amateurish lot admittedly, and all they could say afterwards was that he made a call from a phone box, but there was no time for them to do anything about it.

'Bloody queer moment to take a holiday, isn't it?' Enderby remarked petulantly, when this intelligence was brought to him, together with a string of moans from the staff-side about overtime, travelling time, and allowances for unsocial hours. Then he remembered, and said, 'Oh my Christ, he's visiting his bitch goddess. Hasn't he got enough problems, taking on Karla single-handed?' The whole episode annoyed Enderby strangely. He fumed all day and insulted Sam Collins in front of everyone. As a former diplomat, he had great contempt for abstracts, even if he took refuge in them constantly.

The house stood on a hill, in a coppice of bare elms still waiting for the blight. It was granite and very big, and crumbling, with a crowd of gables that clustered like torn black tents above the tree tops. Acres of smashed greenhouses led to it; collapsed stables and an untended kitchen garden lay below it in the valley. The hills were olive and shaven, and had once been hillforts. 'Harry's Cornish heap,' she called it. Between the hills ran the line of the sea, which that morning was hard as slate under the lowering cloud banks. A taxi took him up the bumpy drive, an old Humber like a wartime staff car. This is where she spent her childhood, thought Smiley; and where she adopted mine. The drive was very pitted: stubs of felled trees lay like yellow tombstones either side. She'll be in the main house, he thought. The cottage where they had passed their holidays together lay over the brow, but on her own she stayed in the house, in the room she had had as a girl. He told the driver not to wait, and started towards the front porch, picking his way between the puddles with his London shoes, giving the puddles all his attention. It's not my world any more, he thought. It's hers, it's theirs. His watcher's eyes scanned the many windows of the front façade, trying to catch a glimpse of her shadow. She'd have picked me up at the station, only she muddled the time, he thought, giving her the benefit of the doubt. But her car was parked in the stables with the morning frost still on it; he had spotted it while he was still paying off the taxi. He rang the bell and heard her footsteps on the flagstones, but it was Mrs Tremedda who opened the door and showed him to one of the drawing-rooms – smoking-room, morning-room, drawing-room, he had never worked them out. A log fire was burning.

'I'll get her,' Mrs Tremedda said.

At least I haven't got to talk about Communists to mad Harry, Smiley thought, while he waited. At least I haven't got to hear how all the Chinese waiters in Penzance are standing by for the order from Peking to poison their customers. Or how the bloody strikers should be put up against a wall and shot – where's their sense of service, for Christ's sake? Or how Hitler may have been a blackguard, but he had the right idea about the Jews. Or some similar monstrous, but seriously held, conviction.

She's told the family to keep clear, he thought.

He could smell honey through the wood-smoke and wondered, as he always did, where it came from. The furniture
wax? Or was there, somewhere in the catacombs, a honey
room, just as there was a gunroom and a fishing-room and a
box-room and, for all he knew, a love room? He looked for the
Tiepolo drawing that used to hang over the fireplace, a scene
of Venice life. They've sold it, he thought. Each time he came,
the collection had dwindled by one more pretty thing. What
Harry spent the money on was anybody's guess – certainly not
the upkeep of the house.

She crossed the room to him and he was glad it was she
who was doing the walking, not himself, because he would
have stumbled into something. His mouth was dry and he had
a lump of cactus in his stomach; he didn't want her near him,
her reality was suddenly too much for him. She was looking
beautiful and Celtic, as she always did down here, and as she
came towards him her brown eyes scanned him, looking for
his mood. She kissed him on the mouth, putting her fingers
along the back of his neck to guide him, and Haydon's shadow
fell between them like a sword.

'You didn't think to pick up a morning paper at the station,
did you?' she enquired. 'Harry's stopped them again.'

She asked whether he had breakfasted and he lied and said
he had. Perhaps they could go for a walk instead, she suggested, as if he were someone wanting to see round the estate. She took him to the gunroom where they rummaged for
boots that would do. There were boots that shone like conk-
ers and boots that looked permanently damp. The coast footpath led in both directions out of the bay. Periodically, Harry
threw barbed-wire barricades across it, or put up notices saying 'DANGER LANDMINES'. He was fighting a running battle
with the Council for permission to make a camping site, and

their refusal sometimes drove him to a fury. They chose the north shoulder and the wind, and she had taken his arm to listen. The north was windier, but on the south you had to go single file through the gorse.

'I'm going away for a bit, Ann,' he said, trying to use her name naturally. 'I didn't want to tell you over the telephone.' It was his wartime voice and he felt an idiot when he heard himself using it. 'I'm going off to blackmail a lover,' he should have said.

'Away to somewhere particular, or just away from me?'

'There's a job I have to do abroad,' he said, still trying to escape his Gallant Pilot rôle, and failing. 'I don't think you should go to Bywater Street while I'm away.'

She had locked her fingers through his own, but then she did those things: she handled people naturally, all people. Below them in the rocks' cleft, the sea broke and formed itself furiously in patterns of writhing foam.

'And you've come all this way just to tell me the house is out of bounds?' she asked.

He didn't answer.

'Let me try it differently,' she proposed when they had walked a distance. 'If Bywater Street had been *in* bounds, would you have suggested that I *did* go there? Or are you telling me it's out of bounds for good?'

She stopped and gazed at him, and held him away from her, trying to read his answer. She whispered, 'For goodness' sake,' and he could see the doubt, the pride, and the hope in her face all at once, and wondered what she saw in his, because he himself had no knowledge of what he felt, except that he belonged nowhere near her, nowhere near this place; she was like a girl on a floating island that was swiftly moving away from him with the shadows of all her lovers gathered round her. He loved her, he was indifferent to her, he observed her with the curse of detachment, but she was leaving him. If I do not know myself, he thought, how can I tell who you are? He saw the lines of age and pain and striving that their life together had put there. She was all he wanted, she was nothing, she reminded him of someone he had once known a long time ago; she was remote to him, he knew her entirely. He saw the gravity in her face and one minute wondered that he could ever have taken it for profundity; the next, he despised her dependence on him, and wanted only to be free of her. He wanted to call out 'Come back' but he didn't do it; he didn't even put out a hand to stop her from slipping away.

'You used to tell me never to stop looking,' he said. The statement began like the preface to a question, but no question followed.

She waited, then offered a statement of her own. 'I'm a comedian, George,' she said. 'I need a straight man. I need you.'

But he saw her from a long way off.

'It's the job,' he said.

'I can't live with them. I can't live without them.' He supposed she was talking about her lovers again. 'There's one thing worse than change and that's the status quo. I hate the choice. I love you. Do you understand?' There was a gap while he must have said something. She was not relying on him, but she was leaning on him while she wept, because the weeping had taken away her strength. 'You never knew how free you were, George,' he heard her say. 'I had to be free for both of us.'

She seemed to realise her own absurdity and laughed.

She let go his arm and they walked again while she tried to right the ship by asking plain questions. He said weeks, perhaps longer. He said, 'In a hotel,' but didn't say which city or country. She faced him again, and the tears were suddenly running anywhere, worse than before, but they still didn't move him as he wished they would.

'George, this is all there is, I promise you,' she said, halting to make her entreaty. 'The whistle's gone, in your world and in mine. We're landed with each other. There isn't any more. According to the averages, we're the most contented people on earth.'

He nodded, seeming to take the point that she had been somewhere he had not, but not regarding it as conclusive. They walked a little more, and he noticed that when she didn't speak he was able to relate to her, but only in the sense that she was another living creature moving along the same path as himself.

'It's to do with the people who ruined Bill Haydon,' he said to her, either as a consolation, or an excuse for his retreat. But he thought: 'Who ruined you.'

He had missed his train and there were two hours to kill. The tide was out so he walked along the shore near Marazion, scared by his own indifference. The day was grey, the seabirds were very white against the slate sea. A couple of brave children were splashing in the surf. I am a thief of the spirit, he thought despondently. Faithless, I am pursuing another man's convictions; I am trying to warm myself against other people's fires. He watched the children, and recalled some scrap of poetry from the days when he read it:

> *To turn as swimmers into cleanness leaping,*
> *Glad from a world grown old and cold and weary.*

Yes, he thought glumly. That's me.

'Now, George,' Lacon demanded. 'Do you think we set our women up too high, is *that* where we English middle-class chaps go wrong? Do you think – I'll put it this way – that we English, with our traditions and our schools, expect our womenfolk to stand for *far* too much, then *blame* them for not standing up at all – if you follow me? We see them as *concepts*, rather than flesh and blood. Is that our hangup?'

Smiley said it might be.

'Well, if it *isn't*, why does Val *always* fall for shits?' Lacon snapped aggressively, to the surprise of the couple sitting at the next-door table.

Smiley did not know the answer to that either.

They had dined, appallingly, in the steak-house Lacon had suggested. They had drunk Spanish burgundy out of a carafe, and Lacon had raged wildly over the British political dilemma. Now they were drinking coffee and a suspect brandy. The anti-Communist phobia was overdone: Lacon had declared himself sure of it. Communists were only people, after all. They weren't red-toothed monsters, not any more. Communists wanted what everyone wanted: prosperity and a bit of peace and quiet. A chance to take a breather from all this damned hostility. And if they didn't – well, what could we do about it anyway? he had asked. Some problems – take Ireland – were insoluble, but you would never get the Americans to admit *anything* was insoluble. Britain was ungovernable; so would everywhere else be in a couple of years. Our future was with the collective, but our survival was with the individual, and the paradox was killing us every day.

'Now, George, how do *you* see it? You're out of harness after all. You have the objective view, the overall perspective.'

Smiley heard himself muttering something inane about a spectrum.

And now the topic that Smiley had dreaded all evening was finally upon them: their seminar on marriage had begun.

'*We* were always taught that women had to be cherished,'

Lacon declared resentfully. 'If one didn't make 'em feel loved every minute of the day, they'd go off the rails. But this chap Val's with – well, if she annoys him, or speaks out of turn, he'll like as not give her a black eye. You and I never do that, do we?'

'I'm sure we don't,' said Smiley.

'Look here. Do you reckon if I went and saw her – bearded her in his house – took a really tough line – threatened legal action and so forth – it might tip the scales? I mean I'm bigger than he is, God knows. I'm not without clout, whichever way you read me!'

They stood on the pavement under the stars, waiting for Smiley's cab.

'Well, have a good holiday anyway. You've deserved it,' Lacon said. 'Going somewhere warm?'

'Well, I thought I might just take off and wander.'

'Lucky you. My God, I envy you your freedom! Well, you've been jolly useful, anyway. I shall follow your advice to the letter.'

'But, Oliver, I didn't *give* you any advice,' Smiley protested, slightly alarmed.

Lacon ignored him. 'And that other thing is all squared away, I hear,' he said serenely. 'No loose ends, no messiness. Good of you, that, George. Loyal. I'm going to see if we can get you a bit of recognition for it. What have you got already, I forget? Some chap the other day in the Athenaeum was saying you deserve a K.'

The cab came, and to Smiley's embarrassment Lacon insisted on shaking hands. 'George. Bless you. You've been a brick. We're birds of a feather, George. Both patriots, givers, not takers. Trained to our services. Our country. We must pay the price. If Ann had been your agent instead of your wife, you'd probably have run her pretty well.'

*

The next afternoon, following a telephone call from Toby to say that 'the deal was just about ready for completion', George Smiley quietly left for Switzerland, using the work-name Barraclough. From Zurich airport he took the Swissair bus to Berne and made straight for the Bellevue Palace Hotel, an enormous, sumptuous place of mellowed Edwardian quiet, which on clear days looks across the foothills to the glistening Alps, but that evening was shrouded in a cloying winter fog. He had considered smaller places; he had considered using one of Toby's safe flats. But Toby had persuaded him that the Bellevue was best. It had several exits, it was central, and it was the first place in Berne where anyone would think to find him, and therefore the last where Karla, if he was looking out for him, would expect him to be. Entering the enormous hall, Smiley had the feeling of stepping onto an empty liner far out at sea.

21

His room was a tiny Swiss Versailles. The *bombé* writing-desk had brass inlay and a marble top, a Bartlett print of Lord Byron's Childe Harold hung above the pristine twin beds. The fog outside the window made a grey wall. He unpacked and went downstairs again to the bar where an elderly pianist was playing a medley of hits from the fifties, things that had been Ann's favourites, and, he supposed, his. He ate some cheese and drank a glass of Fendant, thinking: *Now*. Now is the beginning. From now on there is no shrinking back, no space for hesitation. At ten he made his way to the old city, which he loved. The streets were cobbled; the freezing air smelt of roast chestnuts and cigars. The ancient fountains advanced on him through the fog, the medieval houses were the backdrop to a play he had no part in. He entered the arcades, passing art galleries and antique shops, and doorways tall enough to ride a horse through. At the Nydegg Bridge he came to a halt, and stared into the river. So many nights, he thought. So many streets still here. He thought of Hesse: *strange to wander in the fog . . . no tree knows another*. The frozen mist curled low over the racing water; the weir burned creamy yellow.

An orange Volvo estate car drew up behind him, Berne registration, and briefly doused its lights. As Smiley started towards it, the passenger door was pushed open from inside, and by the interior light he saw Toby Esterhase in the driving seat and, in the back, a stern-looking woman in the uniform of a Bernese housewife, dandling a child on her knee. He's using them for cover, Smiley thought; for what the watchers called the silhouette. They drove off and the woman began talking to the child. Her Swiss German had a steady note of indignation: 'See there the crane, Eduard . . . Now we are passing the bear-pit, Eduard . . . Look, Eduard, a tram . . .' Watchers are always dissatisfied, he remembered; it's the fate of every voyeur. She was moving her hands about, directing the child's eye to anything. *A family evening, Officer*, said the scenario. *We are going visiting in our fine orange Volvo, Officer. We are going home*. And the men, naturally, Officer, seated in the front.

They had entered Elfenau, Berne's diplomatic ghetto. Through the fog, Smiley glimpsed tangled gardens white with frost, and the green porticos of villas. The headlights picked out a brass plate proclaiming an Arab state, and two bodyguards protecting it. They passed an English church and a row of tennis-courts; they entered an avenue lined with bare beeches. The street lights hung in them like white balloons.

'Number eighteen is five hundred metres on the left,' said Toby softly. 'Grigoriev and his wife occupy the ground floor.' He was driving slowly, using the fog as his excuse.

'Very rich people live here, Eduard!' the woman was singing from behind them. 'All from foreign places.'

'Most of the Iron Curtain crowd live in Muri, not Elfenau,' Toby went on. 'It's a commune, they do everything in groups. Shop in groups, go for walks in groups, you name it. The Grigorievs are different. Three months ago, they moved out of Muri and rented this apartment on a personal basis. Three thousand five hundred a month, George, he pays it in person to the landlord.'

'Cash?'

'Monthly in one-hundred notes.'

'How are the rest of the Embassy hirings paid for?'

'Through the Mission accounts. Not Grigoriev's. Grigoriev is the exception.'

A police-patrol car overtook them with the slowness of a river barge; Smiley saw its three heads turned to them.

'Look, Eduard, police!' the woman cried, and tried to make the child wave at them.

Toby too was careful not to stop talking. 'The police boys are worried about bombs,' he explained. 'They think the Palestinians are going to blow the place sky high. That's been good and bad for us, George. If we're clumsy, Grigoriev can tell himself we're local angels. The same doesn't go for the police. One hundred metres, George. Look for a black Mercedes in the forecourt. Other staff use the Embassy car pool. Not Grigoriev. Grigoriev drives his own Mercedes.'

'When did he get it?' Smiley asked.

'Three months ago, second-hand. Same time as he moved out of Muri. That was a big leap for him, George. Like a birthday, so many things. Car, house, promotion from First Secretary to Counsellor.'

It was a stucco villa, set in a large garden that had no back because of the fog. In a bay window at the front Smiley glimpsed a light burning behind curtains. There was a children's slide in the garden, and what appeared to be an empty swimming-pool. On the gravel sweep stood a black Mercedes with CD plates.

'All Soviet Embassy car numbers end with 73,' said Toby. 'The Brits have 72. Grigorieva got herself a driving licence two months ago. There are only two women in the Embassy with licences. She's one and she's a terrible driver, George. And I mean terrible.'

'Who occupies the rest of the house?'

'The landlord. A professor at Berne University, a creep. A while ago the Cousins got alongside him and said they'd like to run a couple of probe mikes into the ground floor, offered him money. The professor took the money and reported them to the Bundespolizei like a good citizen. The Bundespolizei got a scare. They'd promised the Cousins to look the other way in exchange for a sight of the product. Operation abandoned. Seems the Cousins had no particular interest in Grigoriev, it was just routine.'

'Where are the Grigoriev children?'

'In Geneva at Soviet Mission School, weekly boarders. They get home Friday nights. Weekends, the family make excursions. Romp in the woods, langlauf, play badminton. Collect mushrooms. Grigorieva's a fresh-air freak. Also they have taken up bicycling,' he added, with a glance.

'Does Grigoriev go with the family on these excursions?'

'Saturdays he works, George – and, I am certain, only to escape them.' Toby had decided views on the Grigoriev marriage, Smiley noticed. He wondered whether it had echoes of one of Toby's own.

They had left the avenue and entered a side-road. 'Listen, George,' Toby was saying, still on the subject of Grigoriev's weekends. 'Okay? Watchers imagine things. They got to, it's their job. There's a girl works in the Visa Section. Brunette and, for a Russian, sexy. The boys call her "little Natasha". Her real name's something else but for them she's Natasha. Saturdays she comes in to the Embassy. To work. Couple of times, Grigoriev drives her home to Muri. We took some pictures, not bad. She got out of the car short of her apartment and walked the last five hundred metres. Why? Another time he took her nowhere – just a drive round the Gurten, but talking very cosy. Maybe the boys just want it to be that way, on account of Grigorieva. They like the guy, George. You know how watchers are. It's love or hate all the time. They like him.'

He was pulling up. The lights of a small café glowed at them through the fog. In its courtyard stood a green Citroën deux chevaux, Geneva registration. Cardboard boxes were heaped on the back seat, like trade samples. A foxtail dangled from the radio aerial. Springing out, Toby pulled open the flimsy door and hustled Smiley into the passenger seat: then handed him a trilby hat, which he put on. For himself, Toby had a Russian-style fur. They drove off again, and Smiley saw their Bernese matron climbing into the front of the orange Volvo they had just abandoned. Her child waved at them despondently through the back window as they left.

'How is everyone?' Smiley said.

'Great. Pawing the earth, George, every one of them. One of the Sartor brothers had a sick kid, had to go home to Vienna. It nearly broke his heart. Otherwise great. You're Number One for all of them. This is Harry Slingo coming up on the right. Remember Harry? Used to be my sidekick back in Acton.'

'I read that his son had won a scholarship to Oxford,' Smiley said.

'Physics. Wadham, Oxford. The boy's a genius. Keep looking down the road, George, don't move your head.'

They passed a blue van with '*Auto-Schnelldienst*' painted in breezy letters on the side, and a driver dozing at the wheel.

'Who's in the back?' Smiley asked when they were clear.

'Pete Lusty, used to be a scalp-hunter. Those guys have been having it very bad, George. No work, no action. Pete signed up for the Rhodesian Army. Killed some guys, didn't care for it, came back. No wonder they love you.'

They were passing Grigoriev's house again. A light was burning in the other window.

'The Grigorievs go to bed early,' Toby said in a sort of awe.

A parked limousine lay ahead of them with Zurich consular plates. In the driving seat, a chauffeur was reading a paperback book.

'That's Canada Bill,' Toby explained. 'Grigoriev leaves the house, turns right, he passes Pete Lusty. Turns left, he passes Canada Bill. They're good boys. Very vigilant.'

'Who's behind us?'

'The Meinertzhagen girls. The big one got married.'

The fog made their progress private, very quiet. They descended a gentle hill, passing the British Ambassador's residence on their right, and his Rolls-Royce parked in the sweep. The road led left and Toby followed it. As he did so, the car behind overtook them and conveniently put up its headlights. By their beam, Smiley found himself looking into a wooded cul-de-sac ending in a pair of tall closed gates guarded on the inside by a small huddle of men. The trees cut off the rest entirely.

'Welcome to the Soviet Embassy, George,' Toby said, very softly. 'Twenty-four diplomats, fifty other ranks – cipher clerks, typists, and some very lousy drivers, all home-based. The trade delegation's in another building, Schanzeneckstrasse 17. Grigoriev visits there a lot. In Berne we got also Tass and Novosti, mostly mainstream hoods. The parent residency is Geneva, UN cover, about two hundred strong. This place is a side-show: twelve, fifteen altogether, growing but only slow. The Consulate is tacked onto the back of the Embassy. You go into it through a door in the fence, like it was an opium den or a cat house. They got a closed-circuit television camera on the path and scanners in the waiting-room. Try applying for a visa once.'

'I think I'll give it a miss, thanks,' said Smiley, and Toby gave one of his rare laughs.

'Embassy grounds,' Toby said, as the headlights flashed over steep woods falling away to the right. 'That's where Grigorieva plays her volley-ball, gives political instruction to the kids. George, believe me, that's a very distorting woman. Embassy kindergarten, the indoctrination classes, the Ping-Pong club, women's badminton – that woman runs the whole show. Don't take my word for it, hear my boys talk about her.' As they turned out of the cul-de-sac, Smiley lifted his glance towards the upper window of the corner house and saw a light go out, and then come on again.

'And that's Pauli Skordeno saying "Welcome to Berne,"' said Toby. 'We managed to rent the top floor last week. Pauli's a Reuters stringer. We even faked a press pass for him. Cable cards, everything.'

Toby had parked near the Thunplatz. A modern clock tower was striking eleven. Fine snow was falling but the fog had not dispersed. For a moment neither man spoke.

'Today was a model of last week, last week was a model of the week before, George,' said Toby. 'Every Thursday it's the same. After work he takes the Mercedes to the garage, fills it with petrol and oil, checks the batteries, asks for a receipt. He goes home. Six o'clock, a little after, an Embassy car arrives at his front door and out gets Krassky, the regular Thursday courier from Moscow. Alone. That's a very itchy fellow, a professional. In all other situations, Krassky don't go anywhere without his companion, Bogdanov. Fly together, carry together, eat together. But to visit Grigoriev, Krassky breaks ranks and goes alone. Stays half an hour, leaves again. Why? That's very irregular in a courier, George. Very dangerous, if he hasn't got the backing, believe me.'

'So what do you make of Grigoriev, Toby?' Smiley asked. 'What is he?'

Toby made his tilting gesture with his outstretched palm. 'A trained hood Grigoriev isn't, George. No tradecraft, actually a complete catastrophe. But he's not straight either. A half-breed, George.'

So was Kirov, Smiley thought.

'Do you think we've got enough on him?' Smiley asked.

'Technically no problem. The bank, the false identity, little Natasha, even: technically, we got a hand of aces.'

'And you think he'll burn,' said Smiley, more as confirmation than a question.

In the darkness, Toby's palm once more tilted, this way, that way.

'Burning, George, that's always a hazard, know what I mean? Some guys get heroic and want to die for their countries suddenly. Other guys roll over and lie still the moment you put the arm on them. Burning, that touches the stubbornness in certain people. Know what I mean?'

'Yes. Yes, I think I do,' said Smiley. And he remembered Delhi again, and the silent face watching him through the haze of cigarette smoke.

'Go easy, George. Okay? You got to put your feet up now and then.'

'Good night,' said Smiley.

He caught the last tram back to the town centre. By the time he had reached the Bellevue, the snow was falling heavily: big flakes, milling in the yellow light, too wet to settle. He set his alarm for seven.

22

The young woman they called Alexandra had been awake one hour exactly when the morning bell sounded for assembly, but when she heard it she immediately drew up her knees inside her calico night-suit, crammed her eyelids together, and swore to herself she was still asleep, a child who needed rest. The assembly bell, like Smiley's alarm clock, went off at seven, but already at six she had heard the chiming of the valley clocks, first the Catholics, then the Protestants, then the Town Hall, and she didn't believe in any of them. Not this God, not that God, and least of all the burghers with their butchers' faces, who at the annual festival had stood to attention with their stomachs stuck out while the fire-brigade choir moaned patriotic songs in dialect.

She knew about the annual festival because it was one of the few Permitted Expeditions, and she had recently been allowed to attend it as a privilege, her first, and to her huge amusement it was devoted to the celebration of the common onion. She had stood between Sister Ursula and Sister Beatitude and she knew they were both alert in case she tried to run away or snap inside and start a fit, and she had watched an hour of the most boring speechifying ever, then an hour's singing to the accompaniment of boring martial music by the brass band. Then a march past of people dressed in village costume and carrying strings of onions on long sticks, headed by the village flag-swinger, who on other days brought the milk to the lodge and – if he could slip by – right up to the hostel door, in the hope of getting a sight of a girl through the window, or perhaps it was just Alexandra trying to get a sight of him.

After the village clocks had chimed the six, Alexandra from deep, deep in her bed had decided to count the minutes till eternity. In her self-imposed rôle as a child, she had done this by counting each second in a whisper: 'One-thousand and-*one*, one-thousand-and-*two*.' At twelve minutes past, by her childish reckoning, she heard Mother Felicity's pompous moped snorting down the drive on her way back from Mass, telling everyone that Felicity-Felicity – pop-pop – and no one else – pop-pop – was our Superintendent and Official Starter of the Day; nobody else – pop-pop – would do. Which was funny because her real name was not Felicity at all; Felicity was what she had chosen for the other nuns. Her real name, she had told Alexandra as a secret, was Nadezhda, meaning 'Hope'. So Alexandra had told Felicity that *her* real name was Tatiana, not Alexandra at all. Alexandra was a *new* name, she explained, put on to wear in Switzerland specially. But Felicity-Felicity had told her sharply not to be a silly girl.

After Mother Felicity's arrival, Alexandra had held the white bed sheet to her eyes and decided that time was not passing at all, that she was in a child's white limbo where everything was shadowless, even Alexandra, even Tatiana. White light bulbs, white walls, a white iron bed frame. White radiators. Through the high windows, white mountains against a white sky.

Dr Rüedi, she thought, here is a new dream for you when we have our next little Thursday talk, or is it Tuesday?

Now listen carefully, Doctor. Is your Russian good enough?

Sometimes you pretend to understand more than you really do. Very well, I will begin. My name is Tatiana and I am standing in my white night-suit in front of the white Alpine landscape, trying to write on the mountain face with a stick of Felicity-Felicity's white chalk, whose real name is Nadezhda. I am wearing nothing underneath. You pretend you are indifferent to such things, but when I talk to you about how I love my body you pay close attention, don't you, Dr Rüedi? I scribble with the chalk in the mountain face. I stub with it like a cigarette. I think of the filthiest words I know – yes, Dr Rüedi, *this* word, *that* word – but I fear your Russian vocabulary is unlikely to include them. I try to write them also, but white on white, what impact can a little girl make, I ask you, Doctor?

Doctor, it's terrible, you must never have my dreams. Do you know I was once a whore called Tatiana? That I can do no wrong? That I can set fire to things, even myself, vilify the State, and *still* the wise ones in authority will not punish me? But instead, they let me out of the back door – 'Go, Tatiana, go' – did you know this?

Hearing footsteps in the corridor, Alexandra pulled herself deeper under the bedclothes. The French girl is being led to the toilets, she thought. The French girl was the most beautiful in the place. Alexandra loved her, just for her beauty. She beat the whole system with it. Even when they put her in the coat – for clawing or messing herself or smashing something – her angel's face still gazed at them like one of their own icons. Even when she wore her shapeless night-suit with no buttons, her breasts lifted it up in a crisp bridge and there was nothing anyone could do, not even the most jealous, not even Felicity-Felicity whose secret name was Hope, to prevent her from looking like a film star. When she tore her clothes off, even the nuns stared at her with a kind of covetous terror. Only the American girl had matched her for looks, and the American girl had been taken away, she was too bad. The French girl was bad enough with her naked tantrums and her wrist-cutting and her fits of rage at Felicity-Felicity, but she was nothing beside the American girl by the time she left. The sisters had to fetch Kranko from the lodge to hold her down, just for the sedation. They had to close the entire rest-wing while they did it, but when the van took the American girl off, it was like a death in the family and Sister Beatitude wept all through evening prayers. And afterwards, when Alexandra forced her to tell, she called her by her pet name, Sasha, a sure sign of her distress.

'The American girl has gone to Untersee,' she said through her tears when Alexandra forced her to tell. 'Oh, Sasha, Sasha, promise me you will never go to Untersee.' Just as in the life she could not mention, they had begged her: 'Tatiana, do not do these mad and dangerous things!'

After that, Untersee became Alexandra's worst terror, a threat that silenced her at any time, even her naughtiest: 'If you are bad you will go to Untersee, Sasha. If you tease Dr Rüedi, pull up your skirt, and cross your legs at him, Mother Felicity will have to send you to Untersee. Hush, or they'll send you to Untersee.'

The footsteps returned along the corridor. The French girl was taken to be dressed. Sometimes she fought them and ended up in the coat instead. Sometimes Alexandra would be sent to calm her, which she did by brushing the French girl's hair over and over again, not talking, till the French girl relaxed and started to kiss her hands. Then Alexandra would be taken away again because love was not, was not, was *not* on the curriculum.

The door flew open and Alexandra heard Felicity-Felicity's courtly voice, harrying her like an old nurse in a Russian play:

'Sasha! You must get up immediately! Sasha, wake up immediately! Sasha, wake up! Sasha!'

She came a step nearer. Alexandra wondered whether she was going to pull back the sheets and yank her to her feet. Mother Felicity could be rough as a soldier, for all her aristocratic blood. She was not a bully, but she was blunt and easily provoked.

'Sasha, you will be late for breakfast. The other girls will look at you and laugh and say that we stupid Russians are always late. Sasha? Sasha, do you want to miss prayers? God will be very angry with you, Sasha. He will be sad and He will cry. He may have to think of ways of punishing you.'

Sasha, do you want to go to Untersee?

Alexandra pressed her eyelids closer together. I am six years old and need my sleep, Mother Felicity. God make me five, God make me four. I am three years old and need my sleep, Mother Felicity.

'Sasha, have you forgotten it is your special day? Sasha, have you forgotten you have your *visitor* today?'

God make me two, God make me one, God make me nothing and unborn. No, I have not forgotten my visitor, Mother Felicity. I remembered my visitor before I went to sleep. I dreamt of him, I have thought of nothing else since I woke. But, Mother Felicity, I do not want my visitor today, or any other day. I cannot, cannot live the lie, I don't know how, and that is why I shall not, shall not, *shall* not let the day begin!

Obediently, Alexandra clambered out of bed.

'*There*,' said Mother Felicity, and gave her a distracted kiss before bustling off down the corridor, calling 'Late again! Late again!' and clapping her hands – 'Shoo, shoo!' – just as she would to a flock of silly hens.

23

The train journey to Thun took half an hour and from the station Smiley drifted, window-shopping, making little detours. *Some guys get heroic and want to die for their countries*, he thought . . . *Burning, that touches the stubbornness in people* . . . He wondered what it would touch in himself.

It was a day of darkening blankness. The few pedestrians were slow shadows against the fog, and lake steamers were frozen in the locks. Occasionally the blankness parted enough to offer him a glimpse of castle, a tree, a piece of city wall. Then swiftly closed over them again. Snow lay in the cobbles and in the forks of the knobbly spa trees. The few cars drove with their lights on, their tyres crackling in the slush. The only colours were in shop-windows: gold watches, ski clothes like national flags. 'Be there eleven earliest,' Toby had said; 'eleven is already too early, George, they won't arrive till twelve.' It was only ten-thirty but he wanted the time, he wanted to circle before he settled; time, as Enderby would say, to get his ducks in a row. He entered a narrow street and saw the castle lift directly above him. The arcade became a pavement, then a staircase, then a steep slope, and he kept climbing. He passed an English Tea-Room, an American-Bar, an Oasis Night-Club, each hyphenated, each neon-lit, each a sanitised copy of a lost original.

But they could not destroy his love of Switzerland. He

entered a square and saw the bank, the very one, and straight across the road the little hotel exactly as Toby had described it, with its café-restaurant on the ground floor and its barracks of rooms above. He saw the yellow mail van parked boldly in the no-parking bay, and he knew it was Toby's static post. Toby had a lifelong faith in mail vans; he stole them wherever he went, saying nobody noticed or remembered them. He had fitted new number-plates but they looked older than the van. Smiley crossed the square. A notice on the bank door said 'OPEN MONDAY TO THURSDAY 07.45–17.00, FRIDAY 07.45–18.15'. 'Grigoriev likes the lunch hour because in Thun nobody wastes his lunch hour going to the bank,' Toby had explained. 'He has completely mistaken quiet for security, George. Empty places, empty times, Grigoriev is so conspicuous he's embarrassing.' He crossed a foot-bridge. The time was ten to eleven. He crossed the road and headed for the little hotel with its unencumbered view of Grigoriev's bank. Tension in a vacuum, he thought, listening to the slip of his own feet and the gurgle of water from the gutters; the town was out of season and out of time. *Burning, George, that's always a hazard.* How would Karla do it? he wondered. What would the absolutist do which we are not doing ourselves? Smiley could think of nothing, short of straight physical abduction. Karla would collect the operational intelligence, he thought, then he would make his approach – risking the hazard. He pushed the café door and the warm air sighed to him. He made for a window table marked 'RESERVED'. 'I'm waiting for Mr Jacobi,' he told the girl. She nodded disapprovingly, missing his eye. The girl had a cloistered pallor, and no expression at all. He ordered *café-crème* in a glass, but she said that if it came in a glass, he would have to have schnapps with it.

'Then in a cup,' he said, capitulating.

Why had he asked for a glass in the first place?

Tension in a vacuum, he thought again, looking round. Hazard in a blank place.

The café was modern Swiss antique. Crossed plastic lances hung from stucco pillars. Hidden speakers played harmless music; the confiding voice changed language with each announcement. In a corner, four men played a silent game of cards. He looked out of the window, into the empty square. Rain had started again, turning white to grey. A boy cycled past wearing a red woollen cap, and the cap went down the road like a torch until the fog put it out. The bank's doors were double, he noticed, opened by electronic eye. He looked at his watch. Eleven-ten. A till murmured. A coffee machine hissed. The card-players were dealing a new hand. Wooden plates hung on the wall: dancing couples in national costume. What else was there to look at? The lamps were wrought iron but the illumination came from a ring of strip lighting round the ceiling and it was very harsh. He thought of Hong Kong, with its Bavarian beer cellars on the fifteenth floor, the same sense of waiting for explanations that would never be supplied. And today is only preparation, he thought: today is not even the approach. He looked at the bank again. Nobody entering, nobody leaving. He remembered waiting all his life for something he could no longer define: call it resolution. He remembered Ann, and their last walk. Resolution in a vacuum. He heard a chair squeak, saw Toby's hand held out for him, Swiss style, to shake, and Toby's bright face sparkling as if he'd just come in from a run.

'The Grigorievs left the house in Elfenau five minutes ago,' he said quietly. 'Grigorieva's driving. Most likely they die before they get here.'

'And the bicycles?' Smiley asked anxiously.

'Like normal,' said Toby pulling up a chair.

'Did she drive last week?'

'Also the week before. She insists. George, I mean, that woman is a monster.' The girl brought him a coffee unbidden. 'Last week, she actually hauled Grigoriev out of the driving seat, then drove the car into the gate post, clipped the wing. Pauli and Canada Bill were laughing so much we thought we'd get static on the whisperers.' He put a friendly hand on Smiley's shoulder. 'Listen, it's going to be a nice day. Believe me. Nice light, a nice layout, all you got to do is sit back and enjoy the show.'

The phone rang, and the girl called 'Herr Jacobi!' Toby walked easily to the counter. She handed him the receiver and blushed at something he whispered to her. From the kitchen, the chef came in with his small son: 'Herr Jacobi!' The chrysanthemums on Smiley's table were plastic but someone had put water in the vase.

'*Ciao*,' Toby called cheerfully into the phone, and came back. 'Everyone in position, everyone happy,' he announced with satisfaction. 'Eat something, okay? Enjoy yourself, George. This is Switzerland.'

Toby stepped gaily into the street. *Enjoy the show*, thought Smiley. That's right. I wrote it, Toby produced it, and all I can do now is watch. No, he thought, correcting himself: Karla wrote it, and sometimes that worried him quite a lot.

Two girls in hiking kit were entering the double doors of the bank. A moment later and Toby had followed them in. He's packing the bank, thought Smiley. He'll man every counter two-deep. After Toby, a young couple, arm in arm, then a stubby woman with two shopping bags. The yellow mail van had not budged: nobody moves a mail van. He noticed a public phone box, and two figures huddled into it, perhaps sheltering from the rain. Two people are less conspicuous than one, they liked to say at Sarratt, and three are less conspicuous than a pair. An empty tour coach passed. A clock struck twelve and, right on cue, a black Mercedes lurched out of the fog, its dipped headlights glittering on the cobble. Bumping clumsily on to the kerb, it stopped outside the bank, six feet from Toby's mail van. *Soviet Embassy car numbers end with 73*, Toby had said. *She drops him and drives round the block a couple of times till he comes out.* But today, in the filthy weather, the Grigorievs had apparently decided to flout the parking laws and Karla's laws too, and rely on their CD plates to keep them out of trouble. The passenger door opened and a stocky figure in a dark suit and spectacles scampered for the bank entrance, carrying a briefcase. Smiley had just time to record the thick grey hair and rimless spectacles of Grigoriev's photographs before a lorry masked his view. When it moved on, Grigoriev had disappeared, but Smiley had a clear sight of the formidable bulk of Grigorieva herself, with her red hair and learner-driver scowl, seated alone at the steering-wheel. *George, believe me, that's a very distorting woman.* Seeing her now, her jaw set, her bullish glare, Smiley was able for the first time, if cautiously, to share Toby's optimism. If fear was the essential concomitant of a successful burn, Grigorieva was certainly someone to be afraid of.

In his mind's eye, Smiley now imagined the scene that was playing inside the bank, exactly as he and Toby had planned. The bank was a small one, a team of seven could flood it. Toby had opened a private account for himself: Herr Jacobi, a few thousand francs. Toby would take one counter and occupy it with small transactions. The foreign-exchange desk was also no problem. Two of Toby's people, armed with a spread of currencies, could keep them on the run for minutes. He imagined the hubbub of Toby's hilarity, causing Grigoriev to raise his voice. He imagined the two girl hikers doing a double act, one rucksack dumped carelessly at Grigoriev's feet, recording whatever he happened to say to the cashier; and the hidden cameras snapping away from toggle bags, rucksacks, brief-cases, bedrolls, or wherever they were stowed. 'It's the same as the firing-squad, George,' Toby explained, when Smiley said he was worried about the shutter noise. 'Everybody hears the click except the quarry.'

The bank doors slid open. Two businessmen emerged, adjusting their raincoats as if they had been to the lavatory. The stubby woman with the two shopping bags followed them out, and Toby came after her, chatting volubly to the girl hikers. Next came Grigoriev himself. Oblivious of everything, he hopped into the black Mercedes and planted a kiss on his wife's cheek before she had time to turn away. He saw her mouth show criticism of him, and Grigoriev's placatory smile as he replied. Yes, Smiley thought, he certainly has something to be guilty about; yes, he thought, remembering the watchers' affection for him: yes, I understand that too. But the Grigorievs did not leave; not yet. Grigoriev had hardly closed his door before a tall, vaguely familiar woman in a green Loden coat came striding down the pavement, tapped fiercely on the passenger window and delivered herself of what seemed to be a homily upon the sins of parking on pavements. Grigoriev was embarrassed. Grigorieva leaned across him and bawled at her – Smiley even heard the word *Diplomat* in heavy German rise above the sound of the traffic – but the woman remained where she was, her handbag under her arm, still swearing at them as they drove away. She'll have snapped them in the car with the bank doors in the background, he thought. They photograph through perforations: half a dozen pinholes and the lens can see perfectly.

Toby had returned and was sitting beside him at the table. He had lit a small cigar. Smiley could feel him trembling like a dog after the chase.

'Grigoriev drew his normal ten thousand,' he said. His English had become a little rash. 'Same as last week, same as the week before. We got it, George, the whole scene. The boys are very happy, the girls too. George, I mean they are fantastic. Completely the best. I never had so good. What do you think of him?'

Surprised to be asked, Smiley actually laughed.

'He's certainly henpecked,' he agreed.

'And a nice fellow, know what I mean? Reasonable. I think he'll act reasonable too. That's my view, George. The boys are the same.'

'Where do the Grigorievs go from here?'

A sharp male voice interrupted them. 'Herr Jacobi!'

But it was only the chef, holding up a glass of schnapps to drink Toby's health. Toby returned the toast.

'Lunch at the station buffet, first-class,' he continued. 'Grigorieva takes pork chop and chips, Grigoriev steak, a glass of beer. Maybe they take also a couple of vodkas.'

'And after lunch?'

Toby gave a brisk nod, as if the question required no elucidation.

'Sure,' he said. 'That's where they go. George, cheer up. That guy will fold, believe me. You never had a wife like that. And Natasha's a cute kid.' He lowered his voice. 'Karla's his meal ticket, George. You don't always understand the simple things. You think she'd let him give up the new apartment? The Mercedes?'

Alexandra's weekly visitor arrived, always punctual, always at the same time, which was on Fridays after rest. At one o'clock came lunch, which on Fridays consisted of cold meat and *Rösti* and *Kompott* of apples or perhaps plums, depending on the season, but she couldn't eat it and sometimes she made a show of sicking it up or running to the lavatory or calling Felicity-Felicity and complaining, in the basest language, about the quality of the food. This never failed to annoy her. The hostel took great pride in growing its own fruit, and the hostel's brochures in Felicity-Felicity's office contained many photographs of fruit and blossom and Alpine streams and mountains indiscriminately, as if God, or the sisters, or Dr Rüedi, had grown the whole lot specially for the inmates. After lunch came an hour's rest and on Fridays this daily hour was Alexandra's worst, her worst of the whole week, when she had to lie on the white iron bedstead and pretend she was relaxing, while she prayed to any God that would have her that Uncle Anton might be run over or have a heart attack, or, best of all, cease to exist – locked away with her own past and her own secrets and her own name of Tatiana. She thought of his rimless spectacles and in her imagination she drove them into his head and out the other side, taking his eyes with them, so that instead of his soggy gaze to stare at, she would see straight through him to the world outside.

And now at last rest had ended, and Alexandra stood in the empty dining hall in her best frock, watching the lodge through the window while two of the Marthas scoured the tiled floor. She felt sick. Crash, she thought. Crash on your silly bicycle. Other girls had visitors, but they came on Saturdays and none had Uncle Anton, few had men of any sort; it was mainly wan aunts and bored sisters who attended. And none got Felicity-Felicity's study to sit in, either, with the door closed and nobody present but the visitor; that was a privilege which Alexandra and Uncle Anton enjoyed alone, as Sister Beatitude never tired of pointing out. But Alexandra would have traded all of those privileges, and a good few more beside, for the privilege of not having Uncle Anton's visit at all.

The lodge gates opened and she began trembling on purpose, shaking her hands from the wrists as if she had seen a mouse, or a spider, or a naked man aroused for her. A tubby figure in a brown suit began cycling down the drive. He was not a natural cyclist, she could tell from his self-consciousness. He had not cycled here from any distance, bringing a breath of outside. It could be baking hot, but Uncle Anton neither sweated nor burned. It could be raining heavily, but Uncle Anton's mackintosh and hat, when he reached the main door, would scarcely be wet, and his shoes were never muddied. Only when the giant snowfall had come, three weeks ago, or call it years, and put a metre's thickness of extra padding round the dead castle, did Uncle Anton look anything like a real man living in the real elements; in his thick knee-boots and anorak and fur hat, skirting the pine trees as he plodded up the track, he stepped straight out of the memories she was never to mention. And when he had embraced her, calling her 'my little daughter', slapping his big gloves down on Felicity-Felicity's highly polished table, she felt such a surge of kinship and hope that she would catch herself smiling for days afterwards.

'He was so warm,' she confided to Sister Beatitude in her bit of French. 'He held me like a friend! Why does the snow make him so fond?'

But today there was only sleet and fog and big floppy flakes that would not settle on the yellow gravel.

He comes in a car, Sasha – Sister Beatitude told her once – with a *woman*, Sasha. Beatitude had seen them. Twice. Watched them, naturally. They had two bicycles strapped to the roof of the car, upside down, and the woman did the driving, a big strong woman, a bit like Mother Felicity but not so Christian, with hair red enough to scare a bull. When they reached the edge of the village, they parked the car behind Andreas Gertsch's barn, and Uncle Anton untied his bicycle and rode it to the lodge. But the woman stayed in the car and smoked, and read *Schweizer Illustrierte*, sometimes scowling at the mirror, and her bicycle never left the roof; it stayed there like an upturned sow while she read her magazine! And guess what! Uncle Anton's bicycle was *illegal*! The bicycle – as a good Swiss, Sister Beatitude had checked the point quite naturally – Uncle Anton's bicycle had no *plaque*, no licence, he was a criminal at large, and so was the woman, though she was probably too fat to ride it!

But Alexandra cared nothing for illegal bicycles. It was the car she wanted to know about. What type? Rich or poor? What colour, and above all, where did it come from? Was it from Moscow, from Paris, where? But Sister Beatitude was a country girl and simple, and in the world beyond the mountains most foreign places were alike to her. Then what letters were on the number-plate, for goodness' sake, silly? Alexandra had cried. Sister Beatitude had not noticed such matters. Sister Beatitude shook her head like the dumb dairymaid she was. Bicycles and cows she understood. Cars were beyond her mark.

Alexandra watched Grigoriev arrive, she waited for the moment when he leaned his head forward over the handlebars and raised his ample bottom in the air and swung one short leg over the crossbar as if he were climbing off a woman. She saw how the short ride had reddened his face, she watched him unfasten the brief-case from the rack over the back wheel. She ran to the door and tried to kiss him, first on the cheek, then on the lips, for she had an idea of putting her tongue into his mouth as an act of welcome, but he scurried past her with his head down as if he were already going back to his wife.

'Greetings, Alexandra Borisovna,' she heard him whisper, all of a flurry, uttering her patronymic as if it were a state secret.

'Greetings, Uncle Anton,' she replied; then Sister Beatitude caught her by the arm and whispered to her to behave herself or else.

*

Mother Felicity's study was at once both sparse and sumptuous. It was small and bare and very hygienic, and the Marthas scrubbed it and polished it every day so that it smelt like a swimming-pool. Yet her little pieces of Russia glistened like caskets. She had icons, and she had richly framed sepia photographs of princesses she had loved, and bishops she had served, and on her saint's day – or was it her birthday or the bishop's? – she had taken them all down and made a theatre of them with candles and a Virgin and a Christ-child. Alexandra knew this because Felicity had called her in to sit with her, and had read old Russian prayers to her aloud, and chanted bits of liturgy in a marching rhythm to her, and given her sweet cake and a glass of sweet wine, all to have Russian company on her saint's day – or was it Easter or Christmas? Russians were the best in the world, she said. Gradually, though she had had a lot of pills, Alexandra had realised that Felicity-Felicity was stone drunk, so she lifted up her old feet and put a pillow for her, and kissed her hair and let her fall asleep on the tweed sofa where parents sat when they came to enrol fresh patients. It was the same sofa where Alexandra sat now, staring at Uncle Anton while he pulled the little notebook from his pocket. He was having one of his brown days, she noticed: brown suit, brown tie, brown shirt.

'You should buy yourself brown cycle clips,' she told him in Russian.

Uncle Anton did not laugh. He kept a piece of black elastic like a garter round his notebook and he was unwinding it with a shrewd, reluctant air while he moistened his official lips. Sometimes Alexandra thought he was a policeman, sometimes a priest disguised, sometimes a lawyer or schoolmaster, sometimes even a special kind of doctor. But whatever he was, he clearly wished her to know, by means of the elastic and the notebook, and by the expressions of nervous benevolence, that there was a Higher Law for which neither he nor she was personally responsible, that he did not mean to be her jailer, that he wished her forgiveness – if not her actual love – for locking her away. She knew also that he wished her to know that he was sad and even lonely, and assuredly that he was fond of her, and that in a better world he would have been the uncle who brought her birthday presents, Christmas presents faithfully, and each year chucked her under the chin, 'My-*my*, Sasha, aren't you growing up,' followed by a restrained pat on some rounded part of her, meaning 'My-*my*, Sasha, you'll soon be ready for the pot.'

'How is your reading progressing, Alexandra?' he asked her, while he flattened the notebook in front of him and turned the pages looking for his list. This was small talk. This was not the Higher Law. This was like talk about the weather, or what a pretty dress she was wearing, or how happy she appeared today – not at all like last week.

'My name is Tatiana and I come from the moon,' she replied.

Uncle Anton acted as though this statement had not been made, so perhaps she only said it to herself, silently in her mind, where she said a lot of things.

'You have finished the novel by Turgenev I brought you?' he asked. 'You were reading *Torrents of Spring*, I think.'

'Mother Felicity was reading it to me but she has a sore throat,' said Alexandra.

'So.'

This was a lie. Felicity-Felicity had stopped reading to her as a punishment for throwing her food on the floor.

Uncle Anton had found the page of his notebook with the list on it, and he had found his pencil too, a silver one with a top you pressed; he appeared inordinately proud of it.

'So,' he said. '*So* then, Alexandra!'

Suddenly Alexandra did not want to wait for his questions. Suddenly she could not. She thought of pulling down his trousers and making love to him. She thought of messing in a corner like the French girl. She showed him the blood on her hands where she had chewed them. She needed to explain to him, through her own divine blood, that she did not want to hear his first question. She stood up, holding out one hand for him while she dug her teeth into the other. She wanted to demonstrate to Uncle Anton, for once and for ever, that the question he had in mind was obscene to her, and insulting, and unacceptable, and mad, and to do this she had chosen Christ's example as the nearest and best: did He not hang on Felicity-Felicity's wall, straight ahead of her, with blood running down His wrists? *I have shed this for you, Uncle Anton,* she explained, thinking of Easter now, of Felicity-Felicity going round the castle breaking eggs. *Please. This is my blood, Uncle Anton. I have shed it for you.* But with the other hand jammed in her mouth, all she could manage in her speaking voice was a sob. So finally she sat down, frowning, with her hands linked on her lap, not actually *bleeding*, she noticed, but at least wet with her saliva.

Uncle Anton held the notebook open with his right hand and was holding the pop-top pencil in his left. He was the first left-handed man she had known and sometimes, watching him write, she wondered whether he was a mirror image, with the real version of him sitting in the car behind Andreas Gertsch's barn. She thought what a wonderful way that would be of handling what Doctor Rüedi called the 'divided nature' – to send one half away on a bicycle while the other half stayed put in the car with the red-headed woman who drove him. Felicity-Felicity, if you lend me your pop-pop bicycle, I will send the bad part of me away on it.

Suddenly she heard herself talking. It was a wonderful sound. It made her like all the strong healthy voices around her: politicians on the radio, doctors when they looked down on her in bed.

'Uncle Anton, where do you come from, please?' she heard herself enquire, with measured curiosity. 'Uncle Anton, pay attention to me, please, while I make a statement. Until you have told me who you are and whether you are my real uncle, and what is the registration number of your big black car, I shall refuse to answer any of your questions. I regret this, but it is necessary. Also, is the red-headed woman your wife or is she Felicity-Felicity with her hair dyed, as Sister Beatitude advises me?'

But too often Alexandra's mind spoke words which her mouth did not transmit, with the result that the words stayed flying around inside her and she became their unwilling jailer, just as Uncle Anton pretended to be hers.

'Who gives you the money to pay Felicity-Felicity for my detention here? Who pays Dr Rüedi? Who dictates what questions go into your notebook every week? To whom do you pass my answers which you so meticulously write down?'

But once again, the words flew around inside her skull like the birds in Kranko's greenhouse in the fruit season, and there was nothing that Alexandra could do to persuade them to come out.

'*So*, then?' said Uncle Anton a third time, with the watery smile that Dr Rüedi wore when he was about to give her an injection. 'Now first you must please tell me your full name, Alexandra.'

Alexandra held up three fingers and counted on them like a good child. 'Alexandra Borisovna Ostrakova,' she said in an infantile voice.

'Good. And how have you been feeling this week, Sasha?'

Alexandra smiled politely in response: 'Thank you, Uncle Anton. I have been feeling much better this week. Dr Rüedi tells me that my crisis is already far behind me.'

'Have you received by any means – post, telephone, or word of mouth – any communication from outside persons?'

Alexandra had decided she was a saint. She folded her hands on her lap, and tilted her head to one side, and imagined she was one of Felicity-Felicity's Russian Orthodox saints on the wall behind the desk. Vera, who was faith; Liubov, who was love; Sofia, Olga, Irina or Xenia – all the names that Mother Felicity had taught her during that evening when she had confided that her own real name was Hope – whereas Alexandra's was Alexandra or Sasha, but never, never Tatiana, and just remember it. Alexandra smiled at Uncle Anton and she knew her smile was sublime, and tolerant, and wise; and that she was hearing God's voice, not Uncle Anton's; and Uncle Anton knew it too, for he gave a long sigh and put away his notebook, then reached for the bell button to summon Mother Felicity for the ceremony of the money.

Mother Felicity came hastily and Alexandra guessed she had not been far from the other side of the door. She had the account ready in her hand. Uncle Anton considered it and frowned, as he always did, then counted notes onto the desk, blue ones and orange ones singly, so that each was for a moment transparent under the beam of the reading lamp. Then Uncle Anton patted Alexandra on the shoulder as if she were fifteen instead of twenty-five, or twenty, or however old she was when she had clipped away the forbidden bits of her life. She watched him waddle out of the door again and on to his bike. She watched his rump strive and gather rhythm as he rode away from her, through the lodge, past Kranko, and away down the hill towards the village. And as she watched she saw a strange thing, a thing that had never happened before: not to Uncle Anton, at least. From nowhere, two purposeful figures materialised – a man and a woman, wheeling a motor-bike. They must have been sitting on the summer bench the other side of the lodge, keeping out of sight, perhaps in order to make love. They moved into the lane, and stared after him, but they didn't mount the motor-bike, not yet. Instead, they waited till Uncle Anton was almost out of sight before setting off after him down the hill. Then Alexandra decided to scream, and this time she found her talking voice and the scream split the whole house from roof to floor before Sister Beatitude bore down on her to quell her with a heavy smack across the mouth.

'They're the same people,' Alexandra shrieked.

'Who are?' Sister Beatitude demanded, drawing back her hand in case she needed to use it again. 'Who are the same people, you bad girl?'

'They're the people who followed my mother before they dragged her away to kill her.'

Sister Beatitude gave a snort of disbelief. 'On black horses, I suppose!' she sneered. 'Dragged her on a sledge, too, didn't he, all across Siberia!'

Alexandra had spun these tales before. How her father was a secret prince more powerful than the Czar. How he ruled at night, as the owls rule while the hawks are at rest. How his secret eyes followed her wherever she went, how his secret ears heard every word she spoke. And how, one night, hearing her mother praying in her sleep, he sent his men for her and they took her into the snow and she was never seen again: not even by God, He was looking for her still.

24

The burning of Tricky Tony, as it afterwards became known in the Circus mythology – such being Grigoriev's whimsical codename among the watchers – was one of those rare operations where luck, timing and preparation come together in a perfect marriage. They had all known from early on that the problem would be to find Grigoriev alone at a moment which allowed for his speedy reintroduction into normal life a few hours later. Yet by the weekend following the coverage of the Thun bank, intensive researches into Grigoriev's behaviour pattern had produced no obvious pointers as to when this moment might be. In desperation, Skordeno and de Silsky, Toby's hard-men, dreamed up a wildcat scheme to snatch him on his way to work, along the few hundred metres of pavement between his house and the Embassy. Toby killed it at once. One of the girls offered herself as a decoy: perhaps she could hitch a lift from him somehow? Her altruism was applauded, but it did not answer the practicalities.

The main problem was that Grigoriev was under double guard. Not only did the Embassy security staff keep check on him as a matter of routine; so did his wife. The watchers had no doubt that she suspected him of a tenderness for little Natasha. Their fears were confirmed when Toby's listeners contrived to tamper with the junction box at the corner of the road. In one day's watch, Grigorieva telephoned her husband no less than three times, to no apparent purpose other than to establish that he was indeed at the Embassy.

'George, I mean that woman is a total monster,' Toby stormed when he heard this. 'Love – I mean, all right. But possession, for its own sake, this I absolutely condemn. It's a matter of principle for me.'

The one chink was Grigoriev's Thursday-afternoon drives to the garage, when he took the Mercedes to have it checked. If a practised car coper such as Canada Bill could introduce an engine fault during the Wednesday night – one that kept the car mobile, but only just – then might not Grigoriev be snatched from the garage while he was waiting for the mechanic to trace it? The plan bristled with imponderables. Even if everything worked, how long would they have Grigoriev to themselves? Then again, on Thursdays Grigoriev must be back home in time to receive his weekly visit from the courier Krassky. Nevertheless, it remained the only plan they had – their worst except for the others, said Toby – and accordingly they settled to an apprehensive wait of five days while Toby and his team leaders plotted fallbacks for the many unpleasant contingencies should the plot abort: everyone to be signed out of his hotel and packed; escape papers and money to be carried at all times; radio equipment to be boxed and cached under American identity in the vaults of one of the major banks, so that any clues left behind would point to the Cousins rather than themselves; no forms of assembly other than walk-and-talk encounters on the pavement; wavelengths to be changed every four hours. Toby knew his Swiss police, he said. He had hunted here before. If the balloon went up, he said, then the fewer of his boys and girls around to answer questions, the better. 'I mean, thank God the Swiss are only neutral, know what I mean?'

As a somewhat forlorn consolation, and as a boost to the delicate morale of the watchers, Smiley and Toby decreed that the surveillance of Grigoriev should be kept at full pitch throughout the expected days of waiting. The observation post in the Brunnadernain would be manned round the clock; car and cycle patrols would be increased; everyone should be on his toes for the remote chance that God, in an uncharacteristic moment, would favour the just.

What God did, in fact, was send idyllic Sunday weather, and it proved decisive. By ten o'clock that Sunday it was as if the Alpine sun had come down from the Oberland to brighten the lives of the fog-ridden lowlanders. In the Bellevue Palace, which on Sundays has a quite overwhelming calm, a waiter had just spread a napkin on Smiley's lap for him. He was drinking a leisurely coffee, trying to concentrate on the weekend edition of the *Herald Tribune*, when, looking up, he saw the gentle figure of Franz the head porter standing before him.

'Mr Barraclough, sir, the telephone, I am sorry. A Mr Anselm.'

The cabins were in the main hall, the voice was Toby's and the name Anselm signified urgency: 'The Geneva bureau has just advised us that the managing director is on his way to Berne at this very moment.'

The Geneva bureau was word code for the Brunnadernain observation post.

'Is he bringing his wife?' said Smiley.

'Unfortunately, Madame is obliged to make an excursion with the children,' Toby replied. 'Perhaps if you could come down to the office, Mr Barraclough?'

Toby's office was a sun pavilion situated in an ornamental garden next to the Bundeshaus. Smiley was there in five minutes. Below them lay the ravine of the green river. In the

distance, under a blue sky, the peaks of the Bernese Oberland
lifted splendidly in the sunlight.

'Grigoriev left the Embassy on his own five minutes ago,
wearing a hat and coat,' Toby said as soon as Smiley arrived.
'He's heading for the town on foot. It's like the first Sunday
we watched him. He walks to the Embassy, ten minutes later
he sets off for the town. He's going to watch the chess game,
George, no question. What do you say?'

'Who's with him?'

'Skordeno and de Silsky on foot, a back-up car behind, two
more ahead. One team's heading for the Cathedral Close right
now. Do we go, George, or don't we?'

For a moment, Toby was aware of that disconnection
which seemed to afflict Smiley whenever the operation gathered speed: less indecision, than a mysterious reluctance to
advance.

He pressed him: 'The green light, George? Or not? George,
please! We are speaking of seconds here!'

'Is the house still covered for when Grigorieva and the children get back?'

'Completely.'

For a moment longer Smiley hesitated. For a moment, he
weighed the method against the prize, and the grey and distant
figure of Karla seemed actually to admonish him.

'The green light, then,' said Smiley. 'Yes. Go.'

He had barely finished speaking before Toby was standing
in the telephone kiosk not twenty metres from the pavilion.
'With my heart going like a complete steam engine,' as he
later claimed. But also with the light of battle in his eyes.

There is even a scale model of the scene at Sarratt, and occasionally the directing staff will dig it out and tell the tale.

The old city of Berne is best described as a mountain, a fortress, and a peninsula all at once, as the model shows. Between the Kirchenfeld and Kornhaus bridges, the Aare runs in a horseshoe cut into a giddy cleft, and the old city roosts prudently inside it, in rising foothills of medieval streets, till it reaches the superb late-Gothic spire of the Cathedral, which is both the mountain's peak and its glory. Next to the Cathedral, at the same height, stands the Platform, from whose southern perimeter the unwary visitor may find himself staring down a hundred feet of sheer stone face, straight into the swirling river. It is a place to draw suicides and no doubt there have been some. It is a place where, according to popular history, a pious man was thrown from his horse and, though he fell the whole awesome distance, survived by God's deliverance to serve the church for another thirty years, dying peacefully at a great age. The rest of the Platform makes a tranquil spot, with benches and ornamental trees and a children's playground – and, in recent years, a place for public chess. The pieces are two foot or more in height, light enough to move, but heavy enough to withstand the occasional thrust of a south wind that whips off the surrounding hills. The scale model even runs to replicas of them.

By the time Toby Esterhase arrived there that Sunday morning, the unexpected sunshine had drawn a small but tidy body of the game's enthusiasts, who stood or sat around the chequered pavement. And at their centre, a mere six feet from where Toby stood, as oblivious to his surroundings as could be wished, stood Counsellor (Commercial) Anton Grigoriev of the Soviet Embassy in Berne, a truant from both work and family, intently following, through his rimless spectacles, each move the players made. And behind Grigoriev stood Skordeno and his companion de Silsky, watching Grigoriev. The players were young and bearded and volatile – if not art students, then certainly they wished to be taken for them. And they were very conscious of fighting a duel under the public gaze.

Toby had been this close to Grigoriev before, but never when the Russian's attention was so firmly locked elsewhere. With the calm of impending battle, Toby appraised him and confirmed what he had all along maintained: Anton Grigoriev was not a fieldman. His rapt attention, the unguarded frankness of his expressions as each move was played or contemplated, had an innocence which could never have survived the infighting of Moscow Centre.

Toby's personal appearance was another of those happy chances of the day. Out of respect for the Bernese Sunday, he had donned a dark overcoat and his black fur hat. He was therefore, at this crucial moment of improvisation, looking exactly as he would have wished had he planned everything to the last detail: a man of position takes his Sunday relaxation.

Toby's dark eyes lifted to the Cathedral Close. The getaway cars were in position.

A ripple of laughter went out. With a flourish, one of the bearded players lifted his queen and, pretending it was a most appalling weight, reeled with it a couple of steps and dumped it with a groan. Grigoriev's face darkened into a frown as he considered this unexpected move. On a nod from Toby, Skordeno and de Silsky drew one to either side of him, so close that Skordeno's shoulder was actually nudging the quarry's, but Grigoriev paid no heed. Taking this as their signal, Toby's watchers began sauntering into the crowd, forming a second echelon behind de Silsky and Skordeno. Toby waited no longer. Placing himself directly in front of Grigoriev, he smiled and lifted his hat. Grigoriev returned the smile – uncertainly, as one might to a diplomatic colleague half-remembered – and lifted his hat in return.

'How are you today, Counsellor?' Toby asked in Russian, in a tone of quiet jocularity.

More mystified than ever, Grigoriev said thank you, he was well.

'I hope you enjoyed your little excursion to the country on Friday,' said Toby in the same easy, but very quiet voice, as he slipped his arm through Grigoriev's. 'The old city of Thun is not sufficiently appreciated, I believe, by members of our distinguished diplomatic community here. In my view it is to be recommended both for its antiquity, and its banking facilities. Do you not agree?'

This opening sally was long enough, and disturbing enough, to carry Grigoriev unresisting to the crowd's edge. Skordeno and de Silsky were packing close behind.

'My name is Kurt Siebel, sir,' Toby confided in Grigoriev's ear, his hand still on his arm. 'I am chief investigator to the Bernese Standard Bank of Thun. We have certain questions relating to Dr Adolf Glaser's private account with us. You would do well to pretend you know me.' They were still moving. Behind them, the watchers followed in a staggered line, like rugger players poised to block a sudden dash. 'Please do not be alarmed,' Toby continued, counting the steps as Grigoriev kept up his progress. 'If you could spare us an hour, sir, I am sure we could arrange matters without troubling your domestic or professional position. Please.'

In the world of a secret agent, the wall between safety and extreme hazard is almost nothing, a membrane that can be burst in a second. He may court a man for years, fattening him for the pass. But the pass itself – the 'will you, won't you?' – is a leap from which there is either ruin or victory, and for a moment Toby thought he was looking ruin in the face. Grigoriev had finally stopped dead and turned round to stare at him. He was pale as an invalid. His chin lifted, he opened his mouth to protest a monstrous insult. He tugged at his captive arm in order to free himself but Toby held it firm. Skordeno and de Silsky were hovering, but the distance to the car was still fifteen metres, which was a long way, in Toby's book, to drag one stocky Russian. Meanwhile, Toby kept talking; all his instinct urged him to.

'There are irregularities, Counsellor. Grave irregularities. We have a dossier upon your good self which makes lamentable reading. If I placed it before the Swiss police, not all the diplomatic protests in the world would protect you from the most acute public embarrassment, I need hardly mention the consequence to your professional career. Please. I said *please.*'

Grigoriev had still not budged. He seemed transfixed with indecision. Toby pushed at his arm, but Grigoriev stood rock solid and seemed unaware of the physical pressure on him. Toby shoved harder, Skordeno and de Silsky drew closer, but Grigoriev had the stubborn strength of the demented. His mouth opened, he swallowed, his gaze fixed stupidly on Toby.

'What irregularities?' he said at last. Only the shock and the quietness in his voice gave cause for hope. His thick body remained rigidly set against further movement. 'Who is this Glaser you speak of?' he demanded huskily, in the same stunned tone. 'I am not Glaser. I am a diplomat. Grigoriev. The account you speak of has been conducted with total propriety. As Commercial Counsellor I have immunity. I also have the right to own foreign bank accounts.'

Toby fired his only other shot. *The money and the girl,* Smiley had said. *The money and the girl are all you have to play with.*

'There is also the delicate matter of your marriage, sir,' Toby resumed with a show of reluctance. 'I must advise you that your philanderings in the Embassy have put your domestic

367

arrangements in grave danger.' Grigoriev started, and was heard to mutter '*banker*' – whether in disbelief or derision will never be sure. His eyes closed and he was heard to repeat the word, this time – according to Skordeno – with a particularly vile obscenity. But he started walking again. The rear door of the car stood open. The back-up car waited behind it. Toby was talking some nonsense about the withholding tax payable on the interest accruing from Swiss bank accounts, but he knew that Grigoriev was not really listening. Slipping ahead, de Silsky jumped into the back of the car and Skordeno threw Grigoriev straight in after him, then sat down beside him and slammed the door. Toby took the passenger seat; the driver was one of the Meinertzhagen girls. Speaking German, Toby told her to go easy and for God's sake remember it was a Bernese Sunday. No English in his hearing, Smiley had said.

Somewhere near the station Grigoriev must have had second thoughts, because there was a short scuffle and when Toby looked in the mirror Grigoriev's face was contorted with pain and he had both hands over his groin. They drove to the Länggass-strasse, a long dull road behind the university. The door of the apartment house opened as they pulled up outside it. A thin housekeeper waited on the doorstep. She was Millie McCraig, an old Circus trooper. At the sight of her smile, Grigoriev bridled and now it was speed, not cover, that mattered. Skordeno jumped on to the pavement, seized one of Grigoriev's arms and nearly pulled it out of its socket; de Silsky must have hit him again, though he swore afterwards it was an accident, for Grigoriev came out doubled up, and between them they carried him over the threshold like a bride, and burst into the drawing-room in a bunch. Smiley was seated in a corner waiting for them. It was a room of brown chintzes and lace. The door closed, the abductors allowed themselves a brief show of festivity. Skordeno and de Silsky burst out laughing in relief. Toby took off his fur coat and wiped the sweat away.

'*Ruhe*,' he said softly, ordering quiet. They obeyed him instantly.

Grigoriev was rubbing his shoulder, seemingly unaware of anything but the pain. Studying him, Smiley took comfort from this gesture of self-concern: subconsciously, Grigoriev was declaring himself to be one of life's losers. Smiley remembered Kirov, his botched pass at Ostrakova and his laborious recruitment of Otto Leipzig. He looked at Grigoriev and read the same incurable mediocrity in everything he saw: in the new but ill-chosen striped suit that emphasised his portliness; in the treasured grey shoes, punctured for ventilation but too tight for comfort; in the prinked, waved hair. All these tiny, useless acts of vanity communicated to Smiley an aspiration to greatness which he knew – as Grigoriev seemed to know – would never be fulfilled.

A former academic, he remembered, from the document Enderby had handed him at Ben's place. *Appears to have abandoned university teaching for the larger privileges of officialdom.*

A pincher, Ann would have said, weighing his sexuality at a single glance. *Dismiss him.*

But Smiley could not dismiss him. Grigoriev was a hooked fish: Smiley had only moments in which to decide how best to land him. He wore rimless spectacles and was running to fat round the chin. His hair oil, warmed by the heat of his body, gave out a lemon vapour. Still kneading his shoulder, he started peering round at his captors. Sweat was falling from his face like raindrops.

'Where am I?' he demanded truculently, ignoring Smiley and selecting Toby as the leader. His voice was hoarse and high pitched. He was speaking German, with a Slav sibilance.

Three years as First Secretary (Commercial), Soviet Mission to Potsdam, Smiley remembered. *No apparent intelligence connection.*

'I demand to know where I am. I am a senior Soviet diplomat. I demand to speak to my Ambassador immediately.'

The continuing action of his hand upon his injured shoulder took the edge off his indignation.

'I have been kidnapped! I am here against my will! If you do not immediately return me to my Ambassador there will be a grave international incident!'

Grigoriev had the stage to himself, and he could not quite fill it. Only George will ask questions, Toby had told his team. Only George will answer them. But Smiley sat still as an undertaker; nothing, it seemed, could rouse him.

'You want ransom?' Grigoriev called, to all of them. An awful thought appeared to strike him. 'You are terrorists?' he whispered. 'But if you are terrorists, why do you not bind my eyes? Why do you let me see your faces?' He stared round at de Silsky, then at Skordeno. 'You must cover your faces. Cover them! I want no knowledge of you!'

Goaded by the continuing silence, Grigoriev drove a plump fist into his open palm and shouted 'I demand' twice. At which point Smiley, with an air of official regret, opened a notebook on his lap, much as Kirov might have done, and gave a small, very official sigh: 'You are Counsellor Grigoriev of the Soviet Embassy in Berne?' he asked in the dullest possible voice.

'Grigoriev! I am Grigoriev! Yes, well done, I am Grigoriev! Who are you, please? Al Capone? Who are you? Why do you rumble at me like a commissar?'

Commissar could not have described Smiley's manner better: it was leaden to the point of indifference.

'Then, Counsellor, since we cannot afford to delay, I must

ask you to study the incriminating photographs on the table behind you,' Smiley said, with the same studied dullness.

'Photographs? What photographs? How can you incriminate a diplomat? I demand to telephone my Ambassador immediately!'

'I would advise the Counsellor to look at the photographs first,' said Smiley, in a glum, regionless German. 'When he has looked at the photographs, he is free to telephone whomever he wants. Kindly start at the left,' he advised. 'The photographs are arranged from left to right.'

A blackmailed man has the dignity of all our weaknesses, Smiley thought, covertly watching Grigoriev shuffling along the table as if he were inspecting one more diplomatic buffet. A blackmailed man is any one of us caught in the door as we try to escape the trap. Smiley had arranged the layout of the pictures himself; he had imagined, in Grigoriev's mind, an orchestrated succession of disasters. The Grigorievs parking their Mercedes outside the bank. Grigorieva, with her perpetual scowl of discontent, waiting alone in the driving seat, clutching the wheel in case anyone tried to take it from her. Grigoriev and little Natasha in long shot, sitting very close to each other on a bench. Grigoriev inside the bank, several pictures, culminating in a superb over-the-shoulder shot of Grigoriev signing a cashier's receipt, the full name Adolf Glaser clearly typed on the line above his signature. There was Grigoriev looking uncomfortable on his bicycle, about to enter the sanatorium; there was Grigorieva roosting crossly in the car again, this time beside Gertsch's barn, her own bicycle still strapped to the roof. But the photograph that held Grigoriev longest, Smiley noticed, was the muddy long shot stolen by the Meinertzhagen girls. The quality was not good but the two heads in the car, though they were locked mouth to mouth, were recognisable enough. One was Grigoriev's. The other, pressed down on him as if she would eat him alive, was little Natasha's.

'The telephone is at your disposal, Counsellor,' Smiley called to him quietly, when Grigoriev still did not move.

But Grigoriev remained frozen over this last photograph, and to judge by his expression, his desolation was complete. He was not merely a man found out, thought Smiley; he was a man whose very dream of love, till now vested in secrecy, had suddenly become public and ridiculous.

Still using his glum tone of official necessity, Smiley set about explaining what Karla would have called the pressures. Other inquisitors, says Toby, would have offered Grigoriev a choice, thereby inevitably mustering the Russian obstinacy in him, and the Russian *penchant* for self-destruction: the very impulses, he says, which could have invited catastrophe. Other inquisitors, he insists, would have menaced, raised their voices, resorted to histrionics, even physical abuse. Not George, he says: never. George acted out the low-key official time-server, and Grigoriev, like Grigorievs the world over, accepted him as his unalterable fate. George by-passed choice entirely, says Toby. George calmly made clear to Grigoriev why it was that he had no choice at all: The important thing, Counsellor – said Smiley, as if he were explaining a tax demand – was to consider what impact these photographs would have in the places where they would very soon be studied if nothing was done to prevent their distribution. There were first the Swiss authorities, who would obviously be incensed by the misuse of a Swiss passport on the part of an accredited diplomat, not to mention the grave breach of banking laws, said Smiley. They would register the strongest official protest, and the Grigorievs would be returned to Moscow overnight, all of them, never again to enjoy the fruits of a foreign posting. Back in Moscow, however, Grigoriev would not be well regarded either, Smiley explained. His superiors in the Foreign Ministry would take a dismal view of his behaviour, 'both in the private and professional spheres'. Grigoriev's prospects for an official career would be ended. He would be an *exile* in his own land, said Smiley, and his family with him. All his family. 'Imagine facing the wrath of Grigorieva twenty-four hours a day in the wastes of outer Siberia,' he was saying in effect.

At which Grigoriev slumped into a chair and clapped his hands on to the top of his head, as if scared it would blow off.

'But finally,' said Smiley, lifting his eyes from his notebook, though only for a moment – and what he read there, said Toby, God knows, the pages were ruled but otherwise blank – 'finally, Counsellor, we have also to consider the effect of these photographs upon certain organs of State security.'

And here Grigoriev released his head and drew the handkerchief from his top pocket and began wiping his brow, but as hard as he wiped, the sweat came back again. It fell as fast as Smiley's own in the interrogation cell in Delhi, when he had sat face to face with Karla.

Totally committed to his part as bureaucratic messenger of the inevitable, Smiley sighed once more and primly turned to another page of his notebook.

'Counsellor, may I ask you what time you expect your wife and family to return from their picnic?'

Still dabbing with the handkerchief, Grigoriev appeared too preoccupied to hear.

'Grigorieva and the children are taking a picnic in the Elfenau woods,' Smiley reminded him. 'We have some questions to ask you, but it would be unfortunate if your absence from home were to cause concern.'

Grigoriev put away the handkerchief. 'You are spies?' he whispered. 'You are Western spies?'

'Counsellor, it is better that you do not know who we are,' said Smiley earnestly. 'Such information is a dangerous burden. When you have done as we ask, you will walk out of here a free man. You have our assurance. Neither your wife, nor even Moscow Centre, will ever be the wiser. Please tell me what time your family returns from Elfenau—' Smiley broke off.

Somewhat half-heartedly, Grigoriev was affecting to make a dash for it. He stood up, he took a bound towards the door. Paul Skordeno had a languid air for a hard-man, but he caught the fugitive in an armlock even before he had taken a second step, and returned him gently to his chair, careful not to mark him. With another stage groan, Grigoriev flung up his hands in vast despair. His heavy face coloured and became convulsed, his broad shoulders started heaving as he broke into a mournful torrent of self-recrimination. He spoke half in Russian, half in German. He cursed himself with a slow and holy zeal, and after that, he cursed his mother, his wife and his bad luck and his own dreadful frailty as a father. He should have stayed in Moscow, in the Trade Ministry. He should never have been wooed away from academia merely because his fool wife wanted foreign clothes and music and privileges. He should have divorced her long ago but he could not bear to relinquish the children, he was a fool and a clown. He should be in the asylum instead of the girl. When he was sent for in Moscow, he should have said no, he should have resisted the pressure, he should have reported the matter to his Ambassador when he returned.

'Oh, Grigoriev!' he cried. 'Oh, Grigoriev! You are so weak, so weak!'

Next, he delivered himself of a tirade against conspiracy.

Conspiracy was anathema to him, several times in the course of his career he had been obliged to collaborate with the hateful *'neighbours'* in some crackpot enterprise, every time it was a disaster. Intelligence people were criminals, charlatans and fools, a masonry of monsters. Why were Russians so in love with them? Oh, the fatal flaw of secretiveness in the Russian soul!

'Conspiracy has replaced religion!' Grigoriev moaned to all of them, in German. 'It is our mystical substitute! Its agents are our Jesuits, these swine, they ruin everything!'

Bunching his fists now, he pushed them into his cheeks, pummelling himself in his remorse, till with a movement of the notepad on his lap, Smiley brought him dourly back to the matter in hand: 'Concerning Grigorieva and your children, Counsellor,' he said. 'It really is essential that we know what time they are due to return home.'

In every successful interrogation – as Toby Esterhase likes to pontificate concerning this moment – there is one slip which cannot be recovered; one gesture, tacit or direct, even if it is only a half smile, or the acceptance of a cigarette, which marks the shift away from resistance, towards collaboration. Grigoriev, in Toby's account of the scene, now made his crucial slip. 'She will be home at one o'clock,' he muttered, avoiding both Smiley's eye, and Toby's.

Smiley looked at his watch. To Toby's secret ecstasy, Grigoriev did the same.

'But perhaps she will be late?' Smiley objected.

'She is never late,' Grigoriev retorted moodily.

'Then kindly begin by telling me of your relationship with the girl Ostrakova,' said Smiley, stepping right into the blue – says Toby – yet contriving to imply that his question was the most natural sequel to the issue of Madame Grigorieva's punctuality. Then he held his pen ready, and in such a way, says Toby, that a man like Grigoriev would feel positively obliged to give him something to write down.

For all this, Grigoriev's resistance was not quite evaporated. His *amour propre* demanded at least one further outing. Opening his hands, therefore, he appealed to Toby: '*Ostrakova!*' he repeated with exaggerated scorn. 'He asks me about some woman called *Ostrakova*? I know no such person. Perhaps he does, but I do not. I am a diplomat. Release me immediately, I have important engagements.'

But the steam, as well as the logic, was fast going out of his protests. Grigoriev knew this as well as anyone.

'Alexandra Borisovna Ostrakova,' Smiley intoned, while he polished his spectacles on the fat end of his tie. 'A Russian girl, but has a French passport.' He replaced his spectacles. 'Just as you are Russian, Counsellor, but have a Swiss passport. Under a false name. Now how did you come to get involved with her, I wonder?'

'*Involved*? Now he tells me I was *involved* with her! You think I am so base I sleep with mad girls? I was blackmailed. As you blackmail me now, so I was *blackmailed*. Pressure! Always pressure, always Grigoriev!'

'Then tell me how they blackmailed you,' Smiley suggested, with barely a glance at him.

Grigoriev peered into his hands, lifted them, but let them drop back on to his knees again, for once unused. He dabbed his lips with his handkerchief. He shook his head at the world's iniquity.

'I was in Moscow,' he said, and in Toby's ears, as he afterwards declared, angel choirs sang their hallelujahs. George had turned the trick, and Grigoriev's confession had begun.

*

Smiley, on the other hand, betrayed no such jubilation at his achievement. To the contrary, a frown of irritation puckered his plump face.

'The *date*, please, Counsellor,' he said, as if the place were not the issue. 'Give the *date* when you were in Moscow. Henceforth, please give dates at all points.'

This too is classic, Toby likes to explain: the wise inquisitor will always light a few false fires.

'September,' said Grigoriev, mystified.

'Of which year?' said Smiley, writing.

Grigoriev looked plaintively to Toby again. 'Which year! I say September, he asks me *which* September. He is a historian? I think he is a historian. This September,' he said sulkily to Smiley. 'I was recalled to Moscow for an urgent commercial conference. I am an expert in certain highly specialised economic fields. Such a conference would have been meaningless without my presence.'

'Did your wife accompany you on this journey?'

Grigoriev let out a hollow laugh. 'Now he thinks we are capitalists!' he commented to Toby. 'He thinks we go flying our wives around for two-week conferences, first class Swissair.'

'"In September of this year, I was ordered to fly alone to Moscow in order to attend a two-week economic conference,"' Smiley proposed, as if he were reading Grigoriev's statement aloud. '"My wife remained in Berne." Please describe the purpose of the conference.'

'The subject of our high-level discussions was extremely secret,' Grigoriev replied with resignation. 'My Ministry wished to consider ways of giving teeth to the official Soviet attitude towards nations who were selling arms to China. We were to discuss what sanctions could be used against the offenders.'

Smiley's faceless style, his manner of regretful bureaucratic necessity, were by now not merely established, says Toby, they were perfected: Grigoriev had adopted them wholesale, with philosophic, and very Russian, pessimism. As to the rest of those present, they could hardly believe, afterwards, that he had not been brought to the flat already in a mood to talk.

'Where was the conference held?' Smiley asked, as if secret matters concerned him less than formal details.

'At the Trade Ministry. On the fourth floor . . . in the conference room. Opposite the lavatory,' Grigoriev retorted, with hopeless facetiousness.

'Where did you stay?'

At a hostel for senior officials, Grigoriev replied. He gave the address and even, in sarcasm, his room number. Sometimes, our discussions ended late at night, he said, by now liberally volunteering information; but on the Friday, since it was still summer weather and very hot, they ended early in order to enable those who wished to leave for the country. But Grigoriev had no such plans. Grigoriev proposed to stay in Moscow for the weekend and with reason: 'I had arranged to pass two days in the apartment of a girl called Evdokia, formerly my secretary. Her husband was away on military service,' he explained, as if this were a perfectly normal transaction among men of the world, one which Toby at least, as a fellow soul, would appreciate even if soulless commissars would not. Then, to Toby's astonishment, he went straight on. From his dalliance with Evdokia he passed without warning or preamble to the very heart of their enquiry:

'Unfortunately, I was prevented from adhering to these arrangements by the intervention of members of the Thirteenth Directorate of Moscow Centre known also as the Karla Directorate. I was summoned to attend an interview immediately.'

*

At which moment the telephone rang. Toby took the call, rang off, and spoke to Smiley.

'She's arrived back at the house,' he said, still in German.

Without demur, Smiley turned straight to Grigoriev: 'Counsellor, we are advised that your wife has returned home. It has now become necessary for you to telephone her.'

'Telephone her?' Horrified, Grigoriev swung round on Toby. 'He tells me, telephone her! What do I say? "Grigorieva, here is loving husband! I have been kidnapped by Western spies!" Your commissar is mad! Mad!'

'You will please tell her you are unavoidably delayed,' Smiley said.

His placidity added fuel to Grigoriev's outrage: 'I tell this to my wife? To Grigorieva? You think she will believe me? She will report me to the Ambassador immediately. "Ambassador, my husband has run away! Find him!"'

'The courier Krassky brings your weekly orders from Moscow, does he not?' Smiley asked.

'The commissar knows everything,' Grigoriev told Toby, and wiped his hand across his chin. 'If he knows everything, why doesn't he speak to Grigorieva himself?'

'You are to adopt an official tone with her, Counsellor,' Smiley advised. 'Do not refer to Krassky by name, but suggest that he has ordered you to meet him for a conspiratorial discussion somewhere in the town. An emergency. Krassky has changed his plans. You have no idea when you will be back, or what he wants. If she protests, rebuke her. Tell her it is a secret of State.'

They watched him worry, they watched him wonder. Finally, they watched a small smile settle over his face.

'A secret,' Grigoriev repeated to himself. 'A secret of State. Yes.'

Stepping boldly to the telephone, he dialled a number. Toby stood over him, one hand discreetly poised to slam the cradle should he try some trick, but Smiley with a small shake of the head signalled him away. They heard Grigorieva's voice saying 'Yes?' in German. They heard Grigoriev's bold reply, followed by his wife – it is all on tape – demanding sharply to know where he was. They saw him stiffen and lift his chin, and put on an official face; they heard him snap out a few short phrases, and ask a question to which there was apparently no answer. They saw him ring off again, bright-eyed and pink with pleasure, and his short arms fly in the air with delight, like someone who has scored a goal. The next thing they knew, he had burst out laughing, long, rich gusts of Slav laughter, up and down the scale. Uncontrollably, the others began laughing with him – Skordeno, de Silsky, and Toby. Grigoriev was shaking Toby's hand.

'Today I like very much conspiracy!' Grigoriev cried, between further gusts of cathartic laughter. 'Conspiracy is very good today!'

Smiley had not joined in the general festivity, however. Having cast himself deliberately as the killjoy, he sat turning the pages of his notebook, waiting for the fun to end.

'You were describing how you were approached by members of the Thirteenth Directorate,' Smiley said, when all was quiet again. 'Known also as the Karla Directorate. Kindly continue with your narrative, Counsellor.'

25

Did Grigoriev sense the new alertness round him – the discreet freezing of gestures? Did he notice how the eyes of Skordeno and de Silsky both hunted out Smiley's impassive face and held it in their gaze? How Millie McCraig slipped silently to the kitchen to check her tape-recorders yet again, in case, by an act of a malevolent god, both the main set and the reserve had failed at once? Did he notice Smiley's now almost Oriental self-effacement – the very opposite of interest – the retreat of his whole body into the copious folds of his brown tweed travelling coat, while he patiently licked his thumb and finger and turned a page?

Toby, at least, noticed these things. Toby in his dark corner by the telephone had a grandstand seat from which he could observe everyone and remain as good as unobserved himself. A fly could not have crossed the floor, but Toby's watchful eyes would have recorded its entire odyssey. Toby even describes his own symptoms – a hot feeling around the neck-band, he says, a knotting of the throat and stomach muscles – Toby not only endured these discomforts, but remembered them faithfully. Whether Grigoriev was responsive to the atmosphere is another matter. Most likely he was too consumed by his central rôle. The triumph of the telephone call had stimulated him, and revived his self-confidence; and it was significant that his first statement, when he once more had the floor, concerned not the Karla Directorate, but his prowess as the lover of little Natasha: 'Fellows of our age *need* a girl like that,' he explained to Toby with a wink. 'They make us into young men again, like we used to be!'

'Very well, you flew to Moscow alone,' Smiley said, quite snappishly. 'The conference got under way, you were approached for an interview. Please continue from there. We have not got all afternoon, you know.'

The conference started on the Monday, Grigoriev agreed, obediently resuming his official statement. When the Friday afternoon came, I returned to my hostel in order to fetch my belongings and take them to Evdokia's apartment for our little weekend together. Instead of this, however, I was met by three men who ordered me into their car with even less explanation than you did – a glance at Toby – saying to me that I was required for a special task. During the journey they advised me that they were members of the Thirteenth Directorate of Moscow Centre, which everybody in official Moscow knows to be the élite. I formed the impression that they were intelligent men, above the common run of their profession, which, saving your presence, sir, is not high. I had the impression they could be officers rather than mere lackeys. Nevertheless I was not unduly worried. I assumed that my professional expertise was being required for some secret matter, that was all. They were courteous and I was even somewhat flattered . . .

'How long was the journey?' Smiley interrupted, as he continued writing.

Across town, Grigoriev replied vaguely. Across town, then into countryside till dark. Till we reached this one little man like a monk, sitting in a small room, who seemed to be their master.

*

Once again, Toby insists on bearing witness here to Smiley's unique mastery of the occasion. It was the strongest proof yet of Smiley's tradecraft, says Toby – as well as of his command of Grigoriev altogether – that throughout Grigoriev's protracted narrative, he never once, whether by an over-hasty follow-up question or the smallest false inflection of his voice, departed from the faceless rôle he had assumed for the interrogation. By his self-effacement, Toby insists, George held the whole scene 'like a thrush's egg in his hand'. The slightest careless movement on his part could have destroyed everything, but he never made it. And as the crowning example, Toby likes to offer this crucial moment, when the actual figure of Karla was for the first time introduced. Any other inquisitor, he says, at the very mention of a 'little man like a monk who seemed to be their master' would have pressed for a description – his age, rank, what he was wearing, smoking, how did you know he was their master? Not Smiley. Smiley with a suppressed exclamation of annoyance tapped his ballpoint pen on his pad, and in a long-suffering voice invited Grigoriev, then and for the future, kindly *not* to foreshorten factual detail:

'Let me put the question again. How long was the journey? Please describe it precisely as you remember it and let us proceed from there.'

Crestfallen, Grigoriev actually apologised. He would say they drove for four hours at speed, sir; perhaps more. He remembered now that they twice stopped to relieve themselves. After four hours they entered a guarded area – no, sir, I saw no shoulder-boards, the guards wore plain clothes – and drove for at least another half hour into the heart of it. Like a nightmare, sir.

Yet again, Smiley objected, determined to keep the temperature as low as possible. How could it have been a nightmare, he wanted to know, since Grigoriev had only a moment before claimed that he was not frightened?

Well, not a nightmare exactly, sir, more a dream. At this stage, Grigoriev had had an impression he was being taken to the *landlord* – he used the Russian word, and Toby translated it – while he himself felt increasingly like a poor peasant. Therefore he was not frightened, sir, because he had no control over events, and accordingly nothing for which to reproach himself. But when the car finally stopped, and one of the men put a hand on his arm, and addressed a warning to him: at this point, his attitude changed entirely, sir: 'You are about to meet a great Soviet fighter and a powerful man,' the man told him. 'If you are disrespectful to him, or attempt to tell lies, you may never again see your wife and family.'

'What is the name of this man?' Grigoriev had asked.

But the men replied, without smiling, that this great Soviet fighter had no name. Grigoriev asked whether he was Karla himself; knowing that Karla was the code name for the head of the Thirteenth Directorate. The men only repeated that the great fighter had no name.

'So that was when the dream became a nightmare, sir,' said Grigoriev humbly. 'They told me also that I could say goodbye to my weekend of love. Little Evdokia would have to get her fun elsewhere, they said. Then one of them laughed.'

Now a great fear had seized Grigoriev, he said, and by the time he had entered the first room and advanced upon the second door, he was so scared his knees were shaking. He even had time to be scared for his beloved Evdokia. Who could this supernatural person be, he wondered in awe, that he could know almost before Grigoriev himself knew, that he was pledged to meet Evdokia for the weekend?

'So you knocked on the door,' said Smiley, as he wrote:

And I was ordered to enter! Grigoriev went on. His enthusiasm for confession was mounting, so was his dependence upon his interrogator. His voice had become louder, his gestures more free. It was as if, says Toby, he was trying physically to coax Smiley out of his posture of reticence; whereas in reality it was Smiley's feigned indifference which was coaxing Grigoriev into the open. And I found myself not in a large and splendid office at all, sir, as became a senior official and a great Soviet fighter, but in a room so barren it would have done duty for a prison cell, with a bare wood desk at the centre, and a hard chair for a visitor to sit on:

'Imagine, sir, a great Soviet fighter and a powerful man! And all he had was a bare desk, which was illuminated only by a most inferior light! And behind it sat this priest, sir, a man of no affectation or pretence at all – a man of deep experience, I would say – a man from the very roots of his country – with small, straight eyes, and short grey hair, and a habit of holding his hands together while he smoked.'

'Smoked *what*?' Smiley asked, writing.

'Please?'

'What did he smoke? The question is plain enough. A pipe, cigarettes, cigar?'

'Cigarettes, American, and the room was full of their aroma. It was like Potsdam again, when we were negotiating with the American officers from Berlin. "If this man smokes American all the time," I thought, "then he is certainly a man of influence."' Rounding on Toby again in his excitement, Grigoriev put the same point to him in Russian. To smoke American, chain smoke them, he said: imagine the cost, the influence necessary to obtain so many packets!

Then Smiley, true to his pedantic manner, asked Grigoriev to demonstrate what he meant by 'holding his hands together'

while he smoked. And he looked on impassively while Grigoriev took a brown wood pencil from his pocket and linked his
chubby hands in front of his face, and held the pencil in both
of them, and sucked at it in caricature, like someone drinking
two-handed from a mug.

'So!' he explained, and with another volatile switch of
mood, shouted something in high laughter to Toby in Russian, which Toby did not see fit, at the time, to translate, and
in the transcription is rendered only as 'obscene'.

The priest ordered Grigoriev to sit, and for ten minutes described to him the most intimate details of Grigoriev's love affair
with Evdokia, and also of his indiscretions with two other girls,
who had both worked for him as secretaries, one in Potsdam and
one in Bonn, and had ended up, unbeknown to Grigorieva, by
sharing his bed. At which point, if Grigoriev was to be believed,
he made a show of courage, and rose to his feet, demanding to
know whether he had been brought half-way across Russia in
order to attend a court of morals: 'To sleep with one's secretary
was not an unknown phenomenon, I told him, even in the polit-
buro! I assured him that I had never been indiscreet with foreign
girls, only Russians. "This too I know," he says. "But Grigorieva
is unlikely to appreciate the distinction."'

And then, to Toby's continuing amazement, Grigoriev gave
vent to another burst of throaty laughter; and though both de
Silsky and Skordeno discreetly joined in, Grigoriev's mirth out-
lived everybody's, so that they had to wait for it to run down.

'Kindly tell us, please, why the man you call the priest summoned you,' Smiley said, from deep in his brown overcoat.

'He advised me that he had special work for me in Berne
on behalf of the Thirteenth Directorate. I should reveal it to
nobody, not even to my Ambassador, it was too secret for any
of them. "But," says the priest, "you shall tell your wife. Your

personal circumstances render it impossible for you to make a conspiracy without the knowledge of your wife. This I know, Grigoriev. So tell her." And he was right,' Grigoriev commented. 'This was wise of him! This was clear evidence that the man was familiar with the human condition.'

Smiley turned a page and continued writing. 'Go on, please,' he said.

First, said the priest, Grigoriev was to open a Swiss bank account. The priest handed him a thousand Swiss francs in one hundred notes and told him to use them as the first payment. He should open the account not in Berne, where he was known, nor in Zurich, where there was a Soviet trade bank.

'The Vozhod,' Grigoriev explained gratuitously. 'This bank is used for many official and unofficial transactions.'

Not in Zurich, then, but in the small town of Thun, a few kilometres outside Berne. He should open the account under the name of Glaser, a Swiss subject: 'But I am a Soviet diplomat!' Grigoriev had objected. 'I am not Glaser, I am Grigoriev!'

Undeterred, the priest handed him a Swiss passport in the name of Adolf Glaser. Every month, said the priest, the account would be credited with several thousand Swiss francs, sometimes even ten or fifteen. Grigoriev would now be told what use to make of them. It was very secret, the priest repeated patiently, and to the secrecy belonged both a reward, and a threat. Very much as Smiley himself had done an hour before, the priest boldly set out each in turn. 'Sir, you should have observed his composure towards me,' Grigoriev told Smiley incredulously. 'His calmness, his authority in all circumstances! In a chess game he would win everything, merely by his nerves.'

'But he was not playing chess,' Smiley objected drily.

'Sir, he was not,' Grigoriev agreed, and with a sad shake of his head resumed his story.

A reward, and a threat, he repeated.

The threat was that Grigoriev's parent Ministry would be advised that he was unreliable on account of his philandering, and that he should therefore be barred from further foreign postings. This would cripple Grigoriev's career, also his marriage. So much for the threat.

'This would be extremely terrible for me,' Grigoriev added, needlessly.

Next the reward, and the reward was substantial. If Grigoriev acquitted himself well, and with absolute secrecy, his career would be furthered, his indiscretions overlooked. In Berne he would have an opportunity to move to more agreeable quarters, which would please Grigorieva; he would be given funds with which to buy himself an imposing car which would be greatly to Grigorieva's taste; also he would be independent of Embassy drivers, most of whom were *neighbours*, it was true, but were not admitted to this great secret. Lastly, said the priest, his promotion to Counsellor would be accelerated in order to explain the improvement in his living standards.

Grigoriev looked at the heap of Swiss francs lying on the desk between them, then at the Swiss passport, then at the priest. And he asked what would happen to him if he said he would rather not take part in this conspiracy. The priest nodded his head. He too, he assured Grigoriev, had considered this third possibility, but unfortunately the urgency of the need did not provide for such an option.

'So tell me what I must do with this money,' Grigoriev had said.

It was routine, the priest replied, which was another reason why Grigoriev had been selected: 'In matters of routine, I am told you are excellent,' he said. Grigoriev, though he was by now scared half-way out of his skin by the priest's words, had felt flattered by this commendation.

'He had heard good reports of me,' he explained to Smiley with pleasure.

Then the priest told Grigoriev about the mad girl.

Smiley did not budge. His eyes as he wrote were almost closed, but he wrote all the time – though God knows *what* he wrote, said Toby, for George would never have dreamed of consigning anything of even passing confidentiality to a notepad. Now and then, says Toby, while Grigoriev continued talking, George's head lifted far enough out of his coat collar for him to study the speaker's hands, or even his face. In every other respect he appeared remote from everything and everybody inside the room. Millie McCraig was in the doorway, de Silsky and Skordeno kept still as statues, while Toby prayed only for Grigoriev to 'keep talking, I mean talking at any price, who cares? We were hearing of Karla's tradecraft from the horse's mouth.'

The priest proposed to conceal nothing, he assured Grigoriev – which, as everyone in the room but Grigoriev at once recognised, was a prelude to concealing something.

In a private psychiatric clinic in Switzerland, said the priest, there was confined a young Russian girl who was suffering from an advanced state of schizophrenia: 'In the Soviet Union this form of illness is not sufficiently understood,' said the priest. Grigoriev recalled being strangely touched by the priest's finality. 'Diagnosis and treatment are too often complicated by political considerations,' the priest went on. 'In four years of treatment in our hospitals, the child Alexandra has been accused of many things by her doctors. "Paranoid reformist and delusional ideas . . . An overestimation of her own personality . . . Poor adaptation to the social environment . . .

Over-inflation of her capabilities . . . A bourgeois decadence in her sexual behaviour." Soviet doctors have repeatedly ordered her to renounce her incorrect ideas. This is not medicine,' said the priest unhappily to Grigoriev. 'It is politics. In Swiss hospitals, a more advanced attitude is taken to such matters.' It was essential that the child Alexandra should go to Switzerland.

It was by now clear to Grigoriev that the high official was personally committed to the girl's problem, and familiar with every aspect of it. Grigoriev himself was already beginning to feel sad for her. She was the daughter of a Soviet hero – said the priest – and a former official of the Red Army who, in the guise of a traitor to Russia, was living in penurious circumstances among counter-revolutionary Czarists in Paris.

'His name,' the priest said, admitting Grigoriev to the greatest secret of all, 'his name,' he said, 'is Colonel Ostrakov. He is one of our finest and most active secret agents. We rely on him totally for our information regarding counterrevolutionary conspirators in Paris.'

Nobody in the room, said Toby, showed the least surprise at this sudden deification of a dead Russian deserter.

The priest, said Grigoriev, now proceeded to sketch the manner of the heroic agent Ostrakov's life, at the same time initiating Grigoriev into the mysteries of secret work. In order to escape the vigilance of imperialist counter-intelligence, the priest explained, it was necessary to invent for an agent a legend or false biography which would make him acceptable to anti-Soviet elements. Ostrakov was therefore in appearance a Red Army defector who had 'escaped' into West Berlin, and thence to Paris, abandoning his wife and one daughter in Moscow. But in order to safeguard Ostrakov's standing among the Paris émigrés, it was logically necessary that the wife should suffer for the traitorous actions of her husband.

'For after all,' said the priest, 'if imperialist spies were to re-port that Ostrakova, the wife of a deserter and renegade, was living in good standing in Moscow – receiving her husband's sal-ary, for example, or occupying the same apartment – imagine the effect this would have upon the credibility of Ostrakov!'

Grigoriev said he could imagine this well. The priest, he explained in parenthesis, was in no sense authoritarian in his manner, but rather treated Grigoriev as an equal, doubtless out of respect for his academic qualifications.

'Doubtless,' Smiley said, and made a note.

Therefore, said the priest somewhat abruptly, Ostrakova and her daughter Alexandra, with the full agreement of her hus-band were transferred to a far province and given a house to live in, and different names, and even – in their modest and self-less way – of necessity, their own legend also. Such, said the priest, was the painful reality of those who devoted themselves to special work. And consider, Grigoriev – he went on intently – consider the effect that such deprivation, and subterfuge, and even duplicity, might have upon a sensitive and perhaps already unbalanced daughter: an absent father whose very name had been eradicated from her life! A mother who, before being re-moved to safety, was obliged to endure the full brunt of public disgrace! Picture to yourself, the priest insisted – you, a father – the strains upon the young and delicate nature of a maturing girl!

Bowing to such forceful eloquence, Grigoriev was quick to say that as a father he could picture such strains easily and it occurred to Toby at that moment, and probably to everybody else as well, that Grigoriev was exactly what he claimed to be: a humane and decent man caught in the net of events beyond his understanding or control.

For the last several years, the priest continued in a voice heavy with regret, the girl Alexandra – or, as she used to call herself, Tatiana – had been, in the Soviet province where she lived, a wanton and a social outcast. Under the pressures of her situation she had performed a variety of criminal acts, including arson and theft in public places. She had sided with pseudo-intellectual criminals and the worst imaginable antisocial elements. She had given herself freely to men, often several in a day. At first, when she was arrested, it had been possible for the priest and his assistants to stay the normal processes of law. But gradually, for reasons of security, this protection had to be withdrawn, and Alexandra had more than once been confined to State psychiatric clinics that specialised in the treatment of congenital social malcontents – with the negative results which the priest had already described.

'She has also on several occasions been detained in a common prison,' said the priest in a low voice. And, according to Grigoriev, he summed up this sad story as follows: 'You will readily appreciate, dear Grigoriev, as an academic, a father, as a man of the world, how tragically the ever-worsening news of his daughter's misfortunes affected the usefulness of our heroic agent Ostrakov in his lonely exile in Paris.'

Yet again, Grigoriev had been impressed by the remarkable sense of feeling – he would call it even a sense of direct personal responsibility – that the priest, through his story, inspired.

His voice arid as ever, Smiley made another interruption.

'And the mother is by now *where*, Counsellor, according to your priest?' he asked.

'Dead,' Grigoriev replied. 'She died in the province. The province to which she had been sent. She was buried under another name, naturally. According to the story as he told it to me, she died of a broken heart. This also placed a great burden on the priest's heroic agent in Paris,' he added. 'And upon the authorities in Russia.'

'Naturally,' said Smiley, and his solemnity was shared by the four motionless figures stationed round the room.

At last, said Grigoriev, the priest came to the precise reason why Grigoriev had been summoned. Ostrakova's death, coupled with the dreadful fate of Alexandra, had produced a grave crisis in the life of Moscow's heroic foreign agent. He was even for a short time tempted to give up his vital work in order to return to Russia and take care of his deranged and motherless child. Eventually, however, a solution was agreed upon. Since Ostrakov could not come to Russia, his daughter must come to the West, and be cared for in a private clinic where she was accessible to her father whenever he cared to visit her. France was too dangerous for this purpose, but in Switzerland across the border, treatment could take place far from the suspicious eye of Ostrakov's counterrevolutionary companions. As a French citizen, the father would claim the girl and obtain the necessary papers. A suitable clinic had already been located and it was a short drive from Berne. What Grigoriev must now do was take over the welfare of this child, from the moment she arrived there. He must visit her, pay the clinic, and report weekly to Moscow on her progress, so that the information could at once be relayed to her father. This was the purpose of the bank account, and of what the priest referred to as Grigoriev's Swiss identity.

'And you agreed,' said Smiley, as Grigoriev paused, and they heard his pen scratching busily over the paper.

'Not immediately. I asked him first two questions,' said Grigoriev, with a queer flush of vanity. 'We academics are not deceived so easily, you understand. First, I naturally asked him why this task could not be undertaken by one of the many Swiss-based representatives of our State Security.'

'An excellent question,' Smiley said, in a rare mood of congratulation. 'How did he reply to it?'

'It was too secret. Secrecy, he said, was a matter of compartments. He did not wish the name of Ostrakov to be associated with the people of the Moscow Centre mainstream. As things were now, he said, he would know that if ever there was a leak, Grigoriev alone was personally responsible. I was not grateful for this distinction,' said Grigoriev, and smirked somewhat wanly at Nick de Silsky.

'And what was your second question, Counsellor?'

'Concerning the father in Paris: how often he would visit. If the father was visiting frequently, then surely my own position as a substitute father was redundant. Arrangements could be made to pay the clinic directly, the father could visit from Paris every month and concern himself with his own daughter's welfare. To this the priest replied that the father could come only very seldom and should never be spoken of in discussions with the girl Alexandra. He added, without consistency, that the topic of the daughter was also acutely painful to the father and that conceivably he would never visit her at all. He told me I should feel honoured to be performing an important service on behalf of a secret hero of the Soviet Union. He grew stern. He told me it was not my place to apply the logic of an amateur to the craft of professionals. I apologised. I told him I indeed felt honoured. I was proud to assist however I could in the anti-imperialist struggle.'

'Yet you spoke without inner conviction?' Smiley suggested, looking up again and pausing in his writing.

'That is so.'

'Why?'

At first, Grigoriev seemed unsure why. Perhaps he had never before been invited to speak the truth about his feelings.

'Did you perhaps not *believe* the priest?' Smiley suggested.

'The story had many inconsistencies,' Grigoriev repeated

with a frown. 'No doubt in secret work this was inevitable. Nevertheless I regarded much of it as unlikely or untrue.'

'Can you explain why?'

In the catharsis of confession, Grigoriev once more forgot his own peril, and gave a smile of superiority.

'He was emotional,' he said. 'I asked myself. Afterwards, with Evdokia, next day, lying at Evdokia's side, discussing the matter with her, I asked myself: What was it between the priest and this Ostrakov? Are they brothers? Old comrades? This great man they had brought me to see, so powerful, so secret – all over the world he is making conspiracies, putting pressure, taking special action. He is a ruthless man, in a ruthless profession. Yet when I, Grigoriev, am sitting with him, talking about some fellow's deranged daughter, I have the feeling I am reading this man's most intimate love letters. I said to him: "Comrade. You are telling me too much. Don't tell me what I do not need to know. Tell me only what I must do." But he says to me: "Grigoriev, you must be a friend to this child. Then you will be a friend to me. Her father's twisted life has had a bad effect on her. She does not know who she is or where she belongs. She speaks of freedom without regard to its meaning. She is the victim of pernicious bourgeois fantasies. She uses foul language not suitable to a young girl. In lying, she has the genius of madness. None of this is her fault." Then I ask him: "Sir, have you met this girl?" And he says to me only, "Grigoriev, you must be a father to her. Her mother was in many ways not an easy woman either. You have sympathy for such matters. In her later life she became embittered, and even supported her daughter in some of her anti-social fantasies."'

Grigoriev fell silent a moment and Toby Esterhase, still reeling from the knowledge that Grigoriev had discussed Karla's proposition with his mistress within hours of its being made, was grateful for the respite.

'I felt he was dependent on me,' Grigoriev resumed. 'I felt he was concealing not only facts, but feelings.'

There remained, said Grigoriev, the practical details. The priest supplied them. The overseer of the clinic was a White Russian woman, a nun, formerly of the Russian Orthodox community in Jerusalem, but a good-hearted woman. In these cases, we should not be too scrupulous politically, said the priest. This woman had herself met Alexandra in Paris and escorted her to Switzerland. The clinic also had the services of a Russian-speaking doctor. The girl, thanks to the ethnic connections of her mother, also spoke German, but frequently refused to do so. These factors, together with the remoteness of the place, accounted for its selection. The money paid into the Thun bank would be sufficient for the clinic's fees and for medical attention up to one thousand francs a month, and as a hidden subsidy for the Grigorievs' new lifestyle. More money was available if Grigoriev thought it necessary; he should keep no bills or receipts; the priest would know soon enough if Grigoriev was cheating. He should visit the clinic weekly to pay the bill and inform himself of the girl's welfare; the Soviet Ambassador in Berne would be informed that the Grigorievs had been entrusted with secret work, and that he should allow them flexibility.

The priest then came to the question of Grigoriev's communication with Moscow.

'He asked me: "Do you know the courier Krassky?" I reply, naturally I know this courier; Krassky comes once, sometimes twice a week to the Embassy in the company of his escort. If you are friendly with him, he will maybe bring you a loaf of black bread direct from Moscow.'

In future, said the priest, Krassky would make a point of

contacting Grigoriev privately each Thursday evening during his regular visit to Berne, either in Grigoriev's house or in Grigoriev's room in the Embassy, but preferably his house. No conspiratorial discussions would take place, but Krassky would hand to Grigoriev an envelope containing an apparently personal letter from Grigoriev's aunt in Moscow. Grigoriev would take the letter to a safe place and treat it at prescribed temperatures with three chemical solutions freely available on the open market – the priest named them and Grigoriev now repeated them. In the writing thus revealed, said the priest, Grigoriev would find a list of questions he should put to Alexandra on his next weekly visit. At the same meeting with Krassky, Grigoriev should hand him a letter to be delivered to the same aunt, in which he would pretend to be writing in detail about his wife Grigorieva's welfare, whereas in fact he would be reporting to the priest on the welfare of the girl Alexandra. This was called word code. Later, the priest would if necessary supply Grigoriev with materials for a more clandestine communication, but for the time being the word code letter to Grigoriev's aunt would do.

The priest then handed Grigoriev a medical certificate, signed by an eminent Moscow doctor.

'While here in Moscow, you have suffered a minor heart attack as a consequence of stress and overwork,' said the priest. 'You are advised to take up regular cycling in order to improve your physical condition. Your wife will accompany you.'

By arriving at the clinic by bicycle or on foot, the priest explained, Grigoriev would be able to conceal the diplomatic registration of his car.

The priest then authorised him to purchase two second-hand bicycles. There remained the question of which day of the week would be best suited for Grigoriev's visits to the clinic.

Saturday was the normal visiting day but this was too dangerous; several of the inmates were from Berne and there was always the risk that 'Glaser' would be recognised. The overseer had therefore been advised that Saturdays were impracticable, and had consented, exceptionally, to a regular Friday-afternoon visit. The Ambassador would not object, but how would Grigoriev reconcile his Friday absences with Embassy routine?

There was no problem, Grigoriev replied. It was always permissible to trade Fridays for Saturdays, so Grigoriev would merely apply to work on Saturdays instead; then his Fridays would be free.

His confession over, Grigoriev treated his audience to a swift, over-lit smile.

'On Saturdays, a certain young lady also happened to be working in the Visa Section,' he said, with a wink at Toby. 'It was therefore possible we could enjoy some privacy together.'

This time the general laughter was not quite as hearty as it might have been. Time, like Grigoriev's story, was running out.

They were back where they had started, and suddenly there was only Grigoriev himself to worry about, only Grigoriev to administer, only Grigoriev to secure. He sat smirking on the sofa, but the arrogance was ebbing from him. He had linked his hands submissively and he was looking from one to the other of them, as if expecting orders.

'My wife cannot ride a bicycle,' he remarked with a sad little smile. 'She tried many times.' Her failure seemed to mean whole volumes to him. 'The priest wrote to me from Moscow: "Take your wife to her. Maybe Alexandra needs a mother, also."' He shook his head, bemused. 'She cannot ride it,' he said to Smiley. 'In such a great conspiracy, how can I tell Moscow that Grigorieva cannot ride a bicycle?' Perhaps there was no greater test of Smiley's rôle as the responsible functionary in charge, than the way in which he now almost casually transformed Grigoriev the one-time source into Grigoriev the defector-in-place.

'Counsellor, whatever your long-term plans may be, you will please remain at the Embassy for at least another two weeks,' he announced, precisely closing his notepad. 'If you do as I propose, you will find a warm welcome should you elect to make a new life somewhere in the West.' He dropped the pad into his pocket. 'But next Friday you will not visit the girl Alexandra. You will tell your wife that this was the substance of today's meeting with Krassky. When Krassky the courier brings you next Thursday's letter, you will accept it normally but you will afterwards continue to maintain to your wife that Alexandra is not to be visited. Be mysterious towards her. Blind her with mystery.'

Accepting his instructions, Grigoriev nodded uneasily.

'I must warn you however that if you make the smallest error or, on the other hand, try some trick, the priest will find out and destroy you. You will also forfeit your chances of a friendly reception in the West. Is that clear to you?'

There were telephone numbers for Grigoriev to ring, there were call-box to call-box procedures to be explained, and against all the laws of the trade, Smiley allowed Grigoriev to write the whole lot down, for he knew that he would not remember them otherwise. When all this was done, Grigoriev took his leave in a spirit of brooding dejection. Toby himself drove him to a safe dropping point, then returned to the flat and held a curt meeting of farewell.

Smiley was in his same chair, hands clasped on his lap. The rest of them, under Millie McCraig's orders, were busily tidying up the traces of their presence, polishing, dusting, emptying ashtrays and waste-paper baskets. Everyone present except himself and Smiley was getting out today, said Toby, the surveillance teams as well. Not tonight, not tomorrow. Now. They were sitting on a king-sized time bomb, he said: Grigoriev might at this very moment, under the continued impulse of confession, be describing the entire episode to his awful wife. If he had told Evdokia about Karla, who was to say he would not tell Grigorieva, or for that matter little Natasha, about his pow-wow with George today? Nobody should feel discarded, nobody should feel left out, said Toby. They had done a great job, and they would be meeting again soon to set the crown on it. There were handshakes, even a tear or two, but the prospect of the final act left everybody cheerful at heart.

And Smiley, sitting so quiet, so immobile, as the party broke up around him, what did he feel? On the face of it, this was a moment of high achievement for him. He had done everything he had set out to do, and more, even if he had resorted to Karla's techniques for the purpose. He had done it alone; and today, as the record would show, he had broken and turned Karla's hand-picked agent in the space of a couple of hours. Unaided, even hampered by those who had called him back to service, he had fought his way through to the point where he could honestly say he had burst the last important lock. He was in late age, yet his tradecraft had never been better; for the first time in his career, he held the advantage over his old adversary.

On the other hand, that adversary had acquired a human face of disconcerting clarity. It was no brute whom Smiley was pursuing with such mastery, no unqualified fanatic after all, no automaton. It was a man; and one whose downfall, if Smiley chose to bring it about, would be caused by nothing more sinister than excessive love, a weakness with which Smiley himself from his own tangled life was eminently familiar.

26

To every clandestine operation, says the folklore, belong more days of waiting than are numbered in Paradise, and for both George Smiley and Toby Esterhase, in their separate ways, the days and nights between Sunday evening and Friday seemed often numberless, and surely bore no relation to the Hereafter.

They lived not so much by Moscow Rules, said Toby, as by George's war rules. Both changed hotels and identities that same Sunday night, Smiley decamping to a small *hôtel garni* in the old town, the Arca, and Toby to a distasteful motel outside the town. Thereafter the two men communicated between call-boxes according to an agreed rota, and if they needed to meet, they selected crowded outdoor places, walking a short distance together before parting. Toby had decided to change his tracks, he said, and was using cars as sparingly as possible. His task was to keep the watch on Grigoriev. All week he clung to his stated conviction that, having so recently enjoyed the luxury of one confession, Grigoriev was sure to treat himself to another. To forestall this, he kept Grigoriev on as short a rein as possible, but to keep up with him at all was a nightmare. For example, Grigoriev left his house at quarter to eight each morning and had a five-minute walk to the Embassy. Very well: Toby would make one car sweep down the road at seven-fifty exactly. If Grigoriev carried his brief-case in his right hand,

Toby would know that nothing was happening. But the left hand meant 'emergency', with a crash meeting in the gardens of the Elfenau palace, and a fallback in the town. On the Monday and Tuesday, Grigoriev went the distance using his right hand only. But on the Wednesday it was snowing, he wished to clear his spectacles, and therefore he stopped to locate his handkerchief, with the result that Toby first saw the briefcase in his left hand, but when he raced round the block again to check, Grigoriev was grinning like a madman and waving the brief-case at him with his right. Toby, according to his own account, had 'a total heart attack'. The next day, the crucial Thursday, Toby achieved a car meeting with Grigoriev in the little village of Allmendigen, just outside the town, and was able to talk to him face to face. An hour earlier, the courier Krassky had arrived, bringing Karla's weekly orders: Toby had seen him enter the Grigoriev residence. So where were the instructions from Moscow? Toby demanded. Grigoriev was cantankerous and a little drunk. He demanded ten thousand dollars for the letter, which so enraged Toby that he threatened Grigoriev with exposure then and there; he threatened to make a citizen's arrest and take him straight down to the police station and charge him personally with posing as a Swiss national, abusing his diplomatic status, evading Swiss tax laws, and about fifteen other things, including venery and espionage. The bluff worked, Grigoriev produced the letter, already treated, with the secret writing showing between the handwritten lines. Toby took several photographs of it, then returned it to Grigoriev.

Karla's questions from Moscow, which Toby showed to Smiley late that night in a rare meeting at a country inn, had a beseeching ring: ' . . . report more fully on Alexandra's appearance and state of mind . . . Is she lucid? Does she laugh and does her laughter make a happy or a sad impression? Is she clean in her personal habits, clean finger-nails, brushed hair? What is the doctor's latest diagnosis; does he recommend some other treatment?'

But Grigoriev's main preoccupations at their rendezvous in Allmendigen turned out not to be with Krassky, nor with the letter, nor its author. His lady-friend of the Visa Section had been demanding outright to know about his Friday excursions, he said. Hence his depression and drunkenness. Grigoriev had answered her vaguely, but now he suspected her of being a Moscow spy, put there either by the priest or, worse, by some other frightful organ of Soviet Security. Toby, as it happened, shared this belief, but did not feel that much would be served by saying so.

'I have told her I shall not make love to her again until I completely trust her,' Grigoriev said earnestly. 'Also I have not yet decided whether she shall be permitted to accompany me in my new life in Australia.'

'George, this is a madhouse!' Toby told Smiley in a furious mixture of images, while Smiley continued to study Karla's solicitous questions, even though they were written in Russian. 'Listen, I mean, how long can we hold the dam? This guy is a total crazy!'

'When does Krassky return to Moscow?' Smiley asked.

'Saturday midday.'

'Grigoriev must arrange a meeting with him before he leaves. He's to tell Krassky he will have a special message for him. An urgent one.'

'Sure,' said Toby. 'Sure, George.' And that was that.

Where had George gone in his mind? Toby wondered, watching him vanish into the crowd once more. Karla's instructions to Grigoriev seemed to have upset Smiley quite

403

absurdly. 'I was caught between one total loony and one complete depressive,' Toby claims of this taxing period.

While Toby, however, could at least agonise over the vagaries of his master and his agent, Smiley had less substantial fare with which to occupy his time, which may have been his problem. On the Tuesday, he took a train to Zurich and lunched quietly at the Kronenhalle with Peter Guillam, who had flown in by way of London at Saul Enderby's behest. Their discussion was restrained, and not merely on the grounds of security. Guillam had taken it upon himself to speak to Ann while he was in London, he said, and was keen to know whether there was any message he might take back to her. Smiley said icily that there was none, and came as near as Guillam could remember to bawling him out. On another occasion – he suggested – perhaps Guillam would be good enough to keep his damned fingers out of Smiley's affairs? Guillam switched the topic hastily to business. Concerning Grigoriev, he said, Saul Enderby had a notion to sell him to the Cousins as found rather than process him at Sarratt. How did George feel about that one? Saul had a sort of hunch that the glamour of a senior Russian defector would give the Cousins a much-needed lift in Washington, even if he hadn't anything to tell, while Grigoriev in London might, so to speak, mar the pure wine to come. How did George feel on that one, actually?

'Quite,' said Smiley.

'Saul also rather wondered whether your plans for next Friday were strictly necessary,' said Guillam, with evident reluctance.

Picking up a table-knife, Smiley stared along the blade.

'She's worth his career to him,' he said at last, with a most unnerving tautness. 'He steals for her, lies for her, risks his neck for her. He has to know whether she cleans her finger-nails and brushes her hair. Don't you think we owe her a look?'

Owe to whom? Guillam wondered nervously as he flew back to London to report. Had Smiley meant that he owed it to himself? Or did he mean to Karla? But he was far too cautious to air these theories to Saul Enderby.

From a distance, it might have been a castle, or one of those small farmsteads which sit on hilltops in the Swiss wine country, with turrets, and moats with covered bridges leading to inner courtyards. Closer to, it took on a more utilitarian appearance, with an incinerator, and an orchard, and modern outbuildings with rows of small windows rather high. A sign at the edge of the village pointed to it, praising its quiet position, its comfort, and the solicitude of its staff. The community was described as 'interdenominational Christian theosophist', and foreign patients were a speciality. Old, heavy snow cluttered fields and roof-tops, but the road which Smiley drove was clear. The day was all white; sky and snow had merged into a single, unchart-ed void. From the gatehouse a dour porter telephoned ahead of him and, receiving somebody's permission, waved him through. There was a bay marked 'DOCTORS' and a bay marked 'VISITORS' and he parked in the second. When he pressed the bell, a dull-looking woman in a grey habit opened the door to him, blush-ing even before she spoke. He heard crematorium music, and the clanking of crockery from a kitchen, and human voices all at once. It was a house with hard floors and no curtains.

'Mother Felicity is expecting you,' said Sister Beatitude in a shy whisper.

A scream would fill the entire house, thought Smiley. He noticed pot plants out of reach. At a door marked 'office' his escort thumped lustily, then shoved it open. Mother Felicity was a large, inflamed-looking woman with a disconcerting worldliness in her gaze. Smiley sat opposite her. An ornate cross rested on her large bosom, and while she spoke, her heavy hands consoled it with a couple of touches. Her German was slow and regal.

'So,' she said. 'So, you are Herr *Lachmann*, and Herr Lachmann is an acquaintance of Herr *Glaser*, and Herr Glaser is this week indisposed.' She played on these names as if she knew as well as he did they were lies. 'He was not so indisposed that he could not telephone, but he was so indisposed that he could not bicycle. That is correct?'

Smiley said it was.

'Please do not lower your voice merely because I am a nun. We run a noisy house here and nobody is the less pious for it. You look pale. You have a flu?'

'No. No, I am well.'

'Then you are better off than Herr Glaser who has succumbed to a flu. Last year we had an Egyptian flu, the year before it was an Asian flu, but this year the *malheur* seems to be our own entirely. Does Herr Lachmann have documents, may I ask, which legitimise him for who he is?'

Smiley handed her a Swiss identity card.

'Come. Your hand is shaking. But you have no flu. "By occupation, *professor*,"' she read aloud. 'Herr Lachmann hides his light. He is *Professor* Lachmann. Of which subject is he professor, may one ask?'

'Of philology.'

'So. Philology. And Herr *Glaser*, what is *his* profession? He has never revealed it to me.'

'I understand he is in business,' Smiley said.

'A businessman who speaks perfect Russian. You also speak perfect Russian, Professor?'

'Alas, no.'

'But you are friends.' She handed back the identity card. 'A Swiss-Russian businessman and a modest professor of philology are friends. So. Let us hope the friendship is a fruitful one.'

'We are also neighbours,' Smiley said.

'We are all neighbours, Herr Lachmann. Have you met Alexandra before?'

'No.'

'Young girls are brought here in many capacities. We have god-children. We have wards. Nieces. Orphans. Cousins. Aunts, a few. A few sisters. And now a Professor. But you would be very surprised how few daughters there are in the world. What is the family relationship between Herr Glaser and Alexandra, for example?'

'I understand he is a friend of Monsieur Ostrakov.'

'Who is in Paris. But is invisible. As also is Madame Ostrakova. Invisible. As also, today, is Herr Glaser. You see how difficult it is for us to come to grips with the world, Herr Lachmann? When we ourselves scarcely know who we are, how can we tell *them* who *they* are? You must be very careful with her.' A bell was ringing for the end of rest. 'Sometimes she lives in the dark. Sometimes she sees too much. Both are painful. She has grown up in Russia. I don't know why. It is a complicated story, full of contrasts, full of gaps. If it is not the cause of her malady, it is certainly, let us say, the framework. You do not think Herr Glaser is the father, for instance?'

'No.'

'Nor do I. Have you *met* the invisible Ostrakov? You have not. Does the invisible Ostrakov exist? Alexandra insists he is a phantom. Alexandra will have a quite different parentage. Well, so would many of us!'

'May I ask what you have told her about me?'

'All I know. Which is nothing. That you are a friend of Uncle Anton, whom she refuses to accept as her uncle. That Uncle Anton is ill, which appears to delight her, but probably it worries her very much. I have told her it is her father's wish to have someone visit her every week, but she tells me her father is a brigand and pushed her mother off a mountain at dead of night. I have told her to speak German but she may still decide that Russian is best.'

'I understand,' said Smiley.

'You are lucky, then,' Mother Felicity retorted. 'For I do not.'

Alexandra entered and at first he saw only her eyes: so clear, so defenceless. In his imagination, he had drawn her, for some reason, larger. Her lips were full at the centre, but at the corners already thin and too agile, and her smile had a dangerous luminosity. Mother Felicity told her to sit, said something in Russian, gave her a kiss on her flaxen head. She left, and they heard her keys jingle as she strode off down the corridor, yelling at one of the sisters in French to have this mess cleared up. Alexandra wore a green tunic with long sleeves gathered at the wrists and a cardigan over her shoulders like a cape. She seemed to carry her clothes rather than wear them, as if someone had dressed her for the meeting.

'Is Anton dead?' she asked, and Smiley noticed that there was no natural link between the expression on her face and the thoughts in her head.

'No, Anton has a bad flu,' he replied.

'Anton says he is my uncle but he is not,' she explained. Her German was good, and he wondered whether, despite what Karla had said to Grigoriev, she had that from her mother too, or whether she had inherited her father's gift for languages, or both. 'He also pretends he has no car.' As her father had once done, she watched him without emotion, and without commitment. 'Where is your list?' she asked. 'Anton always brings a list.'

'Oh, I have my questions in my head.'

'It is forbidden to ask questions without a list. Questions out of the head are all completely forbidden by my father.'

'Who is your father?' Smiley asked.

For a time he saw only her eyes again, staring at him out of their private lonely place. She picked up a roll of Scotch tape from Mother Felicity's desk, and lightly traced the shiny surface with her finger.

'I saw your car,' she said. '"BE" stands for Berne.'

'Yes, it does,' said Smiley.

'What kind of car does Anton have?'

'A Mercedes. A black one. Very grand.'

'How much did he pay for it?'

'He bought it second-hand. About five thousand francs, I should imagine.'

'Then why does he come and see me on a bicycle?'

'Perhaps he needs the exercise.'

'No,' she said. 'He has a secret.'

'Have *you* got a secret, Alexandra?' Smiley asked.

She heard his question, and smiled at it, and nodded a couple of times as if to someone a long way off. 'My secret is called *Tatiana*.'

'That's a good name,' said Smiley. '*Tatiana*. How did you come by that?'

Raising her head, she smiled radiantly at the icons on the wall. 'It is forbidden to talk about it,' she said. 'If you talk about it, nobody will believe you, but they put you in a clinic.'

'But you are in a clinic already,' Smiley pointed out.

Her voice did not lift, it only quickened. She remained so

409

absolutely still that she seemed not even to draw breath between her words. Her lucidity and her courtesy were awesome. She respected his kindness, she said, but she knew that he was an extremely dangerous man, more dangerous than teachers or police. Dr Rüedi had invented property and prisons and many of the clever arguments by which the world lived out its lies, she said. Mother Felicity was too close to God, she did not understand that God was somebody who had to be ridden and kicked like a horse till he took you in the right direction.

'But you, Herr Lachmann, represent the forgiveness of the authorities. Yes, I am afraid you do.'

She sighed, and gave him a tired smile of indulgence, but when he looked at the table he saw that she had seized hold of her thumb, and was forcing it back upon itself till it looked like snapping.

'Perhaps *you* are my father, Herr Lachmann,' she suggested with a smile.

'No, alas, I have no children,' Smiley replied.

'Are you God?'

'No, I'm just an ordinary person.'

'Mother Felicity says that in every ordinary person, there is a part that is God.'

This time it was Smiley's turn to take a long while to reply. His mouth opened, then with uncharacteristic hesitation closed again.

'I have heard it said too,' he replied, and looked away from her a moment.

'You are supposed to ask me whether I have been feeling better.'

'Are you feeling better, Alexandra?'

'My name is Tatiana,' she said.

'Then how does Tatiana feel?'

She laughed. Her eyes were delightfully bright. 'Tatiana is the daughter of a man who is too important to exist,' she said. 'He controls the whole of Russia, but he does not exist. When people arrest her, her father arranges for her to be freed. He does not exist but everyone is afraid of him. Tatiana does not exist either,' she added. 'There is only Alexandra.'

'What about Tatiana's mother?'

'She was punished,' said Alexandra calmly, confiding this information to the icons rather than to Smiley. 'She was not obedient to history. That is to say, she believed that history had taken a wrong course. She was mistaken. The people should not attempt to change history. It is the task of history to change the people. I would like you to take me with you, please. I wish to leave this clinic.'

Her hands were fighting each other furiously while she continued to smile at the icons.

'Did Tatiana ever meet her father?' he asked.

'A small man used to watch the children walk to school,' she replied. He waited but she said no more.

'And then?' he asked.

'From a car. He would lower the window but he looked only at me.'

'Did you look at him?'

'Of course. How else would I know he was looking at me?'

'What was his appearance? His manner? Did he smile?'

'He smoked. Feel free, if you wish. Mother Felicity likes a cigarette occasionally. Well, it's only natural, isn't it? Smoking calms the conscience, I am told.'

She had pressed the bell: reached out and pressed it for a long time. He heard the jingle of Mother Felicity's keys again, coming towards them down the corridor, and the shuffle of her feet at the door as she paused to unlock it, just like the sounds of any prison in the world.

'I wish to come with you in your car,' said Alexandra.

Smiley paid her bill and Alexandra watched him count the notes out under the lamp, exactly the way Uncle Anton did it. Mother Felicity intercepted Alexandra's studious look and perhaps she sensed trouble, for she glanced sharply at Smiley as if she suspected some misconduct in him. Alexandra accompanied him to the door and helped Sister Beatitude open it, then shook Smiley's hand in a very stylish way, lifting her elbow up and outward, and bending her front knee. She tried to kiss his hand but Sister Beatitude prevented her. She watched him to the car and she began waving, and he was already moving when he heard her screaming from very close, and saw that she was trying to open the car door and travel with him, but Sister Beatitude hauled her off and dragged her, still screaming, back into the house.

Half an hour later in Thun, in the same café from which he had observed Grigoriev's visit to the bank a week before, Smiley silently handed Toby the letter he had prepared. Grigoriev was to give it to Krassky tonight or whenever they met, he said.

'Grigoriev wants to defect tonight,' Toby objected.

Smiley shouted. For once in his life, shouted. He opened his mouth very wide, he shouted, and the whole café sat up with a jolt – which is to say, that the barmaid looked up from her marriage advertisements, and of the four card-players in the corner, one at least turned his head.

'Not yet!'

Then, to show that he had himself completely under

control, he repeated the words quietly: 'Not yet, Toby. Forgive me. Not yet.'

Of the letter which Smiley sent to Karla by way of Grigoriev, no copy exists, which is perhaps what Smiley intended, but there can be little doubt of the substance, since Karla himself was anyway a self-professed exponent of the arts of what he liked to call pressure. Smiley would have set out the bare facts: that Alexandra was known to be his daughter by a dead mistress of manifest anti-Soviet tendencies, that he had arranged her illegal departure from the Soviet Union by pretending that she was his secret agent; that he had misappropriated public money and resources; that he had organised two murders and perhaps also the conjectured official execution of Kirov, all in order to protect his criminal scheme. Smiley would have pointed out that the accumulated evidence of this was quite sufficient, given Karla's precarious position within Moscow Centre, to secure his liquidation by his peers in the Collegium; and that if this were to happen, his daughter's future in the West – where she was residing under false pretences – would be uncertain, to say the least. There would be no money for her, and Alexandra would become a perpetual and ailing exile, ferried from one public hospital to another, without friends, proper papers, or a penny to her name. At worst, she would be brought back to Russia, to have visited upon her the full wrath of her father's enemies.

After the stick, Smiley offered Karla the same carrot he had offered him twenty years before, in Delhi: save your skin, come to us, tell us what you know, and we will make a home for you. A straight replay, said Saul Enderby later, who liked a sporting metaphor. Smiley would have promised Karla immunity from prosecution for complicity in the murder of Vladimir, and there is evidence that Enderby obtained a similar concession through his German liaison regarding the murder of Otto Leipzig. Without a question, Smiley also threw in general guarantees about Alexandra's future in the West – treatment, maintenance, and if necessary, citizenship. Did he take the line of kinship, as he had done before, in Delhi? Did he appeal to Karla's humanity, now so demonstrably on show? Did he add some clever seasoning, calculated to spare Karla humiliation, and knowing his pride, head him off perhaps from an act of self-destruction?

Certainly, he gave Karla very little time to make up his mind. For that too is an axiom of pressure, as Karla was well aware: time to think is dangerous, except that in this case, there is reason to suppose that it was dangerous to Smiley also, though for vastly different reasons; he might have relented at the eleventh hour. Only the immediate call to action, says the Sarratt folklore, will force the quarry to slip the ropes of his restraint, and against every impulse born or taught to him, sail into the blue. The same, on this occasion, may be said to have applied equally to the hunter.

27

It's like putting all your money on black, thought Guillam, staring out of the window of the café: everything you've got in the world, your wife, your unborn child. Then waiting, hour by hour, for the croupier to spin the wheel.

He had known Berlin when it was the world capital of the cold war, when every crossing point from East to West had the tenseness of a major surgical operation. He remembered how on nights like these, clusters of Berlin policemen and Allied soldiers used to gather under the arc lights, stamping their feet, cursing the cold, fidgeting their rifles from shoulder to shoulder, puffing clouds of frosted breath into each other's faces. He remembered how the tanks waited, growling to keep their engines warm, their gun barrels picking targets on the other side, feigning strength. He remembered the sudden wail of the alarm klaxons and the dash to the Bernauerstrasse or wherever the latest escape attempt might be. He remembered the fire brigade ladders going up; the orders to shoot back; the orders not to; the dead, some of them agents. But after tonight, he knew that he would remember it only like this: so dark you wanted to take a torch with you into the street, so still you could have heard the cocking of a rifle from across the river.

'What cover will he use?' he asked.

Smiley sat opposite him across the little plastic table, a cup of cold coffee at his elbow. He looked somehow very small inside his overcoat.

'Something humble,' Smiley said. 'Something that fits in. Those who cross here are mostly old-age pensioners, I gather.' He was smoking one of Guillam's cigarettes and it seemed to take all his attention.

'What on earth do pensioners want here?' Guillam asked.

'Some work. Some visit dependants. I didn't enquire very closely, I'm afraid.'

Guillam remained dissatisfied.

'We pensioners tend to keep ourselves to ourselves,' Smiley added, in a poor effort at humour.

'You're telling me,' said Guillam.

The café was in the Turkish quarter because the Turks are now the poor whites of West Berlin, and property is worst and cheapest near the Wall. Smiley and Guillam were the only foreigners. At a long table sat a whole Turkish family, chewing flat bread and drinking coffee and Coca-Cola. The children had shaven heads and the wide, puzzled eyes of refugees. Islamic music was playing from an old tape-recorder. Strips of coloured plastic hung from the hardboard arch of an Islamic doorway.

Guillam returned his gaze to the window, and the bridge. First came the piers of the overhead railway, next the old brick house that Sam Collins and his team had discreetly requisitioned as an observation centre. His men had been moving in surreptitiously these last two days. Then came the white halo of sodium arc lights, and behind it lay a barricade, a pillbox, then the bridge. The bridge was for pedestrians only, and the only way over it was a corridor of steel fencing like a bird walk, sometimes one man's width and sometimes three.

Occasionally one crossed, keeping a meek appearance and a steady pace in order not to alarm the sentry tower, then stepping into the sodium halo as he reached the West. By daylight the bird walk was grey; by night for some reason yellow, and strangely bright. The pillbox was a yard or two inside the border, its roof just mastering the barricade, but it was the tower that dominated everything, one iron-black rectangular pillar at the bridge's centre. Even the snow avoided it. There was snow on the concrete teeth that blocked the bridge to traffic, snow swarmed round the halo and the pillbox and made a show of settling on the wet cobble; but the sentry tower was immune, as if not even the snow would go near it of its own free will. Just short of the halo, the bird walk narrowed to a last gateway and a cattle pen. But the gateway, said Toby, could be closed electrically at a moment's notice from inside the pillbox.

The time was ten-thirty but it could have been three in the morning, because along its borders, West Berlin goes to bed with the dark. Inland, the island-city may chat and drink and whore and spend its money; the Sony signs and rebuilt churches and conference halls may glitter like a fair-ground; but the dark shores of the borderland are silent from seven in the evening. Close to the halo stood a Christmas tree, but only the upper half of it was lit, only the upper half was visible from across the river. It is a place of no compromise, thought Guillam, a place of no third way. Whatever reservations he might occasionally have about the Western freedom, here, at this border, like most other things, they stopped dead.

'George?' said Guillam softly, and cast Smiley a questioning glance.

A labourer had lurched into the halo. He seemed to rise into it as they all did the moment they stepped out of the bird walk, as if a burden had fallen from their backs. He was carrying a small brief-case and what looked like a railman's lamp. He was slight of build. But Smiley, if he had noticed the man at all, had already returned to the collar of his brown overcoat and his lonely, far-away thoughts. 'If he comes, he'll come on time,' Smiley had said. Then why do we get here two hours early? Guillam had wanted to ask. Why do we sit here, like two strangers, drinking sweet coffee out of little cups, soaked in the steam of this wretched Turkish kitchen, talking platitudes? But he knew the answer already. Because we *owe*, Smiley would have said if he had been in a talking mood. Because we owe the caring and the waiting, we owe this vigil over one man's effort to escape the system he has helped create. For as long as he is trying to reach us, we are his friends. Nobody else is on his side.

He'll come, Guillam thought. He won't. He may. If this isn't prayer, he thought, what is it?

'More coffee, George?'

'No, thank you, Peter. No, I don't think so. No.'

'They seem to have soup of some sort. Unless that was the coffee.'

'Thank you. I think I've consumed about all I can manage,' said Smiley, in quite a general tone, as if anyone who wished to hear was welcome.

'Well, maybe I'll just order something for rent,' said Guillam.

'Rent? I'm sorry. Of course. God knows what they must live on.'

Guillam ordered two more coffees and paid for them. He was paying as he went, deliberately, in case they had to leave in a hurry.

Come for George's sake, he thought; come for mine. Come for all our damn sakes, and be the impossible harvest we have dreamed of for so long.

'When did you say the baby was due, Peter?'

'March.'

'Ah. March. What will you call it?'

'We haven't really thought.'

Across the road, by the glow of a furniture shop that sold reproduction wrought iron and brocade and fake muskets and pewter, Guillam made out the muffled figure of Toby Esterhase in his Balkan fur hat, affecting to study the wares. Toby and his team had the street, Sam Collins had the observation post: that was the deal. For the escape cars, Toby had insisted on taxis, and there they stood, three of them, suitably shabby, in the darkness of the station arches, with notices in their windscreens saying 'out of service', and their drivers standing at the *Imbiss*-stand, eating sausages in sweet sauce out of paper dishes.

The place is a total minefield, Peter, Toby had warned. *Turks, Greeks, Yugoslavs, a lot of crooks – even the damn cats are wired, no exaggeration.*

Not a whisper anywhere, Smiley had ordered. *Not a murmur, Peter. Tell Collins.*

Come, thought Guillam urgently. We're all rooting for you. Come.

From Toby's back, Guillam lifted his gaze slowly to the top-floor window of the old house where Collins' observation post was sited. Guillam had done his Berlin stint, he had been part of it a dozen times. The telescopes and cameras, the directional microphones, all the useless hardware that was supposed to make the waiting easier; the crackle of the radios, the stink of coffee and tobacco; the bunk-beds. He imagined the co-opted West German policeman who had no idea why he had been brought here, and would have to stay till the operation was abandoned or successful – the man who knew the bridge by heart and could tell the regulars from the casuals and spot the smallest bad omen the moment it occurred: the silent doubling of the watch, the Vopo sharpshooters easing softly into place.

And if they shoot him? thought Guillam. If they arrest him? If they leave him – which they would surely like to, and had done before to others – bleeding to death, face downward in the bird walk not six feet from the halo?

Come, he thought, less certainly, willing his prayers into the black skyline of the East. Come all the same.

A fine, very bright pin-light flitted across the west-facing upper window of the observation house, bringing Guillam to his feet. He turned round to see Smiley already half-way to the door. Toby Esterhase was waiting for them on the pavement.

'It's only a possibility, George,' he said softly, in the tone of a man preparing them for disappointment. 'Just a thin chance, but he could be our man.'

They followed him without another word. The cold was ferocious. They passed a tailor's shop with two dark-haired girls stitching in the window. They passed wall posters offering cheap ski holidays, death to Fascists, and to the Shah. The cold made them breathless. Turning his face from the swirling snow, Guillam glimpsed a children's adventure playground made of old railway sleepers. They passed between black, dead buildings, then right, across the cobbled road, in pitch-frozen darkness to the river bank, where an old timber bullet-shelter with rifle slits offered them the whole span of the bridge. To their left, black against the hostile river, a tall wooden cross, garnished with barbed wire, bore memory to an unknown man who had not quite escaped.

Toby silently extracted a pair of field-glasses from his overcoat and handed them to Smiley.

'George. Listen. Good luck, okay?'

Toby's hand closed briefly over Guillam's arm. Then he darted away again, into the darkness.

The shelter stank of leaf-mould and damp. Smiley crouched to the rifle slit, the skirts of his tweed coat trailing in the mud, while he surveyed the scene before him as if it held the very reaches of his own long life. The river was broad and slow, misted with cold. Arc lights played over it, and the snow danced in their beams. The bridge spanned it on fat stone piers, six or eight of them, which swelled into crude shoes as they reached the water. The spaces between them were arched, all but the centre, which was squared off to make room for shipping, but the only ship was a grey patrol boat moored at the Eastern bank, and the only commerce that it offered was death. Behind the bridge, like its vastly bigger shadow, ran the railway viaduct, but like the river it was derelict, and no trains ever crossed. The warehouses of the far bank stood monstrous as the hulks of an earlier barbaric civilisation, and the bridge with its yellow bird walk seemed to leap from half-way up them, like a fantastic light-path out of darkness. From his vantage point, Smiley could scan the whole length of it with his field-glasses, from the floodlit white barrack house on the Eastern bank, up to the black sentry tower at the crest, then slightly downhill again towards the Western side: to the cattle pen, the pillbox that controlled the gateway, and finally the halo.

Guillam stood but a few feet behind him, yet Guillam could have been back in Paris for all the awareness Smiley had of him: he had seen the solitary black figure start his journey; he had seen the glimmer of the cigarette-end as he took one last pull, the spark of it comet towards the water as he tossed it over the iron fencing of the bird walk. One small man, in a worker's half-length coat, with a worker's satchel slung across his little chest, walking neither fast nor slowly, but walking like a man who walked a lot. One small man, his body a fraction too long for his legs, hatless despite the snow. That is all that happens, Smiley thought; one little man walks across a bridge.

'Is it him?' Guillam whispered. 'George, tell me! Is it Karla?'

Don't come, thought Smiley. *Shoot*, Smiley thought, talking to Karla's people, not to his own. There was suddenly something terrible in his foreknowledge that this tiny creature was about to cut himself off from the black castle behind him. Shoot him from the sentry tower, shoot him from the pillbox, from the white barrack hut, from the crow's-nest on the prison warehouse, slam the gate on him, cut him down, your own traitor, kill him! In his racing imagination, he saw the scene unfold: the last-minute discovery by Moscow Centre of Karla's infamy; the phone calls to the frontier – 'Stop him at any cost!' And the shooting, never too much – enough to hit a man a time or two, and wait.

'It's him!' Guillam whispered. He had taken the binoculars from Smiley's unresisting hand. 'It's the same man! The photograph that hung on your wall in the Circus! George, you miracle!'

But Smiley in his imagination saw only the Vopo's searchlights converging on Karla as if he were like a hare in the headlights, so dark against the snow; and Karla's hopeless old man's run before the bullets threw him like a rag doll over his own feet. Like Guillam, Smiley had seen it all before. He looked across the river into the darkness again, and an unholy vertigo seized him as the very evil he had fought against seemed to reach out and possess him and claim him despite his striving, calling him a traitor also; mocking him, yet at the same time applauding his betrayal. On Karla has descended the curse of

Smiley's compassion; on Smiley the curse of Karla's fanaticism. I have destroyed him with the weapons I abhorred, and they are his. We have crossed each other's frontiers, we are the no-men of this no-man's-land.

'Just keep moving,' Guillam was murmuring. 'Just keep moving, let nothing stop you.'

Approaching the blackness of the sentry tower, Karla took a couple of shorter steps and for a moment Smiley really thought he might change his mind and give himself up to the East Germans. Then he saw a cat's tongue of flame as Karla lit a fresh cigarette. With a match or a lighter? he wondered. *To George from Ann with all my love.*

'Christ, he's cool!' said Guillam.

The little figure set off again, but at a slower pace, as if he had grown weary. He is stoking up his courage for the last step, thought Smiley, or he is trying to damp his courage down. He thought of Vladimir and Otto Leipzig and the dead Kirov; he thought of Haydon and his own life's work ruined; he thought of Ann, permanently stained for him by Karla's cunning, and Haydon's scheming embrace. He recited in his despair a whole list of crimes – the tortures, the killings, the endless ring of corruption – to lay upon the frail shoulders of this one pedestrian on the bridge, but they would not stay there: he did not want these spoils, won by these methods. Like a chasm, the jagged skyline beckoned to him yet again, the swirling snow made it an inferno. For a second longer, Smiley stood on the brink at the smouldering river's edge.

They had started walking along the tow-path, Guillam leading, Smiley reluctantly following. The halo burned ahead of them, growing as they approached it. *Like two ordinary pedestrians*, Toby had said. *Just walk to the bridge and wait, it's normal.* From the darkness around them, Smiley heard

whispered voices and the swift, damped sounds of hasty movement under tension. 'George,' someone whispered. 'George.'
From a yellow phone box, an unknown figure lifted a hand in
discreet salute, and he heard the words 'triumph' smuggled to
him on the wet freezing air. The snow was blurring his glasses,
he found it hard to see. The observation post stood to their
right, not a light burning in the windows. He made out a van
parked at the entrance, and realised it was a Berlin mail van,
one of Toby's favourites. Guillam was hanging back. Smiley
heard something about 'claiming the prize'.

They had reached the edge of the halo. An orange rampart
blocked the bridge and the chicane from sight. They were out
of the eye-line of the sentry-box. Perched above the Christmas tree, Toby Esterhase was standing on the observation
scaffold with a pair of binoculars, calmly playing the cold war
tourist. A plump female watcher stood at his side. An old notice warned them they were there at their own risk. On the
smashed brick viaduct behind them Smiley picked out a forgotten armorial crest. Toby made a tiny motion with his hand:
thumbs up, it's our man now. From beyond the rampart, Smiley
heard light footsteps and the vibration of an iron fence. He
caught the smell of an American cigarette as the icy wind wafted it ahead of the smoker. There's still the electric gateway, he
thought; he waited for the clang as it slammed shut, but none
came. He realised he had no real name by which to address
his enemy: only a codename and a woman's at that. Even his
military rank was a mystery. And still Smiley hung back, like a
man refusing to go on stage.

Guillam had drawn alongside him and seemed to be trying
to edge him forward. He heard soft footsteps as Toby's watchers one by one gathered to the edge of the halo, safe from
view in the shelter of the rampart, waiting with bated breath

for a sight of the catch. And suddenly, there he stood, like a man slipping into a crowded hall unnoticed. His small right hand hung flat and naked at his side, his left held the cigarette timidly across his chest. One little man, hatless, with a satchel. He took a step forward and in the halo Smiley saw his face, aged and weary and travelled, the short hair turned to white by a sprinkling of snow. He wore a grimy shirt and a black tie: he looked like a poor man going to the funeral of a friend. The cold had nipped his cheeks low down, adding to his age.

They faced each other; they were perhaps a yard apart, much as they had been in Delhi jail. Smiley heard more footsteps and this time it was the sound of Toby padding softly down the wooden ladder of the scaffold. He heard soft voices and laughter; he thought he even heard the sound of gentle clapping, but he never knew; there were shadows everywhere, and once inside the halo, it was hard for him to see out. Paul Skordeno slipped forward and stood himself one side of Karla; Nick de Silsky stood the other. He heard Guillam telling someone to get that bloody car up here before they come over the bridge and get him back. He heard the ring of something metal falling on to the icy cobble, and knew it was Ann's cigarette-lighter, but nobody else seemed to notice it. They exchanged one more glance and perhaps each for that second did see in the other something of himself. He heard the crackle of car tyres and the sounds of doors opening, while the engine kept running. De Silsky and Skordeno moved towards it and Karla went with them, though they didn't touch him; he seemed to have acquired already the submissive manner of a prisoner; he had learned it in a hard school. Smiley stood back and the three of them marched softly past him, all somehow too absorbed by the ceremony to pay attention to him. The halo was empty. He heard the quiet closing of the car's doors and the sound of it driving away. He heard two other cars leave after it, or with it. He didn't watch them go. He felt Toby Esterhase fling his arms round his shoulders, and saw that his eyes were filled with tears.

'George,' he began. 'All your life. Fantastic!'

Then something in Smiley's stiffness made Toby pull away, and Smiley himself stepped quickly out of the halo, passing very close to Ann's lighter on his way. It lay at the halo's very edge, tilted slightly, glinting like fool's gold on the cobble. He thought of picking it up, but somehow there seemed no point and no one else appeared to have seen it. Someone was shaking his hand, someone else was clapping him on the shoulder. Toby quietly restrained them.

'Take care, George,' Toby said. 'Go well, hear me?'

Smiley heard Toby's team leave one by one until only Peter Guillam remained. Walking a short way back along the embankment, almost to where the cross stood, Smiley took another look at the bridge, as if to establish whether anything had changed, but clearly it had not, and though the wind appeared a little stronger, the snow was still swirling in all directions.

Peter Guillam touched his arm.

'Come on, old friend,' he said. 'It's bedtime.'

From long habit, Smiley had taken off his spectacles and was absently polishing them on the fat end of his tie, even though he had to delve for it among the folds of his tweed coat.

'George, you won,' said Guillam as they walked slowly towards the car.

'Did I?' said Smiley. 'Yes. Yes, well, I suppose I did.'